THE KYBE

'The Kybe' is a cluster of fishermen's cottages taking its name from the rough marsh grass that separates it from the town of Skerries. Beyond is the deceptively peaceful sound and the island dominated by its squat Martello tower. Within this idyllic scene is set a love story, elemental in its simplicity — the tale of Eileen Mullen, her love for her husband and children and her passion for the foreign soldier. The story of this small Fingal community is silhouetted vividly against the backdrop of the Napoleonic Wars. The author portrays the domestic intimacy of the Mullen home and the activities of the local community as vividly as he does the terrible battle of Waterloo. The story is told with the pace and poignancy of an old ballad.

Hugh Fitzgerald Ryan was born in Skerries in 1941 where he now teaches. This is his first novel.

To Margaret
for all her encouragement

THE KYBE

Hugh Fitzgerald Ryan

A novel of Ireland
in Napoleonic times

Hugh F. Ryan.

WOLFHOUND PRESS

© 1983 Hugh Fitzgerald Ryan
Text and illustrations.

The people and events depicted in this novel are entirely fictitious with the
exception of Luke Ryan — a legendary smuggler. The author has felt free to take
chronological liberties with this elusive and intriguing character.

First published 1983
WOLFHOUND PRESS
68 Mountjoy Square, Dublin 1

British Library Cataloguing in Publications Data
   Ryan, Hugh Fitzgerald
     The Kybe
     I. Title
     823'.914 [F] PR6058.Y/

     ISBN 0 86327 011 5
     ISBN 0 86327 021 2 P6k

This book is published with the assistance of
The Arts Council (An Chomhairle Ealaíonn), Dublin, Ireland.

Cover design: Michael O'Brien
Cover illustration: Hugh Fitzgerald Ryan
Typesetting by Design & Art Facilities, Dublin.

CHAPTER 1

"If we hurry", said Lucy, "we might catch up on Skip. I know he's gone for crabs today because I saw him on the dorn a while ago".

Matt stretched his short legs to keep pace with his sister. They splashed through the tidal pools in their bare feet, stepping now and again on the banks of bootlace weed and laughing in high excitement, waving their arms to recover their balance.

Before them the dorn, a causeway of shingle and small boulders, carpeted at this time of year with bright green seaweed, stretched back towards the island. Here and there were larger black rocks covered in growth of brown leathery weed and clumps of mussels almost obscured in mud and barnacles. Beyond was the island, long and low with its squat, grey Martello tower. One small field had been cleared from the thistles and rank waist-high grass where a crop of young oats, green, turning yellow, reflected the sun.

"We'll be murdered if we're caught," said Matt, his heart thumping both with exertion and the delicious fear involved in doing something so dangerously wrong. It was hard to believe that this exciting summery island could be the same sinister place which their mother had forbidden under pain of direst punishment.

"There he is." Lucy pointed to the reef at the north end of the island where a cloud of gulls wheeled like dust in a sunbeam, their distant cries coming thin and faint in protest at the threat to their newly hatched young. A stooping figure moved along the outer ledges of rock near the edge of the tide. Occasionally the tiny figure straightened and pressed hands to the small of its back, then bent again, rooting in the weed.

"Skip, Skip, wait for us," they both shouted as they scrambled towards him.

I wish I had my boots, Matt thought to himself and smiled at the idea. Who ever heard of children having boots for clambering on rocks or wading in the pools to catch crabs? Boots are for Sundays and big occasions and for the men who worked on the land or the carters walking beside their big brown horses. Even the men on the schooners went barefoot a lot of the time. But still they don't have barnacles and limpets all over the schooners.

"So there yiz are," said Skipper as they slithered and crawled up to where he stood, using the unexpected visit as an excuse for a rest, a chance to take the stiffness out of old bones and to gaze contemplatively at the work already done. To Skipper the joy of work usually consisted of having enough done to justify knocking off and maybe going for a glass of porter or a smoke with a few cronies.

"Youse shouldn't be here at all. If your Mammy finds out there'll be hell to pay and if she sees you with me I'll be blempt." He smiled all the same and the children smiled back. At eight and nine years of age it is good to know that there is someone, a grown up, who can deflect even a mother's anger and make everything all right. And nobody could do this like Skip.

Undoubtedly he had a presence. Five foot six inches at the very most, he wore nondescript homespun trousers, rolled up to the knee, a collarless linen shirt of indeterminate colour and an old broadcloth coat bereft of its tails – an outfit ill designed for the business of catching crabs, but as he had never been seen wearing anything else he looked perfectly at home. His straggling white moustache was stained yellow at the eaves from the habitual clay pipe which now protruded from his top pocket. The lined and weatherbeaten face suggested a life of toil before the mast, though his title indicated a more exalted station, but in fact nobody could ever recall Skip ever having held gainful employment for any appreciable length of time. He enjoyed the rank of retired sea captain apparently without having had to go through the tedious business of going to sea. He was a gentleman of leisure, dispossessed by an accident of birth, deprived by a twist of fate of the accoutrements of the gentry but possessed of the same ability to enjoy the good things of life if in a somewhat lower key, without the trouble of earning a living.

"I have about a dozen," he said indicating a large wooden bucket, "a few good hens and some big fellas with claws on them that would take the leg off you. There's another one here now but I can't get at him with the gaff. I'll have to get me hand in after him." With this he removed his jacket, folded it carefully and handed it to Lucy. He rolled up his right shirtsleeve, exposing a skinny arm, white, but none too clean and knelt down on the weed to thrust his hand into a small cleft in the rock.

"He's a big one all right, be the jings! That's it me lad. Back you go. Easy does it," – all this apparently to the crab which seemed to have wedged itself in the crack. "He can't get me as long as I hold his claw but as soon as he tries to move further back – yes, yes, now we have you."

The white arm withdrew, streaked with little red gashes from the barnacles and the children drew back with fright as Skip quickly transferred his grip from the claw to the crab's back and triumphantly waved it in front of their faces, a monstrous clashing thing with a spread of claws fully twelve inches across.

"Now, Matt me son, what do you think of that fella? Spit in his eye now and that will quieten him down."

"Not me. I wouldn't go near him." Matt could see the eyes of the crab and the malevolent, almost human expression on the creature and fancied that the eyes on their little stalks were focussing exclusively on him.

"All right so," said Skip and accurately directed a salvo into the mandibles at which the monster immediately folded its claws and legs in under itself for all the world like a hedgehog rolling up in the face of danger.

"Wouldn't life be just grand if you could shut everyone up as easy as that when they get difficult?" laughed Skip as he tucked the crab into the bucket and dropped a handful of wrack on it. "Just to keep them occupied so they won't tear each other to bits."

"Skip, can we go up to the tower when you're finished?" asked Lucy pleadingly. To go up to the tower was something that they had often longed to do. Some of their friends had even climbed up to the door about ten feet up but it had been locked. One or two claimed to have got inside but they were generally regarded as liars anyway, the type that would scale all the eggs from a nest if you showed them one. They were the ones that the harbour master always aimed a kick at or chased off the quay when the fishing boats came in. Yet there lingered the suspicion that maybe they had been inside. How else could you account for the soldier's button and the pack of dogeared cards that Larry Donovan had shown them once outside Morris's shop? He had been up there with his da after collecting eggs around the island. The cards proved how bad some of the soldiers were or so his da said. There were things written on the walls too, but they couldn't read them but his da said they were probably bad as well. There were even bottles that his da had brought back to Morris's after washing them in the tide and got a tanner for them from Mr. Morris.

"Well," said Skip, "we can walk around it and yiz can look at it and maybe I'll have a sit down in the sun for a while. Take a hold of the bucket there. The crabs won't bite yiz." He led the way back to the small beach by way of a long narrow gully floored with coarse sand, fragments of shells, fingernails of old limpets, ruined winkles and whelks with walls fallen away leaving only the spiral staircase open to the public gaze, empty carapaces of small green crabs now bleached in the sun and the occasional dead starfish dried into rigour by the hot June sun. Occasionally, in an inch or two of weedy water, a hermit crab lumbered along dragging his borrowed shell behind him.

"What is he doing?" asked Matt, watching one of the tiny creatures manoeuvring his shell alongside another slightly larger white winkle.

"Watch him now," replied Skip, bending close and leaning on his gaff. "He's going to move house." Sure enough after advancing cautiously once or twice from his black, shiny fortress, displaying formidable claws and shell, like a miniature lobster, the hermit crab emerged, exposing the brown pulpy vulnerable tail. With a quick flick of the tail he inserted himself into the vacant shell and resumed his defensive posture. Lucy watched fascinated and with a vague embarrassment. The crab made her think of a helmeted soldier with armour to the waist but naked from there down. It seemed cruel even to her young mind that a creature should be created so imperfectly that all its life it must drag a great weight after it simply to avoid being eaten alive by its neighbours.

Under the grassy bank the man and the children stepped carefully over the scattered nests of seabirds. They could hardly be dignified with the term nests when compared to the beautiful bowl of the thrush, wedged in the fork of a whitethorn or the mossy orb of the wren, tucked into an ivy covered wall like a soft green womb for the tiny eggs lying secure in the feathery darkness. The gulls were satisfied with a few ribs of hay and some twigs tossed into a shallow depression in which the eggs lay, almost invisible, bluegrey and mottled with umber. Only slightly more visible were the chicks already hatched. The shoddy workmanship could not be taken as evidence of careless parents for the gulls screamed and dived at the intruders, coming within inches of their heads and pulling away sharply with a violent flapping of wings, so close that their angry yellow eyes gave warning that trespass was not treated lightly and anyone tampering with their small furry, disgruntled looking offspring did so at their peril. Skip, in reply, waved his gaff and shouted good natured abuse particularly at the great black-backs which spattered the warm, rounded rocks with increasing accuracy, like gunners bracketing their target in preparation for the coup de grace.

Laughing and a little alarmed, the two children broke into a run, hauling themselves one-handed up the grassy slope by the stringy grass and crackling cow parsley, with the old man fighting a noisy rearguard action behind them, hooshing the heavy bucket and gesticulating with the gaff, while the gulls, confident now of victory, gradually left off their screaming and glided down to land beside their nests with a few short hops and a businesslike folding of the great wings, for all the world, thought Lucy, like Mrs. Morris smoothing her crackling starched apron behind the counter, subduing an awkward customer or admonishing a tardy delivery man with her withering glare.

"Why was the tower put here anyway Skip? Did soldiers really live in it? Had they guns?" Matt wanted to know all about it. "Did you ever see them? Was there battles in them days? Maybe the men in that other tower would fire at the men in this one." He pointed back towards the headland that stood out beyond the town and the white wall of the harbour, visible now behind the dunes, as they reached the high part of the island. Another Martello tower of identical design commanded the height over the harbour. This one was still used mainly as a store house by the coastguard and being more accessible to the village children, had not the same magic as its island counterpart.

"Well," said Skip, "we'll sit down for a while but keep your eye on the tide there. We don't want to be stuck out here for the night and your mother going demented lookin' for yiz all over the barony." He seated himself with a few grunts and a long sigh of contentment, with his back to the warm, massive limestone blocks of the tower and groped awkwardly with his left hand for the pipe in his top pocket. The sun stood high in a cloudless sky strained of colour and the old man closed his eyes against the glare from the wet sand beyond the dorn. The long low promontories to the south stood in silhouette against the light, with Lambay long and graceful in shades of purple and violet with a gash of yellow cornfield on the landward side. Beyond lay Howth in pale violet outline and the faint blue suggestion of Wicklow and its mountains.

He began slowly and carefully to fill the broken-stemmed clay pipe with a few shreds of tobacco which he pared from a short piece of plug with a small bone handled knife. Matt watched with interest this essentially masculine occupation. He had envied the men who stood at the corner of the square smoking their pipes, laughing among themselves and spitting elaborately on the cobblestones to emphasise a point or express an opinion on the gentlemen who came occasionally to hire them for a day's labour. There were even some more flamboyant characters who smoked with pipes upside down in the rain and little perforated lids to prevent the loss of the valuable and aromatic contents.

"Do you see this tinder box? Now I got this a present from one of the soldiers in this very tower. A friend of mine he was and a strange character indeed. Oh aye, a remarkable character". Skipper held out a small metal box to the wondering gaze of the children. He opened the lid with a small flourish and exposed the contents, small bits of paper, some dry moss, a piece of flint, brown with white spots, a steel striker and, wonder of wonders, a small burning glass in a brass ring.

"Now watch this," he said and began to focus a white spot of sun through the glass onto a pinch of the dry tinder. Matt could not resist putting his finger over the glass to feel the heat but there was nothing unusual.

"It doesn't seem to be much use," he remarked in a superior tone.

"Put your finger under the glass, stupid," his sister scoffed. "That's where the heat is."

Matt gave a yelp when the white spot settled on the back of his finger. It stung like a wasp and he quickly put his finger in his mouth and laughed, a little too loud, for fear that tears might come. The moss began to smoke, a thin wraith of blue. The spot turned brown, writhed and burst into flame which Skip fed with some wisps of dried grass and a few small twigs. Then with a reddened twig he lit his pipe, puffed a few times to ensure success and settled back against the wall with a faraway look of content in his eyes. The small fire consumed its tiny store of fuel. Grey ghosts of grass curled and lifted in the air, drifting upwards against the tower wall only to fall under their own weight or whip sideways in the slight breeze that had sprung up from the south east.

"Did yiz ever hear of a man called Napoleon Bonaparte?" asked the old man.

"Yes," answered Lucy, "well at least I heard a song about him once. Was he the King of France, or something?"

"Oh, better by half than the king of France. He was an emperor of France. Emperors, you see," Skip went on, "is bigger than kings. Them lads make themselves emperors but kings is only born.

Emperors can own a lot of countries but kings only own the one".

"That isn't true," exclaimed Lucy, surprised at herself for interrupting but sure in the knowledge that she was justified. "Our king owns four countries and I know that because Mammy has a half crown with the king's head on it, King George, she said, and lions on it and a harp and she said it was because he owns England and Ireland and Scotland and Wales. The lions were lying down and some were standing up and the harp . . . " She stopped, fearing that she had gone too far.

"A half a crown," Skip, unruffled, sucked thoughtfully on his pipe. "Now that's a brave amount of money. But the lions and harps and so on was all together on a kind of shield like they used to have in the old days, isn't that right? Now that's because he made all them countries into the one. The United Kingdom it's called. But Napoleon Bonaparte had so many countries that he could give them away to his brothers and his friends to be kings in them. He even gave one to his little babby and called him the King of Rome. Now there's a quare one, the King of Rome and he not half the size of young Matt there."

"But the crown would be too big and heavy and it would slip down over his eyes." Matt didn't think it would be a very comfortable business being a king at that age. Skipper and Lucy laughed at his innocence of the ways of kings and emperors.

"You don't have to wear the crown all the time Matt," explained his sister patiently. "You can order someone to carry it around for you. You only have to wear it when you're sitting on your throne."

It still didn't seem such a good idea for a small baby to be sitting on a big throne with a heavy gold crown on his head and sure how could he give orders anyway and wasn't the Pope the King of Rome, but Matt thought it wiser to be quiet and maybe these questions would be answered in the course of the story.

"Anyway," continued Skip brushing aside the technicalities of majesty, "kings and emperors is always enemies like cats and dogs and they fight wars to take each other's countries. That's why there are soldiers you see." The children nodded at the logic of it all. "Now this Napoleon had a mind to take England away from King George and this country too, invade them it's called. He was going to bring all his soldiers over here in big ships and kill all the English soldiers and take over the whole country."

"And maybe give it to one of his other babies," suggested Lucy, completely taken up with the story.

"Aye, or maybe come over and be king himself and live in a big house in Dublin and rule all the countries from up there." Matt understood that Dublin was a very big place with a lot of grand houses and maybe even a palace for the emperor to live in. "Well maybe he would at that," conceded Skip. "However King George decided to put a stop to any such plans. Now do you see anything down there to the south, just to the right of Lambay." He pointed a gnarled and stained finger at the furthest headland visible from where they sat and the children peered into the haze, squinting their eyes against the glare.

"Why! It's another tower," exclaimed Lucy in surprise, "just like this one and the one on the headland."

"That's right, exactly the same and if you climbed up on that far tower you would see another one further on and so on nearly all the way around Ireland. That's what King George did. He put a whole line of towers with big guns on them to fire on any ships that came from France and sink them. They could send signals to each tower with big fires and the soldiers would come from Dublin and kill the French soldiers if they swam ashore."

Matt thought that King George was a very clever man to think of such a plan. "Did the French soldiers ever come?" he asked.

"Only a few came a long time ago but they was all captured or killed. They didn't come near the towers though because they knew they couldn't get past the big guns."

"Where did all the other French soldiers go then?" asked Lucy.

"To a place called Russia," replied Skip pronouncing it Roossia, "to fight another emperor but they all froze to death in the snow and was ate be bears and wolves. Froze still as statues they did, except Napoleon. Being an emperor you see, he had big fur coats and a coach and horses."

"What happened to him then? Did he give up being an emperor?" Lucy could see little hope of continuing without an army.

"Well after another big battle King George's soldiers caught him and put him in prison on an island out in the middle of the ocean and that's where he remains to this day." Wondering to some extent, how Napoleon managed a last battle with all his soldiers frozen like statues, Matt thought it not such a bad fate to live on an island maybe in a tower like this and spend the time catching crabs and fish, even for a man who had given away kingdoms to his friends.

By this time two arms of the flowing tide had begun to reach around the island, reclaiming it from the land and a stream had broken across beyond the dorn. The stagnant pools became revitalised and began to reach towards each other linking together with silver threads. The old man roused himself and with uncharacteristic alacrity headed down the slope onto the shingle causeway, carrying the bucket and urging the children along with warnings of what the rats and gulls would do to them that night if they were prevented from getting to the mainland.

The stream had become a respectable river about twenty yards across by the time they reached the end of the dorn. Skip doffed his boots and put them in the bucket. Lucy hitched her petticoat up beyond her knees and held onto the bucket with her other hand. Matt had little to worry about in his old knee breeches but was glad to hold the man's hand when he felt the rush of the water piling up against his legs. It was no easy task for them as they waded slowly landwards with bootlace weed, come alive again, brushing against their legs and unseen shards of shell stabbing into their feet.

"Now," said Skip, when they reached the strand, "run along home and I'll come around later with a few crabs for the mammy. And mind the wee fella," he added as an afterthought. He watched them running on the wet beach, their reflections splintering on the ripple marks and their piping voices shrill with excitement as they jumped over the pools and rivulets which had begun to take on an orange tinge from the lowering sun.

As good as his word the old man brought half a dozen of his catch later in the evening. They lay dull red on the white deal table, still steaming from the pot. Matt had seen crabs boiled before and heard them struggling in the pot, lifting the lid in desperation and getting a leg or two over the rim only to be thrust back into the warm water where they gradually gave up the fight. It worried him to imagine their fear and in his mind he could hear their voices crying for help. He had felt the urge to reprieve them but had never done so, feeling guilty but rationalising it with Skipper's remark "The crabs wouldn't worry if the boot was on the other foot." A crude philosophy perhaps but there was no denying that they were good to eat. The cat also agreed and investigated the smell but drew back with a sniff and a twitch of the head from the hot shells. He sprang to the floor and set about sharpening his claws nonchalantly on a leg of the table which had sprouted hairs as evidence of his constant attention.

Eileen Mullen loved this time of evening most of all when the work of the day was over. Winter and summer there was always a fire on the hearth, essential, of course, for cooking but certainly a luxury on this

June evening when there was no more than the slightest chill in the air. Nevertheless, it gave her a sense of security, a focal point to sit with her children or the occasional caller, or by herself, reviewing the events of the day. This evening had started badly because of the trip to the island but Skip had assured her that the children had been with him at all times, so gradually her agitation eased and at last she was satisfied with a promise that they would never go again without permission.

"I don't like that place at all Skip, as well you know, but I won't forbid the children as long as they are in good hands."

They sat now in the half light by the fire, Skip busy with his pipe and discoursing amiably on the happenings of the town or the comings and goings of the boats at the harbour. The life of the town continued on an even keel. The great events of the world did not touch it. Schooners came with coal or salt perhaps and departed with barrels of fish to far off ports in Britain or the Continent. Eileen rocked the little boy Peter on her lap and spoke of her day in the shop, how the customers were in good spirits with the fine weather, how the heat had even begun to melt the butter on the cool slate shelves at the back of the shop, how even Mrs. Morris had laughed as her husband wrestled with the striped canvas canopy which, he insisted, attracted trade to his door.

Skipper grunted. "A great man for business but a terrible man with his hands." Credit where it was due. "But where did he get that young lad of his at all? I never saw anyone take to the carpentering the way he did. Beautiful work he put into that little yawl of his. I dare say he'll be in the business in a big way sometime." He looked across at the woman sitting quietly now in the glow of the fire. A fine woman he thought to himself. Not yet thirty four and a widow these five or six years. Striped canvas me arse. That's not what brings customers to old Morris's door but the eyes of Eileen Mullen, beautiful green eyes that a man would drown in. He indulged in a moment of fantasy. If I was twenty years younger meself, stories or no stories . . . He didn't pursue the thought. Indeed he was justified in his assessment of the woman who was at that moment sending her children off to bed in the two small attic rooms which they reached by means of a stairs, more of a ladder, from the kitchen. He could hear the murmur of their prayers over his head and the creak of the woman's steps on the boards. As a young widow she could have withdrawn into her black weeds and become indistinguishable from the old shawlies who shuffled the village streets like ragged jackdaws. She would have had reason to withdraw or so it was whispered by the same old jackdaws. But Eileen

Mullen had survived. She no longer wore black. She earned her living and looked people in the eye. Her three children were as well looked after as any and the older ones even had some learning. She had earned respect, grudging at first, and hardly a man in Fingal hadn't thought about her at some time or other.

"Skip Garrigan, you're an old scoundrel and no mistake." Her voice interrupted his reverie and he looked up to see her descending the ladder holding a fold of her long petticoat in one hand so that her bare feet were visible on the rungs. Mrs Morris would never permit bare feet in the shop. Skipper spread his hands helplessly, admitting the truth of her remark. "I don't suppose you would be interested in a bottle of porter," she added. "I just happen to have one or two in the cupboard."

"Well it wouldn't go amiss," he replied, indicating that perhaps he would be prepared to oblige if only out of courtesy. "Tell me," he said as he watched her pouring the dark frothing contents carefully into a mug, the light of the fire glowing through the blue green bottle, "did you ever consider marrying again? I'm not asking on my own behalf now you'll understand," joking to remove any risk of offence, "but a fine young woman like yourself shouldn't be alone lookin' after her childer."

Eileen gave a short laugh, with a touch of irony. "I've made my own way in the world for a few years now and sure maybe the men would be afraid of me."

"Maybe the boys would, Eileen, but there must be a man or two left in the country somewhere, though the men aren't what they were when I was on the go."

"Skip," said Eileen softly and looking at him levelly, "when I've known only the best, why would I settle for less?"

"Aye, aye, indeed," he murmured and stared into the coals. "How could you settle for less?"

They sat in silence again for a few moments until Eileen smiled at him attempting to break the spell that threatened to cast a chill over the evening. "Unless, of course, you would consider leaving off your wicked ways and make an honest woman of me."

Skipper drained his mug at a gulp and rapped it on the mantlepiece. "Be the jings now but I'm off to the races. Anytime I get a chance to rest me legs the women do be throwin' themselves at me. Us bachelors lead a fierce dangerous existence."

He left with instructions to leave the crabs to cool overnight and a muttered curse at the cat which darted between his legs as he closed the door. The woman sat for a long time after he left, gazing into the fire, unmoving. A tear slipped from the corner of her eye and trickled like liquid gold down her cheek until she brushed it from her upper lip with the back of her hand.

CHAPTER 2

The coastguard cutter slipped quietly between Lambay and the point in a light easterly air although the sergeant, looking landwards, could discern only a long grey bank of mist. As a landsman Peter Howlett did not enjoy the rolling sensation of the long oily green swell from the east, but had long ago come to accept discomfort as one of the many occupational hazards of soldiering. In the lee of the island now the swell had abated and the sergeant felt sufficiently at ease for his natural civility to reassert itself. Turning from the rail he engaged the lieutenant in desultory conversation. The officer, with the collar of his broadcloth coat turned up against the morning chill, was glad to enlighten him on the nature of his new station.

"Over there," he indicated the bank of mist, "is the most civilised part of this God-forsaken country. At least there is very little talk of sedition as far as I can make out and I've served on this section for a good number of years now. It's a reasonably prosperous region. Fingal they call it, and I gather that the landlords are enlightened gentlemen."

"How do you mean enlightened? Are landlords a problem in Ireland?" Landlords and gentry were much the same all over as far as the sergeant was concerned. Most officers were gentlemen as was only the natural thing. Some admittedly were fools and squandered mens' lives but, in general, officers knew their business and presumably handled their estates with reasonable efficiency.

The lieutenant laughed. "Sergeant," he said, "you have much to learn about Ireland then. In this country a ditch is a bank and a dyke is a channel and the farmers build gaps between their fields. They use the king's English to conceal what they are thinking, not to communicate."

Sensing a diatribe on the exotic nature of the Irishry the sergeant returned to the original point. "Why should landlords be a cause of sedition? Have the people been converted to the French way of thinking?" The officer interrupted his disquisition temporarily to oversee the tightening of the jib sheet in what seemed to the sergeant a surprisingly polite manner. The lieutenant noticed his expression.

"It's not like the regular navy here – all that 'belay there' and shouting. I wouldn't be able for all that. Tell a man what to do and save cursing for when you really need it. Better for the nerves."

"Perhaps you have a point but I can't see His Majesty's navy taking on the Frogs like a bunch of gentlemen boating on the Thames." Reorganisation of the navy was tacitly left to the Lords of the Admiralty who no doubt would see to it in their own good time. A century here or there should make precious little difference.

"You were telling me about landlords".

"Ah yes. Now that's exactly what I was saying. The Irish landlord feels obliged by divine ordinance to oppress and plunder his tenants while the tenant in turn hates his landlord and thwarts him at every opportunity – and all in the name of religion".

The sergeant whose acquaintance with divine worship consisted of the Lord's Prayer and frequent witnessing of the burial service nevertheless knew that the bulk of Irish people were obstinate in their adherence to popish superstition, which if not legal was nevertheless tolerated by the government. He remarked that in his trade a man's way of worshipping or not worshipping his Maker was less important than his ability to stay alive and help his companions to do likewise.

"It seems to me that the situation you describe could result only in the pauperising of both classes. Is this not the case?"

The lieutenant frowned, admitting some puzzlement. "The funny thing is though, most gentry live in the most sumptuous manner while their tenants appear to be as impoverished as the slaves in the sugar islands". The paradox made him ruminate while his eyes roved constantly, checking aloft and watching the easy instinctive movements of his crew as they trimmed sail here and there to catch the light air.

By now the mist had begun to clear and landward the sergeant could make out three or four low islands lying like whales or rather as he imagined whales would lie if left undisturbed. He smiled inwardly thinking that his acquaintance with whales consisted of a woodcut in some book dimly recalled from childhood, a gigantic whale with a small piggy eye, emerging from the maelstrom of its own wake to devour a boatload of sailors who looked, some at the monster and some directly at the reader, with expressions of comic alarm as their flimsy craft stood on its transom and oars and men spilled from it in disarray. Their surprise was scarcely justified he thought even now, considering that they had roused the monster themselves with a dozen or so harpoons thrust into the great grey side which rose like a citadel above them.

Like passing from one climate to another a gust of warm humid air greeted them and the smell of the land reached their nostrils.

"Now," said the lieutenant, "you can see your new kingdom. Captain Osgood's company has overall responsibility for the towers in this area. He's billeted with us at the harbour at the moment."

"Yes, I know. His name is on my orders here," replied Howlett. "I must report to him on arrival."

"Good, good. He's a reasonable fellow I must say. He shan't cause you much trouble. You'll catch him after lunch so he should be in a good temper. Spends most of his time riding around the district. He claims that he is doing a survey in preparation for mapping but I suspect it's mainly in the interests of his liver. Clever fellow all the same. He was involved in the original siting of the towers and apparently made some useful emendations to the old maps." The lieutenant made some derogatory comments on the quality of the coastal charts and maps with which he was obliged to ply his trade and on the need for a comprehensive survey. "Were it not for my extremely sensitive nose, I think I should have ended up on the grey mare rock times out of number." He tapped the organ in question and chuckled to himself.

"Why are there three towers in such close proximity?" Howlett asked.

"Indeed there are four," said the lieutenant. "In a little while you should be able to descry another about three miles northward of the harbour. They had to build two martelloes quite close together to get a clear line around the headland. The village itself you see is at the point of a triangle. In fact we have to give that outer island a wide berth, the one with the ruin on it, before we head into the harbour." Howlett felt the uncomfortable watering of his eyes that had troubled him for some time and groped for a kerchief to dry them. He could not make out any ruin on the outer island and reached into an inner pocket for the spectacles he had recently acquired. It was absurd he felt for an artillery man to have to depend on spectacles but he had been assured by the battalion surgeon that the condition was temporary. He would have felt happier if the surgeon had not been regarded as occupying a position in the medical profession about two steps below that of the farrier.

"Try this," the lieutenant handed him a short brass-bound spy glass, with the aid of which he swept the low-lying coast beyond the islands. He could make out now a cluster of white cottages on the foreshore and behind them a low church with a square tower or belfry, perhaps, nearby. On a knoll beyond the church stood a windmill, to his professional eye the salient feature of the whole area. The village seemed to consist of two segments for between the white cottages on the foreshore and the more imposing looking buildings nearer the headland, lay an extent of what he took to be marshland and a line of sand dunes.

"We must go seaward of that mark there," the lieutenant broke in, "before going about for the harbour." He pointed again with the offhand assurance of the seaman sure of his skill and the sergeant swept the glass along the line of the shore until he located a metal cross protruding from the water beyond a ridge of black rocks dusted white with raucous gulls and accumulated droppings.

By now the cutter was knifing along parallel to the line of rocks, reaching on the freshening breeze which had swung round to the west. The tower on the headland slipped astern, then the white wall of a coalyard and the small grey coastguard station with the flag whipping at the yard arm.

"I don't imagine Bonaparte will cause you much trouble in your new home at this stage," remarked the lieutenant, "but you're more familiar with his problems than I am. To tell the truth these towers were an expensive piece of folly; locking the stable door and all that. If the French couldn't do it properly in '98 when the country was in turmoil, we won't need martelloes to keep them out now."

The sergeant was about to maintain that it was too soon to write Bonaparte off as a threat when to a cry of 'Lee ho!' the heavy boom swung across and he ducked in some alarm, to the obvious amusement of the sailors. The cross went by to port and another short reach brought the cutter level with the harbour wall where she turned into the wind and let go the anchor about a cable's length from the pier head with a staccato rattling of chains. For a moment confusion prevailed as halyards were released and hands reached to haul in and furl the canvas and then, suddenly, the cutter lay swinging gently in the roadstead and the sergeant became aware for the first time of noises carrying from the land.

"Give the coastguard those towers and twenty four pounders and we could put paid to all the smugglers in the kingdom. Sink a few fishing smacks now and again and the occasional schooner. Never mind the French." The lieutenant outlined a strategy which, to Howlett, savoured of some of the irrational ferocity which he had so criticised in the Irish landlords and their tenants.

"Is smuggling a serious problem hereabouts?" he asked.

"Well, it's not as bad as it was a few years back but, on principle, the heavy hand is a sovereign way to ensure good behaviour. There isn't a man in Fingal over the age of twelve who wouldn't put his hand to a bit of contraband, given half a chance. Look at this old rogue for example. If he had his deserts he'd have been hanged a dozen times over already." The lieutenant indicated a figure standing in the stern of a punt and sculling lazily towards them with a single oar, using his weight rather than any muscular effort to push the oar from side to side.

"Avast there Captain Garrigan," called the lieutenant, visibly transforming himself into a representative of His Britannic Majesty. "Stand by to take us ashore." In a lower voice he added, "You'll excuse the formality, sergeant, but they expect it of us you see. We'll go ashore with this gentleman and my men will bring your trunk later in the gig. Perhaps you'll have something to wet your whistle before proceeding to the island."

With consummate mastery, Captain Garrigan brought his punt about and laid it against the side of the cutter, holding on to a strake with his left hand and saluting elaborately with his right.

"A pleasure sir, a pleasure, as one captain to another, and will the grand major be disembarking with you?" This with a nod in the direction of the sergeant whose amusement at his rapid promotion was to an extent offset by the alarming rise and fall of the punt into which he would shortly be expected to lower himself.

"Sergeant Howlett and myself are here on His Majesty's business and would appreciate if you would place us on shore with the utmost dispatch, even to the extent of unshipping a second oar." The lieutenant could not resist a sly wink at his own scintillating wit.

"Be the holy, then, yiz better come aboard gentlemen, if it's King George himself as sent yiz." Garrigan cleared his throat and spat over the gunwale, an equivocal spit, arguably a comment on King George and his affairs but in any court of law a defensible side-effect of the tobacco from which the same monarch drew a considerable part of his revenue. With more luck than skill Howlett transferred to the punt and found himself, to his relief, sitting on the after thwart, facing the little captain who pulled now on two oars in view of the urgency of the situation. The lieutenant, more at home in small craft, chose to stand in the bow, to some extent out of affectation but more likely out of fastidious concern for his uniform trousers. Captain Garrigan's vessel, it must be admitted, seemed to have accumulated more than its share of dried fish guts and bird droppings, the former undoubtedly the primary cause of the latter.

"A veteran, do ye tell me?" remarked the oarsman after a few short questions between breaths, "and does that mean that we can be expecting great goin's on and manoeuvres?"

The sergeant shrugged, unsure of how to answer so direct an enquiry into the conduct of the war but further discussion was forestalled as Skipper swung the punt, backwatering with his right oar and slipped behind two small wherries which stood aground in the shallow water near the pier head, beside a flight of rough steps let into the limestone wall.

"Watch your step on the hairy woar there, sergeant," volunteered Skipper but the import of this advice was lost on Howlett who was more concerned with keeping his footing on the slippery green weed. At the top of the steps he stood for a moment getting accustomed to the unfamiliar stability of the ground and looking around at the cluster of cottages and unprepossessing houses and thought, wryly, that it looked an unlikely place for 'great goin's on and manoeuvres'.

"John Mullen, carrier by trade, at your service, sergeant. I understand that you want to get over to the island." Howlett turned to look at the speaker as he emerged from the coastguard station. John Mullen was a heavyset man of about his own age, thirty-one or two at the most and dressed in rough homespun tweed breeches and a linen shirt. He wore heavy brown boots and leather gaiters buckled at the side. At first glance the impression was of a formidable looking character who, in England, would have been most unlikely to escape the attentions of the recruiting sergeant or the press gang. But on closer examination the first impression was belied by the frank and cheerful expression on his freckled face or at least that part of it that could be seen above the bushy reddish beard.

"Ah good. Captain Osgood sent for you, I take it."

Mullen indicated a pony and cart standing by a bollard at the near end of the quay. "I'll just get my car and we can be away whenever you're ready. We have another couple of hours before the flow so there'll be plenty of time to get over and back." Mullen unhitched the reins which were twisted loosely around the bollard and led the pony over to where Howlett stood beside his black military chest.

"Give us that box there sergeant," said he, grasping the heavy trunk with powerful arms and swinging it up onto the back of the cart, securing it by lifting and chaining the tailboard into place.

Howlett instinctively took the pony's head to prevent her rearing or skittering as the shafts lifted under the weight. He patted her nose and spoke softly to her, enjoying the feel of the animal. Horses and even mules were the aspect of his job that he enjoyed most of all and he felt a justified pride in his gentle mastery of them.

Mullen put his foot on the shaft and sat up onto the cart. "I can see that you know a bit about animals," he remarked approvingly as Howlett climbed aboard.

"Aye, I've had dealings with horses for a long time now. That's a fine pony you have there." He sensed a common ground.

"She's not the worse, I will admit," agreed Mullen, "good for this kind of thing and taking folk over to the coaching inn in the trap, but you should see my Clydesdales. Now them are the horses for you."

Having lived most of his live in close proximity to other men, with little opportunity for privacy for even the most basic functions, Peter Howlett had developed a habit of reticence, generally keeping his opinions to himself. However, on this fine summer afternoon with the benefit of a good meal of beef, pickles and bread, courtesy of the coastguard service, not to mention a couple of tankards of the local ale from the same source, he felt himself relaxing and responding to the enthusiasm and good nature of this big outgoing man beside him.

"I hardly expected to find Clydesdales in this part of the world. No disrespect, but I thought Ireland had nothing but wild mountain ponies." He had a general notion of Ireland as a land of bog and rainswept mountain, and was having difficulty accommodating his preconception to this apparently prosperous lowland which put him in mind of the Lincolnshire of his childhood.

"His lordship up there breeds all sorts of horses," said Mullen pointing vaguely towards the two hills beyond the town. "Sure if it wasn't for the likes of him your army would be leggin' it around Europe instead of ridin' in style on the finest horse flesh."

Howlett laughed aloud at how little this picture consorted with his experience of jouncing over rutted tracks on a gun limber, choking in the stifling dust of a peninsular summer or wading up to the knees in the mud of the low countries, hauling recalcitrant mules, the whites of their eyes showing in terror, as they struggled through the viscid morass.

The road led past a yard where some men were repairing a small fishing smack and Mullen raised an index finger to his forehead in salute. He turned off the cobbled road at a gap in the wall and they emerged onto the strand opposite the island with the tower. Half a mile of wet sand lay between them and the dorn and the pony broke into a trot at the command 'mup there' and a slap of the reins on its haunches.

"It's a wonder now Mullen you never thought of soldiering yourself. You look to me like a man who could handle himself in a fight." Howlett reflected that there must be a recruiting sergeant inside every soldier.

"John's the name, John." Mullen bridled at being addressed by his surname. The English and the gentry, not that there is any real distinction, always used a man's surname, as if keeping him at a distance, or in his place. He pronounced it 'Jawn' in the nasal drawl of Fingal, that was so strange and comical to the ear of the Englishman. "Now why would I put meself out fightin' for anybody? This war is for to make the gentry rich, what with prices risin' and good harvests, so I'll get what I can out of the carryin' while it lasts and maybe put a bit by for when the peace comes. And the French say they're friends to the Irish and we should rise up again the king, but sure everyone knows they're a crowd of heathen blasphemers. No, bad cess to the lot of them, no disrespect to your callin' now, but I'll look after me own family and me own business and come out of this war with a bit of land and a few shillin's in me pocket."

Mullen had turned the war like a cut stone to expose facets of which Howlett had no previous notion. The concept of family was so vague to him, a drunken father who disappeared at an early stage and a slattern of a mother who raised no objection to his joining the colours as a bandboy, that he had come to think of the army as his home irrespective of where it might send him. It seemed indecent that a working man should think in terms of profiting from the war, whereas this was the natural function of a gentleman. As for the religion of one's antagonist, this was a notion that eluded him altogether. A soldier's profit was forty shillings a month and lucky to escape with all his limbs intact.

"But if you wake up some fine morning to see a French fleet lying out there, who do you think will protect your family and your business then? Your Clydesdales would pull French guns as well as any other!" Howlett's animation matched that of the Irishman as he pointed to an imaginary line of tricoloured ships on the horizon.

"By Jaysus, then I'll fight, Frenchman or blackymoor," and Mullen's hands tightened on the reins till the knuckles showed white under the freckles. "By Christ I'd go for them with the gevell."

"With the what?" Howlett had been warned about the use of the king's English.

"The gevell, the pitchfork." And suddenly the comic aspect of the situation struck Mullen and he gave a roar of laughter and slapped his passenger on the back. "By Jaysus, but that would put the heart across oul Bonaparte, meself and yourself up on the car with a couple of gevells and chargin' the hell out of his army." The tension broke and Howlett could picture it clearly. Tears rolled down his face as he laughed at the absurdity of it. Mullen slapped the pony into a canter and then into a gallop and with a wild yell splashed through the shallow pools until the iron rims crunched on the gravel of the dorn.

"Whoa there, whoa there," he called to the pony as he reined her in, slowing her to a gentle walk. "If Eileen sees me gallopin' on them stones she'll have me hide. She's that fond of the pony."

The sergeant felt unaccountably exhilarated by the boyish pleasure of the ride. Mullen reached behind him to an old coat folded in the corner of the cart. "Maybe we don't agree on everything, sergeant, but I'll wager you won't argue with a drop of the real stuff." He produced a small stoneware bottle and passed it to his passenger. "That's the lad that'll keep you warm if you have to spend the winter in your tower, the best of Irish whiskey".

Howlett uncorked the bottle and took a swig of the contents, letting it burn down his throat and take his breath away. Mullen retrieved the bottle and took a long pull on it. "What do you think of that then?" He looked sideways at his passenger and raised an eyebrow interrogatively.

"It's good stuff all right," agreed the sergeant. 'I'm a beer drinker myself but I can appreciate good liquor. Now if you hadn't told me what it was I would have sworn it was French brandy." He wondered fleetingly if he was already absorbing the habit of circumlocution from the atmosphere of the place.

"The best malt has always a sugestion of the brandy right enough. That's how you can tell the quality." Mullen smiled behind his beard but the humour showed in his eyes. He suggested that as they were now approaching the grassy slope of the island proper, they should dismount "and take the weight off Eileen's little friend", so together they made their way up the incline in high good humour, passing the bottle back and forth until it was empty, whereupon Mullen tossed it into his coat and wiped his beard with the back of his hand.

"Anyway, sergeant, you won't mind me askin' but what brings yourself to this part of the world? Surely an experienced gunner like yourself would be better employed in Spain on somewhere like that. You don't look to me like the kind of man they send to these parts, pensioners most likely and fellows wore out be the war."

"I suppose you could say I'm a bit like that too, now that I think of it." Howlett had never allowed himself to consider the longterm consequences of his injury nor had he anyone in whom he could confide his deeper fears, but the liquor had loosened his tongue and he found himself responding to the genuine interest of his new acquaintance. He explained as well as his untrained mind could, the condition as the surgeon had explained it. In Spain the previous year he had received a splinter of steel in his right eye. The surgeon had managed to remove it by means of a magnet but some weeks later the left eye had become inflamed. Since then both eyes had suffered periodic inflammation and were prone to infection. The surgeon had suggested the drastic expedient of removing the injured eye which Howlett had refused, considering that it was actually in better condition than the other. Since then, he explained, he was obliged to bathe his eyes in clean water and avoid as much strain on them as he could. To this end he had acquired spectacles, which he used for the little reading he did, particularly his music, or for examining maps or diagrams. He patted the pocket of his waistcoat to reassure himself that the spectacles were still safe.

Mullen showed instant concern. "And how do you manage at all?"

"Well I get along fairly well and I'm hopeful that things will improve. For the moment though, I've been sent here, I suppose," he made light of it, "until my aim gets better." They had by now reached the tower and halted at the ladder leading up to the door through which a man appeared buttoning his blue artillery coat in haste and adjusting his belt.

Within the shadow of the old church tower, between the graveyard and the sea, lay the Kybe with its cluster of white cottages that Peter Howlett had observed from the deck of the coastguard cutter. The Kybe, being almost an island in its own right, stood aloof from the village and was inhabited mostly by fisherfolk. Nets festooned the straggling driftwood fences and lobster cages were piled here and there by the limewashed gables. On the shingle foreshore small boats were drawn up above the high watermark, their black sides gleaming in the afternoon sun. Small children and the inevitable dogs cavorted in the pools, watched by the women who had taken the fine weather as an excuse for a break from the daily toil.

Eileen Mullen sat with her two young children, Lucy an independent young lady of three years and Matt, almost two now and just big enough to wander into mischief, tripping over stones or climbing on the crumbling grassy breakwater. She had, she reflected, the ideal life. At twenty-seven she was mistress of her own home and had a husband with his own business through his own hard work and beholden to no one. Their cottage on the Kybe was regarded as one of the finest and she took great pride and pleasure in keeping it and her trim vegetable garden in good order. What with a bit of land at Balcunnin, inherited from her father and the carrying business, she and John had little opportunity for idleness, but even in the bad times they were never short of something to put on the table.

She thought about her husband now as she watched him returning from the island, the water rising to the hubs of the cart and the little pony making a long vee shaped ripple as it breasted the flowing tide. She supposed that she had always wanted John Mullen, at least since she had begun to come into the village with her parents to deliver the buttermilk or the salty country butter which her mother used to make for Mr Morris of the Square. It was there she had first seen him, she remembered, laughing with the other barefooted boys and gazing at the unattainable sweet things in the shop window. He could not have been more than ten at the time and when her father had gone inside he had sat up on the car beside her and asked her name. The other boys had grinned in envy or admiration at his daring and nudged each other, muttering under their breath until a scuffle broke out and off they went, cuffing each other and pulling at ragged shirt-tails.

She had offered him an apple from the wooden tub.

"It's very small," he said.

"It's a Bath apple. Bath apples are always small."

There was a silence while John puzzled this out. Finally he asked, although he knew that he would appear foolish, "Are they called bath apples because you keep them in a tub?"

She had laughed then although she had no desire to ridicule this open and pleasant boy and he, hurt at first, had laughed with her.

"No, but what's so funny? Why are they bath apples?"

"Bath is a place where they grow little apples and we have some of those trees." All the same Eileen admitted it was a funny name for a place and an even funnier name for an apple. He had gone then, rejoining his friends who crowded around to see the wonder of the tiny apple, more like a crab apple to their eyes but a world away from crab apples in terms of sweetness. Off they went then as something else took their interest but he had turned and waved to her as they rounded the corner of Quay Street and, somehow, he had been part of her life ever since.

Looking back at her life on Lord Balcunnin's estate, it seemed almost idyllic, living in the gatelodge where the great people of the country came and went in their carriages and his lordship himself clattered by with his troop of militia, magnificent, if not exactly uniform, in their scarlet coats. In winter, even more exciting, the hunt met at Balcunnin house and the same gentlemen, now in hunting pink, took their stirrup cups, while hounds yelped and snorting horses stamped on the frosty ground impatient to be off.

Balcunnin himself rarely passed the lodge without a friendly wave and sometimes dismounted to discuss farming matters with her father and usually slipped a few pennies to herself and her brothers as they stood back shyly, staring with wide eyes at their important visitor. Her father, too, grew in stature on these occasions and was visibly proud of his position as chief herdsman on the greatest estate in Fingal.

Best of all, however, was when John Mullen, now growing into a sturdy young man, arrived with his father's great horses to haul timber from his lordship's woods or at harvest time to bring the grain to the harbour. Sometimes he delivered coal to the house and on these occasions she did not climb on the cart with him because of the risk to her petticoats but they would walk the length of the tree-lined drive, laughing and talking and sometimes holding hands, as if absent-mindedly. During the time that she worked in the shop for Mrs Morris John had been there in the evening, when his work permitted, to drive her home in his trap and even the irascible Mrs Morris responded to his cheerful good nature, although she pretended to disapprove of Eileen's stravagin' the roads at all hours with young scamps like John Mullen. She had refused offers from several suitors over the years, thinking them awkward and gangling by comparison with her John and it came as no surprise to anyone when, four years ago now, he led her to the mass house in Church Street where Father Clare pronounced them man and wife.

Eileen called her children to her and walked out to meet her husband as he turned the pony around the mussel rocks and veered towards the Kybe. John spotted them and slapped the pony into a trot.

When he reached the little group he jumped down, holding the reins and took the baby from Eileen and threw him in the air to Matt's delighted alarm.

"And how have all my chickens been today?" he asked, giving Eileen a playful slap on the rump as she climbed onto the cart. Lucy climbed up by the wheel and sat swinging her feet over the tail board.

"Now you stop and behave like a proper gentleman," Eileen scolded.

"But sure a gentleman would always help a lady into her carriage, wouldn't he? And what gentleman could resist such a severe temptation?"

"Now none of that talk, John Mullen. Do you want to scandalise your young daughter?" They laughed together as the pony once more broke into a trot and Eileen told him about her day. "And what brought you to the island today, anyway?" she asked.

"There's a new sergeant arrived today with the coastguard. A comical strange poor lad and nearly half blind, according to himself. Plays music too, he told me, on a fife or a flute or something, just like a Protestant, but I don't think he goes in much for religion. He seemed a dacent sort of man though, strangely enough". John was prepared to admit that there could be a 'dacent man' in the king's army, put there no doubt through no fault of his own, but he would have preferred if the king had deployed them in Spain or France where they would be of more use. "He says they're here to protect us but I told him that in some parts of the country they had caused more trouble than they cured."

"What did he say to that?" Eileen was not particularly interested in the loutish talk of soldiers but hoped that John had not left his bone with the dog in the discussion.

"Oh he didn't like that at all, at all. Talked about us bein' glad of them if old Bonaparte ever decided to come over here."

"I'm sure when his friends have introduced him to the widow Clooney, he'll have enough to occupy him without protectin' us from Bonaparte" Eileen replied archly.

"Now there's no need to talk like that about the poor woman and her just tryin' to feed all them childer of hers. And isn't it better that she keeps the soldiers occupied than havin' them around the place botherin' people." Mrs Clooney's public house was known to supply more than strong liquor to soldiers or visiting seamen. John did not wish to commit himself too strongly on her side, "but all the same I don't think it's charitable for Father Clare to be always prayin' for the poor woman off the altar like he does be doin'."

"Now that's enough about Mrs Clooney," said Eileen slapping the back of his hand, "or I'll think you've been goin' there yourself with your drinkin' friends."

"Now wouldn't there be the brave talk if I did and I with the finest lookin' girl in Fingal in me bed at home. Wouldn't they take me for the right amadhaun?" Eileen supposed that she should be gratified at coming out best in the comparison with the widow Clooney. "Well I'm very glad that you think you have a better deal and I dare say the sheets are cleaner too."

John was in no position to contest that. "Well, we won't worry about the army's problems. I'm starvin' with the hunger and I have to be away with the fish to Dublin whenever the boats get in. Now if you're a good girl and get me somethin' to eat, I'll bring you a present from the big city."

This was the aspect of John's business that she liked least, for when the tides were full in the evening, he had to travel all night to get the fish to the market and she missed the security of his presence in the house and the warmth of his hairy body in the wide featherbed in the inner room. On the other hand she loved the occasions when he returned early in the morning with presents for herself and the children, and she rose to stir the fire into a blaze and heat the porridge for him. She often went back to the bed with him then and they made love together before the children woke to demand attention and usher in the day with shrieks and yells. This was the warmest, safest time of all, with John beside her, asleep now and smelling slightly of fish and horses and sometimes a faint whiff of whiskey on his breath. He was entirely hers then and she would think, selfishly, no friends or children to make claims upon him.

"How would new potatoes and a couple of fresh mackerel suit you?"

"We dug the potatoes today," Lucy called from the back of the cart, "and Matt only pulled the flowers off," and she laughed at her little brother.

"That should go down very well, and how were the spuds?" It was always a matter of concern to see how the new potatoes looked.

"They're fine this year again and I have some grand butter to put on them. My mother sent some in with one of the estate men." Eileen's mother was what they called a well doin' woman and although her Eileen and John now worked their fields at Balcunnin she still lived at the lodge and made the butter in the dairy. Not everybody, she explained, had the gift or the prayers necessary to make the butter come just right.

The sun was beginning to sink behind the old church and in the distance the windmill, its arms stationary now, stood out against the reddening sky. On arriving at the cottage Eileen hurried inside to prepare the evening meal. John, meanwhile, drew water from the well for the pony and washed himself energetically in a wooden tub by the back door, shaking a spray of drops from his beard like a great hairy dog, much to the amusement of the children.

"Right so," he said, "let's get some food and then I'll pack you two off to bed before I go." He carried them inside and sat them on stools at the table leaving the top half-door open to let in the light and the cool air of the evening.

CHAPTER 3

Peter Howlett stood on the firing step on top of the tower and surveyed his area of responsibility. He leaned his elbows on the stone breastwork and levelled his spy glass as the small boat approached from behind the headland. Beneath the single russet coloured sail he could make out the figure of the old reprobate whom he had met on his arrival. There was a boy sitting in the bow, with his bare legs dangling in the spray. He watched idly as there was not a great deal else to do. Life on the island was restful enough but dull to a man more accustomed to marches and the bustle of the camp with, occasionally, the visceral excitement of battle thrown in. After service under Wellesley in the Peninsula, the thought of blowing Captain Garrigan from the water seemed tame entertainment, yet Howlett found himself instinctively calculating range and trajectory.

Below him on the shore he could see two of the gunners in their shirtsleeves, Bateson a stolid man nearing fifty and Laidlaw, a caustic short-tempered Scot, casting lines into the water in the hope of catching something for the evening meal. As yet they had succeeded only in catching large wriggling green crabs which Laidlaw dashed to pieces on the stones to use as further bait. The experiment, however, only established the cannibalistic and self-destructive tendencies of the crabs. The remaining gunner, Thurston, a young and enthusiastic fellow sent there by some administrative quirk, was asleep in the guardroom below, dreaming no doubt of cannonades and the glory that so far had eluded him. If Bonaparte could begin as a humble gunner why not Emperor Thurston, though he admitted that he would be moderately satisfied with a generalship as a start. Meanwhile, he chafed at the restrictions placed on his ambition by the straitness of the island station.

Howlett had instituted regular drill, a practice neglected by his predecessor. At first his gunners had resented the seemingly pointless drill and Laidlaw had grumbled sullenly under his breath. Gradually they had come to see it as a useful relief in the tedium and a sort of punctuation of their days. It had given their small community a cohesion that had previously been lacking, and while not making them boon companions, they were able to co-exist in reasonable harmony. Howlett was relieved that they did not find his music unduly irksome, although he rarely played in the guardroom, preferring when on watch to take his instrument up to the roof or when anyone was asleep, down to the beach, where the sound of the music merged agreeably with the constant murmur of the sea.

Skip Garrigan had brought his boat into the wind to the north of the island and was hauling on a line of corks. Howlett watched with interest as three or four cages were handled aboard and the boy removed a number of lobsters and crabs, which he dropped into the bilges of the little craft. He then rebaited the cages and dropped them over the stern with a series of splashes, the sound of which carried on the breeze to the watcher on the tower. Skip turned the small boat towards the shelving beach with the obvious intention of landing. Howlett snapped the spy glass shut and made his way down by the spiral staircase set into the massive eight foot thick wall. Thurston was sleeping like a babe on his low wooden bed and the sergeant quietly stepped out the door and stood at the top of the ladder, unwilling to leave his post, although the likelihood of Bonaparte seizing this opportunity for a surprise invasion was slight indeed.

On the boat the boy was already furling the sail and Skip stood on the beach with his trousers rolled up to the knee. He made the painter fast to a large stone and the boy waded ashore with a small cask under his arm. The boat swung easily in the curve of the beach, out of reach of the waves which broke over the submerged dorn. Laidlaw and Bateson abandoned their fruitless task and wandered over to engage the visitor in conversation.

"Yiz won't catch much there at this time o' day," volunteered Garrigan, looking at their makeshift lines. "Wait till evening and the mackerel might come in after the fry. I was jiggin' for them meself and I have a few in the boat there that might make a supper, if yiz'd like to buy them."

Since they could hardly take their custom elsewhere, Bateson agreed to take a half dozen and produced a fourpence from his fob reflecting no doubt that the laws of supply and demand operated nowhere more harshly than on a small rocky island among men accustomed to spartan military fare.

"Go you," said Garrigan to the boy, while deftly pocketing the groat, "and get six of the best for these gentlemen and throw in a crab or two for good measure and I'll bring the cask on up to the sergeant." Laidlaw eyed the cask with interest, thinking that perhaps the sergeant had more concern for their welfare than he had realised. Howlett also wondered about the cask as Garrigan arrived at the foot of the ladder. "What have you there for us sir," he called, trying to recall the old man's name and rank, "not some of your famous Irish malt I suppose."

"Well indeed it isn't," admitted Garrigan. "It's a present from a friend of mine John Mullen, the carrier, though I told him I didn't think it would do you much good."

"What is it then?" Howlett could not imagine what it could be. Casks were for powder, liquor, water or salt pork. His curiosity was aroused.

"Well as a matter of fact it's water. It's from the holy well at Balcunnin that's supposed to be great for the eyes, providin', of course, you say the right prayers. Now, I said to him, savin' your presence now sergeant, that you would most likely be a Protestant gentleman and probably damned already and that water would have no effect seein' as how you wouldn't know any real prayers but he says there's quare properties in the water and he would say the prayers for you himself. John does be passin' the well on his way to Dublin every couple o' days and sure he thought it couldn't do any harm."

Howlett was amused and struggled to hide a smile. "Convey my thanks to Mr Mullen for me then and tell me, do I drink this water or do I apply it to the eyes? Perhaps a combination of spirits and water would produce the desired effect." He regretted his tone immediately on seeing the offended look on Garrigan's face. "No, I'm sorry for smiling but I hope I'm not completely damned yet all the same. Tell Mr Mullen that I am truly grateful and shall certainly try the water."

Garrigan was mollified sufficiently to explain further about the holy well and the great patterns that were held there in the old days before the risings at the end of the century when the authorities put a stop to any such large gatherings in the interests of law and order. "We had fierce sport too in them days with drinkin' and prayin' and cripples leppin' up on their two legs and dancin' jigs for further orders. There was great fightin' too with the factions all batin' the hell out of each other. Many's the good stick I broke on me own head or someone else's," and he fingered his crown in reminiscence of happier times.

Howlett listened with interest, wondering about these people who could combine politics, music, liquor and prayer into one great, composite country festival.

"Aye, there'd be women too in the tinkers' tents." A faraway look came into the old man's eyes, "and the priests liftin' us out of there with his big blackthorn. Ah well," he finished and rose to go, "them was the days all right. Times has got fierce quiet nowadays. I tell you what, I'll be bringin' some lads over in a week or two to get the oats in for his lordship and maybe the oul eyes will be feelin' a bit better be then."

Howlett thanked him again for his trouble and walked with him to the edge of the beach. They met Bateson and Laidlaw coming up the slope with the mackerel on a string through the gills and three or four large crabs tied together at the claws, Laidlaw holding them gingerly at arm's length.

"Good luck to yiz now, gentlemen," called Garrigan as he hauled on the painter and stepped dryshod with surprising agility onto the deck of his little craft. The boy hauled on a halyard and the sail took the wind immediately. The boat came alive, falling back from the shore and heading into the strong running tide with spray breaking white over the bow.

Howlett returned to his station on the roof and peered through the glass at the towers to the north and south. No unusual signal replaced the flag on the flagstaff. He thought about the cask of holy water and resolved to try it anyway, although Laidlaw's ribald comments had made him feel a bit diffident about the whole thing. Laidlaw prided himself on his catholic tastes in matters of strong drink, but rejected superstition with all the vehemence of an unlettered John Knox. Be it said, however, that he differed from his great mentor in the matter of women. Howlett too had felt a twinge at the thought of the tinker women in the tents. It had been a long time now since he had encountered a woman and the tinker women somehow sounded more fresh and wholesome than the raddled whores supplied by the sutlers at Torres Vedras during the long winter of three years ago. In fact the joke went about that the rancid meat in the sutlers' cauldrons derived from those ladies who had completed their term of service and could be put to no other use. Whether true or not, the thought of the women of the camp even now filled him with a certain revulsion. Since then there had been village girls. Poets might describe them as sloe-eyed señoritas who, out of gratitude, offered their favours to the dashing English liberators, but to Howlett the reality was that they were hungry and were prepared to sell themselves for a loaf of bread or a few silver shillings. He resolved to investigate the premises in the town where Laidlaw intimated there was hospitality in plenty for His Majesty's soldiers. It crossed his mind that the thought was incongruous in a man who intended to bathe his eyes in holy water and perhaps make a fist of the Lord's Prayer, sheepishly from lack of practice. From below came the smell of frying fish and, as if to hint at dinner, the cat came and wound himself around his legs with low guttural whimpers. He lifted him onto the parapet where he paced back and forth regarding him with a knowing eye. He was a handsome ginger and Howlett had taking an instant liking to him. He was a ferocious hunter and kept the rats, which abounded on the island, well away from the tower. In early summer he fed royally on the newly fledged gulls, but bore the scars of several fierce encounters with the outraged parents. Bateson came slowly up the spiral stairs and emerged on the roof slightly out of breath.

"I reckon as how you could do with something to eat sergeant. The mackerel are good when you get 'em fresh."

"Aye, that I could, Bateson. I'll leave things in your hands then. Give us a hail if you spy the French." The standard joke raised the expected smile.

"Or Luke maybe," added Bateson. "We could put a shot across his bows."

"Who's Luke?" This was a new name to Howlett.

"Oh he's a notorious smuggler they say around here, but I don't know if anyone 'ave ever seen him. Others say he's a French privateer, but I don't know much about that either." Bateson scratched his head. He had not given the matter a great deal of thought, accepting the folklore at face value.

"Well he might make interesting sport for us sometime, but for the moment my friend and I shall concentrate on our supper". Howlett gathered up the cat and made his way below to the small semi-circular kitchen on the ground floor. The room, lit only by a small high window in the massive wall, was already quite dark and pungent with the smoke of frying mackerel. Laidlaw acted in the capacity of cook much of the time, maintaining that 'army vittles were bad enough without havin' some ignorant gunner muckin' them up even worser.' He handed Howlett a tin plate of potatoes boiled in their jackets and flipped a fried fish out of the blackened pan. They sat down at the rough wooden table and Laidlaw remarked, "Get that into ye sergeant; as good as your Lowestoft herrings any day."

Howlett was not prepared to let provincial loyalties interrupt his meal and concentrated on a careful dissection of the fish. The skin and bones he dropped on the flagstone where they were pounced on by the cat. Thurston appeared, still bleary eyed from his long sleep, and applied himself to the food with his customary enthusiasm. Thurston's conversation, carried on with great volubility, ranged widely over the conduct of the war, the art of gunnery, the personal lives of the great on which he professed to be an expert, while particles of food fell from his lips in quantities comparable to his gems of wisdom. Laidlaw's more scabrous sense of humour tried to stem the flow with footnotes on the more pressing realities of life in the service, the lack of 'weemin', diseases of soldiers, the paucity of money and the stupidity of the high command, not on any particular point of strategy, but the general, all pervading, ineluctable ineptitude of all officers at all times since war began.

Howlett found the exchange entertaining but felt at the same time that the argument veered close enough to personal abuse. He sensed an undercurrent of violence in Laidlaw which he supposed could be attributed to living in cramped quarters with men of different viewpoints. The situation was hardly helped by Thurston's alarming table manners. He showed total incompetence in dealing with the bonier parts of the fish, producing a pile of mangled remains which seemed to exceed in volume the original mackerel, much to the delight of the cat. Again Howlett noted how Laidlaw cleared away the plates and swept the floor with a kind of repressed savagery, leaving the place clean enough but muttering under his breath. He thanked him for his efforts, deciding that Laidlaw was due for some time ashore.

It was then that he thought of Mullen and remembered the cask. As his eyes were bothering him again he went up to the guardroom and drew off a cup of water and sniffed at it. He wondered whether he should boil it as the surgeon had recommended but he was reluctant to disturb Laidlaw who was still muttering below. As regards prayers, Howlett felt that it would be a bit unreasonable of him to be disturbing God after so long and decided to rely on the properties which the little captain had claimed for the well.

It stung his eyes slightly with an agreeable tingling sensation. He dabbed gently with a cloth. It was well known that medicine which stung or tasted foul was good for you. He replaced the bung in the cask and walked to the door to empty the contents of the cup. There was no miraculous improvement but his eyes felt less gritty. Westwards, he could dimly make out the low hills of the mainland in the twilight with, here and there, a light in the cottages on the Kybe.

Summer ripened gradually into autumn and the fields on the headland turned golden yellow with corn. The men and women came to the island with the little skipper to cut and bind the oats. The soldiers ambled over to watch them, the men standing to the waist-high oats, their scythes swinging rhythmically, levelling the stalks with a sound like tearing cloth and the women and boys bending to gather and bind the sheaves and build them into stooks.

At the time of the low spring tides in early September, Eileen stood at the kitchen window watching the heavy carts laden with sheaves lumbering landwards along the dorn. She thought of the excitement of 'drawin' in' when she lived at Balcunnin, when the stooks were gathered into the haggard from all parts of the estate and the men built the towering ricks in preparation for the threshing. There would be strangers from the town, hired for the week and the wild looking countrymen who migrated from one threshing to another. Then there would be dancing and drinking with refreshments for the children. Her reverie was interrupted as the room darkened and someone knocked at the half door. She turned and saw to her surprise a soldier in blue artillery uniform, his musket slung over his left shoulder.

"Is this the house of John Mullen, the carrier?" he asked and she noticed for the first time the sergeant's stripes on his sleeve.

"Yes," she replied with some alarm. "Is there something wrong?" She moved towards the door and the sergeant saw her more clearly in the light. He noticed her long hair falling over the simple white collar and, in particular, he was struck by her eyes, a deep shade of green and wide now with apprehension.

"No ma'am. You must forgive me for startling you. My name is Howlett and I am sergeant on the island there. I called to thank your husband for a kindness he did me."

"Oh, you must be the man with the sore eyes." Realisation dawned on her face and she smiled. "And how are they now?" "Well, that's just it. They feel much better and I would say that the sight has improved. Is your husband about?" Howlett felt confused for no reason that he could pinpoint and wished that the carrier would appear from somewhere.

"He's in the town but he should be back presently. Maybe you would like to wait." Eileen did not invite him inside. Soldiers were not the kind of people you would entertain in your home. She did, however, make the concession of asking him to sit down on the tub upturned outside the door but he declined, preferring to pace on the small gravel path with the thumb of his left hand hooked into the strap of his musket. The children came shyly to stare at the tall dark-skinned soldier with the neat black moustache, Matt and Lucy and some of their friends.

Eileen resumed her work self consciously, paying no overt attention to the visitor. She found that she fumbled with the dishes and fell to wiping down the white deal table. She wished that John would return and resolve the awkwardness. Soon she became conscious of the murmur of voices and secretively she contrived to look out through the upper half of the door. To her surprise she saw the sergeant squatting on his heels talking to a group of small children who crawled around obviously regaling him with information about themselves and their locality. Some reached out timidly to touch the uniform and its insignia or to run their hands along the pipeclayed webbing, while the boys in particular stared enviously at the huge brown musket. The sergeant was nodding seriously although Eileen doubted very much if he could understand their chatter.

Howlett would have liked to talk with her but no pretext occurred to him. He wondered what she was doing and pictured her going about her duties within. After a while it struck him as strange that she did not reappear even to speak to her children, as presumably some of these were hers. He felt uncomfortable and in the way and decided to leave, disengaging himself without gruffness from the group of small children. He walked to the door and knocked again. Eileen felt a stab of fear in her belly. "Yes sergeant." She sounded more hostile than she had intended. She put down her brush and wiped her hands on her apron, self-consciously busy.

"I must be off ma'am, so perhaps you would tell your husband that I called. Again thank him for me and tell him that I feel a considerable improvement in the eyes." He was tempted to make some joke about the prayers but thought wiser of it. There was no knowing how she might take it. Women, he had noticed, tended to be more proprietorial about the Almighty than most of the men he had met. God, he thought, that sounds pompous. Why not say that my eyes are better? Considerable improvement!

"Very well, sergeant, and goodbye to you," like dismissing a beggar from the door. Eileen was ashamed of her abruptness and glad to see him go. She watched him walking down the little path and bending to close the wooden gate behind him. She noticed the tan of his hand against the white paint, the curve of his back with the light falling on his shoulder and the dark shadow on his face from the peak of his shako. For such a mild spoken man there was something dangerous about him. Perhaps it was his complete self assurance, an air of authority. He had a certain coldness, she thought. He was obviously a man who was used to getting his own way.

Christ, Howlett thought to himself, I almost tripped. I must have looked a complete fool, fumbling at that blasted gate. He felt her eyes boring into his back as he stepped along the cobbled track, careful not to trip on the worn stones, his legs feeling stiff and awkward. It was a relief to get around the corner of the next cottage and he relaxed, knowing that he was safely out of her line of vision. He glanced back to check. There was no one to be seen. He slung his musket more comfortably and set off towards the town. Soon he began to whistle pensively through his teeth. The track linking the Kybe to the town led over a small footbridge where the stream widened out before meeting the sea. In the stream John Mullen had halted to let the pony drink. The carrier was sitting relaxed on the cart, smoking the inevitable clay pipe. Howlett felt embarrassed for no reason that he could explain. He leaned on the low parapet of the bridge as Mullen raised a hand in salute.

"That's a fine evening sergeant, and how are things with yourself?" said the carrier, removing his pipe and tapping it on the side of the cart.

"I'm very well and thank you for your concern," replied Howlett, adding casually, "I called to your home beyond and your wife told me you were in town. I came to tell you that my eyes are much better". He checked himself for fear that he might be prattling conspicuously. Why should he feel guilty for a simple act of civility?

"Well that's just great, just great." Mullen was genuinely pleased. "The well is a powerful man all right. Of course, I threw in the few prayers just to be on the safe side." He looked sideways at Howlett with an amused twinkle in his eye. "We might not have the bells or the steeples like youse folk, but we have the powerful prayers."

"They seem to be working for me all right. I can't deny that." Howlett found it easy to fit in with the carrier's good humour.

"So you must have met my family above then. Did herself give you a bite to eat?" asked Mullen. Howlett replied that he was in a bit of a hurry and had not been able to wait for long. That was not strictly true.

"You could come back with me now and have a bit of dinner with us if you like. Maybe you could tell us a bit about your travels and so on." Mullen was intrigued to know more about a life so different from his own.

"That's very civil of you, John." The familiarity of the name sounded strange to Howlett, "but I must report to Captain Osgood." That was another lie.

More likely report to Mrs Clooney, the carrier thought but held his tongue. "I suppose you've heard all about the great battles in Austria. It looks like you may be hearing from Bonaparte after all."

"We hear very little on our island I'm afraid but I know that he has concentrated his army around Dresden, or what's left of his army after Russia."

"Well, he's on the go again or so they're saying over at the boats. He's runnin' rings around them Austrians be all accounts."

"A remarkable man, there's no doubt. He has the luck of the devil."

"Are you sure now you won't come back with me for somethin' to eat? Ye must be tired of army rations over beyond."

"No thank you. I must get into town directly." Howlett hoped that Mullen would not ask about his accommodation for the night. As yet he had only the vaguest notion of where he would stay being more in search of diversion than rest and presumed that he could bed down if necessary at the tower by the harbour.

"Well then, I'm sure we'll be seein' you around the place. Mup there," this to the pony who raised her head from the stream and shook it vigorously with a jingle of harness. "Good luck to you then sergeant. I'm glad to hear about the oul eyes." The cart rumbled from the stream and Mullen slapped the pony into a trot. Howlett turned to watch him go and felt a pang of envy for this man whose life seemed so straightforward and comfortable compared with his own. What must it be like to arrive home at evening to a dinner prepared for you and a wife and children to bid you welcome, particularly a wife like Eileen Mullen?

Beyond the stream to the left lay some market gardens and swampy ground while to the right lay the dunes covered with tall spiky grass. Howlett stepped out smartly towards Church Street which soon led him to The Square. He noted the curious looks of the group of men standing at the corner of Quay Street. An elderly man was busily removing baskets of vegetables from the flagstones in front of the most imposing premises which bore the legend 'W. Morris, General Grocer, Wines and Spirits.' A woman, presumably his wife, swept away the dust and scraps of leaves, pursuing every speck of dust with meticulous care. Howlett touched the peak of his cap courteously.

"Good evening," he said. "Perhaps you can direct me to an eating house belonging to a woman by the name of Clooney." He was indeed hungry as well as thirsty. The woman visibly stiffened and brushed more vigorously, her lips set in a firm line of disapproval. The man put down the baskets he had just that moment lifted and looked at the sergeant. "Oh aye, Clooneys. It's on the right, down Quay Street just before you come out on the harbour road. Just be careful not to drink the whiskey though," and the man chuckled knowingly. "Tell him to be careful about a few other things too," said the woman to the small cloud of dust that rose in front of her, "a young fellow like that."

"Aye and the porter too," and the man winked conspiratorially, two men of the world together. The sergeant somehow was touched by the woman's remark. It was a long time since anyone had regarded him as a young fellow, some gruff bandsmen perhaps in his early days. Since then it had been his responsibility to look after young fellows, stemming their panic under fire, while concealing his own fear, or encouraging them on the long sweltering soul-destroying treks from one battle-ground to another. For the second time that evening he felt awkward and embarrassed about his destination, feeling that his thoughts lay open to any observer. "I'm obliged to you sir, ma'am." He tipped the peak of his cap again. "Good night to you."

"Good night sergeant," replied the man, "and remember about the whiskey." His laugh carried on the soft night air as also did the sharp reprimand of his wife.

The loungers at the corner who had caught every word of the exchange, smirked and nudged one another. One or two spat or wrung out their pipes. Others muttered a 'good night sergeant', as he passed. "Be jasus sergeant but haven't youse the fine time of it with boots on your feet and money in your pockets, eh?" volunteered one of the men.

"Well now, I can arrange for all of you gentlemen to enjoy the same comforts." This was a situation with which Howlett was familiar, the easy banter among men in which his rank always gave him an advantage.

"Oh, we wouldn't be thinking of anything extreme like. Donovan's the name by the way, Larry Donovan. Maybe I'll walk along with you and enjoy the night air as I'm going your way anyhow." So saying the man fell into step beside Howlett, appointing himself official guide and interpreter, commenting on the people they met, the size and customs of the town and the extensive voyages of its trading vessels. As if by instinct they turned in the open door of the public house, the sergeant stooping under the low doorway. Donovan steered him through the smoke and the throng of seamen until they reached the bar.

CHAPTER 4

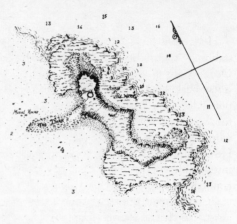

Mrs Clooney's establishment was typical of seamen's public houses in any port. Drinking was the main concern of the customers but for a few coppers a plate of fish or bacon and cabbage could be obtained. Mrs Clooney prided herself on the quantity of her food if not on hygiene. The customers were a mixed lot as befitted a sea port. Hunched at the bar was a group of northern fishermen, their musical accents rising and falling as they laughed over some professional matter. Donovan explained that the Kilkeel men often found themselves detained in these parts due to weather conditions or particularly good fishing, although he suspected himself that they were more likely running from shelter from their dour calvinistic wives, to do some serious drinking in the depraved and idolatrous south. This was explained in short asides while supervising the pouring of the porter, a complicated matter involving a barrel, some jugs and a tray 'to catch the ullage.' Again the language problem arose for Howlett who understood ullage to be a gap between the contents and the top of the barrel. All the same he admitted that the word sounded appropriate for the evil looking fluid swilling about in the tray. Mrs Clooney thriftily and dexterously, poured the 'ullage' into a jug and topped up the two pints.

He had to admit that the taste was not bad at all and Donovan downed his pint with speed, wiping the foam from his upper lip with the back of his hand. Again in his capacity as guide and mentor, he ordered two more for which Howlett also paid, thinking it a small price for his education. Donovan raised his voice over the roar of voices and continued his exposition. The African looking men in the corner were just after discharging the cargo of a coal boat from Wales. They sat in black clothes, with black pints in black hands and the lamplight gleamed on their oily black faces.

Here and there groups of local fishermen talked and argued, stabbing with forefingers and swearing to emphasise a point. Occasionally a singer broke into song only to abandon the effort after a few bars. Two dragoons and a coast-guard rating sat at a long table to one side, the red uniforms making a splash of colour in the fog of tobacco smoke. They were, as Donovan remarked, in good form and working diligently at large plates of the celebrated bacon and cabbage. Howlett joined them and ordered the same for himself and his now inseparable companion. "And what brings dragoons to this part of the country?" he asked.

"Coast guard duties," replied one of the dragoons. "We have to assist our friend here," slapping the rating on the shoulder, "in apprehending smugglers. At the moment we're gathering intelligence and this appears the most likely place." The soldiers guffawed and ordered another round.

"Oh yiz've come to the right place all right," broke in Donovan. "This place does be alive with them all the same. I seen scads o' them here in me time. Dangerous they are."

"What about Luke? I heard mention of some fellow by that name."

"A desperate man sergeant. A real cut throat. I seen him in here time and again. We'd be well rid of him now if youse men could lay hold of him. Hey Skip, come over here a minute." Donovan waved to the familiar figure of Garrigan who approached through the fog. "Skip, these men is after smugglers. They're collectin' intelligence now, isn't that a good one?"

"Smugglers is it?" said Garrigan, sitting down with a mug of ale. Aye we know about them lads all right." He rolled his eyes heavenward.

"Tell them about Luke, Skip. You've met him haven't ye?" The coastguard and the soldiers leaned forward intently.

"The scourge o' the seas gentlemen, the scourge o' the seas." Skip thumped the table with clenched fist. "He does be in and out along this coast like a ghost. He could be in here tonight for all we know." Garrigan surveyed the room furtively and then relaxed. "I wouldn't want it to get about that we was discussin' Luke with youse gentlemen but I know yiz are discreet." He tapped the side of his nose significantly and embarked on a colourful account of the notorious privateer, cut throat, agent provocateur and general subversive whose activities had apparently done much to further the French cause during the previous fifteen years of war.

The rapid succession of pints, some of them now by courtesy of

Donovan who had managed to negotiate credit with the formidable Mrs Clooney, had begun to fog Howlett's brain but certain inconsistencies niggled at the back of his mind. Firstly the depredations of this buccaneer had apparently gone unnoticed in the rest of the kingdom and secondly Garrigan had picked a strange place to impart secret information to His Majesty's forces, since every word was audible to the occupants of the nearest table, as villainous looking a crew as he had ever seen, their knives flashing as they hacked at their food. He noticed how they muttered among themselves and leaned sideways occasionally to catch some of the more lurid parts of Garrigan's account.

If, technically, Mrs Clooney's was a disorderly house, the disorder was strictly on her own terms. She was a large and muscular woman with a raucous laugh and a round of language to match that of her customers. Undoubtedly, she had been a good looking woman at one time; the seven or eight children of various complexions testified to her attractiveness to a variety of men since her husband died. She was a sore trial to poor Father Clare who had tried without success on numerous occasions to persuade her to marry but he retreated always before her good humoured dictum 'Better ten bastards nor one bad husband'. The demise of her husband was by now lost in the mists of legend, a small forgotten, domestic tragedy, dismissed in ribaldry and laughter. When Mrs Clooney ejected a customer for whatever reason took her fancy, that customer left without demur. When she took a liking to a customer that fortunate man was treated as a favourite son. She found herself approving of the young sergeant who sat at the table with the soldiers and the two local men. He was not noisy like the others, although he drank as much as they. Neither did he treat the locals with the patronising good humour of the dragoons, nor was he fooled by them. She noticed how they tended to turn to him for corroboration and how he responded with a native courtesy, measuring his remarks before committing himself.

It was well after midnight when she came over to ask if anyone needed a room for the night. The dragoons laughed and asked whether the usual comforts were available. Mrs Clooney indicated that everything was taken care of. Garrigan rose unobtrusively and shuffled unsteadily towards the door. Donovan nudged the sergeant and recommended the hospitality with a salacious leer.

"Get out of here Larry Donovan, ye little scut ye. And what would you know about it?" Mrs Clooney snapped and aimed a cuff at the unfortunate Donovan's ear. "Your knees will be knockin' if I tell your missus you was in here spendin' money ye haven't got." Donovan fled. She turned again to the sergeant. "And will you be stayin' the night yourself sergeant?"

"Well, yes. I had intended to enquire about lodgings earlier but the time slipped by." He noticed how his words slurred and he spoke with the elaborate care of the inebriate. "If you would be so kind as to conduct me to a room." He seemed to be standing to one side observing the scene as she took him by the arm and steered him towards the door at the back of the bar from which most of the customers had departed. The Kilkeel men had lapsed into silence and were drinking with the sullen desperation of men on too short a holiday, determined to extract the maximum pleasure from the occasion. She led him up a twisting flight of stairs to a landing, from which opened six or seven doors. From behind the doors came the sound of snores and furtive rustlings. Occasional grunts and laughter could be heard and the clink of glasses. Through an open door he caught sight of several children sleeping on mattresses on the floor. Outside somewhere a dog barked, fell silent and barked again. The room was small and barely furnished. A small window opened onto the street.

"I'll leave you now sergeant to make yourself comfortable. You'll be wantin' breakfast early no doubt." Mrs Clooney placed a lighted candle on the stool and closed the door. Howlett stood for a moment at the open window and breathed the cool night air. His head felt light and for some reason he felt sad. Down in the street he could see a figure, which he reckoned to be Garrigan, standing in the dim light from the bar, holding an animated conversation with two or three seamen. He wondered vaguely if it had something to do with the conversation about smugglers.

His thoughts were interrupted by the sound of the door closing. He had almost forgotten the business of the house. He turned to see a girl of about sixteen standing with her back to the door. She was dressed only in a short white shift and she looked at him with a frightened smile. "Missus sent me," she said and stood nervously watching him. In the candle light she looked sallow like the village girls in Spain. Howlett felt his need of a woman and his heart began to thump audibly so that he felt she must surely hear it. There was a taste of salt in his mouth. He sat down on the side of the bed and beckoned to her.

"You can give me a hand with these boots for a start. What's your name?"

"Bridie sir." What else had he expected? She knelt in front of him and wrestled with the boots. He could see the whiteness of her young breasts through the open neck of her shift.

"And how old are you, Bridie?"

"I dunno, sir. About fifteen or sixteen, sir."

Always the sir, he thought. I can buy her and throw her away and she still calls me sir. It wasn't right. He could see now that her eyes were green as she looked up at him. This child was not what he wanted. Like it was said of drowning men, his life passed before his eyes. It was a bleak prospect both past and future. He had never really wanted anything, he realised, except the immediate gratification of an appetite, a drink, a woman, a dry pair of stockings, the comfort of a fire or a refuge from the rain. He had never had any concept of ambition, something to work for like Mullen the carrier. He was, he realised with dismay, as valueless as this child, someone to be used and forgotten when his usefulness was over, perhaps to end his days like the other limbless scarecrows who littered the streets and roads of the kingdom. The pointlessness of it struck him like a blow. To his astonishment he felt his eyes stinging with tears and turned aside with embarrassment.

The child was frightened. "What is it sir? Did I do something wrong?"

"No, no, not at all". Christ, I'm nearly old enough to be her father, he thought. "Nothing at all." It must be the drink that was affecting him. It was a long time since he had had so much. "But I tell you what you can do Bridie. Go along to bed yourself and bring me some hot water for shaving in the morning." He groped awkwardly in his coat pocket. "Here's a shilling for yourself and mind you don't say a word to anyone."

"I won't tell a soul sir." Bridie still kneeling on the floor gazed at the coin in her hand in amazement. Impulsively he took her face between his hands and kissed her on the forehead with a gentleness he had never suspected in himself. "Off you go now and see that you're early in the morning with the water." She leaped up with a delighted smile of relief and opened the door. "Oh yes sir, and thank you for the shillin'."

He lay back on the bed after the door closed. I must be going soft in the head, he thought. He closed his eyes. Still he could see the eyes clearly as he drifted off to sleep, green eyes that gazed at him as if they could see into his soul. He knew somehow that he had seen those eyes before and that they were not the eyes of the child.

Peter Howlett was conscious of a dull pain in the back of his head as he walked towards the harbour. The events of the previous night seemed unreal in the early morning light and he turned his mind towards his meeting with his Commanding Officer. He had formed no impression of Osgood on their first brief meeting and since then they had not met as Osgood had been away in the southern part of his sector towards Howth. Now it was time to relieve the gunners on the island and Howlett was intrigued to make the further acquantance of his captain who was by report no ordinary artillery officer. He had apparently made himself at home at the coastguard station where he had billeted a dozen of his company. Others were distibuted in the vicinity in stable lofts and houses near the harbour. His activities had expanded to such an extent that the coastguard officers seized any opportunity to put to sea, for breathing space as they said, but generally everyone appeared to rub along pretty well together.

The tide was low and fishing smacks lay, with slanted masts, on the hard wet sand. Others stood on their stumpy keels against the harbour wall. Drying nets and ropes littered the roadside and festooned the bollards. As yet there was little activity. One or two figures moved on the quay side and a troop of gulls picked idly around the edge of the tide. The sharp salty smell had an astringent effect on Howlett's nerves and he felt his spirits improving as his head cleared.

Captain Osgood was sitting at his large work table when Howlett entered the room and saluted. "Ah, good morning, sergeant. Welcome to my centre of operations," he greeted him. "You're changing the tower details, I presume." That disposed of the main business of Howlett's call without preliminaries. "The corporal below will give you the names."

"Very good, sir" replied Howlett, "I shall send the men over directly by boat."

The captain had taken what must have been the finest room in the coastguard station as his centre of operations, whatever they might be and that was none too clear at first glance. A large oriel window overlooking the anchorage, lit the long upstairs room, offering abundant light for the business of mapping which appeared to be the captain's main concern. Three of the walls were covered with beautifully executed maps of the locality, backed with coarse linen for protection. The fourth wall supported shelving on which Howlett could see a variety of rocks and stones of different shapes and colours. The table itself was littered with pots of ink and paste, a jar containing a sheaf of writing and drawing implements and a box of instruments, protractors and the like. The box struck Howlett as a particularly fine piece of work and bore the maker's name, 'James Simon, London', on a brass plate inside the open lid.

"Well sergeant," the captain looked up again from the map he had been studying. "What do you think of my maps?"

"Very fine, sir" replied Howlett. It seemed a strange question.

"Ah, you don't understand. You see, I draw them myself. One of the benefits of this damned war is that it has given me the use of sufficient men to indulge my passion for cartography."

"Now I understand, sir. I beg your pardon." Howlett leaned forward to inspect the map on which the captain had been working. He was impressed by the neatness of the detail and recognised his island, shaped like a footprint, immediately. Fine brown hachures indicated the clay cliffs at the northern end and a small black circle denoted the tower. The dorn, indicated by dots, stood out from the western side like a blade.

"You see what we have here," said Osgood, pleased to have an interested listener. "I have almost completed my survey of the immediate area of the coast down to the high water mark. I shall require your men to measure below that mark." He indicated the heavy black line with his ink stained finger, "down to the low water mark at spring tide level. Uncomfortable work I'll be bound, but it can wait a while."

Howlett pictured for a moment the present detail clambering over wet rocks and seaweed with surveyor's chains and poles and imagined Laidlaw's comments on the business. He repressed a smile.

"You see how important your island is in the matter of visibility. I can calculate most of the altitudes of the district from there. You have noticed the stakes marking the various vantage points?"

"Yes sir. I wondered why there were four of them."

"Precision sergeant. The time has come for a complete mapping survey of the whole kingdom. Now Vallencey's maps are good but I hope to go one better. I haven't been granted any funds as yet but I offset that by making use of his majesty's troops. As you can see I have based my maps on a scale of eight inches to the mile, which allows for convenient subdivision into furlongs and rods." Howlett nodded. "Now come and look at these." He took Howlett by the arm and brought him to inspect some of the maps on the wall, indicating the beauty of his work with enthusiasm. "These are my pride and joy. Thirty two inches to the mile." Large sections of the district appeared in beautifully watercoloured detail. "I'm recommending that this should be adopted as standard practice, brown for the lower areas, suggesting rock and sand and green for the higher zones for obvious reasons. I expect that my scales will also become standard in time." He moved along the line of maps, commenting as he went, on the coastline as far as Howth. "The coastline is the easiest part. When we move inland our real difficulties will begin. It will probably take a century, if we ever get started at all."

"But sir, would there be a need for a survey of the whole country? I mean we are hardly likely to get involved in major campaigns in Ireland, are we?" Howlett felt that a lot of this dedicated effort might be unnecessary. Captain Osgood did not allow sceptics to dampen his enthusiasm.

"There you see. The military mind! We were not put upon this world merely to blow each other to pieces. Commerce, sergeant. People need maps for land purchase, road building, canals." His voice rose with the ardour of a preacher. "Navigation. Where would our navy be if we had no charts?" A rhetorical question for which Howlett could think of no answer.

"But all the same, sir, just supposing you print these maps and make them generally available, might not the French or some other power lay hold of them and use them to our disadvantage." It seemed to Howlett a bit like sticking out your chin and inviting the enemy to let drive at it.

"A detail, sergeant, a detail. I doubt if maps would make much difference. Most generals can contrive to get themselves lost just as well with maps as without them." Laidlaw and the Captain subscribed to the same creed it seemed, although expressed in different idioms. "The benefits will far outweigh the temporary disadvantages. However, let the next generation worry about that. I shall concentrate on the coastal area, constructing the framework as it were. Being the instigator of a scheme has certain advantages in that one can pick the most interesting parts for one's self."

"How do you mean sir?"

"The coastline is fascinating, sergeant. There you may descry the very structure of the land torn open to view, almost like the handprint of the Almighty." Again the missionary tone crept into his voice.

"Well I don't rightly understand about all that sir," muttered Howlett at a loss to see where it was all leading. Osgood could see his confusion and paused. "Perhaps I am overstating things a bit," he smiled. "But let me show you my collection of fossils. I can see that you take me for an eccentric, sergeant, but rest assured that this is not the case. I feel sure that these elegant objects hold some secret which may prove to be of importance."

"I dare say, sir" replied Howlett. "Some of them look like insects, sir, don't they? And some look rather like leaves." He leaned closer, intrigued. Certainly some of the items looked for all the world like the imprint of leaves or snails in the grey lumps of rock but he could not imagine how a soft body could leave a mark on a rock.

"Look at this beauty, sergeant" said Osgood and handed him a spiral of grey stone about the size of the palm of his hand. Beauty and elegance were not words that would have occurred to Howlett to describe a representation of a large snail but the object had an undeniable beauty in the perfection of its spiral and the translucence of the glazed, grey stone. "I don't claim to understand about them myself but I have made a practice of collecting the most striking specimens in the hope of finding out a bit about them. If you should happen across any further specimens in the course of your surveys, I should be obliged if you would let me have them."

"I shall certainly do that, sir," said Howlett.

"No, seriously, sergeant, I am interested in expanding my collection although, of course, this activity must take second place to our military duties." The captain laughed. "You need not fear that I am going to turn you and your men into pioneers."

"That is a relief, sir. I was never overfond of digging." Howlett began to feel that the captain was after all sane and that his interest was a harmless diversion. Osgood he supposed was most likely one of those scientific gentlemen who had found himself in the artillery more or less by accident.

"You see sergeant, I believe that at some time in the past these objects were in fact alive." This was a bit too much for Howlett to accept but he raised no argument. The captain was standing by the window and glanced down at the sound of approaching hooves. "Now sergeant, here's another interesting specimen." Howlett looked down to see a tall spare man dressed in a dark riding habit approaching.

"This is Balcunnin. He owns the town and most of the land hereabouts, and God knows how much land in Somerset and elsewhere. A very fine fellow as you will probably learn." There was the sound of boots on the stair and the door opened. The corporal announced, "Lord Balcunnin to see you, captain."

His lordship stooped to enter the room and handed his hat and riding crop to the corporal who looked about him and placed the objects on a chest near the door. "Good morning to you captain", said his lordship in a sharp voice that crackled like twigs breaking underfoot. "I find you well, I trust."

"Yes, thank you, your lordship. May I introduce my new sergeant, Peter Howlett." Artillery companies had long been noted for the paternalistic command structure and Osgood saw no incongruity in introducing Howlett as a friend.

"Sir," responded Howlett and saluted.

"The sergeant has come here to recuperate, sir" went on the captain. "I think the sea air is doing him good."

"Excellent, captain, excellent." His lordship having disposed of the social niceties produced a roll of papers and parchment from under his arm. "Now these are the maps of my lands I was telling you about. I shall be happy to place them at your disposal if they are of any use to you." He unrolled the outer map, a quaint piece of work of over a century before, with trees and buildings drawn in and some attempt at perspective. Osgood bent to examine it. "It's a beautiful piece of work sir, but none too accurate I'm afraid. I expect that when we have completed our survey inland, your maps will look less decorative and more useful."

"I shall leave them in your hands at that rate. You and your men have access to my grounds at any time, of course, and make use of my workers if they should appear idle."

"You can expect us quite soon then, sir, as I must employ my men as much as possible. We don't want any conflict with the townspeople."

"Indeed, we do not captain and may I say that we have been fortunate here in that respect. Certainly in other places the idleness of the soldiers has contributed in no small way to outbreaks of sedition. As magistrate I appreciate your contribution to public order."

"A great pleasure, sir, when I can follow my own particular interests at the same time." The captain was gratified that his work did not pass unnoticed.

"And what of yourself sergeant? How have you adapted to our peaceful backwater?" Balcunnin turned to Howlett.

"Well sir, it makes a change from the wars." Howlett replied careful to avoid comment on the tedium of the island station.

"The sergeant is musical, my lord, like yourself, if I may say so," broke in Osgood with a certain pride.

"Do you tell me?" His lordship was immediately interested. "And what do you play?"

"Clarinet, sir. I played a fife as a youngster but I prefer the clarinet." Howlett shuffled slightly in disparagement of his talent. "I acquired one of my own as a matter of fact and it has given me much pleasure over the years."

"I hope you can say the same for your comrades in arms." His lordship's manner suggested that he would expect proficiency in anyone claiming to have a skill. "Perhaps we shall have the opportunity of hearing you play sometime." Abruptly Balcunnin changed the subject. "Well Captain Osgood, I must see to my men."

"Are you on manoeuvres, sir?" Osgood strove to keep any trace of superciliousness from his voice. Regular troops tended to regard the local militias in Ireland with amused contempt. The popular picture was of a raggle-taggle of debauched minor squires on sway-backed nags, harrying their own people, a view beloved of cartoonists on the other side of the water, where the internecine quarrels of the simian Irish were a source of constant entertainment. Indeed, it would be true to say that in the troubled times, at the turn of the century, the behaviour of militiamen more than any action of the regular army, had turned the people of all persuasions against the Dublin government. In all fairness Balcunnin's troop was not typical. The area had always been peaceful, being inside the Pale and his lordship tended to regard manoeuvres as a means of keeping his men in condition for the hunting season.

"Yes," he replied with a laugh, "but if I don't keep an eye on my brother, he'll have the thatch from over my tenants' heads." His lordship's brother Ned conformed more closely to the popular picture of the Irish squire, and was known to be a trial to the head of the family. Their father had given Ned a seat in the old parliament in Dublin where he had distinguished himself as a roaring boy among the bucks of that city but Balcunnin on inheriting the estate had baulked at the idea of sending Ned to Westminster. Consequently, Ned divided his time between the estates in Ireland and England with forays into London society for light relief from his responsibilities. When at home, which, fortunately, was not too often, he held the rank of major in the militia.

In response to Howlett's expression of puzzlement Balcunnin expanded on his remark. "You see I have lands in Mayo, which is on the west coast. It's a much poorer area than this and I must admit a more disaffected area I have never come across. Fit only for sheep, if I could persuade the people to go elsewhere. It is unfortunately necessary to keep a sharp eye on the populace and this has entailed searching for weapons with some stringency. I go there as little as possible myself."

"They hide weapons in the thatch", added Osgood by way of further explanation.

"I leave it to my agent to look after such matters." Balcunnin dismissed the subject and retrieved his hat and crop from the chest. "Good day to you captain, sergeant. Have a look at my maps. Obliged, obliged." The door closed and his lordship's boots sounded on the wooden stairs. Osgood looked at the sergeant.

"A very capable fellow, his lordship. Nobody's fool I can tell you."

"I can see that," admitted Howlett, "but why is there such a difference between the easterners and the people of Mayo?" Osgood was impressed at the way Howlett penetrated to the nub of the question.

"Climate," he explained. "This is a fertile region around here. People are moderately comfortable. It pays them to be loyal. Peace and prosperity as they say. Mayo and the most of the west is bleak and overcrowded. You need no Jacobins to sow the seeds of revolt in such conditions. His lordship is right in saying the land is fit only for animals. I daresay he'll move in that direction some day. He's something of an expert on agriculture you see."

"But what of the people? If the area is overpopulated, where can he send them?"

"That is the problem. They won't just die off and he cannot ship them off to colonies in the Americas, so I fear matters will simply get worse and worse. Fortunately, it is not our immediate concern, sergeant Howlett. I fear I have detained you too long from your duties. You'll be wanting to return to your men."

"Yes, sir." Howlett replaced his headgear and slung his musket over his shoulder. "And thank you for your instructive conversation." He was surprised to reflect how easy and informal the interview with the captain had been.

"We are all learning as we go along, sergeant. I shall be over to see your island shortly and don't forget my fossils." He returned Howlett's salute.

Outside on the quay three gunners who had been lounging at ease came to attention as Howlett approached. However eccentric Osgood might have appeared at first sight, it was obvious that he tolerated no slovenly behaviour in his men. Howlett directed them to the waiting boat, crewed inevitably by old Garrigan and the small boy. "And how are you this morning sergeant," greeted Garrigan with a conspiratorial wink. The three soldiers looked interested. "I'm well enough Captain Garrigan." Howlett had no desire to share confidences with him. "Perhaps you would cast off and let us be on our way."

"Oh aye, aye, right away sergeant." Garrigan realised that officers and the like would not be able to chat like a christian in front of their men. He was not offended and signalled to the boy to hop ashore and cast off. He settled comfortably in the stern with his elbow resting on the tiller while the boy officiously hauled on the halyard to raise the heavy canvas. Howlett pushed the boat away from the pier and the sail filled with wind.

CHAPTER 5

It was October and the weather was still surprisingly mild. The schooners had returned at last from their long summer on the Newfoundland banks with barrels of salted cod, and the herring fishing had begun in earnest. John Mullen found himself trudging to the market several nights a week, a task which he did not resent, his cart laden with boxes of herring or whiting. The beginnings of winter frost gave a sharp nip to the night air and he had taken to stopping briefly along the way for a drop to keep the cold at bay. The road took him through the village of Tyrrelstown and it was inevitable that he should encounter the local men over a pint of porter at the Man O' War. They were decent men in their way and John Mullen never objected to doing a favour in the city for any of them or dropping off a bit of fish in return for the excellent vegetables which they grew on the light sandy soil, but coming up to the time of the annual game, local pride tended to make relations a bit strained. He would not give them the satisfaction of passing through without stopping. A man has his pride, but he had promised Eileen that he would not be provoked into violence by remarks about goat eaters or bearded ladies. These remarks were occasioned by the mysterious disappearance of the saint's goat from the island in bygone days and the belief, still widely held in defiance of all evidence, that the women of the town were condemned, as was the way with saints in the old days, to go through all eternity with whiskers on their chins.

Now that the schooners had returned, there were enough men to field a respectable team and John felt that his town could acquit itself with honour. As nobody kept track of the victories to date both sides felt entitled to lord it over their rivals and in truth the winning of the game was to a large extent irrelevant. In the true spirit of sportman-ship, the important thing was to compete and what happened to the ball in the course of the day was a mystery to most of the participants. In some parts of the country the game was discouraged where religious or political overtones might inflame the passions but, in fact, his lordship was known to favour the event, as a lightning rod, so he said, to channel the energies of the young men into harmless pursuits. Whatever damage might be done was done therefore, not in the name of God or Holy Ireland, but in defence of the good name of a man's native soil. At the same time he thought it prudent to maintain some military presence during the game and to this end he sent a detachment of militia to keep an eye on the spectators, with instructions to his brother to observe impartiality no matter how the game should turn out. Captain Osgood sent a dozen men under Howlett, remarking that it would make an interesting change from island duty. He cautioned him to keep his men well away from the refreshment booths, saying that some of the soldiers after a few drinks were inclined to forget that they were still in the United Kingdom and tended to behave with the insolence of an occupying force.

The rules of the game were simple. Between the round tower of Tyrrelstown and the big tree on the corner of his lordship's private grounds, lay a good two miles of pasture and ploughed land, divided by high banks and hedges of whitethorn and bramble. Beside the banks were ditches of stagnant water overgrown with weeds, and green scum. Midway between the two landmarks, which served as goals, the ball, a pigskin bag stuffed with rags and straw, was thrown in and a local dignitary, usually Balcunnin himself, signalled the start of hostilities with a pistol shot. Whichever team carried the ball to the opponents' goal was declared the winner. Ashplants and blackthorns, by common consent, were left at home in the interests of friendly relations, but it was noticeable that the contestants generally wore heavy boots and gaiters which sometimes inadvertently connected with something other than the ball. It had been known for a game to end in a matter of hours but usually the contest stretched into the hours of darkness which tended to preclude a clear-cut decision. This could lead to weeks of argument and accusations of fraud or cowardice until feelings abated sufficiently for normal life and commerce to resume.

The Mullen family drove in style in the trap, while Larry Donovan followed in the cart with some of the neighbours. John liked to establish a sort of redoubt for his family near the hawkers' booths and safely out of the way of the game. The cart was also useful for bringing home some of those overcome by their exertions either on the field of play or in the subsequent celebrations or otherwise, in the beer tents. Donovan because of his size did not take part in the game but was invaluable as mentor and strategist, at least in his own estimation. In truth as there was no overall captain on either side, team strategy was not as highly prized as individual initiative.

"Now Eileen, keep them childer in the trap whatever ye do. Larry will keep yiz in touch with the game." John was anxious to get to work and stood impatiently, rolling up his sleeves. His team-mates likewise impatient, stood in groups, sharing a bottle and shouting ribald insults at the sixty or seventy Tyrrelstowners who replied in kind. A few relieved themselves furtively behind a hedge or a cart as the tension got to them. Balcunnin rode from group to group offering good natured encouragement. At last he gestured to the opposing teams and upwards of a hundred and fifty men jostled in the centre of the field. Balcunnin held the ball in his right hand.

"Now lads, we are all neighbours here. Let's have a good clean game, and let the better team win." He drew a formidable pistol from his saddle holster and pointed it aloft. Absolute silence descended over the field. Eileen standing in the trap saw the puff of white smoke before she heard the report. The ball rose high in the air and the game was on. Immediately she lost sight of John as a melee developed in the centre of the field. Balcunnin's horse reared and kicked as he extricated himself and cantered back towards the booths. Spectators, old men, women and children surged forward to follow the game and flowed back like a tide before the shouting, punching, cursing mob of contestants. The ball was nowhere to be seen. Balcunnin rode in unusually good spirits to where his brother had dismounted within easy reach of refreshments.

"Read your Thucydides Ned." Ned was no scholar. "Almost as many as fought at Plataea though I doubt we'll change the course of history here today." Ned was pleased to see his brother in such good form for generally he was too much inclined to seriousness. "Whatever about Thucydides, we'll have some heads opened here one way or another. What say you to a charge?" Balcunnin laughed at the idea. This was typical of Ned who was quite capable of leading his men with a tally-ho, just for the hell of it.

"Let's not get too partisan Ned. Ah there you are sergeant. And what do you think of our country sport?"

Howlett had stood up on the hub of a cart to get a better view over the heads of the crowd. No pattern had as yet emerged in the game which looked more like a riot. The more limber of the spectators tended to get involved whenever the ball came into view. "I think sir I should prefer to face the French." Howlett stepped down, conscious of his undignified position.

The crowd surged towards the hedge as the ball was kicked free and a gap appeared as the majority of both teams thundered through into the neighbouring field with the spectators in hot pursuit. Here and there men picked themselves up and staggered after the throng. Cheers and shouts of execration arose from all sides. Balcunnin and his entourage set off at a fast trot and Howlett directed his men to follow at the double.

Larry Donovan leapt into the trap and unhooked the reins. "Be jasus, Mrs. Mullen but we can't miss this. Your man is in the lead there. We'll have these hoors bet in no time, beggin' your pardon ma'am." They clattered onto the road, the trap swaying and bouncing and the children shrieking with excitement. Eileen clutched the little boy.

"Easy with my pony Larry Donovan or I'll have your hide." Donovan slowed the pace at once, although it was imperative that he should be on hand to direct the thrust of his team. They could follow the action of the game over the tops of the hedges until eventually the players emerged into a wide open stubble field still awaiting the plough. Sure enough she could see John pounding along, roaring advice and fending off all comers. Occasionally he aimed a kick at the ball sending it skittering over the stubble.

"Come on John," she screamed. "You have it now."

"Christ, woman, sit down or you'll have us all in the ditch." Donovan reined in the pony as Eileen jumped up and down with excitement. At that point a Tyrrelstowner with courage beyond the call of duty, dived on the ball to stem the headlong rush and the carrier hurtled over the prone body and disappeared beneath the feet of those who had been close on his heels.

"Oh Jesus, Mary and Joseph he'll be killed." The inclusion of the whole family turned blasphemy into a pious ejaculation. The advance was stopped and the Tyrrelstown men saved the situation, ploughing through the mob in a spearhead formation, the ball safely hidden somewhere in their midst. A couple of gigantic red-bearded assassins led the counter charge, striking down all before them as the surge of bodies was reversed and spectators scrambled out of the way.

"Somebody get them red bastards." Donovan was standing in the trap and gesticulating with the whip like a general, but his shouting was lost in the tumult.

"Mind the children Larry, I have to find John." Eileen sprang down by the shaft and ran to where she had last seen her husband. He was still lying under a pile of his teammates, and she was relieved to hear him roaring at them to get up. At least his lungs had survived. The water in the stubble squirted upwards as she ran, startlingly cold on her legs below her raised skirts and she was laughing with surprise and relief by the time she reached where her husband now stood, bent double with his hands on his knees. He was caked in mud and blood ran from his nose and the briar scratches on his arms.

"Just winded girl," he managed between gasps. "I'll claim one of them Nolan brothers before this day is out." She reached up to dab at the blood and he took the kerchief from her. "Give us that for luck, like the oul' knights in the story books." He wiped his face and smiled at her. "Would you have any water in the trap? The lads and meself could do with a drink." Eileen waved to Larry to come over. "I have surely, though it's more of a wash ye need."

"Where are they now Larry?" He grabbed the jar of water, drank some and splashed some more over his face and neck. "Are youse lads all right?" He turned to the two young fishermen who had followed them over and passed the jar to them. "I'd rather be back on The Banks, baitin' lines and it blowin' frost," said one ruefully, rinsing blood from his mouth. "They're two fields away," reported Donovan "and goin' like the hammers for the tree. Them Nolan hoors is knockin' all before them. Hold it, hold it, they've turned again. The lads have it again. Head across that way and yiz'll catch them in the field beyond." He indicated that a flanking movement was in progress and that they could rejoin their comrades by cutting across a field of young turnips. "Right lads, we're off again." John set off at a trot with his two apprentices.

Surely enough they could see a small group haring along, presumably with the ball, relying this time on fleetness of foot rather than the brute force of the Nolans. The crowd streamed along the road and through the fields, parallel to the game, shouting encouragement as before. Even the gentry had become so caught up in the game as to shout with the best, spurring their horses and waving their hats. And so it went on, the game fluctuating across the countryside with no sign of a decision until the light began to fade. Similarly the dedication of the followers flagged under the killing pace and more and more people began to congregate at the tinkers' booths and stalls where business was brisk.

Howlett abandoned the pursuit, figuring that whatever the result he would be bound to hear it eventually. He had noticed John Mullen's wife Eileen in a trap at an early stage of the game and now he watched with interest as Donovan hitched the pony to the back of the big red cart and departed in search of diversion. She looked tired, he thought. The little boy was asleep on her lap and the other child, the girl, had become cranky and restless. On impulse Howlett turned to the stall behind him and picked out a couple of apples, dropping a few pence into the creased and grubby hand of the hawker.

"Excuse me, Mrs Mullen." She turned with a start and looked at him. "I thought maybe the children would care for an apple." There was no hostility this time. She smiled at him as he stood awkwardly rubbing an apple on his coat. She thought he looked like a little boy. How had she ever thought him menacing?

"That is kind of you sergeant. No doubt Lucy would be glad of an apple, but this little fellow wouldn't manage it at all." She rocked the little boy who clutched at her shawl in his sleep.

"Maybe yourself then?" and his stomach churned suddenly and alarmingly with the fear of rejection.

"I will and thank you," she said and took the proffered apple. Her fingers touched his momentarily and he felt the touch, like a burn. With an effort he restrained himself from looking for the mark. Howlett felt a kind of elation. It was so easy. He had offered her an apple and she had just accepted it, like that. Now he watched furtively as she bit into it with strong white teeth. There was something unself-consciously animal about her actions. In a detached way he was amused by his own reaction to this woman, at his age to be acting like a schoolboy, not that he had been a schoolboy for very long. He waited to see if she would say anything else, conscious of his hand resting on the side of the trap and wondering idiotically how to remove it without awkwardness.

"Have you seen my husband anywhere sergeant? I lost track of him a while back."

"No ma'am, but I think the game must be nearly over now."

Groups of men were making their way towards them in the gathering dusk, supporting each other or groaning or arguing loudly about the finer points of the game. Their breaths hung around them in clouds of steam as they gasped. The lowering sun highlighted the sweat and blood on their faces and limbs. By all accounts it had been a memorable day's sport.

"Have any of you seen John?" Eileen called to the groups as they passed.

"Aye missus, he's on his way in," answered one bedraggled figure whose right arm hung limply at his side.

"Is he all right? It's the same every year," she added to Howlett. "He'll be killed one of the days."

"Ah he's not too bad missus." She felt cold at the understatement. "Well, it's like this missus," went on the man, wincing in pain and holding his injured limb with his good hand. "Them Nolans was havin' a go at John but we had a word with them. Two desperate hoors. It took five of us to put manners on them and I nearly had me arm pulled out at the roots. John'll be all right though, he's just a bit knocked about."

"Shouldn't we go and look for him, Mrs Mullen? I can get some of my men to scout around." Howlett thought that a burial detail might be required as well.

"Wait sergeant," replied Eileen. "Here he is now. I'd know his boots anywhere. If the Nolans haven't killed him I'll finish the job."

Coming towards them was a group of survivors carrying three limp forms by the shoulders and feet. Except that his beard was darker, Mullen could have passed for a brother of the other two.

"Put them up in the cart till I have a look at them," called Eileen, testily, her anxiety relieved by the fact that the three men had begun to groan and kick themselves free. The bearers carefully handed their charges up and laid them on the straw on the floor of the cart. Eileen handed the still sleeping child to Howlett and went to succour the wounded. He watched as she bathed the bruised and bloody heads with a wet cloth, her capable hands working deftly until one after another they regained consciousness. "Oh ye big fools," she berated them. "Ye must have heads of solid wood. Here drink some o' this." She thrust the jar angrily at each of them in turn. The Nolan boys looked just as shamefaced as her husband.

"We're sorry for causin' you this trouble missus," volunteered one of them grinning sheepishly. "It wasn't anythin' personal like." He indicated the battered visage of her husband who was watching the exchange in some trepidation.

"I know your mother well, you two, and if I speak to her ye'll know all about trouble. Now get off with ye if ye're able to walk and don't be behavin' like savages – as for you, ye eejit, I'll have somethin' to say to you too." The Nolans climbed stiffly from over the tailboard and began to limp away. After a few steps the spokesman turned and came back diffidently. "Eh, you wouldn't happen to know missus who won the game?"

Mullen sat up in the straw. "Oh yes, I forgot clean about the game."
Eileen pushed him down. "Lie down ye fool before ye bleed to
death. No I don't know who won. I suppose ye'll all claim victory as
usual." The Nolans retreated in disorder.

"Well now, opinions differ as to who won." Donovan had
reappeared, swaying slightly and obviously with drink taken.
"Touchdowns was definitely made at both ends but one was with a
turnip, or so they say, though which team scored with the turnip I
don't rightly know. So ye see," he paused judicially for effect, "the
result remains inconclusive."

Mullen laughed a ghastly gurgle from the depths of the straw and
Howlett was overcome by a paroxysm of laughter so that the child
woke in his arms and began to cry for his mother. Even Eileen had to
see the funny side of it against her will. "Right now Larry, get the cart
filled up and let's be off home. You'll do no drinkin' here John Mullen
and the state you're in." Eileen was firmly in control.

"Ah now Eileen don't be so hard. At least offer the sergeant a jant
home and he can have a drop with us in town. Isn't that right Larry?"
Mullen instinctively sought security in numbers.

"I'd be glad of the lift right enough but I must send my men on ahead.
I could use a drop of something after today." Larry agreed that it
would be the civil thing to do and Eileen looked askance at them as at
three conspirators. "Well ye better get a move on then. I have to get
these children to bed sometime, not to mention that big baby in the
straw there." The cart lurched out onto the hard road with Larry in
command again, ordering the neighbours' children to sit down and be
quiet, an impossible task, and swiping with the whip at the boys who
jumped up on the protruding shafts at the back. "Stop that scuttin'
there or yiz will break the belly band," but the boys followed,
laughing and ducking to sneak a ride.

It was more or less assumed that Howlett would drive the pony and
trap with Eileen and the children. The gunners marching with muskets
slung easily over their shoulders, saluted him good humouredly as he
drove past, feeling a bit conspicuous. He was tempted to clown a little
by the holiday atmosphere, but he contented himself with waving to
them. There was little conversation in the trap and he glanced now and
again at Eileen sitting opposite. She caught his eye and smiled at him,
but looked quickly away.

He thought she had been about to say something but changed her
mind. All at once he wished the journey over or that he was walking
with his men. His mouth felt dry and he searched his brain for

something to say.

"And how are your eyes nowadays sergeant?" Eileen felt foolish when she heard herself asking the same question again. He must think her stupid, saying the same thing any time they met, but anything was better than the awkward silence.

"They were never better, Mrs Mullen. The soreness has gone completely." He saw the flicker of a smile again and wondered if he was being pompous or was it his accent that sounded funny amid the Fingallian drawl? She was about to point out the site of the holy well in a coppice near the big tree when the deep rumble of gunfire made her pause. The cavalcade ground to a halt and people looked at each other in alarm. Howlett knew immediately that they were naval guns and further ahead people near the top of the rise were pointing in great excitement towards the town. People began to surge forward fearfully, urging one another on. Howlett slapped the reins on the pony's back and forced a way through the crowd to the top of the hill. By standing and craning his neck he could see what he reckoned must be a frigate, although he was not too sure, just beyond the harbour. Even at that distance he could see that the sails, orange in the later afternoon sun, were being taken in and the sound of another gun came rumbling to them over the fields.

"What is it sergeant?" Eileen asked apprehensively.

"Oh it's just a warship firing a salute." Was he just a bit too offhand, he wondered. "It's probably some important visitor on a tour of inspection."

The tension in the crowd had eased and further ahead Balcunnin's party could be seen in animated conversation with a horseman in coastguard uniform. Suddenly his lordship waved his hat and several of the militia hurled theirs aloft. Pistol shots and hurrahs could be heard and the cheering spread through the crowd. "Where?" "Leipzig" "Never heard of it" "Napoleon is bet" "Finished" "Resounding victory" "Blucher" "Who?" "Must be in France". A babble of confused voices and cheers. The war must surely be over. Was Napoleon dead or captured? No one could say. Howlett felt a twinge of fear. After twenty years as a soldier what would become of him in peacetime? He looked down at Eileen. She seemed more confused than elated by the news.

John Mullen sitting up in the cart felt unaccountably saddened by the news. There was no doubt Napoleon had given them a good run for their money. Life without the familiar backdrop of the war would be very strange from now on.

"Where to John? This calls for a celebration." Donovan was impatient. "The redcoats will be cock o' the walk tonight and no mistake."

"Just take us home Larry. I've had enough for today. Eileen," he raised himself up on his elbows, "bring the sergeant in for a bite to ate."

Howlett thought he heard him say something about conquerors. Feeling somehow embarrassed by the remark he declined the invitation as gracefully as he could. He would have given anything to stay for the evening with the Mullens but suddenly he resented the idea of being with the woman on her husband's terms. Better to spend the evening in Clooney's with his own kind. Anger boiled in him and he slapped the pony into a trot. Eileen looked up and was shocked to see the expression on his face. She wondered what had happened to upset him so much and concluded that it must be something to do with the war. They travelled the rest of the way in silence and finally arriving at the Kybe, the sergeant lifted the children down and touched his cap.

"I'll say goodnight then, Mrs Mullen." He spoke coldly, angry with himself.

"Goodnight sergeant," she answered in puzzlement as he strode quickly into the darkness without looking back, then she shrugged and lifted the latch of the cottage door.

Napoleon was not dead apparently and winter settled upon the town
with its full fury. For weeks during November and December easterly
gales lashed the coast keeping the fleet in port and the townspeople
crouching by their fires. Poverty was felt in its full misery in houses
where no money was coming in and fuel and food became scarce. The
old took to their beds to keep warm, rising only for a short time each
day to cook the one meal. Here and there children could be seen
scouring the strand for driftwood, their coats streaming behind them
and the pelting sand stinging their bare legs. People rose to clear ice
from the insides of their windows and to chafe at the enforced
idleness.

Peter Howlett's men shivered in their island tower, huddled by the
small guardroom fire when possible and stamping their feet and
blowing on frozen fingers during their shortened spells on watch.
Relief was delayed for weeks and Howlett, who had retreated into
himself, was glad that Laidlaw and Thurston were ashore. Had they
been there he had no doubt they would have come to blows. He found
some relief in his music and fortunately the three gunners were glad of
the entertainment.

The main consolation to his morose spirit was paradoxically the
violence of the storm. He derived a perverse pleasure from standing at
the parapet for hours on end with the collar of his coat turned up,
watching the tremendous combers rolling in from the east, great grey
masses of water building up and up, with the spray whipping from the
ridges, until they seemed ready to sweep the island before them. Then
on reaching the long flat ledges of the reef they toppled and collapsed
in a seething avalanche of foam, driven relentlessly in to the beach and
tossing great flecks of spume as high as the tower itself. On the
westward side the conflicting waves swept around the island to meet at

the dorn, thrusting up into a ridge and slashing landwards like a great
white blade. Further west, the town lay inaccessible beyond the line of
thundering surf. Seagulls, translucent against the scudding grey clouds,
hung, buffetted by the rising winds, or rode the gale landwards with
consummate mastery of their element to forage in the distant fields.
Only the farmers profited from the bounty of the storm as great drifts
of woar, wrack and leathery fronds torn from the ocean bed were cast
up on the beach to feed the following year's crops. During temporary
lulls in the storm Howlett could see the men with their carts gathering
the weed along the length of the beach. He watched them through his
spyglass and could see the familiar figure of Balcunnin's agent, who
also acted as proctor, riding on the beach and keeping tally of the
loads. His lordship was by now in London and Howlett reflected
wryly that the coppers collected from the woar gatherers would go a
long way towards the upkeep of Balcunnin's London establishment.

Frequently he allowed his glass to swing along the line of the Kybe
and with a guilty feeling he allowed it to settle on the familiar cottage.
Sometimes he could see a shawl-wrapped figure at the well or for a
brief instant in the doorway and he persuaded himself that it was she.
He imagined sometimes that she stood and looked towards the island
but it was impossible to be sure. At night when rain or sleet did not
obscure the view he could see a light which he reckoned to be in her
window and he felt the jealousy rise in him like bile, thinking of her
husband there, snug and warm at the kitchen table or by the fire.
Although there was no need to watch through the night in this wild
weather, he often found himself in the small hours of the morning
peering into the dark, imagining them asleep together in bed and then
the sweat broke out on his forehead and the injustice of everything
made the blood pound in his head and he gripped the parapet in
misery with his numbed hands.

John Mullen hated the east wind. It got under every door and through
every crack. It carried off more old people than ever consumption did
and it played hell with trade. Worse still it made Eileen miserable. For
the first time ever she snapped at the children and at himself and
turned to him grudgingly in the bed at night. Things hadn't been the
same since the night of the football game, the night when people were
saying the war was over. He remembered how she had taken him
urgently to bed and damn nearly devoured him so that in the end he
had laughed and begged for quarter.

"Be Christ," he had said "but you're more danger to a man than
the Nolans. Amn't I wounded enough?" And then the tears had come

and she didn't know why and he had held her to him gently. "I was only jokin' girl," he had said and she had talked, it seemed for hours, about her childhood, and her brother lost at sea, and her father lifting her up on the great horses, all rambling stuff until he thought she had a fever. But in the morning she was up and busy about the house as usual and everything was grand again. Now she had taken to walking, not just an errand to the shop or a visit to a neighbour, but walking in all weathers with a shawl clutched about her and her wet hair clinging to her face and a vacant look in her eyes. Several times he had seen her watching him when he went to draw woar for the farmers on the beach, just standing on the breakwater with her shawl clinging to her in the wind. He imagined that his companions looked at him strangely at times and he would wave to her cheerfully to conceal his anxiety.

In the evening all would be well again with a meal prepared and the children washed and ready for the bed, and he would wonder what he had been worried about. It was the weather all right. He decided to bring her mother down for a few days for the company. There would be little enough to do in the dairy at that time of year. He longed for the fishing to start again as he felt that he was in her way around the house. It was natural, he supposed, that it should get her down, cooped up all day with children and the wind moaning in the chimney and rain beating on the windows. Still her mother would cheer her up and then there would be Christmas and a bit of fun. After that there would be a stretch in the evenings and things would look up.

In mid-December the storm blew itself out. The day dawned bright and clear with a sharp frost. The air was still and strangely silent after the weeks of wind. The only sound was the rumble of the long swell rolling onto the beach. John felt his spirits soar as he stood outside the door and looked about him. In the low field beyond the graveyard the floodwaters had turned to ice, with grass and rushes thrusting upwards in little frozen clumps. A flock of gulls alighting unawares, skidded in undignified postures and flapped desperately to regain their balance. John laughed aloud.

"I'm off to the yard for the trap Eileen. I'll be back in a few minutes."

"Are we going somewhere?" she called from within. "Why didn't you tell me?"

"We're going to see your mother and maybe she'll come back with us for a few days."

After a moment's silence she emerged. "That would be nice, John. I would like that very much." She looked much better already, he thought, thinner maybe but beautiful as always. He was glad that his suggestion had met with approval. "Hurry now and I'll have the children ready when you get back."

The familiar road to Balcunnin had rarely looked so good to John as on that morning. The wheels crackled through the icy puddles and the pony's shoes clinked on the hard road metal. The hedges, hacked clean for the winter, stood out black and brown against the frosty fields. Old familiar trees stretched their shorn limbs over the road as if in greeting. He pointed to well-known landmarks, and recalled childhood escapades and she responded with animation. The children, pent up in the house for so long, were excited by the outing and the prospect of seeing their grandmother and cousins again.

Balcunnin house, a magnificent Palladian structure, stood amid parkland and woods, with a view of the town and its islands. It was said to have a window for every day of the year and stood as a monument to the dexterity and enterprise of the Balcunnin ancestors in supporting in turn Cromwell, Charles II and his unfortunate brother, and after a short interregnum, the principles of the Great Revolution of 1689. His lordship's father had thrown his influence behind the Act of Union after the alarming years of unrest and revolution and considered the peerage his due for ridding the country of the corrupt cabal in College Green.

It was widely believed that the woods abounded in man traps and that trespassers were shot on sight, but this did not prevent the village boys from making incursions into the bamboo woods in search of fishing rods or birds' nests. As yet nobody had actually been shot, although most people claimed to know someone whose father had known a man etc., etc. In truth his lordship, a classicist by inclination, thought of himself as a liberal and enlightened landlord, privately comparing himself to Horace's man of Argos when restraining the more reactionary views of his brother Ned. "We do not rave Ned; we do not rave over trifles," he used to quote. Ned's philosophy, if he had ever formulated one, lay probably somewhere between Machiavelli and Attila the Hun. He saw the defence of property as the first duty of a gentleman and the harrying of tenants as a necessary part of good government.

The estate employed over twenty families and produced besides milk, beef and corn, the fine horses which were the pride of the district. As well as hunters, the Balcunnin estate bred heavy draught horses for home use and for sale on contract to the army, the prosperous farmers and the Dublin breweries. It was here that John and his father had bought their first Clydesdales and here they brought their mares to be covered by the Balcunnin stallions. He thought affectionately of his horses, great chestnut giants with white blazes and white socks, stamping and snorting in the stables, impatient at their confinement and of his father, a tall gaunt man who kept his views to himself and obviously preferred the society of animals to that of man. It was small wonder that old Mullen had opted for the life of the carrier where he could be alone with his thoughts and his horses on the long dark trudge to the market.

Eileen's mother still lived in the lodge with her married son Jem and his wife and brood of youngsters. The lodge, with its classical facade and pillars was an echo in miniature of the big house. It stood beside the great iron gates of the park which swung open easily at their approach. Two of the young cousins regarded it as their job and their right to open and ride upon the gates whenever the opportunity arose.

Jem's wife Annie emerged to investigate the excited cries of the boys, accompanied as always by three or four of her offspring. Annie because of her fecundity and good nature was generally regarded as placid, if not bovine, a view which Jem did not entirely subscribe to. He was well aware of the sharp intellect and determination of his wife. It was she who saw to it that her children went to the schoolmaster to learn their letters and numbers, determined that they should rise in the world as far as the law would permit them. Jem who was content to follow in his father's footsteps had, as a result, gained a reputation as a 'fierce ambitious man'.

"I thought it must be yourselves," she said by way of greeting. "Come on in and warm yourselves".

Eileen and John always enjoyed visiting the lodge with its warmth and family atmosphere, although John claimed that a large part of the pleasure came from returning to the relative tranquillity of the Kybe. "Is mam here?" asked Eileen, embracing her sister-in-law.

"Aye she's 'ithin' at the soda bread as usual." Annie retained her back country accent which had so amused her in-laws at first.

"Eileen, child, is that you? And Johnny and the childer!" Old Mrs Eavers was the only one who called him Johnny. She came towards them as they entered the room, wiping the flour from her hands with her apron. "Well this is a grand surprise!" In fact she was hardly sixty, a fine well set up woman with her grey hair hidden under her cap. She was simply "old" to distinguish her from Annie, the young Mrs Eavers, but they could have passed for sisters. "I thought ye would be all blun away this last month, what with the wind." She hugged her daughter and grandchildren, leaving floury imprints on their shoulders and backs. "We've had trees down everywhere so people could hardly stir out of doors."

John stood by, watching mother and daughter talking excitedly and laughing as if they had not met for years. The children were immediately taken in tow by their cousins and crawled under the table for a conference.

"Sit down there John," said Annie. "Jem will be in soon for his breakfast. He wants a word with you about the land." She placed a cake of hot bread on the table. "Yiz might as well have somethin' yourselves."

"Well now I won't object to a bowl o' tae and a bit of bread on this could day," said John drawing up a chair. "Have youse two settled it then? Are you comin' to stay with us Gran?"

"Yes Johnny, I will," smiled Mrs Eavers. "As long as you mind your manners and don't be tryin' to marry me off to any of them scoundrels you're always drinkin' with. A respectable old woman like me."

"Are you callin' me poor father a scoundrel, a decent good livin' man? And don't I know a sea captain who would be talkin' nice to ye, given half a chance? Jem come here." Jem was scraping his boots at the doorstep. "What do you say we marry Gran off to Skip Garrigan? I'd say he'd have a nice little bit in the sock." It was an old joke but none the worse for that.

"Go outa that now," said Mrs Eavers. "I could do better than that for meself."

"And what would you want to do that for?" asked Jem, rubbing his hands in front of the stove. "Let the poor divil boy it out in peace. Do you want him to end up like me?"

"There speaks the voice of experience," said John grandiloquently amid general laughter at the picture of Skipper as pater familias. Maybe they were two ships that would do better to pass in the night.

"The hunt is meetin' abroad at the house," Jem informed them. "Maybe you'd like to take the childer along to see the horses."

"Now that's an idea and we can leave these women in peace to set the world to rights," said John. "Finish your breakfast first and we'll walk along with you." It would be presumptuous to drive up to the front door without an invitation.

"You'd better leave Matt behind, John," Eileen put in. "He wouldn't be able for the walk."

"Sure can't I carry him if that's the case and a few others besides. Put coats on them there Annie and we'll have a pack as good as Mr

Ned's any day."

"We'll be ready then when you come back," she said.

"Take your time, John," said Annie. "Advent or no, there's a nice bit of hogget in the pot and you're welcome to stop for dinner. It isn't every day we have company."

"Oh, be God I'll stop for that all right. Is she still tryin' to put a bit of fat on your bones Jem?" John dug his brother-in-law in the ribs. Jem was undeniably thin, although as wiry as a whippet.

"Will ye come on for God's sake. I want to talk to you about the furze." They departed talking of burning and drainage, with a rout of excited children skipping at their heels.

"Now Eileen," said Annie, "sit you there by the stove and rest. I have to say that I don't think you look at all well. Have you been sick at all?"

"I'm fine, I'm fine. Don't be fussin' woman," protested Eileen. "But it will be nice to have Mam with us for a while. Now and again I do get a bit lonely for Balcunnin."

"Aye, them were the good days all right," said her mother, "but we'll have the grand talks below on the Kybe and it will be just like old times again."

CHAPTER 7

"Tell me more about your musical accomplishments, sergeant." Balcunnin paused in the act of mounting his horse, his left foot already in the stirrup.

It seemed an abrupt greeting to Howlett as he emerged from the coastguard station. "Beg pardon sir, what was that sir?"

"Your music, man. What do you play?" His lordship grew testy if kept waiting for an answer.

"Clarinet your lordship, but it's a good while since I played in a band."

"Which clarinet, man? Be specific."

Not everybody in Howlett's experience appreciated the difference between one clarinet and another. Most laymen lumped them all together as fifes or flutes, but there was a world of difference between the mellow sound of the clarinet and the shrill screech of the fife. "B flat sir, although I started on the piccolo."

"Piccolo? No that would be of no use to me. Presumably you read musical notation." It was more a statement than a question, in tone almost a command.

"I do read, sir, quite competently." It was irritating to be put through this interrogation about what was now a private matter. He had transferred from the regimental band to gunnery when still a boy in search of adventure, but there were times when he missed the thrill of a rousing march. His present instrument had come his way years ago at a country fair. He could hardly recall the circumstances, but it had given him pleasure and consolation for many a long year.

"I dare say. You have a good ear?"

"Well, sir, I can pick up an air fairly smartly if that's what you mean." He smiled inwardly recalling how the bandmaster had rejected his application to be a drummer, a vast and terrifying German with bristling moustaches, looking down upon him: 'De ear is nicht gut enough for drums boy. Du muss de voodvind play. De drummer muss haf de musical intelligence und de gut ear.' Strange that the bandmaster's musical ear had never developed a sensitivity for the subtleties of the language. He doubted if his lordship would appreciate the anecdote.

"I shall expect you on Stephen's night. I've already spoken to Osgood." Who the devil was Stephens, Howlett wondered but left the question unasked. Somebody would enlighten him. Balcunnin swung into the saddle and dug in his heels. "And see you bring your instrument." He clattered away along the road in the direction of the boatyard.

Was it an invitation or a command? What difference? It would make a change.

The St Stephen's night dance for the Balcunnin staff and their friends was one of the big events of the year, more formal than the harvest celebrations after the threshing but, of course, not quite as grand as the New Year's Ball in the big house. The long high loft over the stables and tack rooms was cleared and swept and the wooden floor was dusted with fine bran from the mill. Paper streamers and lanterns made gay splashes of colour on the walls and the high oaken rafters. Everywhere wreaths and festoons of holly with bright red berries disguised the austerity of the whitewash. Long benches were laid by the walls and trestle tables at one end supported the dishes of fowl and meat, cakes and other confections prepared amid unbearable excitement by the kitchen staff. Barrels of ale and porter, with something stronger for the older men, were set up downstairs in the tack room.

When the Mullens arrived, having left the children in the lodge under the care of Annie's eldest daughter, the crowd had already begun to build up. A hum of conversation came from behind the lighted windows of the yard and downstairs some of the lads had already begun an assault on the ale. John handed Eileen and her mother from the trap and gave the reins to the boy to take the pony under cover. He braced himself for the ordeal of entering the room in his fine clothes, expecting, with justification, a ribbing from the boys who were already in good form. He looked quite the gentleman in new stovepipe trousers worn in the latest fashion over his boots and a bottlegreen cutaway coat which Eileen had insisted upon for the occasion.

"I'm not goin' up there with you lookin' like a tinker." She had insisted and fair play to her, he was never the most elegant dresser. He would have looked very odd with Eileen in her new dress, with her hair gathered up but for the ringlets which fell over her temples. He was no expert on ladies' fashions, but there was no doubt Eileen could hold her head up in any company. And hadn't she been a new woman lately with all the work on the dresses for herself and her mother. Here goes, he thought, and pushed open the door, standing back with a flourish to allow the ladies to enter.

"Thank you kindly, sir," she smiled at him and took his arm, as heads turned to see the new arrivals.

"Eileen, is it yourself? Mrs Eavers ma'am, but aren't you lookin' well." The room was full of men, grooms and small farmers, tenants on the estate and men from the town, connected by marriage with Balcunnin folk.

"Holy mother o' Jasus Eileen but who is this fine buck ye have in tow? Don't tell me now." Jem was enjoying his brother-in-law's discomfiture to the full.

"It's the lord lef-tenant snakin' in here imbroglio to see how we're gettin' along." There was no doubt but Jem was a comical hoor after a few jars.

"No I'm not the lord bloody lef-tenant, but it's a good thing somebody in this family has a bit of style. We couldn't have your sister dancin' with a long loodheramawn of a scarecrow like yourself." Jem raised his hands in surrender. "And now me son," this with a jab of the forefinger to Jem's shirt front, "ye can pull me a pint of that oul' ale there till I escort these ladies upstairs."

"I will, I will, your honour and Eileen, perhaps you could see your way to savin' a dance for this humble scarecrow." He bowed gallantly as they mounted the stairs. The match was adjudged a draw and Jem returned to the serious business of the evening.

As yet upstairs the dancing had not begun and as was always the way the women and girls had drifted to one side in chattering groups while the men gravitated to the other side, the more forward ones, generally the house staff, eyeing the girls and winking conspiratorially, while the gauche farm boys shuffled awkwardly in their good clothes and shiny boots. The musicians, two fiddlers and a piper, were standing near the small stage which had been made from a few planks laid over boxes. Eileen felt the blood drain from her face as she recognised the figure of the sergeant standing awkwardly beside them with a long black box under his arm. In a flash as she turned to say something incoherent to her mother, she noticed every detail of the scene. His blue coat, freshly brushed, the brass buttons, a white stock around his neck, how he stroked his chin, obviously feeling uncomfortable at being there at all. The fiddlers were ignoring him and the piper was occupied in a wrestling match with his instrument.

Her mother was talking to her and to the other women but she could not understand a word. She smiled and nodded, hoping that her agitation would die down and wondering how she could escape. It was hopeless. Her husband's voice cut through the hubbub of conversation. "Well if it isn't yourself sergeant. Aren't you the great stranger?" She was aware of them shaking hands. John said something about 'no fit state to entertain anyone that night' and then he called them over. "You know me wife, of course, and this is her mother, Mrs Eavers. The sergeant is goin' to give us a tune on the flute, Gran."

Howlett groped for something to say. He avoided looking directly at her and yet was acutely aware of how beautiful she looked, in a sheer cream coloured dress gathered under her breasts by a string, in what he had heard described as the French fashion. She wore no jewellery or rouge he noticed, and he felt pleased for some reason. He relaxed sufficiently to remark that he didn't think the musicians were too pleased to see him.

"Patsy, come over here to me a minute. You too Michael." John could appreciate their professional jealousy. "Now lads, the sergeant here."

"Peter is the name," broke in Howlett to remove some of the formality.

"Pether here is a veteran of all the wars and he's come here to learn some real music and youse are just the men to teach him. Tom, bring them pipes over here and give our friend here a gander at them." The piper grinned shyly and came forward. Eileen and her mother took the opportunity to excuse themselves and drift back to their friends. Howlett looked curiously at the pipes. There was no sign of a mouthpiece, just a little bellows strapped to the piper's elbow. They were quite unlike the war pipes he had seen in the Scottish regiments. He admitted that he had never seen the like.

"Well," said Tom, glad to be able to expound to a new audience, "I'll twist a little tune for you," and played a snatch of an air, in a style completely new to the sergeant's ear, with elbow pumping and fingers flying over the stops.

"And what do you make of that now, Pether?" He could have said that he thought of lonely rain swept fens and the honking of wild

geese in the evening sky, but they might not have understood. "It's
very pleasant. Could I have a look at your music?"

The three looked at each other and grinned. "But sure we carry it
all in here," said Patsy, tapping his head. "Now listen," and he raised
his bow and began to play with little nods and bows. "*The Blackbird*,"
he said. "Learned it from me father as couldn't write his own name."
Michael took up the tune and the piper slipped in beside them. "Now
see if you can folly us."

"I'll leave ye to it then," said John, "and I'll send up a drop o' the
lad to help ye along. No bother to ye Pether." He slapped Howlett on
the shoulder as an encouragement and emboldened him to pick up his
clarinet and attempt a few notes. People moved onto the floor,
looking curiously at first at the motley orchestra, but soon lost
themselves in the whirling dance amid whoops and yells. He could see
Eileen swinging on her husband's arm and laughing excitedly. Lines of
dancers passed through each other and couples swung around so that
he feared that lives would surely be lost in collisions, which miraculously did not happen. He paused and reached for the glass by his
elbow. It was the same brand of Irish malt that he remembered from
his first day in the town and not bad either. The music was coming to
him now, the clarinet blending with the pipes as he improvised. He
tapped his foot in time with the music and now and again Patsy gave
him an encouraging wink or a 'maith an fear Pether, keep it up'.
Occasionally too the fiddlers took off on little virtuoso improvisations
of their own just to let him know his place or cut a little caper, as if
about to join in the dance. With the liquor warming his innards,
Howlett was happy to defer to their expertise and follow where he
could. And all the time he was aware of Eileen no matter where she
was dancing, outshining in his view, every other girl and woman in the
room. At last supper was called and the cheese cloths were removed
from the food table. People sat around balancing plates on their knees
and chatting, and even the hard men from below deigned to come
upstairs for more solid nourishment. The older men sat around
wheezing and mopping their perspiring faces and lighting their pipes
while the younger blades signalled to the girls and slipped quietly
downstairs to the appointed meeting place.

Howlett, feeling more at home with the musicians, was sitting with
a plate of cold meat and a tankard, fascinated by their talk of jigs and
reels and the harpers that used to go around all the big houses in the
old days. Some of the best poets, they told him, had gone into the
army or the navy and had given up the old language. "They had riz out

of it entirely," averred Michael, presumably meaning that they had come up in the world. He was not in a position to talk about poetry, not being much of a reader, but it intrigued him to hear these men, by their own say so, illiterate, arguing about verse forms and rhyme with apparently a degree of technical knowledge.

"Would you play something for us on your pipe, Peter?" He looked up to see her standing there with a hectic flush in her cheeks, obviously from the dancing. He stood up. Although she was a tall woman he found himself looking down into her eyes. "I don't know that my kind of music would fit in here," nodding towards his three companions.

"Please."

"Ah go on Pether, give us an oul bar," put in the piper.

"All I really know are marches and a few bits and pieces I picked up here and there."

"I insist man." It was his lordship himself. People stood back as he approached. "Let's have nothing too political, like Yankee Doodle." He enjoyed his little joke. It would hardly have been Howlett's choice in view of the American war. "Well, then, *The Scottish Archers*" and he began the rousing old march with the fiddlers drumming their fingers on the backs of their instruments. Feet tapped in time to the irresistible rhythm and he concluded to a spontaneous round of applause. "Excellent, excellent," beamed Balcunnin, "although we could have done with horns and bassoon to give it some body. Now, perhaps, something of my choosing. I have adapted one of my favourites by Kreutzer to a clarinet score." He produced a folded paper and opened it on the table. Howlett with some embarrassment took out his spectacles, feeling childishly, that they made him look ridiculous.

Again he played with verve and sensitivity after the initial stiffness and a few stumbles. People gathered around with interest and a hushed silence descended. Balcunnin stood motionless with his head cocked slightly to one side while Eileen, beside him, watched with a proprietorial pride as if she regarded him as her discovery. The three musicians leaned forward with interest, their eyes following the lines of dots in fascination. For a moment when he finished, there was silence and then, again, a burst of applause this time even louder. "The grandest stuff Pether. Powerful," insisted his colleagues slapping him on the back.

"I look forward to seeing you on New Year's Eve". Balcunnin turned abruptly and the crowd opened before him again as he strode to the door, nodding affably to his servants and their guests.

"I think Peter, you have just passed a test." Eileen was smiling broadly at him as he quickly removed his spectacles. "Well done." Further conversation was prevented by shouts of "Wran boys, Wran boys" and a deal of commotion on the stairs.

The noise intensified with sporadic cheers and into the room burst as strange a crew as Howlett had ever set eyes on. Ragged as beggars, they carried an air of ruined grandeur, what with round hats and tailed coats, and one wore what could have passed for a military uniform. There were seven of them, with blackened faces. Three were armed with musical instruments, a fife, a sort of one sided drum and the inevitable fiddle. The other four carried stout ash staves, which they clashed in mock battle back and forth across the room. Strangest of all, the leader, the one in the uniform, carried a pole from which hung a wicker cage. In it a small bird fluttered wretchedly in obvious terror.

The people drew back to the walls and benches to leave room for the entertainment, their faces alight with anticipation. The three musicians of the group stood to one side and set up a strident racket, the drumbeat pulsating, to Howlett's ear rather like the tabor in country dances vaguely recalled from his youth. He presumed that the group bore some relationship to the morris men of his home country.

"Here I am," declaimed the military gentleman striking an aggressive pose in the centre of the room, "the bould Duke George." He launched into a doggerel to the accompaniment of booing and hissing from the audience, the general import of which was that he would deal severely with such of his subjects as did not accept his rule . . . "and if any man," he concluded, "would take my land, I will defend it with this hand." He stamped his foot and glared about him.

The other three performers introduced themselves in turn, Tom the Fool, with straw sticking out of his sleeves and from the ruins of his hat, who spoke a deal of nonsense but declined to challenge the Duke; and Slick Slack the Tinker, whose rhymes, bawdy and crude, were accompanied by gestures of an overtly sexual nature. He spoke mainly of his calling, stopping holes in buckets and cans with the implication that he was not particular as to what kind of holes he stopped in the course of his working days or nights. He drew much laughter from the audience, although some of the ladies affected embarrassment, but he in turn declined to challenge the Duke. Finally, the fourth man threw off his coat and leaped into the centre, brandishing his staff: "And here am I the bould Luke Ryan," at which the crowd erupted with cheers and whistles. Could this, Howlett wondered, be the mythical smuggler he had heard so much about, the local amalgam of Robin Hood and

Captain Flint, of whom Garrigan had spoken with such awe? With a fair amount of strutting and posturing the hero made the round of the room, flexing his muscles and waving his stick to the delight of his audience.

"And now I swear it on the Book

This tyrant will not escape, says Luke

The curse o' Crummel on kings and lords"

with a contemptuous spit on the ground,

"And let's do battle now with our swords."

The vigour of the battle more than compensated for the feebleness of the verse and the tyrant was inevitably slain, to universal satisfaction. The entire troupe then, including the miraculously revived duke, began to caper around the room shaking their hats at the audience and chanting:

"The Wran, the Wran, the king of all birds,

On St Stephen's Day was caught in the furze."

"What is the reason for the bird," asked Howlett quietly of Eileen. She stood in front of him within arms' length and he had almost to restrain himself from reaching out and touching the back of her neck where a curl of hair had escaped during the dancing.

"It's a wran. They catch it and put it in a cage to let it starve. It goes everywhere with them during the week and then they bury it."

"But why? Do you not think it cruel?"

"I do feel sorry for it," she replied, "but if it didn't die there wouldn't be any luck." Howlett shook his head in puzzlement.

"Up with the kittle and down with the pan . . . " — The blackened face was gazing up at him with a gap toothed leer. He was startled by the expression of malevolent glee on the face as the mummer capered in front of him, shaking the cage in which the tiny prisoner shrilled fiercely, "A penny or tuppence to bury the wran . . . and good luck to ye, soldier and you too missus." Howlett put his hand quickly into his pocket and produced a coin, a shilling. He felt that he and Eileen were the centre of attention and, anxious to be rid of the mummer, he dropped the coin into the extended hat. The wran boy moved on to the next group, rattling the coins in his hat and shaking the unfortunate wren, but from time to time he looked back at them and grinned, his few teeth looking startlingly white in the wizened black face.

"Be God he did well outa you all right Pether. Couldn't you recruit him now on the strength of the shillin'?" It was John standing beside them and Howlett flinched, fearing that the mummer somehow had read his mind and that his thoughts were now open to everybody. "I don't like them wran boys John," said Eileen with a shiver. "I sometimes think they're wicked."

"Ah sure we dipped his wing in a barrel o' beer, A Happy Christmas and a bright New Year." — John completed the old rhyme and turned to the piper. "Never mind them oul' pagans Eileen. Here Tom give us *The Fuip o' Dunboyne* and let's get the party movin' again. Get the sergeant another jar and let him hear some dacent music again." He seized his wife and dragged her out onto the floor where the other dancers had begun to move in a circle at the first strains of the old familiar tune. Above the sound of the dance Howlett could hear the wran boys' drum receding out into the yard and away into the night. He wondered where they came from and where they went, and particularly why their visit had left him with such a feeling of unease.

"Pagans", John had called them. That was a strange word to hear in such an aggressively christian country, where even whippets and greyhounds ran for the honour of their masters' particular creed. The dancing became more and more frenzied and Howlett gave up the effort of improvising with the musicians. He contented himself with the role of spectator, his eyes mainly following Eileen Mullen dancing with the young men. He would have given a great deal to dance with her but the dancing was too complicated for him and, anyway, he felt it would have looked very odd. Still it was good to watch and occasionally it seemed that she caught his eye as if aware of him lounging by the wall.

At length people began to drift away, huddling in long coats and cloaks against the cold night air. A light powdery snow had begun to fall, muffling the sound of hooves and wheels in the stable yard. People called goodbyes to each other as fervently as if they were embarking on an Atlantic voyage, and wives collected their husbands from groups of the lads who were determined to make a night of it. Howlett said good night to the Mullen family as they left in their trap for the lodge.

"And a Happy New Year to you sergeant," said Mrs Eavers, "and thank you for the music."

"Maybe this year will see the end of the oul' war, Peter and yourself and the others will be able to go home." John was in a benevolent mood and wished well to all men, even British soldiers.

"Good night Peter," called Eileen, "and maybe you'll play for us again sometime?"

"I would like that very much," he replied, thinking at the same time that he had no particular interest in ending or prosecuting any war if it took him away from the sight of this woman. The trap swung out of the yard, its lamps shining on the snow and he saw her looking back for a moment as he swung into the saddle of his horse.

"Is there somethin' I could do for your honour?" The voice startled him and his horse shied from the tattered figure that scuttled out of the stable doorway.

"What do you mean? Who are you?" Howlett felt instinctively for his sabre under his cloak. "It's only meself", said the voice by way of explanation and he recognised in the dim light the wrinkled face of the wran boy leader. He was still carrying the cage with the bird, and his cunning little eyes sparkled with malicious glee as he reached for the horse's bridle.

"For a consideration now soldier, you can have her," and the little man cackled. "I can arrange it you see."

"I don't know what you are talking about. Get out of my way or I'll run you down." He pulled the horse around viciously and the wizened little man leaped aside. Howlett dug in his heels and the horse leaped forward.

"If you change your mind soldier . . . " the voice trailed off into a cackle of laughter. Howlett felt the blood pounding in his temples. It was impossible that anyone could know what he had been thinking. To hell with it, he thought. Just some drunken peasant being offensive. He gathered his cloak around him, allowing it to trail back over the horse's haunches and set off into the darkness. He thought at times that he heard the soft laughter in the trees by the roadside and the hairs of his neck prickled but he decided that it was the wind rattling the bare boughs. He was glad to catch up with a wagon full of revellers on the road to the town and like a child reaching out for a hand in the dark he rode with them, enjoying their banter and songs but, nevertheless, he could not banish the wren boy entirely from his mind.

Laidlaw did not enjoy life on the island and winter made matters worse. After his weeks ashore the spartan regime seemed more offensive to his fiery spirit. He had spent the Christmas season in revelry insofar as he could afford it. Any money he had been able to acquire at cards went directly to Mrs Clooney for liquor or the girls. He felt it necessary to stock up for the lean times ahead as he explained after each debauch. "We cannae be slippin' ashore like the sergeant," he complained to the others, "goin' off to the big hoose or gettin' it free from wee Bridie or the missus herself, I'll be bound." It simply bore out all his theories on rank. Officers were born to privilege but there was something wrong in a sergeant, one of their own class, being favoured not only by Mrs Clooney but by a peer of the realm too. While his men stood to in the cold and frost or crouched by the fire in the guardroom, their sergeant was hobnobbing with the great people of the county and toasting the New Year with fine French wines. "Aye, and the lassies. He'll do well there. Your fine ladies are very partial tae a week bit o' rough." Laidlaw chuckled salaciously, "but it's no fair all the same. Come on Bateson deal the cards." He returned his full attention to the game. There was little that could be done against the injustices of the world.

Laidlaw was not strictly correct in regarding the Balcunnin New Year's Ball as a bacchanalian orgy. Perhaps if Mr Ned had been in charge this might have been the case, but his lordship and his wife preferred more formal entertainments as befitted their station. Lady Balcunnin, a pale and wraithlike woman, drew her main pleasure in life from agreeing with her husband and in having presented him with three fine children. Her daughter was beautiful in a refined sort of way and was much sought after by the local gentry and the officers of the garrison, but Balcunnin was determined that she should not "throw herself away on any penniless popinjay or some roaring boy of a country squire." The sons, naturally, had gone into the services, the elder to the peninsula where he had covered himself with glory as was to be expected, and the younger to the navy, where they had hoped he would make his fortune if the war held out for a few more years. Unfortunately, with the Austrians and Russians pressing on the eastern borders of France and Wellington thrusting forward from Spain it looked as if their younger boy would not even get his own command before Napoleon was brought to book.

As Howlett approached the house for the second time in a week the difference in the scene struck him forcibly. Every window was ablaze with lights and a succession of carriages described circles in the snow as they swung in under the magnificent, pillared port-cochere to discharge their glittering passengers. Military uniforms were every-where, red and white hussars and dragoons with flashing gold braid, naval officers in blue and white and spectacular aides-de-camp from the Castle, arrogant young men, secure in the knowledge of their superiority. By comparison the civilians looked very dull, the gentlemen of the country in dark frock coats and his lordship's old friends from the university. Howlett made his way in by a back entrance and asked his way to wherever the musicians were to go. He was directed to a passageway which led to one end of the ballroom, a huge room which ran almost the length of the house on one side. Again he found himself in the company of professional musicians who looked at his uniform with no particular interest.

"Clarinet," said one. "You had better sit here. Take a look at this stuff." He thrust a bundle of sheets at Howlett. "The usual minuets and such like. Don't forget to wake me when we're finished." He took a pinch of snuff and began to tune his cello with an elaborate show of boredom. Howlett adjusted his spectacles and looked through the sheets. Scarlatti and Haydn seemed to be in favour. He felt that he would have his work cut out for him as the leader called them to order.

He had forgotten what a ball looked like. Years ago as a young musician he had played at regimental balls on a scale similar to this. The scene was unreal. Like actors on a stage the men moved, stepping and pivoting like automata and bowing to their ladies who tripped and glided like sylphs in diaphanous flowing gowns. It was strange how a people so intent on destroying the empire of Napoleon should copy so slavishly the manners and fashions of his court. Howlett felt like a crow among peacocks. Mercifully out of sight behind the other musicians he watched the glittering scene, but there was no Eileen here to catch his eye or swing through the throng with a merry laugh. He played with half his mind, watching the light playing on the shimmering crystal chandeliers, brittle as the smiles on the faces of the dancers and wondered about his supper.

Balcunnin extricated himself from a group of elderly ladies who had detained him too long behind a hedge of fans and dance programmes. He beckoned to a footman. "Ask the sergeant if he would be good enough to see me in the music room." The footman bowed and withdrew.

The music room was his lordship's retreat when company became insupportable. Its french doors led onto a balcony overlooking the lake and in summer the sound of his playing drifted out over the gardens at unpredictable hours of the day or night. At this time the curtains were drawn and the dozen or so of his personal friends were far enough removed from the ballroom as to be aware only of a distant tinkle of music.

"My God, but those professionals depress me immeasurably. Why cannot someone invent a machine to produce such sounds and spare us the inconvenience of looking at them." One of Balcunnin's commonest complaints was that when society had migrated to London,

Dublin had become a cultural wilderness. He saw it as a duty to try to redress the balance. "Good government need not be bought at the price of bad music," was another of his aphorisms to excuse his support for the very move which many claimed had taken the heart out of Dublin.

"Ah, come in sergeant". He was in an uncommonly mellow humour. "My dear", turning to her ladyship, "this is the young fellow I told you about." The occupants of the music room turned in curiosity to see the newcomer. Balcunnin did not invite everyone to join him in his recitals.

"Well sergeant," said her ladyship graciously coming towards him. "My husband tells me that we shall enjoy your playing."

"That's very kind of him ma'am". Howlett hoped that he would live up to their expectations.

"Let's have some music then before cards." His lordship rubbed his hands. "We can safely leave the youngsters to the dancing. Perhaps you would send for Alicia my dear, to accompany us at some stage." Their daughter had recently acquired one of the new Erhard harps, a magnificent instrument with pedals, and even her father admitted that she had a considerable musical talent. "My old friend here is regrettably unable to join us," Balcunnin bowed to the elderly and portly physician, Dr Cooke, adding by way of explanation and with a sly twinkle, "I cannot understand why so eminent a medical man is unable to find a cure for his own chilblains."

"Because my lord you have the most unhealthy tenants in the land and I am obliged to ride out in all weathers to minister to them." Dr Cooke raised a swollen hand, "but at least you shall be spared my abominable scraping for this evening." The company laughed politely and begged to differ.

"Well then this young fellow must step into the breach if you'll pardon the pun." His lordship was definitely on his mettle, "though I dare say he's more used to opening breaches, what! Well let's make a start. Take the viola Keble and give us plenty of attaque."

The thin ascetic looking parson smiled wanly at the phraseology but in fairness it was acknowledged that although his sermons were as soporific as hemlock, indeed almost fatally dull, he blossomed with his viola into an almost flamboyant virtuoso. Balcunnin, at times had even found it necessary to restrain his ebullience.

"Splendid! We'll give Mozart a canter for a start." Balcunnin sat down to his harpsichord, an instrument he preferred to the pianoforte, although he admitted its limitations. "You have your scores gentlemen. Sergeant, you will work please from first violin as I indicated."

They launched into the opening chords of the overture to Don Giovanni, the thin sound of their little and oddly matched ensemble overlooked in the solemn magnificence of the theme. Howlett experienced again the thrill of letting himself go with the music, moving from the limpid opening passage to the compelling chords of the commendatore's warning and taking flight in the main movement, answering the viola and harpsichord and coming together again in the majestic closing passage. The audience applauded as they finished, with Dr Cooke favouring his swollen hand.

"Delightful gentlemen, delightful." Her ladyship was entranced. "You could all earn your living from your music if you cared."

"Perhaps so my dear." Balcunnin was pleased with their perform-ance. "But I think we should lose much pleasure thereby. Leave us to enjoy our music as amateurs and let us pray that we may never be reduced to earning a living. And now let us attempt something more taxing in *The Magic Flute.* You must try to imagine our young friend here as the scalawag bird catcher, while the good Keble should have little trouble in passing for the virtuous priest." Balcunnin showed surprising animation in combining at once the function of host, conductor and performer.

Again their performance met with universal approbation and Howlett felt relaxed at last. A tall fair haired girl of about twenty slipped into the room and was watching them with interest.

"Finally, the sergeant and I will attempt something rather new. You remember the piece you played for me at the servant's ball, by Kreutzer?" Howlett nodded. "Well this sonata is dedicated to him by Beethoven. A loutish fellow by all accounts but a man of considerable genius as you must agree. I think we should satisfy ourselves with the first movement for the moment."

Howlett began slowly and Balcunnin took up the theme, this time on the pianoforte. Immediately a sense of unison developed between them. The tempo increased, the clarinet conversing this time with the piano. Balcunnin threw himself into the execution of the work with passionate intensity. Howlett scrambled now and again to keep in touch, the rapid tongueing at first giving him some difficulty. Eventually they worked completely in unison, the perspiration breaking out on their brows, swinging into the plaintive passages with sensitivity and moving off again on a completely new theme as one surprise followed another. The audience might not have existed as far as the two were concerned, as the clarinet soared in the closing bars, followed by the insistent piano-forte, pausing softly in a lyrical passage and closing with a flurry to which the pianist gave full bravura expression. His lordship rose immediately spreading his hands and bowing to the applause. He turned to acknowledge Howlett.

"And now ladies and gentlemen I think it is time for supper. Sergeant my congratulations. You have a gift worth cultivating." He offered his arm to his wife. "Shall we go in my dear?" They swept from the room followed by their entourage and Howlett found himself alone.

Damn them, he thought. It's as if I didn't exist. He concluded that his best bet was to go in search of something to eat and make his departure as quietly as possible. The door reopened and the tall fairhaired girl returned with two others of about the same age. The three regarded him curiously. "Papa was pleased with your playing. I have rarely seen him in such good humour." So this was the daughter of the house. "He sent us to see that you are provided for." The others giggled and the fair girl looked at them sternly. Howlett opened his clarinet case and replaced the instrument.

"That's very kind of his lordship," he replied, conscious of their stares.

"We play music too," said one of the girls. "Perhaps you would like to hear us." She draped herself languidly on the piano stool and leaned towards him, displaying ample charms in her low cut ball gown.

"Kitty," broke in the tall girl, "the sergeant is required for supper."

"Oh Alicia you are such a spoil-sport. I just love men with black hair especially on their hands, and he looks such a delicious animal."

Howlett restrained his anger at being discussed like a horse at a fair. He reached for his gloves, conscious of the little tufts of black hairs on the joints of his fingers. "You said something about supper, miss." He addressed Alicia directly, ignoring her friend who pouted in annoyance. He could think of nothing more crushing to say and wanted just to be rid of these tedious children.

"Vanessa," said the girl on the piano stool, "I think it time we returned to our officers." She emphasised the word with a haughty glance at Howlett. "We must leave Alicia to her new friend." They flounced from the room and their tinkling laughter sounded in the corridor.

"I must apologise for my friends. They are very young." Alicia looked at him sympathetically. "It must be awkward for you coming into a place like this."

He was surprised that she should take the trouble to notice and he felt his annoyance subside. "Well yes, miss. It is different from what we are used to on our island." He allowed himself a slight smile at the contrast.

"My father asked me to give you this." She produced two guineas from a small bag. "I hope you will not be offended." To her relief he was not and accepted the gold with a small bow. What would have been patronising in another was graceful coming from her. "He hopes that we may hear you again sometime."

"I should like that very much but I feel I must practise in order to keep up with his lordship."

"Now shall I send someone to show you where your supper is? I must get back to our guests. Good night to you sergeant."

"Good night miss and thank you." He watched her going and turned his mind to his supper with a glow of anticipation. She was undoubtedly a very civil young woman, obviously very self possessed and mercifully without condescension. For the first time that evening he felt at home and the idea flitted through his mind, giving him a start, that perhaps there could be a place for him in this town when the war ended and gunners were no longer in demand. There was no harm in pipe dreams, he supposed and addressed himself to a generous helping of chicken and ham pie. Laidlaw might not be too far wrong. Even non-commissioned officers could belong to the elect once in a while. He jingled the guineas in his pocket and leaned back in his chair with a tankard, watching the flurry of activity as servants raced to cater to the whims of the great ones upstairs. Now if only Eileen were here, he thought, he would ask for nothing more.

CHAPTER 8

For almost three miles along the clay cliffs as far as the southern tower at Monks' Bay there stretched a narrow bridle path, fenced off from the pasture and ploughed land by thorn hedges growing aslant from the constant buffeting of the sea wind. Here on a cold brisk morning in mid-January Captain Osgood had deployed his survey team. Laidlaw and Bateson had charge of the measuring chain which they plied to the accompaniment of the Scot's sotto voce comments on the absurdity of the whole proceeding. Thurston carried the staff with something of a swagger and struck statuesque attitudes where Osgood placed him. The Captain explained the procedure to Howlett as they worked their way along the cliff edge.

"You notice how the cliff has been eroded by the sea in places." He indicated where bites had been taken from the cliffs and where fresh falls of clay and boulders lay on the ledges of limestone below. "That storm in November has caused me to revise some of my boundaries already. I can foresee a time when this path shall fall away completely."

"Will that make your maps useless, sir?" Howlett knew that the captain enjoyed the verbal fencing with regard to his work.

"Antiquarian interest, sir." The captain always had a plausible answer. "Our maps will be looked upon in future years as quarries for antiquarians who would know more about our era. We are chroniclers of but one stage in the constantly changing creation. Never assume that what appears on a map will always be there." It seemed a bizarre reason for such meticulous accuracy thought Howlett, noting down the measurements as they worked their way along. "We shall work as far as that point where the path dips down into the cove." The captain signalled to Thurston to move on ahead and began to set up his theodolite. "I shall make use of the men from Monks' Bay tower from there onwards. Have those men continue as far as the point and go along with them yourself, if you please."

Howlett was glad to descend from the cliff top by the rutted frozen clay track to the beach. At least there was some shelter from the breeze which had numbed his fingers even through his gloves so that he could scarcely hold a pencil. Below him he could see two men with a horse and cart, forking up the brown bank of woar into heaps and with a start he recognised John Mullen and his brother-in-law Jem. They looked up as they saw the soldiers approaching and leaned on their gevells, watching with interested amusement. Laidlaw, walking backwards with the chain and feeling foolish, scowled at their smiling greeting.

"I suppose it's some class of a secret weapon to trip up the enemies and they chargin'," suggested Jem with a nudge.

"No, no, it's how they're goin' to put a fence about the whole country; isn't that the idea soldier?"

Laidlaw grinned sourly. "They'll need no fence tae keep me oot o' this fuckin' country wi' yer watery whiskey and yer skinny weemin."

"Well nobody asked ye to come here ye Scottish git," said John, starting forward with his hands clenched on the shaft of the gevell.

"That will do Laidlaw," called Howlett as he drew near. "Carry on with your work." Laidlaw backed away fingering the handle of his bayonet. "Aye sergeant. I had forgot we were guests here." He looked at the carter belligerently as if to say that there would be some other time to discuss the matter. He moved away with a laugh to rejoin Bateson, who reslung his musket with obvious relief.

"My men do not always see the funny side of things," said Howlett, slightly needled that he should have to explain.

"We were only havin' a laugh Pether," said John, "but that's a truculent hoor, that lad."

"What are you doing here anyway? Did you not get enough of the weed in November?

"Oh that wasn't for ourselves. I was just helpin' out. Jem and me work a bit o' land at Balcunnin and we've cut a few drains in the swampy bit so we'll have to plough in some woar and a bit o' dung if it's ever goin' to be any good."

"I see." Howlett looked at the sheet of squared paper on which he had drawn an outline of the coast. "Has this cove got a name by any chance?"

"Oh aye." Jem leaned over intrigued to see what he was writing. "It used to be called the Divil's Bay but they call it Luke's Bay nowadays. That's his cave over there." He indicated a low tunnel at the base of the cliff.

"Luke's Bay. That should be good enough." Howlett smiled as he wrote, not without difficulty. "Luke appears to get around a bit. Luke's cave too I suppose," and he made a mark on the paper.

"Aye Luke's cave, though I don't see what good it would be to a smuggler if everybody knows about it."

"Why do you pile up the weed instead of just loading up?" It seemed that they were doubling the labour.

"That way we mark it so nobody else will touch it an' we can come back for it again." John fell to loading the cart again. "Look into the house when you're in the town Pether an' we can have a jar together and maybe you'll give us another tune."

"I'd like that, John. And how are your wife and family?"

"Grand. She was very taken with your music. Said you wasn't a bit like a soldier, if you know what I mean. Come in sometime and cheer her up. She gets a bit down in herself in the could weather." Christ, thought Howlett, is the man a simpleton or is he probing? There was no reason for the carrier to suspect the thoughts he had entertained about Eileen.

"We'll be away then Pether. Don't forget to come and see us." The men thrust their gevells into the cartload of weed and set off, leading the horse over the coarse sand. Captain Osgood stood aside to let them pass on the sloping path. "Well sergeant, I think we'll finish for this morning. Let the men have a smoke if they wish. I want to show you something that might interest you." He led the way to the cliff base where horizontal beds of limestone jutted out from beneath the clay. "Beetles and leaves by the looks of things but not like anything I've seen alive." He pointed down at the rock. The rock was a mass of white flecks as if a nest of beetles had become petrified in an instant. In the wet patches and the tiny puddles the rock was almost transparent and the bodies of the fossils stood out with startling clarity. Howlett was amazed at the proliferation of the minute creatures. "It's very puzzling sir, and no mistake."

"The most likely explanation from what I have read on the subject is that the Almighty created these creatures by way of an experiment and, finding that they did not suit His purpose, destroyed them in some great cataclysm which turned them to stone. That would suggest that life had been on this earth in some form for many thousands of years." The captain's pedantic manner did little to enable Howlett to grasp this revolutionary concept.

"Are you saying, sir, that we are looking at the remains of some previous creation? Is that not a heretical notion?"

"I have no doubt it is sergeant. I am a God-fearing man myself but the evidence seems to point to a series of previous creations. We can take it that our own species is a culmination of these celestial experiments." Osgood laughed ironically. "Let us hope that He is satisfied for the moment with His handiwork, eh sergeant." He pointed his toe towards a particularly fine example of a leaf shaped fossil. "Have you any implements in your pouch to knock that out for me? I should like to give it closer scrutiny with my optic glass."

"Certainly sir. I have my hammer and spikes, not that they've seen very much use lately." He unslung his white leather pouch and opened the lid. His hand encountered something soft and yielding and he drew back in alarm. A faint smell of putrefaction reached his nostrils and he tipped the contents out onto the flat rock. There amid the familiar equipment lay the skeletal body of a bird, shrunken and almost mummified, its eyeless sockets gazing at him as if in accusation. A tiny maggot worked its way through the feathers of the bird's cheek. Howlett felt his skin crawling and his stomach lurched in disgust.

"What have you there sergeant? Have you been snipe shooting?" Osgood bent forward and Laidlaw, sensing something out of the ordinary, roused himself from the lee of a rock and ambled over.

"I don't know sir," Howlett was at a loss to explain it. "It's a wren, I think but I have no idea how it got there."

Laidlaw laughed. "I reckon some of your Irish friends have been playin' tricks on ye sergeant." The thought entertained him enormously. Howlett moved the creature away with his foot, furious at whoever had done this and yet struck with guilt that he might have been the cause of its death. He selected a flat stone and laid it over the body, glad not to have to look any more on the empty eyes and the gaping mouth.

"Unsavoury kind of behaviour I must say," Osgood dismissed the matter brusquely, but Laidlaw continued to chuckle. Something in his laugh jarred Howlett's memory and suddenly he saw the little wren boy perched on the mounting block in the dark and the snow of Stephen's night. Damn these people, he thought, rubbing his gloves together, and damn Laidlaw too, blasted Scot – just as bad as the Irish with his mockery. Laidlaw was regaling his mates with an account of what had happened. Thurston looked puzzled while Bateson shook his head. "That's not a very nice thing to do to a body. Right unhealthy I regards it." He derived no pleasure from his sergeant's discomfiture.

Howlett knelt and began to chip at the rock, tapping with the hammer until the fossil fell away. Damn them, he thought, and Mullen too. Is he trying to make a fool of me too? I shall go and visit them by God. He stood up. "Your fossil sir."

"Very good sergeant. We shall return to the town. You will be taking these men over to the island in the morning?"

"Yes sir."

"I have obtained a small boat for your use, you will be pleased to hear. That fellow Garrigan has negotiated with the boat-builder on my behalf and no doubt to his own advantage, so we can go along and inspect it."

Howlett was not particularly overjoyed at this news, as his acquaintance with boats was slight, but he felt that it would give them less of a feeling of imprisonment on their island fastness. They made their way back up onto the cliff where the captain's horse stood cropping the sparse wiry grass. Osgood heaved himself into the saddle. "Meet me at the boatyard in an hour's time sergeant. You men must report to the corporal and then you are free to disport yourself until curfew."

Even Bateson's stolid face broke into a grin at this. It would be a long stint on the island and it behoved a man to make the most of his last evening ashore. Osgood trotted away and the four men followed him in single file, making good time in order not to lose any of the precious moments of freedom. Howlett wondered briefly about the bird but it slipped completely from his mind as they passed through the Kybe. There was no sign of Eileen Mullen as they passed the long cottage but the white sheets on the clothesline showed that she had been busy and he guessed from the smoking chimney that she was indoors, probably making her husband's dinner. Had it not been for the captain's order he would have found some excuse to knock on the door. Howlett dismissed his men and watched them doubling away to the coastguard station in high good spirits like schoolboys unexpectedly released. He turned in at the boatyard. The sign read Bartholomew Morris, Shipwright. Howlett presumed that he must be some connection to the shopkeeper in the Square.

The yard was partially covered by a long high shed from which came the sounds of men at work. Elsewhere stacks of planks separated by wooden slips, were seasoning under covers and piles of ropes and nets were stacked into a lean-to against one of the walls. Several large black boats supported by heavy stocks, stood on cumbersome trailers with rusty iron wheels. A large capstan stood facing the gateway which opened onto the road and the slipway beyond. Captain Osgood's horse was stamping impatiently by the door of the shed.

"Ah, me sweet sergeant, come on in." It was old Garrigan in his capacity of intermediary and master of ceremonies. "This is Tom Morris, the owner of the best pair o' hands in Fingal, when it comes to boats." It was as well to be specific. Howlett looked into the piercing blue eyes of a young fellow of about nineteen or twenty, obviously not the proprietor. "Sergeant," the boy nodded. "You've come to see your boat. Captain Osgood seems satisfied." He gave the impression that he expected no other reaction.

"And why wouldn't he boy?" interjected Garrigan. "Look at her – a little beauty!" Even to Howlett's untechnical eye it was a perfect little craft, twelve feet long, clinker built in pine, with copper nails, rooved on the inside and a graceful rake to the bows. The thwarts were of oak, shining with new varnish, a gem of the shipwright's art. The boy watched expectantly as Howlett ran his hand along the gunwhale. "It looks a fine piece of work," he said lamely, groping for a phrase that would conceal his ignorance of the subject.

"She'll take two rowers if you like, but she should answer very nicely to one. We'll put her down this afternoon and the skipper there," he indicated Garrigan, "can show you the ropes, in a manner of speaking."

"This means, Garrigan," put in Captain Osgood, "that you will lose your contract for conveying his majesty's troops to and from the island."

"Divil a bother, Captain, divil a bother. Sure haven't I enough to be doin' with me lobster cages," replied the old man, " not to mention the odd bit o' fishin'. A body can't always be workin' can he?"

"True, true," assented Osgood. "Perhaps you have some useful advice for the sergeant before he launches out into the deep."

"Oh aye, that I have. First of all keep well clear of the Cross Rock when the tide's on the ebb. If there's a swell runnin' from the east ye'll have to swim for it."

"And secondly?" asked Howlett to forestall the long dissertation that seemed to be developing. "Secondly," Garrigan wagged an admonitory finger, "watch yourself over the dorn when the tide is floodin'. There does be a fierce rip tide there around the springs."

"I'm more worried about hanging on to the oars," admitted Howlett good naturedly. It was better to admit ignorance and learn, that to bluff and be shown up for an idiot.

"I have no doubt our friend here will turn you and your men into a crew of veritable argonauts," said Osgood. "Now, sir, if you will take me to your uncle we can settle the matter of payment. Sergeant, I shall expect you and your men to be capable of bringing me in safety to the other islands when I continue my survey out there." It was obvious that the captain had not intended the boat exclusively for joyriding or skylarking about.

How could a priest understand her trouble? What did they know of anything except what they read in books? She made no mention of it in the dark of the confessional; no mention of how her body ached for the foreign soldier or how she stood for hours at her window looking out through the rain and sleet at the island for a glimpse of a figure moving near the tower – just to know that he was still there. She told the priest of her uncharitableness and neglect of the sacraments and of discord with her husband which had become more frequent, but she could not admit, even to herself, the times in the dead of night when she wished herself free of John to follow her soldier to the wars and to make her life with him wherever his calling brought him. And certainly John was partly to blame, she told herself. He went about his work as usual, never showing consideration if she seemed unwell and always taking the side of the children against her if she told them to be quiet. Why must he always be so noisy and why did he persist in bringing people into the house to see her when all she wanted was to be left alone?

Sometimes she saw the little boat putting out from the island and she imagined that he was coming to see her but the boat bobbed about just off the rocks and eventually returned to the dorn to be drawn up. She hated him for that. He could go fishing without a care for her and probably when he was ashore he went drinking and whoring with never a thought of looking in to see if she was still alive. 'I wish to God he would go somewhere else,' she prayed but she knew that she did not mean it. It looked from the reports of the war that Napoleon was almost finished and the thought that the soldiers would be going away gave her a sick feeling of dread in the pit of her stomach. Father Clare counselled self denial and obedience as the remedy for her troubles, but what use would that be when she kept her worse sins hidden from him? There was no doubt that if she told him more he would have taken direct action himself, but not everything can be solved by a cut of a blackthorn stick or condemnation from the altar. She sat looking into the fire until she heard the sound of boots approaching the door. That would be John looking for his dinner. She stood up and straightened her apron. There was a good stew in the pot and plenty of potatoes so there was no reason why there should be any unpleasantness. She resolved to try very hard to be fair to the man. He was, as everyone said, particularly her mother, the best husband in the barony.

"Eileen, are ye there?" John pushed open the door and entered with a gust of frosty air that set the smoke billowing sideways from the hearth. She was glad to see him and for a moment did not notice the two figures in the doorway behind him. "I've two poor sailors here that could do with somethin' to warm them. Come on in lads". He ushered Howlett and old Garrigan into the room. Skip stood with his cap in one hand and in the other he held a big blue-black lobster that clashed its claws and legs menacingly. Howlett removed his cap and brushed his damp forelock back. His face was white from the cold and his nose glowed a startling red to match Skip's which was usually a healthy reddish purple, even in the best of weather. Eileen began to laugh at the sight of them.

"Ye're like two clowns from the circus," she said between gasps. "John where did you pick them up?" John enjoyed the joke. It was good to hear her spontaneous laughter in the house. He knew he had been right to bring them along and they were pleased to see her too.

"These are some things for the children, Mrs Mullen". Howlett pulled a paper twist of sweets from his coat pocket.

"I think you should call me Eileen," she said smiling, "seein' as how we've known you so long. Now Skip you'll have somethin' to drink and maybe a bit of stew to warm that nose of yours. They should put the two of ye on the Abel Rock to warn the ships." She laughed again, her black mood completely gone. "Pull over to the fire and I'll lay the table for us. The children are over in Donovans' so we can eat in peace."

John poured three glasses for the men and they drew in to the fire, stretching their hands to the blaze. "And how is your little yawl goin' Pether?" he asked.

"I'm getting the hang of it now at last," replied the sergeant. "It's good to be able to get off the island if only to catch a few fish now and again."

"Just keep away from my cages but," put in Garrigan, "or I'll declare war on yiz out there".

"There's no fear of that Skip. I wouldn't want to handle any of those creatures." He gestured towards the pot where the lobster was turning a bright mottled red. The talk then drifted to the war, now apparently in its dying stages. The sergeant was the acknowledged authority on this subject. "He'll have to make peace soon. What with Wellington in France, it can't last much longer."

"Aye but he's still the best man they ever had." John instinctively admired a man who was prepared to take on all comers. "I can't see the French takin' back them oul kings again. Sure didn't they start all the trouble in the first place?"

"And what about yourselves sergeant? Will yiz be leavin' the towers when it's all over?" Garrigan asked the question that Howlett had put to the back of his mind. Eileen, busy at the table, pricked her ears.

"Well we don't rightly know. Captain Osgood says that there is a lot of work to be done on the survey that might keep us here for a while and who knows what way things could turn out." It would be strange to have no war and presumably little need for gunners.

Eileen relaxed at his words. She was happy enough to have this evening and would not let the future cloud it in any way. "If ye have finished setting the world to rights come and have your dinner." She stood while they helped themselves to the potatoes and ladled the stew into their bowls, then she served herself and sat at the table. She noticed how Howlett ate with relish despite his spare figure.

"Your cooking is a lot better than what we're used to in the tower, Eileen." He looked directly across at her. "I'm afraid Laidlaw is rather rough and ready."

"Thank you. I'm sure that is a compliment. And who is Laidlaw by the way?" She wondered why meeting him again had seemed such an alarming prospect. He was really a very pleasant fellow. There was no strain at all.

"Ah Laidlaw! That would be our friend on the beach I suppose." John spoke from behind a mutton bone that he had picked up from his plate. "That's one gentleman I won't be sorry to see the back of."

"Why so?" She turned to her husband. "Have you been fighting with the soldiers?"

"No, not at all Eileen." Howlett saw no cause for alarming her on such a trivial matter. "Friend Laidlaw is a man of violent opinions that's all, but he's the best we have in the way of a cook, I'm afraid."

"He lacks decorum," said John, putting down the bone. "Now when we've finished here we'll have a few jars and maybe a game o' cards. I'll get Larry over to make four."

"Be the jings but this is the life all right," said Garrigan patting his belly. "You don't mind if I have a little smoke Eileen, do ye?"

"You smoke away Skip. I'll clear away and let ye get on with it. I've got darning to do so I won't be in your way. But let's have no more politics and don't you be fightin' with any more soldiers, at least not in my house."

"And sure why would I fight with Pether? Isn't he like one of our own?"

The door opened to admit Larry Donovan, rubbing the hands and looking from one to another with the bright intelligent eyes of a mongrel. "Be the holy, but I could smell the stew from over beyond," he said by way of preamble. "Were ye thinkin' maybe of a game o' cards?"

"Aye, we were. And I bet you could smell the whiskey too."

"Well now that ye mention it I wouldn't object to a drop." Larry slipped onto the form by the table and reached for the cards. "There ye are sergeant. It's as well there's one honest man to keep an eye on ye or these hooks would have ye beggared."

"The sergeant can well afford a couple o' coppers an' he after plunderin' half the gold o' Spain in his time." John pushed a glass across to Larry.

"I fear my plundering days are over now so whatever gold I have will have to last me for the rest of my days. All the same," he patted his waistcoat, "I can certainly risk a shilling or two if you like."

"That's the stuff." Larry rubbed the tips of his fingers together. "Here goes in the name o' God." He flipped the cards expertly into the four little piles.

Eileen found it pleasant to sit and work by the light of the fire and the candles on the table, and listen to the men arguing and disputing each hand. It seemed that the sergeant was losing, mainly to Larry, as was only to be expected. Larry had the instincts of the born survivor, honed to a razor sharpness by years of precarious living. Considering that he had started with a loan of a tanner, a net profit of three shillings and fourpence ha'penny was pretty good going. Howlett did not begrudge the loss. It was small payment for an evening of good fellowship and laughter. Anyway it was largely his own fault, as his mind was not entirely on the cards. He was constantly aware of the woman sitting by the fire, and now and again he stole a covert glance at her, watching the firelight flickering on her features. After a while she rose and went to collect the children, although Larry suggested leaving them for the night. "Sure two more wouldn't make much differ over beyond," he remarked, which was largely true. Larry's unruly clan seemed to increase annually to the point where nobody could be entirely sure as to how many Donovans there were.

Howlett watched as the children came in quietly, peering from behind their mother's skirts at the strange visitor. They had grown since he had seen them at the football game. They came forward shyly to thank him for the toffees at Eileen's bidding and he patted them on the head, at which they retreated quickly to their refuge behind their mother.

"Aye well, put them to bed Eileen or they'll be stuck to everything in a minute," said John, "includin' me whiskers," he added as he hugged them goodnight.

Skip stretched and yawned and the others began to make preparations for leaving. Larry gathered his winnings. "I hope I'll have the pleasure again sometime sergeant," he said with a beaming grin.

"I'll walk as far as the Square with you, sergeant, if you've no objection," offered Garrigan, shrugging himself into his shabby greatcoat. Eileen felt a flush rising to her cheeks. Was he going to spend the night in Clooneys? She had heard in a roundabout way that he was a great favourite there with everyone. She realised that she was jealous. Jealous of the sluts that any man with a couple of shillings could buy for the night.

"We had better hurry then. I don't fancy that harbour road at the best of times, and there's more rain on the way."

It was all right. He was going to the coastguards. He could have made that clear from the beginning. The thought, she knew, was unreasonable but she could not help it. She could feel her black mood returning as the door closed behind the visitors.

"Well now, wasn't that a pleasant bit o' company?" John sensed the change in the atmosphere and sought to prevent her slide into melancholy again.

"It was that, but you should have warned me."

"Aye well, sure I only met them at the harbour and I comin' home. There wasn't any time . . . " he broke off lamely. Somehow he was in the wrong again. "You know," he said changing the subject, "Pether told me a quare one."

"Oh yes?"

"Yes. He found a dead bird in his pooch; a wran he thought. He wondered if I knew anything about it."

Eileen felt a cold clutch of fear at her heart. The wran boys. Who else? She turned away.

"He thought I might have put it there – for a lark." John guffawed. "Can you tie that?" The laugh died in his lips when he saw the shock on her face.

"Oh Jesus can't you see. It's bait. I just know it." He had never seen her so agitated. "Please don't bring him here again."

"Now stop that nonsense. There's none o' them pishogues around here any more. That went out in oul God's time. There's divil a bit wrong with Pether."

"It must have been the wran boys." She collected herself to look at it logically. "They're in with all the movements in the back country."

"That's what it was. Now forget about it. We have nothin' to do with them movements or that oul pagan carry on." She seemed reassured at last. "Sure haven't the priests put a stop to all that class o' thing, straw-boys and wakes and stuff like that. And taken all the fun out o' funerals too while they were at it," he added with an attempt at lightness.

"What are we talkin' about funerals for?" She crossed herself rapidly. "But don't bring any more English soldiers into the house please. What will the neighbours say?"

He could see that she meant it and wisely decided not to argue.

"I'll say my prayers now if you're going to bed."

"Aye well, I'll leave you to it then an' don't be too long. I've an early start in the mornin'." John was not one for excessive piety and confined his prayer to a few mumbled phrases when alone with his horses and, of course, the Sunday Mass. He pulled off his boots and stood them in the chimney corner. "Ye need all the rest ye can get in this could weather lass." He put his hand on her bowed head and withdrew it again, troubled by the lack of response. He left her there with her beads and made his way into the bedroom. A sudden squall of rain lashed viciously against the window panes. It would be a cold road to market in the morning.

102

CHAPTER 9

Howlett leaned on the parapet idly observing the panorama below the tower. March had come with spectacularly low spring tides and the sea had retreated almost beyond the island. Along the edge of the tide several small figures were moving, methodically working their way backwards, bent almost double and every now and again stabbing into the sand with their wire spears. He watched them for a while with curiosity, trying to make out with his glass what it was they were catching. His eyes were back to normal again, and he tried to remember when he had finished the little cask of water. Whatever was in it had certainly done the trick.

"I see they're after the razors again." It was Thurston at his elbow. "Revolting looking things. I wouldn't eat them myself." Howlett was about to ask more about this when Thurston pointed to the shore. "'Ello. It looks like somethin' is goin' on over there."

Howlett trained his glass in the direction of the pointed finger. From behind the churchtower a troop of cavalry was emerging onto the beach. Their bright red coats stood out against the whitewashed walls of the Kybe and through the glass he could see people leaving their houses to watch watever was about to happen. Three officers rode in advance of the column which he identified as heavy dragoons. The column formed up on the beach below the Kybe in ranks of twelve. Presumably they were on training manoeuvres as there was no sign of any opposing force. No sound carried to the watchers on the tower as the lines split again into threes and moved through a series of complex evolutions, forming at last into a long skirmish line. The breakwater rapidly filled with townspeople enjoying the display. It was a sight to stir the blood even if the drawn sabres were only for show as they caught the sunlight. The line moved into a trot, then a canter and finally into a gallop. Now the thunder of hooves could be heard and above it the cheers of the riders. The right wing of the line splashed through the shallows and the razor fishers skipped for their lives into the deeper water. Great clouds of gulls, disturbed from their labours in the estuary, whirled screaming and protesting into the sky as the line swept past, spattering men and horses with sand and spray. The sound died away as the riders reached the furthest point of the beach almost below the headland tower. They wheeled like a line of scarlet ants and began to return again at a trot, then a canter and once more at a full blooded charge. Howlett could not take his eyes off the scene. He realised how much he missed the excitement of campaigning. This might be the last time he would ever see a cavalry charge. The fact that it was merely for sport did not detract from its appeal. He turned to Thurston and the others who had joined them at the parapet. "Well Thurston. That's what it looks like. How do you fancy it?"

"It's a pretty sight sergeant but I warrant we could put a stop to them with a few volleys." Thurston's great mentor would have relied on grapeshot.

"Maybe you'll have your chance to find out someday but not in this war I fear. I still wouldn't fancy meeting those boys on open ground." The charge had slowed again at the southern end of the beach and the dragoons were reforming. With mechanical precision the column reformed and moved off at a walk winding between the white cottages to vanish behind the trees of the graveyard. The people began to drift away and the razor fishers resumed their obsequious posture. The gulls began to settle again. Three riders detached themselves from the knot of people and began to canter towards the island. One was in blue and white; the second in red and the third, in dark riding habit, was obviously a lady, riding sidesaddle.

"It seems we have visitors," remarked Laidlaw. "Some o' the quality by the looks o' things." He handed the glass back to Howlett. Howlett recognised the man in red. It was, he knew, Balcunnin's famous brother, the Hon. Mr Edward, second-in-command of his lordship's militia. He was a heavy-set florid fellow of about fifty whose weight rather than any skill seemed to subdue the horse beneath him. It was difficult to connect him with the more ascetic looking peer. When she turned her head to look up at the tower, he recognised the girl as the lady Alicia, whom he had not seen since the ball at Balcunnin House. She wore a long black riding skirt and a trim spencer jacket with fur at the collar and cuffs. The last was a young fellow in the uniform of a naval officer. He rode his horse with an easy grace and Howlett guessed rightly that this was the younger son of the house. He went below to meet them and saluted as they reined in below the doorway. "Good day to you miss, gentlemen. What can I do for you?" It was unlikely to be a social visit although the girl smiled in a friendly manner.

"Your commanding officer has directed you to admit us to your tower." Mr Ned came directly to the point. "I have his signed order here." Howlett glanced at the paper. It was hardly necessary to go to such lengths but it sounded more serious business this way.

"We would like to examine the terrain from aloft," added the young lieutenant.

"This is my brother Frederick," said the girl. Frederick raised an eyebrow. He had not expected his sister to be familiar with a mere sergeant. "Sergeant Howlett is the musician of whom Papa has spoken so often," she explained.

"Ah, I see. You've made quite an impression by all accounts."

"The gun platform if you please sergeant." Ned had something of his brother's impatience.

"Yes sir." He led them up by the ladder and the spiral stairway in the wall to emerge onto the roof. The girl opted to remain below with the horses.

"How far is it to that cove over there?" Ned pointed to the south where the dark shadow of Luke's Bay cut in the promontory.

"I would say twelve hundred yards or thereabouts sir. I can check it on our charts if you like. May I ask what's afoot?" Howlett was intrigued.

"As you and your men will be required for what we have in mind perhaps we had better explain," said the young lieutenant. "My uncle has decided that it is time to put an end to the activities of this smuggler fellow Ryan."

"Yes and see him kick on the end of a rope too, by God," barked Ned. "My brother takes too lenient a view for a magistrate but this time, by God, we'll have him."

"You see my sloop is putting into Dublin for refitting and I have obtained the use of several guns which we intend to install secretly on these three towers. The major's informants," he nodded to his uncle, "will let us know when Ryan intends to land and we can lay a few shots astern of him and drive him ashore." It seemed to make sense provided Luke agreed to the rules. "Or conversely blow him out of the water."

"I want him alive by God. Just drive him towards my men."

It was fairly simple to Howlett. "What guns will you have for us?"

The cavalry charge had left him feeling elated and eager for some activity.

"Eight pounders. Thirteen hundred yards at least and with maximum depression we can ricochet them a bit further. Enough to frighten a few ragamuffins anyway." Obviously the young man was developing the Nelson touch. Maybe he should have a word with Thurston, thought Howlett. They had much in common, it seemed.

"Let's have no talk of this in the town either." Ned indicated the three gunners who were listening intently at the prospect of some action. "See that you impress this on your men." It struck Howlett as unlikely that the towers could be armed without exciting the curiosity of the townsfolk, a point he put to the two officers.

"I'll have them brought ashore by night. My seamen will swing them aloft in no time," replied the young man. It was all very straight-forward. Nobody would suspect a thing until they were woken by gunfire.

"Very good sergeant." Ned was satisfied with everything. "You'll be hearing from us shortly." He began to descend the stairs and Howlett followed with Mr Frederick. The two men mounted their horses and dug in the heels. The girl paused for a moment. "By the way sergeant, now that the peace appears to be inevitable in Europe, have you thought of where to go from here?"

"No miss. I enlisted for the duration and haven't thought about the future. There wasn't much reason up to now."

Her brother had reined in again at a distance of a few yards and waited, frowning, for his sister to finish her conversation.

"You might be interested to know that my father intends to offer you a position upon your release from the service." This was quite a surprise to him, although he could not imagine what function he could perform in the Balcunnin household, unless it had something to do with horses. "That's very good of his lordship." He did not know whether to indicate acceptance or not as he did not know the nature of the post. Yet it offered the prospect of a home within sight of Eileen Mullen and a solution to the problem of earning a living in a world without war. He patted her horse's neck. "Yes, that's very good of his lordship indeed," he repeated.

"And you still haven't heard me play my new harp," laughed the girl. "Maybe that would put you off the idea of coming to Balcunnin." She swung her horse away from him and rejoined her brother.

"What was all that about?" Howlett heard him ask as they began to descend the grassy slope but her reply was lost to him. Soon they

caught up with their uncle and splashed through the shallows of the
incoming tide as the dorn was once more severed from the mainland.
Howlett stood for a long time watching them swing towards the Kybe
and vanish behind the white cottages. Things seemed to be working
themselves out for him at last. It only remained for Napoleon to see
reason and Howlett's life could begin to settle into an agreeable
routine.

The boat was the pride and joy of the men on the island. They
discussed a suitable name for it and to everyone's surprise the stolid
Bateson came up with *Kittiwake*, revealing a strand of poetry hitherto
unsuspected. So *Kittiwake* it was to be. Bateson surprised them again
by admitting to a knowledge of the sea birds which came to nest on the
island in great numbers. "Any day us'll see the terns comin' home to
nest." He warmed to his subject. "And guillemots. Aye I be right fond
o' the guillemots."

The others looked at each other, tempted to smile and in Laidlaw's
case, to mock. Bateson looked at them seriously. "I reckon I would 'a
run mad on this island the past two year without the birds to keep me
occupied." He smiled shyly. "Didn't see many sea birds in Wiltshire
when I were a lad."

Howlett was intrigued to discover hidden depths. "Where did you
learn so much about them then?"

"Mr Keble the parson gave I a book o' pictures with all the birds in
it and I just got interested."

"Mr Keble? And where did you meet him? I thought us soldiers
were generally given up for damned."

"Well, I were talkin' to him about another matter and he said it
would take my mind off baser things." This was the signal for
uproarious laughter through which Bateson grinned sheepishly. "I
b'aint too old even at my age," he maintained stoutly. Laidlaw
whooped in glee. "I reckon I'd better have a look at that book. I havna
been ashore for weeks and the baser things are beginnin' tae trouble
me somethin' terrible."

"Aye, laugh if ye want to but I've found it a great comfort to watch
what's goin' on around me," Bateson replied with a quiet dignity
which put a stop to their laughter. "I grew up on the land." His a's
broadened agreeably as he recalled his distant boyhood, "an' got to
know a fair bit about birds and animals but I never seen so many in
such a small space till I came to this island."

Howlett found subsequently that Bateson could give an extra dimension to their short fishing trips. He pointed out the different kinds of birds as they skirted the rocks of the island in pursuit of pollack. "Now watch they three shags" he would say. "Come right in close and see what they be at." The three black birds stood erect, their heads turning as if in animated conversation. Sometimes one would stretch its wings to dry them like a great black spreadeagle on some nobleman's coat of arms. At a distance they looked dark and sinister but up close the effect was comical, like minor clergymen taking to each other but constantly looking around for something or someone more interesting. Further out they might spot a mighty gannet resting on the waves or dropping from a tremendous height onto some hapless fish. Sanderlings whirred past in flocks, or a lonely curlew flapped overhead piping its plaintive cry. 'A sure sign of rain,' Bateson invariably added. So much did Howlett become engrossed in watching the birds that he neglected his fishing. Perhaps Mr Keble was right about the baser things. He felt a great contentment at such times. The Kybe gleaming whitely through the haze seemed very far away and life seemed less complicated.

Captain Osgood continued his survey of the islands with the coming of the fine spring weather. The largest island bore the ruins of an ancient monastery, still partly roofed and used as a shelter for the cattle and sheep which grazed the seventeen or so acres of rough grass. To make a landing on the island was not so easy as it was completely girt with jagged weed-covered rocks; but at one point a channel had been cut through the rock, presumably by the monks of old. It was cut at an angle which made it difficult to spot from the sea. In more recent times a small stone hut had been built as a shelter for the shepherd during lambing time. It was evident that the stones of the hut had been obtained by removing part of the old church and here the captain set up his headquarters, such as it was. He directed the three gunners to begin carrying stones from the beach to the topmost point of the island. "We'll build a small mound as our starting point and measure out from there. I have already calculated the altitudes. Private Thurston," he shouted, "don't remove any more stones from that ruin."

Thurston shrugged. It was typical of officers to do things the hard way. Taking stones from the old church would have saved them a climb of several hundred yards down to the beach.

And so they began their survey of the island which occupied them for three days. The fine April weather made it a pleasant task, although the shepherd's hut proved rather cramped during the two nights of their stay. Osgood obtained sufficient measurements from his central point to give him a reasonably accurate drawing of the outline of the island at both high and low watermark. "Unorthodox I'm sure," he confided to Howlett, "but it works fairly well. Be sure to mark in the channel for future reference."

Bateson enjoyed the outing like a child on a protracted picnic. He pointed out the spots where sea birds were preparing to nest and, sitting on the springy close cropped sward, he named the birds wheeling overhead, fulmars, dunlins, red shanks, with the quiet pride of an expert. Captain Osgood took almost as much interest in the ruin as he did in his survey. He measured the structure and drew it from several angles, making detailed drawings of the remaining windows. "It would be interesting to dig around here," he remarked to Howlett. "I have no doubt we should turn up something in time."

"No doubt sir," agreed the sergeant not anxious to get involved in anything so strenuous, "but, unfortunately, we haven't the time, have we?"

"Regrettably no, but perhaps on some other occasion." The matter rested there for the moment as it was time to pack their gear and return to the mainland. Laidlaw and Thurston pulled strongly on the oars, eager to return to the comforts of the shore.

"By the way sergeant." The captain was going over some of his figures in a notebook. "Did you mark the channel on our chart?"

"I did sir," called Thurston between gasps. "The sergeant showed me what to do."

"I'd better have a look at that just to check," said Howlett reaching for the map case. "Dammit Thurston, you've put it in the wrong place. It isn't at the north end of the island."

"Don't worry sergeant," the captain called from the stern. "We can make the necessary adjustments later on. What's that gunfire?" he added raising his head from the figures. The familiar shape of the coastguard cutter came into sight as they rounded the innermost island. Smoke still drifted from the long gun mounted in the bows. Figures waved to them from the deck and from high in the shrouds. The cutter put about and made towards them until it was within hailing distance. Howlett recognised the lieutenant who had brought him to his station almost a year before.

"It's peace, Captain Osgood," the voice called jubilantly. "Bonaparte has abdicated and is on his way to Elba." Cheers came to them over the water. It was definite this time. Osgood raised his hat in acknowledgment and called for three cheers in return. The oarsmen pulled with renewed vigour towards the harbour. There would be some celebrations tonight and no mistake. The matter of Thurston's cartographical error was forgotten in the excitement and in fact remained uncorrected on subsequent maps for over a century and a half thereafter. Few of the fishermen or shepherds had any need of charts, and generations of map makers who rejected Osgood's scales as unworkable enshrined Thurston's mistake with all the authority of antiquity.

CHAPTER 10

For a variety of reasons the bonfires blazed on the eve of May. Loyal subjects construed them as a celebration of the peace and the defeat of a tyrant. The village children saw them as the usual Maybush fires and contributed their share of furze and whitethorn to build up the pyres on beaches and headlands along the coast. Some old people looked back to bygone days when the priests had condemned the lighting of baal fires as a pagan practice but that was all in the past now. Nobody saw anything sinister in having a bit of fun and if a Balrothery dance broke out the worst that could happen would be a few scorched toes, easily cooled in the dewy grass. The fires marked the beginning of summer. From then on it would be safe to leave off the heavy homespun coats and children could think of venturing into the tide without irreparable damage to their health.

It was almost dark when the fire below the breakwater was lit. The children of the Kybe took pride in outdoing all others when it came to building a fire. Furze, driftwood, straw and household refuse were piled ten feet high in a mighty pyramid while piles of extra fuel were reserved to keep it burning far into the night. Some of this fuel no doubt had been obtained by raiding the caches of the town lads, a matter that would be threshed out at a later date. For the moment, however, nobody worried about the future as the flames took a hold on the dry kindling and the furze began to crackle and blaze. Flames thrust upwards, greedily devouring twigs and branches and showers of sparks rose into the inky darkness of the evening sky, always a cause of alarm to older people who feared for the thatch on their cottages not too far away.

The youngsters began to caper around the fire adding twigs and branches, urged on by the cheers of their comrades. Each one advanced, shielding his face from the heat and threw his offering onto the blaze with elaborate casualness. Later on it would be possible to jump over the embers as further proof of bravery. As always Larry Donovan took on the duties of master of ceremonies, taking particular care to see that the smaller children, many of them his own, did not fall headlong into the flames.

"Keep back there or yiz'll all be roasted alive," he shouted as he circled the fire, cuffing the more adventurous boys and driving them back into the ring of onlookers.

"Give us them spuds and we'll put them in to bake." He took the potatoes and pushed them into the hot ashes, not too near the flames. It took a good while for them to bake and many were lost completely as the fire began to collapse.

Eileen stood with some of her neighbours watching the older children playing and keeping a firm hold on the hands of her own two. Some of the boys and girls began to dance holding the ends of long elder branches stretched across the flames. The fire formed the hub of a great wheel, the children dancing and chanting as they went.

"Do ye remember Eileen when we used to do that?" Nora Donovan turned to her, a smile of reminiscence lighting her care-worn face. As usual she held a small baby in her shawl and her lank fair hair hung down on either side of her face. Nora generally looked like a streel from the hard life that Larry gave her, and it was hard to imagine her as a young girl dancing on the beach and Larry Donovan making up to her and trying to entice her to go for a walk up by the cliffs in the darkness. Indeed, he had succeeded too with a persistence that he had never brought to finding regular employment and the upshot of it all was a visit from Fr Clare and a speedy marriage followed by a succession of babies until the juice had been squeezed from Nora and the daily struggle had drained the light from her eyes and the colour from her cheeks.

"Aye, and do you remember how the boys used to pull on the sticks till we thought they'd have us in the fire?" Eileen laughed to think of it now. An uninformed onlooker might have thought she belonged to a younger generation than Nora but they always had been close friends despite the difference in their circumstances.

"D'ye know Eileen, I could still rise to an oul dance if himself would take the bother to ask me." She indicated her husband who caught her eye and grinned back.

"I'm your man Nora, I'm your bloody man," he called, "and I'll dance Eileen off her feet too if she had a mind for it." And Larry executed a few steps on the sand but showed no serious inclination for anything more strenuous.

"Ah Larry, you're all talk," said Eileen. "You'd better look after the spuds. That's about all you're able for at your age."

"Be the holy is that a fact? I wouldn't be too sure about that." Larry left the thought unspoken. He was content to stand on his record.

The dancers fell out of the circle amid shrieks and laughter as their sticks burned through and the dance dissolved in a riot of tumbling bodies and showers of sparks. Larry began to rake out the spuds and distribute them to the children who picked greedily at the steaming floury insides. The fire began to fall in upon itself as the reserves of fuel were used up and people became aware of a chill in the night air.

"It's time I had these children in bed," said Eileen, wiping the remains of potato from their mouths. "I might come over for a while if you would send one of the older ones to sit in the house for me." When John was away she would never leave the house untended.

"Aye, I'll send the girls over. They'll like the change and the bit o'peace." Nora didn't add that the girls would appreciate the good supper that Eileen always gave them, but it was a consideration. They began to walk back towards the Kybe shepherding the children with them. Eileen was glad to have someone to talk to. She had begun to dread the nights when she was alone, and although she was often short with John it was a relief to have him there to distract her from her own thoughts.

When she closed the door behind her about half an hour later she stood for a moment enjoying the cool night air. Beyond the breakwater the moon stood high in the sky and a silver path lay on the full tide. The headland and cliffs stood out clear and black against the light. Occasional bats from the old church tower fluttered above her head with tiny mewing noises, like mice in the wainscotting. She gathered her shawl around her shoulders and turned impulsively from the path to the Donovans' cottage. Suddenly she felt that she wanted to walk by herself in the darkness, just for a little while. She could make some excuse to Nora about being delayed when she came back. She went down onto the beach where the last embers of the fire still glowed. There was no one about. She walked slowly along by the edge of the tide, stepping aside as the small waves washed up on the shelving sand and ran gently downwards with a long sigh. The darkness suited her mood of pensive melancholy and without realising it she found herself at the beginning of the cliff path. It did not occur to her that anyone seeing her would think it strange, a woman unaccompanied walking the cliffs by night. As it was she encountered no one and continued as if in a kind of trance, her shoes swishing through the long wet grass. She was conscious, in a heightened way, of the smells around her, the smell of freshly turned clay, the smell of grass. Even the smell of dung seemed strangely inoffensive. The salt smell of the sea came sharply to her nostrils.

Her step quickened and a sense of urgency overcame her. She felt her heart beating loudly. She must keep going, keep walking as far as possible until she was too tired to think. Then Peter Howlett would be left behind. He would fade into the distance and soon he would be gone altogether and life would return to normal. Briars and thorns tugged at her dress and plucked at her shawl, but she did not notice them in her excitement. Everything was clear to her now. She must avoid seeing him until the soldiers were withdrawn from the towers. She would walk and keep herself occupied until he was taken away out of reach. Already she began in her euphoria to reconstruct the old life of the Kybe, the days of work and laughter with John and the children. In the morning they would begin again.

She came to where the path dipped down into the cove and descended to the little beach. She was warm now from her walk. She threw off her shawl and trailed it over the pebbles. She kicked off her shoes and walked along the edge of the water not caring that her stockings and the hem of her skirt were soaking wet. It occurred to her that she would like to swim in the moonlight by herself.

"Hello Eileen." Someone spoke from within the shadow of a tall rock. She drew back in fear, although she recognised the voice instantly. There was a kind of inevitability about it.

"I hope I didn't frighten you." He stepped forward from the shadow and she could see now the boat drawn up under the rock. She smelled the smoke from his pipe.

"Oh it's you Peter. I didn't expect to see you here." The matter-of-fact nature of her remark struck him as out of place. No more had he expected to see her. He stuttered in confusion. "I . . . was having a smoke. I've been dropping a net out there." He waved his hand vaguely towards the mouth of the cove. "Sea trout or so Skip tells me. It was such a fine night . . . " He trailed off unable to think of anything else to say.

"I've been walking," she explained unnecessarily, moving closer. Something about her struck him as strange, something wild and inexplicable.

"Are you all right?" he asked. He did not want to offend her or make her go away and yet her presence threw him into confusion.

"Yes, I'm perfectly well. In fact I was just thinking of having a swim when you came along."

Christ, he thought, is this really happening? She must be unwell. I should try to get her home. He felt himself beginning to shiver uncontrollably. "Wouldn't that be a bit dangerous?" he asked trying to keep his mind logically calm. He tapped out his pipe on the side of the boat.

"I can see that you think I am mad but that isn't the case. I am also a very good swimmer. You can put your mind at ease on that score." She stood in front of him looking up with a faintly mocking smile. Her eyes glistened in the moonlight. Howlett felt himself slipping like a man on a crumbling slope. His voice sounded thick and coming from a distance. His throat felt painfully constricted.

"I never wanted us to meet like this, Eileen."

"Neither did I. It just happened." She stepped forward and he took her in his arms as naturally as if she had always been with him.

"We could go into the cave," he said feeling that eyes might be watching, possibly from the clifftop. A light showed on the island although it was difficult to make out even the outline against the dark northern sky. What if Laidlaw were watching them through the spy glass? Impossible. He could see nothing at this distance and in the dark of the cove. Yet the light disconcerted him.

"No, here," she said pulling him down on the shingle beside the boat. "No one could see us in here. Quickly. Put your coat on the ground." Howlett was surprised by the urgency and vehemence in her voice. He had never dared hope that she felt as he did. She opened the strings at her throat and shrugged her clothes from her, letting them fall in a pile at her feet. Her body gleamed white in the moonlight like a warm marble statue. She stepped out of the heap of underclothing and the dark pool formed by her dress and lay on the blue coat in the shadow of the rock.

"Hurry," she said.

Howlett fumbled at his clothes with fingers that trembled and refused to answer to his brain.

"Hurry," she said again and laughed. "These stones are cold and I can't stay all night." He lay beside her and she turned to him. "You're cold," she said. "You're trembling."

"No," he answered. He meant he was not cold but it sounded like a refusal. He reached for her, touching her smooth skin and passing his hands over her white body, almost in disbelief. It was really happening. She was holding him. They moved together gently at first

and then frenziedly till he felt her shudder under him with a long sigh
and the tension poured from him in an agonising torrent. All the
loneliness of his lost childhood, the fear, the misery of his solitary
existence, the envy and regret, she drew from him with her soft
enveloping body. Howlett lay exhausted, blinded by a glimpse of an
existence he had never suspected. He could feel her pulse in the
sudden stillness. The ripples swished at his feet as waves crumpled on
the beach. He lay quite still listening to the silence. She did not move
for several minutes. He closed his eyes feeling that he could sleep. He
felt her moving beside him and looked up. She kissed his eyes slowly
and gently.

"Right then. It's time for your swim." She slapped his thigh and
stood upright. He lay back and watched her unselfconsciously. "I'm
not going in there."

"Coward." She was in an elated mood. "Watch me." She ran a few
steps backwards and threw herself into the water. The beach shelved
steeply and when she stood up the water reached to her waist. Her hair
hung loose and wet reaching almost to the tips of her breasts.

"Come in or I'll splash you." She swung her arms like windmill
sails and Howlett scrambled backwards dragging the clothes out of the
range of the spray. She laughed at his undignified posture as he
crouched, feeling rather foolish and vulnerable in the shelter of the
boat.

"I'm not coming in. I can't swim," he mumbled shamefacedly. He
began to pull on his trousers. She turned and swam gracefully with an
easy breaststroke out along the track of the moon. Howlett began to
feel slightly alarmed.

"Come back," he called softly and with relief he saw the white blur
of her face turning towards him. Her hair streamed behind her in the
water as she swam back towards him. He felt himself becoming
aroused again but reality had begun to intrude. She stood up and
emerged from the water and he hobbled towards her with only one
boot on.

"Here, take my shirt and dry yourself, you mad woman." The
strangeness of the encounter struck him clearly for the first time.

"Where is John?" he asked.

"He's away to the market," she said drying herself vigorously. He
turned away as she began to dress herself.

"You are such a gentleman," she said mockingly.

"I don't understand you." He spoke without looking around.

"That doesn't matter. I love you anyway." The word struck him like a physical blow. "You had better go home. I must get back to the island."

"You and Bonaparte and your islands. Don't think about things too long or you will miss your chances." She was laughing at him and he could think of nothing to say. He felt guilty, thinking of John somewhere on the Dublin road, alone with his thoughts. Fear shot through his belly. Where do we go from here, he wondered. "Will you be all right? Shall I see you again?" He had to know if there was hope, though what shape hope might take was a mystery.

"Yes. It can't be helped." She reached her fingers to the side of his face, touched him gently and turned away. He watched her running lightly over the stones until she reached the top of the slope and the cliff path took her out of his sight. He stood for a while, unwilling to leave the cove, trying to make sense of what he felt. He could never recall feeling so happy about anything in his life. Nor could he ever remember feeling so guilty or such a nagging fear of the future, worse than the anxiety before a battle when the enemy gunners wheel into position and the sinister drums begin to roll.

He turned to his boat and slipped the oars into the rowlocks. He rocked the craft from side to side, forming a channel at the stern into which the water began to seep, gradually taking the weight. The keel grated on the shingle and with a quick thrust on the stern he got her afloat and leaped nimbly abroad. Seizing the oars he swung the bow around and pulled strongly towards the pinpoint of light on the island. Beyond the cove he met the incoming swell and spray began to come aboard. Howlett heaved on the oars till the rowlocks groaned in their sockets. He felt the exhilaration of struggling against the sea. He was invincible. Laughter began to bubble up inside him and once or twice he collapsed breathless over the oars. Gradually he calmed and began to steer more carefully, humming softly until he felt the surge of the flood-tide over the dorn and he swung round to starboard and grounded on the island beach.

Immediately Howlett was aware of activity on the island. He heard low voices and the sound of ropes creaking through pulleys. He became conscious of his appearance and quickly pulled his coat on to conceal the fact that he wore no shirt. Damn it, he thought. Of all the nights they choose. It had to be the business of the gun. He bounded up the slope towards the tower. Sure enough a group of seamen stood at the base of the tower with block and tackle and bundles of rope.

Captain Osgood stood by with young Frederick while a bosun supervised the handling of the gun.

"Ah sergeant," called Osgood. "Good of you to join us." There was a tinge of good-natured sarcasm in his voice. "While you have been out fishing the lieutenant and myself have been defending the realm against the king's enemies." The lieutenant nodded to Howlett who had turned his collar up as if for extra warmth.

"I beg pardon sir, but we didn't expect you tonight".

"Obviously sergeant. You are technically off duty, of course". Typically Osgood did not make an issue of it. "Be good enough to go aloft sergeant and supervise the mounting of the gun."

"Sir." He was relieved to be able to escape and grab a shirt from his bunk in the guard room on the way. A tripod stood on the roof with a boom projecting over the parapet. A sailor passed a rope through the block and the low voice came from below: "Careful lads; quiet now; haul away there." Slowly the rope ground through the block.

"How did you get it ashore?" Howlett asked one of the sailors.

"Hogsheads," replied the sailor. "Floated her ashore on a raft o' hogsheads." He pointed to the far side of the island and by straining his eyes Howlett could make out a dark shape lying on the beach. The long rocky ledges were covered by the high tide. Several cables out the sloop lay at anchor, without riding lights but visible in the shimmering moonlight, yet hidden from the town by the island itself.

"Haul away lads," the bosun urged softly from below and the men grunted as they took the strain. With dull thuds and the occasional ringing chime the great bronze gun rose along the side of the tower. The boom groaned under the weight and the men on the roof heaved on their line to sway the gun over the parapet. Gradually they swung it in and heaved it into position on its carriage. For the first time since it was built, all those years before, the tower was armed. The sailors rapidly dismantled the boom and sheer legs and lowered them over the side. The whole operation had been completed in just over an hour with hardly a sound. Now Howlett could appreciate the coastguard lieutenant's remarks about controlling smugglers. The moonlight glinted on the barrel of the gun. For the first time in over a year he was in charge of a lethal engine of war.

"You shall do very well sergeant if you spring this trap for my uncle." The young lieutenant was standing beside him inspecting the siting of the gun. Howlett turned to face him. He was aware of being scrutinised closely and a slight air of hostility in the officer's demeanour. "My sister speaks highly of your skill as a musician. I hope it is matched by your skill in gunnery."

"I know my trade sir, you may rely on that," replied Howlett. "Good, good. By the way my father wishes to speak with you about a project he has in mind, if you could call on him the next time you're ashore." It was a command, not a request, in the family tradition.

"I shall certainly do that sir as soon as this business is finished."

"You could do a lot worse," remarked Frederick. "The Balcunnin servants are generally accounted the most fortunate in the district." Had he emphasised the word servant, Howlett wondered. Was he being put in his place? He shrugged imperceptibly. The gentry were always on their guard against encroachment on their dignity.

The seamen carried up the shot and stacked the balls beside the gun platform. Laidlaw reported the powder safely stowed in the magazine below. "Oh, and I put your sark tae dry by the fire sergeant. You must be gye careless wi' the net tae get sae wet." Howlett felt there was a question implied in the remark and was glad of the darkness that concealed the flush which rose to his cheeks.

"Good man, thanks. I did get a bit tangled up at first." He stopped himself from further explanation.

"Ye know what I'd like to do sergeant?" Laidlaw looked thoughtfully at the gun.

"No, what?" "I'd like to lay some shot on that red bastard Mullen over there and teach him not to insult the king's uniform." Howlett's stomach turned over. Could this caustic Scotsman read his mind? Were they not like gods here on their tower with the power to destroy whom they pleased of the tiny mortals creeping below? They were the lords of life and death. Why should he not take what he wanted?

The lieutenant turned from the parapet. "This is my father's town, gunner. Speak like that again and you'll find yourself on the triangle and no mistake."

"Aye sir, sorry sir," Laidlaw mumbled. "I was just thinking out loud, sir." There was a flavour of insolence, even so, in the 'sir'.

"Sergeant, take care of my gun and use it well." The young man departed with an abruptness doubtless inherited or studied from his father.

"Get a tarpaulin over it. We must conceal it as best we can." Howlett directed his men. "Tomorrow we'll align it on the bay." Below them on the seaward side of the island the landing party was shoving off in a long boat. Oars creaked in the stillness of the night and the dark shape crept over the moonlit water like a great black insect. If Mr Ned's information was reliable the scourge of the seas would soon be dancing on the end of a rope for the entertainment of the crowd. Somehow Howlett wondered if Luke would be so obliging as to step into so obvious a trap. His eye travelled along the dark outline of the land. A light still shimmered on the Kybe. He wondered if she was still awake and his heart ached again with a great loneliness as on winter nights in the cold and storm. He felt the urge to take his boat and go to her and to hell with everything but somehow he feared that she would not even recognise or remember him. By now she would have come to her senses and would see in him only a threat to her security. Howlett took refuge in his sense of duty. The best thing would be to concentrate on the immediate matters and then to speak to Balcunnin. A busy man would have no time to brood on the impossible. A spark of stubborn pride told him that he had survived all right on his own before and could do so again. The argument went round in his brain as he stood there preoccupied, the wrongs cancelled out by the rights until he could make no sense of it. All he could be sure of was that he wanted to see her again more than anything he had ever wanted in his life before.

CHAPTER 11

John Mullen put down his pint and looked at the old captain: "Ye must be mad," he laughed, "do ye want to get yourself kilt?"

Skip grinned, wrinkling his weatherbeaten face mischievously: "Sure it's only the once't and it should be good for a laugh."

"I dunno. If anythin' happened to the horse I could lose me livin', not to mention me life." Nonetheless it sounded crazy enough to work out and he was in such good spirits lately that he felt indestructible.

"Lookit," insisted Garrigan, "all ye're doin' is deliverin' a consignment and sure isn't that yer lawful trade? Ye bring the stuff to Dublin be the Naul road and nobody will put any pass on ye."

"Ye've persuaded me then, but if there's any sign o'trouble I'm off like the hammers and to hell with the consignment as ye call it."

"Aye, that's fair enough, fair enough. There isn't enough of them lads to watch the whole coast so don't worry about a thing."

This was something he wouldn't mention to his father for fear that the old man would lock up the horses and bar the yard against him. Neither would he mention it to Eileen, even though in her present mood she would probably want to come along with him for the laugh. There was no doubt she was in rare form these days, ever since May had come in with unexpectedly hot weather.

Garrigan excused himself and dismounted from the high stool. He shuffled to the door and looked out across the harbour. A yawl was rounding the end of the pier. "That's oul Roche from Arklow. I'd know his yawl anywhere." Garrigan removed his pipe and spat onto the road. "Truculent oul hoor."

"Ah he's not that bad considerin'," said John, joining him in the sunshine. "Them's two decent lads he has. I always get a bit o' work from them with the turf." In his present frame of mind he was prepared to think well of everyone, even the old one-armed sea captain and his hard drinking sons. They leaned against the wall in the sun and watched the activity on the pier. Garrigan lapsed into an unwonted silence, and John thought on the turn his life had taken. Ever since May-Day Eileen had been like a new woman. She was full of laughter as ever before and her eyes were bright and lively. Sometimes, he felt, she was a bit too excitable but this never worried him in the bed at night when her demands upon him became urgent and almost insatiable. Still, he thought, with a private smile, a man should not complain and it had been a long winter.

The swimming was doing her good too. She swam almost every day at the breakwater, in a long shift with her hair streaming behind her. He delighted to sit with the children when he got the chance and watch her, although he was never much of a one for the swimming himself. "I have to do all my swimming before the jelly-fish come in," she explained and indeed she had a right to be afraid of them. For himself the sight of the obscene brown pulpy objects with their hanks of stinging threads was enough to keep him out of the water entirely. Eileen abhorred them too but for the reason that she had been stung badly as a child. Still she was prepared to risk it.

"You know," he said to her once as she emerged from the water, "you remind me of a seal swimming around there." No seal, however, had ever aroused in him the feelings that she aroused as she stood in front of him, pushing her hair back from her face and the wet shift clinging to her. It was like coming home again after a long exile and he felt his love for her almost overpowering, so strengthened did it seem after the long winter of alienation.

"Whatever you do don't start him on the politics." Garrigan broke in on his reverie and John's mind returned to the present. The one subject to be avoided with old Captain Roche was the matter of Ireland's freedom. Although Fingal was not notably a hotbed of revolution, some raw nerves had been touched from time to time and the hunting down of a few pathetic fugitives from Wicklow and Wexford in ninety-eight was an event still remembered in the locality. Roche, himself, had lost his arm during the recapture of Ross, and one would naturally expect him to have harboured a grudge ever since. Strangely Roche's grudge was directed as much against the cause of freedom as against the rough-sharpened Hessian sabre that had caught him on the undefended bridge.

"We weren't worth freedom," he averred, thrusting his views into the face of whoever might disagree and prepared even still to fight against the cause with the same ferocity as he had first espoused it fifteen years previously. "A drunken rabble," he sometimes said, in his more peaceful moods and his eyes would glaze with grief, remembering the lost opportunities, the exhilaration of victory, the garrison in flight, the wild debauch when the town lay open to the victors and the final thunder of hooves on the bridge as the cavalry swept across. "We weren't worth freedom."

This point of view often involved his amiable sons in a conflict of loyalties, defending their father from the attacks of his drinking companions whose republican sentiments were often the same as their own.

"We'd better buy them a drink so, to keep him sweet," said John and went into the bar. Garrigan strolled down onto the pier to greet the Wicklow men. Through the window the carrier observed the tranquil scene. Several schooners lay in the harbour, their black reflections standing in the still water. Seagulls drifted to and fro scavenging for bits of fish. At the end of the pier he could see the soldiers' little boat with the Scotsman lounging on the oars. He wondered briefly about the sergeant. He hadn't seen him for quite a while. Maybe he had been sent away now that the war was definitely over. That would be a pity in a way. He was a fine fellow, for an Englishman, and he regarded him as a friend. 'It's hard on them,' he thought. 'Even the Scotsman must have a home somewhere.'

Out from the coastguard station came Captain Osgood, accompanied by his sergeant. They made their way through the groups of men on the pier and around the stacks of cordage and boxes until they reached the steps. Laidlaw stood up and grasped the rail to steady the boat as the two men stepped aboard. John supposed that the captain was off again on one of his eccentric missions, chipping rocks, or measuring or whatever. He felt a spurt of pleasure at seeing Howlett again and made a note to mention it to Eileen. She had always spoken highly of him as a very civil fellow and she had surely forgotten the episode of the wren. Laidlaw pushed off and pulled on the oars and John had to admit, grudgingly, that he made a reasonable fist of the rowing.

Garrigan appeared at the doorway, followed by the three Wicklow men. Their bulk shut out the sunlight as they entered the low ceilinged room. "How are ye John Mullen?" growled the one-armed man. An attempt at a smile cracked his impassive face, a face as hard and as craggy as the granite of his native mountains. His two sons, behind him, grinned in unfeigned pleasure and reached for the pints that stood ready on the counter. Garrigan, ensconced once again on his stool, reflected on the disadvantages of being small in the company of these enormous men. They were not men to be lightly crossed, he thought irrelevantly, listening to their talk of cargoes and rates for the job.

"Be God John," he put in, "but ye'll need all the horses ye can get if what I hear is true." He paused until they gave him their full attention. "His lordship has decided to make the pier longer and bring it out into the deep water."

This was indeed interesting. The Wicklow men pricked up their ears.

"He'll be needin' stone then," said John seeing the implications for himself. "Be God, this is news all right. I could make me fortune here with a few more carts. I suppose he'll bring the stone from his own quarry."

The Wicklow men made a case for granite, with an eye to their own advantage, pointing out that it had been shipped even to London in preference to land haulage but all agreed eventually that John Mullen could be sitting pretty with Balcunnin's quarry only two miles away from the harbour and himself and his father the leading carriers in the district.

"And another good one," said Garrigan, enjoying the attention, "he's goin' to take on the sergeant to look after the blastin' whenever he can get out of the service. They'll have to open a whole new face in the quarry and Pether is to be the overseer." John was genuinely pleased to hear this. Although the sergeant had set foot in the town only a year before, he had become a familiar figure and was highly thought of in some quarters, particularly in Mrs Clooney's, he thought with a grin. The talk turned to the soldiers and what was to become of them. "I hope to God they don't keep that Scottish lad around here,' said Garrigan. "That's a right jeer that lad. I sometimes think he does be at me cages now that he has the little boat." This was a serious matter and John told them of the encounter on the beach. It was agreed that Laidlaw would not be a welcome addition to the community.

They were joined by old Morris the shipwright and his young nephew Tom, and a good natured argument developed about the merits of the Arklow shipwrights, who, Tom said, had missed their true vocation — making wash tubs and porter barrels, giving the Roches' yawl as indisputable proof of his theory. John left it with them and headed off through the town whistling. He had plenty to think about with regard to the captain's plan and plenty of news for Eileen

Also he would have to speak to his father about getting hold of some
more carts, maybe a couple of drays would be the thing. The da would
have a good idea of what would be needed. And to think that he had
worried about the peace being bad for business. He tipped his cap to
Mr Ned who cantered past obviously in great good humour. A busy
man, thought John, with all his military duties and the whole district to
guard. Well, Luke might put him to the test before very long. They
would have a good laugh about it all in a day or two, himself, and
Eileen and Skip Garrigan.

The watchers on the tower strained their eyes into the darkness. There
it was again, a pinpoint of light flickering to seaward. It must be the
signal to someone on the shore. A fingernail of moon gave only a
glimmer of light. There was no answering light from the shore. The
moon drifted between the high mackerel-scale clouds. The light
flickered again, nearer this time and heading towards the cove.
Howlett sighted along the barrel of the gun, waiting for the light to
appear to landward of the muzzle.

It occurred to him that the tide was half way out and that no boat
could go very far into the cove. It would take nice judgment to trap so
wily a character as Luke without blasting him and his crew to pieces.
Osgood stood at the rampart, never taking his eyes off the cove. At the
sound of three pistol shots and the uncovering of three lanterns they
would know that their quarry was in the trap. Then they would open
fire, sending round after round skimming over the water, effectively
bolting the door against any attempt at escape. The noise itself would
probably be enough to demoralise the smugglers. Thurston stood by
the gun swinging the slow match from side to side, the glowing point
describing an arc in the darkness. He quivered with anticipation.
Action had come at last, somewhat late in the war and not so glorious,
but better than none at all. Laidlaw and Bateson stood by with ramrod
and sponges at the ready. This was better than fishing or filching
lobsters out of the old man's cages.

On the clifftop Major Ned patted his horse's neck and eased his
weight in the saddle. His detachment of twenty picked men stood by
their horses' heads, preserving all possible silence. No sound came
from the harness or hooves which were carefully muffled with rags
and cloth. Below them the sand gleamed a dull silver from the
receding tide. The small craft had come to a halt in the shallows and
the sail was being hauled down and furled. There seemed to be only

two or three men. The light flickered again and moved erratically from side to side as if the men were wading around the boat. Presumably they are preparing to unload whatever they have, thought Ned. He felt it advisable to let them come ashore but they seemed to be in no great hurry. Suddenly below him, to his right, he saw the dim shapes of figures moving in the shadow of the high rock, creeping furtively towards the boat.

"Fire", he roared and three shots echoed around the cove. The three lanterns were hurled over the cliff to smash with gouts of flame on the rocks below. The night erupted with the thunder of the distant gun. Flame issued from the tower, and a shot howled through the air, to smash into the headland cliff. The men mounted rapidly and their major led them at breakneck speed down the slope and onto the wet beach. They spurred their horses on a collision course with the men who had now broken into a run and were heading for the boat.

"I want them alive," Ned's voice carried over the noise. "Use the flat of your sabres." He had not expected to find so many. There must have been about a dozen. Another shot roared across from the tower, this time skipping over the water like a slate making white flashes of spray. The headland again received the impact. The horsemen drove at the runners in the shallows, riding them down and striking blindly at them in the curtain of spray, while Ned and two or three others made for the boat and the men who stood beside it obviously too petrified with fear to try to escape.

"Halt in the King's name," roared Ned.

"Halt in the King's name," echoed a voice behind him.

"Holy Mother o' Jasus we're halted, we're halted," quavered the voice of the man with the lantern.

"Who the devil said that?" roared Ned, again bemused.

"Is that yourself major? I said it. It's me, Dinny Garrigan. Don't murder us for God's sake."

"You are all under arrest. My men will open fire if you resist," came the strange voice again.

"What's going on here?" Ned felt anger taking over from puzzlement. "You are addressing a major of the Fingal militia and I command here."

"Oh I know that sir. I know that" said Garrigan, apparently anxious to remain on good terms.

"Not you, you fool. I'll deal with you presently."

"You are addressing a captain of dragoons and you have made an unwarranted attack on my men while we were apprehending these smugglers."

"While *we* were apprehending these smugglers you mean." Ned
was apoplectic with rage. There was a moment of silence. The gun
boomed again from the tower and the shot whistled past. It
ricocheted off an angular outcrop of rock and skimmed over the
heads of the men on the beach with a derisive whine. Everyone
ducked instinctively from the invisible danger.

"About the smugglers major, sir," Garrigan broke the silence
diffidently, "sure it's only meself and Larry and the young lad after the
flounders. They do come to the light d'ye see," and he held up a gaff
towards the major. A large white flounder flopped feebly from side to
side in the light, impaled and in its final agony. The soldiers moved
closer in curiosity.

"He's right sir," said one of the mounted men from beside the boat.
"There's nothing here but a few fish."

"Damn your flounders sir," said Ned wrenching his horse around
violently, "and damn your dragoons too sir." He dug in his heels
viciously and spurred away, with his troop following sheepishly in his
wake.

"You haven't heard the last of this major," shouted the officer in a
fury, as his men picked themselves up, bruised and bedraggled from
the onslaught. Their horses were brought up from behind the rocks
and they remounted, in some cases with difficulty. The gun on the
tower was silent.

"Is it all right if we go now, captain? We'll get no more fish around
here tonight and we're soaked to the skin."

The dragoon could not trust himself to speak.

"Be the jings Larry but we'll have to have a word with Pether about
firin' cannonballs at his friends and us loyal subjects of his majesty."

Larry had not reckoned on artillery and was still quaking from both
shock and cold.

"Be Jasus Skip, but that's the last time I'll go fishin' with you." His
teeth chattered as he spoke. The boy laughed and dangled his feet in
the water. The horsemen began to move off.

"I think maybe we'll sail over to Elba and drop in on the emperor
seein' as how King George has declared war on us." Garrigan's voice
was heavy with sarcasm. He settled into the stern and reached for the
tiller. "It's a sad state of affairs Larry. Take up the anchor there and
let's be off." The aggrieved tone faded from his voice as they fell back
from the shore and he began to chuckle slyly under his breath. "I'd
fancy a smoke now but I'd be afraid to show a light." Even Larry

began to see the funny side of things although his teeth still chattered from the cold.

Light streamed from the doors and windows of the Kybe as the riders made their way back through the town and the people, alarmed by the cannon fire, stood in anxious groups, wondering what had happened. Some said that Luke had been captured and his ship destroyed, but there was no sign of prisoners. It was remarked that the dragoons looked in worse shape than the militia but neither group looked particularly pleased with their night's work. Nora Donovan, with a blanket wrapped around her, stood watching the procession and talking to Eileen.

"No doubt Larry will have all the news if he's still able to talk when he gets home. He's gone drinkin' again with that oul Garrigan, probably in Clooneys. He'll end up in trouble some day the way he goes on."

The mention of Clooneys gave Eileen a dart of jealousy. At least if Peter was on the island firing his gun in the middle of the night, scarifying people, he couldn't be down in Clooneys consorting with loose women. She felt a sense of satisfaction and relief from the thought. It didn't take gunfire to remind her that she wanted to see him again.

John Mullen turned on his seat as he drove the laden cart off the beach at the mouth of the Delvin. Far out to sea he could just make out the shape of the lugger. The dark sails were being unfurled and already she was under weigh. He leaned back against the straw that covered the barrels and began to relax. In a short while he was on the Naul road where he fell in with a cattle drover. What could be more natural or more innocent than a drover and a carter travelling together for company? Without undue haste they would reach Dublin by first light and he would be home again by midday with money in his pocket. At one point they thought they heard the distant reverberation of gunfire but decided that it must have been thunder. There were no guns around those parts and the lugger was well away by then, even if there had been any pursuit. He thought of the story he would have for Eileen on the morrow and of the presents he would bring from the city. They met not a sinner on the road until the grey light of dawn began to creep over the eastern hills and then it was only a wizened little man with a gap toothed grin, who greeted them from his perch on a gate pillar. Something about him was familiar to John but he could not place him. "One o' them half mad back-country fellas," suggested the drover with the condescension of a much travelled man.

"He looks like a bright little bird perched up there with the sharp little eyes of him," said John and they laughed at the comparison. Shortly afterwards they came within sight of the city and could smell the early morning smoke from the fires. Dublin nestled snug beside its silver river amid trees and gardens, a picturesque sight with its spires standing nobly against the sweeping background of mountains.

"A great morning to be alive," said John to his companion, as they parted from each other at the canal bridge. And it would be a great night too when he reported how he had fared to Garrigan and his cronies.

CHAPTER 12

The town rocked with laughter. The idea of two detachments, regiments, of soldiers and artillery being needed to capture old Garrigan, Larry Donovan and the boy was just too ridiculous for words. This was better than any victory over Tyrrelstown and men felt entitled to partake of a libation to mark the occasion. Members of his majesty's forces were politely asked if any more smugglers had been captured recently or if it was true that Luke had been taken away in chains. For some days the soldiers tended to avoid any contact with the townspeople, even those in whose houses they were billeted, but eventually they found that if any of the normal comforts were to be had they must grin and put up with the joke.

Skip Garrigan maintained his air of injured innocence throughout, insisting still in an aggrieved voice that he was entitled to an apology from all concerned in this unprovoked attack on a loyal subject. Larry on the other hand swelled with pride when recounting his part in the affray and gave a vivid account of what he had said to Major Ned and the dragoon officer. It was unlikely that these two would tamper with Larry Donovan again in a hurry. Indeed, Major Ned did find it necessary to pay a visit to the Balcunnin estates in Mayo where he could enjoy a freer hand in pacifying that turbulent county and not a few hovels were to lose their thatch as a direct result of the action in the cove. His lordship on the other hand seemed to derive a quiet amusement from the whole affair. Perhaps it was merely relief at having his brother out of the way for a time, but he confided to his daughter that he did not believe in coincidence to that extent.

"Somebody, I suspect, has been playing ducks and drakes with our brave lads. I don't think your brother is too pleased either after lending his guns to the cause."

"Surely father you should speak to those men and try to ascertain the facts," suggested Alicia. "After all you are the magistrate."

"My dear I should only bring ridicule upon the law. You will learn that between us and our people there is a barrier of incomprehension which can be raised at a moment's notice. We have been hoodwinked and must accept the fact. These people are like children and must be let enjoy their little triumphs occasionally."

Alicia was pensive for a while. "It was a good joke all the same Papa, don't you think? But is it not sad that we must be separated from those whom we call friends and whom we try so hard to help?" Balcunnin frowned, contemplating the burdens of rank and property. "We must continue to be practical, my dear. Much of the problem lies in superstition but you'll see when work becomes available on the new pier, people will realise where their best interests lie. In our position we do not expect gratitude. The reward lies in doing the job well." In the face of this sound philosophy, the embarrassment of the recent battle could be taken in good part. Alicia's despondency evaporated in the light of her father's common sense. "When do you expect to make a start on the pier, Papa?"

"I intend to bring the matter up when parliament meets in the autumn. It is possible that I may be able to get a subvention for the work but either way it must be done soon. This town could grow and prosper with the proper facilities. I should think that by this time next year we shall see considerable progress."

John Mullen's high spirits did not last as long as he had expected. Eileen had the story of the night's events when he arrived home in the afternoon and he was horrified to hear that there had indeed been great guns involved. Garrigan was definitely mad, he thought, to put himself in that position. Her reaction to his part in the episode was even more violent than he had expected. "You fool, you fool," she screamed and struck at him with clenched fists. "You could have got yourself killed, and then where would we be?"

"Come on." He tried to hold her but she struck at him again. "It was only a favour for Skip and his friends. And I got paid for it handsomely." He showed her the five golden guineas. She slapped them from his hand in fury and they clinked against the kitchen wall. "Do you think I want to see you hanging on some gibbet with smugglers and footpads?" she screamed with spittle forming at the corners of her mouth. "Wouldn't that be a fine sight for your children?"

John felt afraid of her anger. He had never seen her like that before. he could think of nothing to say and turned away to look out of the

window. His shoulders hunched and his eyes stared blankly at the sea
beyond the garden fence. He was conscious of her breath coming in
short quick gasps and then she began to sob, a guttural sound like a
wounded animal. He felt cold and helpless, realising what he had
done. He saw himself, in his mind's eye, swinging from a gallows,
swaying in the breeze. He could almost hear the creaking of the rope.
He could not say how long he stood there or when the sobbing
stopped. He felt her hand on his shoulder and turned to her. Tears still
streamed down her cheeks but she was calmer now. Her hands picked
at his shirt as if removing invisible threads. She looked up at him; all
her anger had gone. "You are a fool and what you did was wrong."

"Aye, maybe ye're right Eileen. I shouldn't 'of done it." His voice
was contrite. "I didn't realise."

A ghost of a smile flickered on her lips. "I do love you, you know
and we need you more than Luke Ryan and Skip Garrigan do."

Nearly home he thought. Say nothin'. He put his arms around her
shoulders.

"Don't think you've heard the last of this. As for that old scoundrel
I'll scratch his eyes out if I catch him."

John thought he had better warn Skip to give Eileen plenty of sea
room for a while until the dust settled. "I'm sorry love," he said.
From now on I'm a solid citizen. You're lookin' at the man who's
goin' to be the biggest carrier in Fingal. Even oul Morris will be
tippin' his hat to me soon." It was safe to introduce a note of levity
now that the storm was over and prudent to change the subject to
more cheerful matters than gibbets and dule trees.

"All right. I'll say no more about it. Your dinner is in the pot and I
must go and find the children." She turned at the door. There was
mischief in her eyes as if they had just been sharing a joke. "By the
way, I'm goin' to keep that money and put it aside for the children. I'll
not have you handing it over to Mrs Clooney." John made no protest.
It was cheap at the price and apparently he was out of trouble again.
There was no doubt but women could look at everything in the most
extraordinary ways. They could make you see things that a man would
never notice. He stooped to gather the coins and placed them on the
mantlepiece. His appetite returned with his escape from her wrath and
he unhooked the big pot from over the fire. After dinner he resolved
to go and find Skip and get the full story of the night's events. It would
be advisable all the same to get home early and mend a few fences
with Eileen to keep her from sliding back into her old moods. The
violence of her temper worried him. It would be necessary to tread
softly for a while yet.

Captain Osgood was delighted with Balcunnin's plan to lengthen the pier. "A capital idea," he confided to Howlett. "This could be the leading haven on the east coast after Dublin itself." Howlett was enthusiastic about the idea, although a little apprehensive about his qualifications for the job of overseer. It sounded more like a job for a pioneer than a gunner and musician. "Nonsense man," Osgood reassured him. "Blasting is merely a logical extension of your present occupation and as a sergeant you should have no difficulty in keeping the men up to scratch." They stood in the oriel window in Osgood's office overlooking the anchorage. The fishing boats vied with the trading schooners for space at the quayside and the pier itself was crowded with men, carts, boxes and piles of nets.

"The need is obvious," said Osgood, indicating the confusion, "but I have put another scheme before his lordship that will probably involve yourself." He turned to a map of the town which he had unrolled on the table. Books and inkpots weighed down the map's four corners, preventing it from rolling up again. "As you see, the town is triangular, with the apex here at the harbour." He traced the shoreline with an ink-stained finger. "Now what strikes you about the land at the base of this triangle?" He looked expectantly at Howlett like a schoolmaster with an apt pupil.

"Well, it's not much use, is it? It seems to be all marsh and sand. I suppose the stream is largely to blame."

"Precisely. Note how this area, the Kybe is almost an island. In fact the whole town could become an island at spring tides if the stream happened to be in spate. I've seen all these fields under water." He drew his finger across between the town and the windmill.

"What have you suggested, sir? Enclosing the stream?"

"No. I think that his lordship should embark on the building of a massive sea wall all along here, to protect these low fields from the high tides."

"But the stream. Will it not back up behind the wall?" It seemed that they would merely lock the water in.

"Baffles, sergeant. We must prevent the tide from getting into the mouth of the stream. A series of baffles will do the job here." He pointed to the little bridge leading onto the Kybe.

"I fear, sir, that you have me baffled too. I hope some engineer undertakes this part of the job."

"You need have no fear sergeant. I shall plan the works myself. I think we'll be here for a little time yet. Let us walk along together and view the site." The captain reached for his hat and a cane. He furled the map and thrust it under his arm. They descended the stairs and strode along the pier. One or two of the men stopped working as they passed. Some remarks were made about disturbing the peace. Howlett had expected something of this sort and replied good-naturedly, "Just a bit of target practice lads. Next time we'll shoot to kill."

"Ye know somethin' sergeant," said one fisherman confidentially, "if ye were any use ye'd have hit the oul so an' so with at least one o' yer shots, but sure they say ye can't kill a bad thing." He chuckled at his own humour. This would be an interesting point of view to put to Garrigan when they next met. He could claim that he had been trying to do a public service. In fact he had not been unduly surprised by the outcome of the whole business and sensed that Garrigan was not the innocent bystander he claimed to be.

Osgood took no notice of these exchanges, so interested was he in the fabric of the pier itself. They walked back and onto the road to the town. "This whole area needs to be fortified," insisted Osgood, "or the dunes could be swept away leaving the headland an island again." They walked along by the dunes as far as the mouth of the stream where Osgood expounded further his theory on baffles. It began to make sense to Howlett. They proceeded onto the breakwater of the Kybe. "Now, from here to the cliffs is where the sea wall is needed. This breakwater will never do."

Howlett's attention had strayed to the cottages and he watched in fearful hope for signs of life around the Mullens' dwelling. He could hear the cries of children at play and occasional shouts of laughter.

"The face is vertical you see. It meets the waves head on." Osgood was expounding again.

"Beg pardon sir, I wasn't following." John Mullen had come into sight with his two children scampering at his heels. Howlett felt his face flushing hot with apprehension. How should he greet the man?

"Ah Mullen," called Osgood "you'll appreciate my point."

John grinned with pleasure. "Well sir I don't know if it's safe to come near the sergeant here. A fierce dangerous man they tell me." Howlett was relieved by the mockery. "He might come at me with that big knife."

The captain smiled tolerantly. "I was explaining to Howlett here how a breakwater should be constructed. You cannot hope to stop the sea head on with a wall like this. You must curve the wall so that the waves are deflected upwards and spend their force that way."

"I see what you mean sir" said Mullen interested.

"The sea is like a woman." Osgood's poetic streak appeared again.

"Immensely powerful and dangerous if not approached with caution. But you can deflect it and render it harmless with a little forethought."

"Be Jasus, you're right there sir. You must be a married man like meself sir. Only trouble is I only think o' the forethought afterwards." Osgood was pleased that his analogy had gone home, however quaintly the Irishman had expressed it.

"Of course Pether here wouldn't know anythin' about that yet." Howlett kept his face impassive with what he imagined to be a noncommital expression. "Though I suppose he'll be on the lookout for a wife when he takes up his new job here." Howlett had listened to all this without saying a word. In fact he could think of nothing coherent to say and stood there feeling foolish and uncomfortable with the sweat breaking out on his forehead.

"Well," he ventured with a dry throat "the captain was explaining about the new sea wall. I suppose you will be interested in the contract for hauling stone." This at least was something they could discuss without strain.

"Aye that I will, and it will be a pleasure workin' with yourself Pether." Howlett felt like a cur and said nothing. The captain took John by the arm and began to point out the line of the new wall. Howlett was conscious of the two children watching him shyly again. He tried to smile at them but they just stared. It unnerved him.

"John." A woman's voice called. "Where are you John?" She came around the corner of the cottage and stopped momentarily in confusion. Howlett looked away towards the sea, pretending not to be aware of her approach.

"Keep away from that lad Eileen," John laughed. "He's the fella that tried to murder poor Larry and the captain." Eileen took up her cue as he turned to greet her. She gathered the children to her skirts in pretended fear.

"I hear you're going to do great things around here," she said by way of conversation. She looked at him levelly, holding his gaze.

"Well, I'll have to wait for my discharge and that might take some time," he mumbled. "There are so many men wanting to get out of the service." John and the captain had moved away a little. "How have you been?" he asked.

"Fine," she answered without elaboration, "and you?"

"All right." His voice carried little conviction to her.

"I must go in now," she said, beginning to turn away. She looked back. "Tomorrow night," she added in a half whisper.

"No," he replied desperately. This was something more easily discussed in the dark, easier to face and easier to explain away.

"Yes," she said, "you must," and then she was gone with her children by the hand. Howlett felt his head reel. He had to sit down to overcome the turmoil inside him. He could not possibly agree to this in cold blood with her husband not more than a few feet away. He would not see her again. It could only end in disaster. It was totally wrong. Yet a voice inside him, small but insistent, told him that he would go, that he had a right to go and that as long as John never knew, there could be no harm in it.

"Sergeant, are you feeling ill?" Osgood's voice cut through his thoughts.

"No sir," he replied standing up again. "I'm all right sir."

"It must be the strain of all the fightin' Pether," volunteered John, slapping him on the shoulder. Would he never hear the end of that? He smiled as best he could at the joke but he could feel the carrier's hand on his shoulder like a hot brand, as he imagined Judas must have felt the kiss until the noose tightened about his neck and his wretched life was extinguished.

CHAPTER 13

Howlett sat at the table in the bar and toyed with his glass. It was evening and the last of the daylight still streamed through the grimy windows. There were few customers in Clooneys at this hour and he had finished his meal undisturbed except for the attention of young Bridie who made it her business to see that he had everything he might need. "Would you like an orange sir?" she asked when he pushed his plate aside.

"An orange? Yes, that would be very nice Bridie and thank you." It was over a year since he had tasted an orange. Bridie produced one from the bulging pocket of her apron and he began to peel it. She watched as he thoughtfully drew longitudinal lines from pole to pole and peeled back the skin with his thumbnail. He stripped off every scrap of pith before dividing the fruit carefully into segments.

"You're very careful, sergeant," said Bridie. "Why don't you just eat it?"

"I like to get the most out of it," he answered. "You know the last time I tasted an orange was in Spain."

"Spain," said Bridie her eyes widening. "What is Spain like? Is it all sunny and happy like people say?" Aye, Spain, he thought. Sunny enough to dry a man out and cold enough to freeze him to death. Long marches over snowy mountain ranges by rutted roads more like torrents than highways. French stragglers impaled and mutilated by the country people, a soldier crawling in a ring of burning straw, driven back like an animal, by the encircling pitchforks. Fever and the bloody flux. Keep moving. Victory within our grasp.

"Aye, Spain is a fine place Bridie, with the sun shining and oranges and grapes growing everywhere, and people dancing and laughing. I think you'd like Spain right enough."

The child's eyes shone. "Yes I think I would like to go there sometime and maybe live there in a little white house on a hill."

"Maybe you will someday, Bridie, and marry a great señor." Everyone should have a dream. "Where did you get the oranges?"

"That sailor over there gave them to me," she said, indicating a tall thin man lounging by the bar. He was dressed in a long brass-buttoned coat and white breeches. Howlett imagined him to be an officer from one of the schooners at present lying in the harbour. "I'm obliged to you sir," he called pointing to the orange by way of explanation. The man nodded civilly in reply. He had been observing the sergeant for some time. "Perhaps you would care to join me in a drink?" Howlett gestured to Bridie who went behind the counter as the man came across to the table. Howlett noticed that the stranger was unarmed except for a silver-topped malacca cane which he laid on the table as he sat down.

"Artillery I see," said the stranger. "I've seen service myself in my time but mostly at sea. What do you find to do in this part of the world?"

Could this be the only man, wondered Howlett, who hasn't heard of the recent business? "Oh, we are kept busy enough," he replied with a wry smile.

"But what guns have you got? I presume you are attached to the Martello towers. You'll forgive my curiosity, but I always understood that the towers were unarmed." Howlett flinched at the man's directness. "We have guns enough sir if need be but law-abiding folk need have no fear." He was not prepared to discuss the disposition of guns with a complete stranger. It began to dawn on him that people were taken aback to find that there were guns on the towers at all. Perhaps all the laughter was intended to conceal their alarm. The thought gave him a feeling of having stolen a march. The man abruptly changed the subject and began to talk of the peace and its effect on trade. He had been to Spain already in the wine trade and expected a great increase in traffic to the continent.

"And how do you find that country since the war?" inquired the sergeant.

"Well I don't know much about politics but I gather that not everyone is happy with the restored monarchy. Some say that King Joseph was in some ways a better king."

Howlett laughed. "Not an easy people to satisfy, the Spaniards. I confess I was sometimes more afraid of our allies than of the French." He described some of his experiences in the peninsula without dwelling too much on the hardships.

"I suppose all the same," said the man, "they had a right to be ill-disposed towards foreign troops in their own land."

"Damn glad they were to have a foreign commander," retorted Howlett, nettled again at the inference. "Anyway I don't complain. I did pretty well out of Spain in the long run, though I have no desire to go back there." At this point they were joined by old Garrigan who approached with elaborate wariness before sitting down and ordering a drink. "All right Skip, I suppose I owe you a drink," said Howlett handing the money to Bridie.

"Aye, that ye do an' all," replied the old man gruffly, "and an explanation too."

"Between the two of us Skip," Howlett looked directly at the old man, "I think you know a lot more than you pretend." He took the mug from Bridie and passed it to Garrigan. "Now what you do is your business but I have to obey orders." He fancied that a quick glance passed between the two men.

"Sure don't I know that sergeant," the old man said quickly, "and am I complainin'? I wouldn't take a few cannonballs as a personal insult." He was anxious to change the subject but Howlett knew he had him.

"I'm not a complete fool Skip, but I won't interfere in your private matters. All the same, if I'm ordered to fire on you in earnest I won't miss." Garrigan took a long and contemplative pull at his drink. He began to stoke his pipe thoughtfully. Eventually he said, "I take your warnin' very kindly." He could see that Howlett meant what he said.

The stranger excused himself and went out into the gathering darkness. It occurred to Howlett that nobody had been introduced, although they had been conversing for almost an hour. "That was a very civil gentleman," he remarked to Garrigan as the door closed. "Did you know him?"

"Oh aye, it's well I know him right enough. A great traveller he is." He leaned forward conspiratorially. "You have been sittin' at the one table with Luke himself. Now isn't that a quare one?" He waited for a reaction from the sergeant. Howlett leaned back on the bench smiling.

"Now that explains a lot of things. No, I'm not going to raise a hue and cry, don't worry. I'm very glad to know that the gentleman is flesh and blood."

"Aw me sweet Pether, I knew a body could trust ye the minute I set eyes on ye. D'ye know, I think we'll make a christian out of ye yet."

The bar began to fill up and the level of noise rose, making conversation more and more difficult. Laidlaw and two other gunners arrived in good shouting form and began to argue with anyone who was prepared to take them on. The Scotsman's rapid fire humour was more than a match for the jibes of his adversaries. It began to emerge that in Laidlaw's eyes the last laugh inevitably rested with the man behind the gun. This was an argument difficult to refute. The locals tended to retreat sullenly behind their drinks as the gunners became more brash. Howlett felt a grudging admiration for the Scotsman who could hold his ground with the best when it came to verbal abuse, but he was not prepared to spend an evening listening to him. He could hardly wait until it was dark enough to go to the cove in safety. No matter how he argued, he knew that he would be there, although he fully expected to find the place deserted. He left the room unobtrusively, leaving Garrigan puffing contentedly on his pipe and observing the exchanges at the bar.

Quickly he made his way through the town to the bridge over the stream. He did not want to be seen going through the Kybe so he made a detour around the old church and the graveyard. This brought him to the marshy ground beyond the trees and he broke into a trot. He was glad that he had left his musket and pack at the coastguard station. The buckles on his belts jingled alarmingly loud in the darkness. Rushes brushed at his legs and he felt his feet sinking into the soft ooze. It was a relief to get onto the cliff path and he began to run, leaping over the outstretched briars in exhilaration like a boy. Now he was certain that she would be there and he grudged the time it took to cover the distance between them. He came suddenly to the top of the slope leading to the beach. The moon was about three-quarters full and the cove was bathed in light except where the cliffs threw dark patches of shadow. He descended more carefully to the beach and looked around. He heard a rippling sound. There she was, swimming quietly towards him just as he remembered her from the last time, with her hair streaming behind her. The water around her boiled with tiny leaping fry. The whole surface of the cove seemed to be alive with little splashes of phosphorus and moonlight. She put him in mind of a mermaid or some sea goddess attended by a million gleaming sprites.

"I knew you'd come," was all she said as she stood up and walked towards him, her body gleaming white and wet in the gloom.

"Where else would I go?" he asked, taking her hands in his own and leading her towards the shadows.

She lay beside him, warm again and drowsy in the soft night air. He pulled his coat over them as far as possible. He could have slept there all night. She wriggled closer, purring almost like a cat. "Keep me warm," she demanded. He laughed gently. "I'm such a bony wretch I can hardly keep myself warm."

"You are you know." She traced his ribs with her fingers. "You need proper feeding to build you up." He said nothing for a few moments. "What are you thinking?" she asked. "Nothing. I refuse to think right now."

"Oh!" She was silent too.

"Will you come here again?" Howlett did not know which answer he wanted to hear.

"If you want me to."

"I want you to but is it not dangerous for you? I have little to lose but you have everything."

"I never wanted this to happen," she said after a while, "but it has and you have made me happier than I ever thought possible — and sadder too," she added. "I know that we have little time together."

"I've wanted you since that first day I called at your cottage," said Howlett.

"I was afraid," she said, "when I saw you then but I never knew why." He laughed softly. "You would never believe how confused I was then. I thought you would take me for a complete fool." He began to shiver slightly and tried to control it. He did not wish to break the spell. Little spasms seized him and then he was still again. She sat up and reached for her dress. "It is time to go. We don't want to be found frozen to death in the morning." Howlett was relieved to pull on his clothes and feel the heat beginning to return to his bones. "I fear I am not built for outdoor lovemaking. Perhaps I am just too old." He laughed wryly. It was ironic how practical considerations kept intruding.

"Will you really take the job with his lordship?" Eileen was pulling on her shoes.

"I think so, but I can't be certain yet."

"And what about us then if you do?"

"I wanted the position at first to be near you, but now I don't know what is for the best."

She hung her head. "Let's not think about it for a little while."

"When will you come here again? I must return to the island tomorrow but I can get the boat at any time."

"You can see our house from the tower?"

"Yes, of course. I think I know every stone of it by now. I've watched you through my spyglass time and again."

"I'll hang a red blanket over the fence on the days that John is away. Let that be my message." The mention of John brought a silence between them. Damn the man, thought Howlett. How much better he would feel if John beat her and treated her badly. "Go now," he said "and I will follow in a while. We don't want to meet anyone at this hour."

"John is a good man and I love him and care about him. He is never to know." She went abruptly, fading rapidly into the darkness. Howlett stood for what seemed hours, trying to make sense of his situation. He could see no way forward except to live from hour to hour postponing any decisions until they might be forced on him. Finally he shrugged and followed her along the cliff, taking care to make a wide detour again around the Kybe. A curlew piped overhead and in the marsh the redshanks trilled a startling ululating sound that made his hair stand on the back of his neck. His footsteps echoed in the dark deserted streets and he was glad to reach his billet at the harbour without encountering another human being.

CHAPTER 14

The Star of Runcorn fled through the darkness as if pursued by all the demons of hell. The gale, intensifying all the time, howled from the east, driving her remorselessly to leeward. For three days the schooner had been beating up channel with her cargo of timber for Liverpool. Now the wind had swung around from the north to due east and had freshened into a whole gale. The skipper had hoped to heave-to in the shelter of Anglesey and ride out the gale but this hope had been dashed. Darkness came upon them, obscuring the distant line of mountains and he decided that his best bet was to run before the wind, with just a reefed mains'l to give him weigh.

"We should fetch up somewhere near Howth by first light," he bellowed over the howling wind to the mate who clung to the rail beside him. The waves in mid-channel lifted the vessel and flung it down again into the troughs with a sickening lurch. Each time it looked as if the following wave would engulf them but each time the stern lifted and the bowsprit sank into the churning mass of foam.

"Be god skipper, if she can take this she'll stand up to anything," confided the mate, grey-faced with fatigue. There was little they could do at this point but struggle with the wheel to prevent her from broaching-to. If they were once caught wallowing broadside by one of these greybeards she would undoubtedly turn turtle. In the short summer night the waves glowed in an eerie light, more frightening because each one was clearly visible as it bore down upon them. The seamen clung to the shrouds, their faces turned towards the stern from whence the main threat came, or aloft where the spars, bare against the luminous overcast, groaned under the strain. The pumps were working frantically to cope with the water that poured, dark and menacing, over the gunwales and spurted unseen through the sprung timbers below.

"The cargo is secure captain," shouted a seaman, working his way aft from the hatch, "but if she takes in much more it could start to move." This was another dimension to their danger, great baulks of timber pounding the sides of the vessel with every rise and fall of the waves.

"Keep an eye on it," the skipper shouted back. "It will be light soon." The sailor retreated below wondering which was preferable – to remain on deck and risk being sent aloft, or brace himself in the darkness of the hold not knowing when the ship might founder leaving him no opportunity to escape. Either way would make little difference to the final outcome, he concluded, turning his thoughts towards his Maker with unwonted fevour. Below in the darkness of the hold he was mercifully unaware of the full fury of the storm. The hours of darkness dragged by interminably. He did not see the mains'l torn away in flitters from the yard or even hear the loud crack as the foremast broke off, clean as a pipestem, but he felt instinctively the change in the motion of the vessel, surely a sign that they were approaching land and that the great ocean rollers were giving way to the white breakers of the shoreline. Now they would swing round into the shelter of some hospitable roadstead. He offered a silent prayer of thanksgiving for their deliverance. A rending crash interrupted his devotions. Cold water drenched him as the timbers were torn asunder. With mute horror he sensed, rather than felt the cargo shifting. A great weight fell on his chest, pinning him to the bulkhead. Was it water or blood that gurgled in his throat, choking the scream? The prayer he thought, I haven't finished the prayer. I haven't finished . . . The timber shifted again and in the darkness of the hold he waited for his mother to come and lift him. He could hear her voice as he died.

Peter Howlett was woken by knocking on the door of the coast-guard house. It was not yet light, he noted, as he pulled on his clothes. Outside he could hear confused shouting above the howling wind and the rattling of the windows. Waves thundered on the foreshore, each impact shaking the building to its foundations. "She'll break up for sure," said a voice as he emerged. The wind cut through his shirt, chilling him to the bone. Coastguards, townspeople and some soldiers were thronging towards the back of the pier where a couple of lanterns threw a yellow pool of light.

"She's stuck fast on the Cross Rock," someone shouted. In the dim first light they could see the schooner. It looked as if her masts had gone by the board. Yards and rigging hung in a tangled mass over the port side, swirling back and forth in the raging sea. The great waves with twenty yards between their tumbling crests reached for the stricken vessel, trying to dash her from her precarious perch. The watchers moved closer, clambering over the slippery rocks in the grey dawn light until they could see the figures clinging desperately to the remains of the rail or the stumps of the masts. Not more than a hundred yards of seething water lay between the wreck and the furthest tip of the Grey Mare but it might just as well have been a hundred leagues.

"Those men will perish if we don't get a line aboard." Someone clutched at his arm and Howlett turned to look at the speaker. He found himself looking into the light blue eyes of the young shipwright Morris. "Come with me," shouted the young fellow urgently. "I need someone to help me."

"You're mad," said Howlett, "nobody could get out on those rocks."

"I mean in a boat. You can handle an oar." "Not me," said Howlett with a hollow laugh. "I'm no seaman." Nevertheless, he found himself running behind the younger man, carried along by the urgency in his voice. "We have got to be first or it's no use."

Willing hands heaved the small skiff down onto the sand. Four short oars were notched onto the thole pins. The shipwright hurled a grapple with a line attached into the stern and leaped aboard. Three or four men waded waist deep in the pounding surf to get them away and Howlett wondered as he heaved on the oars how in God's name he had got himself into this situation. There was nothing for it but to row or be dashed to pieces on the harbour wall. The young man pulled like one possessed, his breath coming in audible grunts. "If we get in the lee of the Grey Mare and stay there till the last minute . . . " Any plan was better than none at all and Howlett resigned himself to following orders. The watchers on the beach became smaller and smaller and he felt fear gripping his vitals. For a moment or two they lay in the lee of the great reef gathering their strength.

"Ready now," shouted Tom. "Keep her into the waves at all costs." His lank fair hair was plastered to his brow with sweat and spray. Wind and sea struck them at once, lifting the frail craft and carrying it along like a twig. It teetered on the crest of a wave until the men on the beach felt sure that it must disappear altogether. The younger man pulled savagely, the tendons on his arms standing out like cords and Howlett followed suit as if in a trance. They slipped down into the trough and the bow rose to meet an even greater onslaught. As if detached from the events, Howlett recollected what Eileen had explained to him about prayer and sin. It was not a subject that had exercised his mind to any extent, although he knew that she went in dread of dying in sin. He went in dread of dying, and he had chafed her, not understanding her fear. Now it seemed like a suitable time to renounce sin. He was afraid and fully expected to die at any moment but it seemed a strange time to try to balance his books with God. Moreover he had a sneaking hope that Tom Morris knew his business well enough to bring them both ashore and in all honesty he could not try to deceive his Maker by renouncing Eileen Mullen when he knew full well that he would renege as soon as his feet touched dry land again. He had never had a close relationship with the Almighty, but Howlett figured that He was entitled to the courtesy of not being taken for a fool. This more honest approach seemed to him the best policy, although he had little time to formulate it in his mind.

They came in under the towering bow of the schooner. She was stuck fast and the waves pounded her mercilessly. Tom reached for a trailing rope and hung on with all his strength. "Get the grapple aboard," he shouted, trying to make the rope fast to the skiff. Howlett swung desperately. The hook clung firmly to the gunwale. The line whipped as unseen hands hauled it in. The great mass of shattered spars and rigging swung perilously towards the little craft. A boom crashed into her side and water spurted through.

"We're sinking." Howlett could not say whether he had spoken aloud or not. He stared at the water washing around his feet. I can't swim, he thought, not for the first time, although it could not have made any difference. "Jump man." Tom was pointing to where the torn shrouds of the foremast hung over the black shining side of the schooner. "Get aboard." The rest of his words were lost. Howlett jumped without argument. His hands grasped the shrouds and he climbed. The wind tore at him and the sea tugged at his feet. Someone hauled him aboard and he lay like a stranded fish on the sloping deck.

As the seamen hauled on the line, the day brightened. A frieze of figures festooned the shoreline and the more accessible rocks. Gradually they pulled in a heavy line with running tackle and made it fast. One by one the survivors attached themselves with ropes and belts to the line and the men on the shore began to haul them across. Some disappeared for endless moments under the waves to emerge again battered and bleeding and in some cases apparently dead. The skipper, unconscious, his arm already broken, was tied to the line and lowered into the water. Howlett looked at his companion. He had no wish to trust himself again to the sea. There appeared to be little choice. "You go next, Tom." The ship heaved beneath him. "No", replied the young man. "Let them get ashore if they can. She's breaking up," he added in a louder voice to the mate.

"For God's sake get ashore", yelled the mate. "We are grateful . . ." He was cut off as he dropped over the side, leaving the two men on the deck above.

"What are we to do?" Howlett turned again to the shipwright. The fellow was beaming with satisfaction. "We do nothing," he shouted with his hand shielding his face. "We hang on till the tide drops. The wind will go down with the tide and then we're sitting pretty." It seemed a strange choice of words but Howlett was in no position to argue. He had sensed the confidence of the young man and it was preferable for the moment to cling to the shuddering deck than to join the panic-stricken seamen in the foaming maelstrom below. "Yourself and meself, sergeant, will be the rich men after this, do ye realise?" He gave a short laugh.

"I'd give a fair share of my wealth to be ashore again," retorted Howlett. "How long do we have to stay here?"

"If she doesn't fall off with the ebb she'll float off with the flood. That is if she doesn't crack up." He rubbed his hands in high glee. "Me uncle will be out to us as soon as the wind drops and it won't hold for long more." Howlett was amazed. "Did you have all this planned from the beginning?"

"Aye well it crossed me mind," admitted Tom, "but we had to do something for the poor mariners anyway. If it wasn't us it would have been Skip Garrigan or someone else and I need the money more than he does." He said nothing more but stood bracing himself against the gale. Howlett crouched by the ruined deck house, frozen in his soaking clothes. He regretted not having taken the time to snatch a coat on the way out. The thought of imminent wealth did little to relieve his apprehension as the great sliding mountains of foam swept in from the east but now they were breaking further out and the water boiled harmlessly around the wreck, causing no more than a slight shudder with each impact. She did not budge from the rock as the tide dropped away from her and the sun broke through the ragged clouds.

For hours they sat on the deck, warmed now by the sun, and watched the activity on the shore. Crowds had come to observe the wonder of a fine ship broken and impaled on the rock. The familiar cross was gone, snapped off by the impact of the bow. The sound between them and the Grey Mare narrowed and narrowed until the observers could come within a stone's throw of them but still the water surged through, impassable though less threatening than before. Gradually the gale began to diminish and they could hail the men who clambered out onto the reef, prominent among them the figure of old Morris the shipwright. Tom shouted to his uncle, giving him an idea of the state of the hull. As yet they had not examined the hold as the water had not gone down far enough and the open hatch cover revealed a dark sinister pool with planks and baulks washing about in the gloom. Howlett recognised the familiar figures of the Mullen family on the foreshore and he waved, a trifle flamboyantly, basking in the sunshine and the newly acquired fame. They waved back and he saw how John turned to his wife and pointed towards the ship. He could not know how Eileen's heart pounded with dread at the thought of the danger he had put himself in and how inwardly she raged at not being able to express her overpowering sense of relief. Howlett paced the sloping deck, conscious of the eyes following his every move.

"Three men drowned," reported Tom, breaking in on his thoughts, "the captain included." They were silent for a time, each of them thinking how they also could so easily be stretched out under a tarpaulin in the yard above. "My uncle says to examine the hold as soon as possible. This timber will come in very handy."

"But can you just claim it like that?"

"The skipper is dead. The owners are in Liverpool and we are aboard, so the law is on our side as I see it." It seemed a conclusive argument, with an Old Testament finality about it and Howlett wondered what it might mean to himself in real terms. It would be a pleasant bonus to start his new life with some cash behind him. "Let's look below," suggested Tom pulling out the remaining battens and rolling away the torn canvas. Daylight streamed into the hold. The timber had torn loose from its lashings and lay strewn everywhere. Obviously the trim of the vessel had been severely upset before she struck. They climbed down to make a closer inspection of their windfall. Tom's experienced eye took in the damage as the water level dropped steadily.

"We can brace these planks enough to get her ashore," he said pointing to where daylight gleamed through the stove-in, starboard side. "By tonight we could have her snug in the harbour." He lifted the end of a plank and peered underneath. Howlett saw him drop the plank and turn away suddenly, crossing himself. "What is it?" he asked, but Tom merely pointed downwards, his face white with shock. Suddenly he was no longer the capable man of affairs but a small boy almost on the verge of tears, Howlett raised the end of the plank again. A face stared up at him from the water, the eyes wide and questioning and the mouth open as if to speak. What had the poor fellow thought in his last moments he wondered. He could not take his eyes off the face. He had seen death before but never like this, alone in the dark wetness of the hold. There was nothing to be done. The mirth had drained out of their adventure. They returned to the deck and sat in glum silence until they saw a boat pulling out from the pier and making towards them in the long rolling swell.

CHAPTER 15

For a time Peter Howlett could not explain the gloom that settled upon him after the salvage of the schooner. It seemed wrong, even ignoble, to profit from the misfortune of the seamen. At night he saw in his dreams the reproachful face of the drowned man in the hold. Sometimes it reminded him of the skull of the little wren, an image that had lurked in his subconscious mind until the dead sailor recalled it in his dreams. He was a hero to the town, along with Tom Morris who had assured him of an equal share in the profit from the wreck. Men came and slapped him on the back and offered to buy him a drink. They had never seen anything like it they assured him. Captain Osgood congratulated him on his part in the rescue and speculated on some more efficient means of getting a line aboard a grounded ship.

"What about these Congreve rockets?" he asked. "Have you ever seen them in use?"

"No sir, I'm glad to say," replied the sergeant. "From what I've heard they are more dangerous to our own side than to the enemy. It's impossible to direct them."

"Still," said the captain thoughtfully, "if a line could be fired across, perhaps by a gun." He considered the problem, rubbing his chin pensively. "We must consider the matter again." He turned to their more immediate problems. "It seems that we must continue to man the towers for a little while more, until everything is settled in France but you should be out of the service before the end of the year."

It was strange for Howlett to be considering any other way of life than the one he had known for almost twenty years and he felt a little stab of apprehension. "However," the captain concluded genially, "with your new wealth you should be quite a man of property around here." Howlett thought of the skipper and his three crewmen buried now in the churchyard by the Kybe, their freshly turned graves like gashes of red under the dark yew trees.

"Well that's not settled yet sir, so I'm not banking on anything for a while."

Tom Morris was more sanguine about the whole matter. Proudly he surveyed the stacks of new timber in the boatyard. "Look at that," he exclaimed, "the best of Norwegian spruce. Pit-props some of it. We can cut them down. Lovely pitch-pine planking. We're in business for years, Pether." He grinned broadly. "You and me can get that schooner into good shape and put her into the coastal trade. We can't go wrong." Howlett frowned. It seemed too easy. *The Star of Runcorn* lay on her port side on the slipway, her damaged planks exhibited like a wound to the world. "When do you hope to start on her?" he asked.

"Just as soon as the case is heard, but the Receiver has to let us keep her. It's a clear case." He went on to paint a rosy picture of the future and Howlett began to succumb to his enthusiasm. A vision of a great trading fleet flying their house flag and ploughing the oceans of the world flashed before him. Why not, he thought. Tom maintained that this new century's prosperity would be built on commodities and the products of the manufactories and whoever controlled the distribution could make real money. Howlett knew nothing of commodities or economies, but he admitted that Tom talked convincingly and seemed to have a good head on his shoulders. The future promised to be interesting.

Eileen met him on the path near the windmill. It was a fine sunny morning and he was whistling as he walked through the long grass. He had been intending to go as far as the quarry and cast his eye over the place. There was no harm in starting to think about his new career and there was little else to do in the relaxed atmosphere of the peace. His heart leapt with delight when he saw her coming towards him, the hem of her skirt brushing the cornflowers on either side of the narrow path. Her two small children followed her at a distance, capering in the long yellowing hay and hiding from each other and their mother. "Isn't it a beautiful morning?" He wanted to reach out for her there and then. How pleasant it would be to be able to sit down in the meadow and just talk together like ordinary lovers on a warm summer's morning.

"Yes it is." Her voice was cold and she made to pass on. Howlett could not imagine what was wrong. "Wait a minute. Can't you talk to me?" He watched her for some sign. Surely nobody could have found out about their meetings. All the same she could be very strange. Maybe she had simply changed her mind. She turned towards him and her voice cut like a whip. "I don't ever want to talk to you again. Just leave me alone."

He felt anger rising inside him, uncontrollable and murderous. He caught her as she stepped by him. "Now hold on. What's happened?" She winced in pain at his grip, alarmed by the expression on his face. "What does it matter? It can't make any difference anyway." The coldness in her manner began to crumble into dumb misery and Howlett's anger subsided as quickly as it had come. More gently he asked her again what was wrong. The children had come up to them and stared from their mother to the soldier and back again in wide-eyed incomprehension. "Tell me please," he insisted. "What have I done?"

She stared past him towards the blue line of the horizon. Her voice seemed to come, dull and lifeless from far away. "You know that I have lived for the sight of you almost since the day we met." He hung his head at a loss for words. "And the other day you could have been killed on that schooner and I couldn't even have shown my grief." Now he understood. He swallowed to remove the pain in his throat. "I'm sorry, I didn't have time to think." It was the truth but it sounded lame.

"Men never take time to think," she leapt on the phrase, "and I had to stand there and laugh and say what great lads you were when I really wanted to be sick." She looked into his face and he believed her. He saw the hurt in her eyes. "If you cared at all you would never have gone and I'm tired of hearing about all the money you and Tom Morris will get." Now the anger flashed from her eyes and Howlett, although the object of her anger, found himself detached from the scene and marvelling at how quickly she changed from one mood to another. Like a small boy in trouble he felt a grin beginning to pull at the corners of his mouth. He knew that this would make matters worse, but at the same time he was relieved to find the cause of her anger.

"Now you're laughing at me. That shows that you don't understand. You don't really care one way or the other."

"That's not so," he smiled broadly. "I'll admit I was showing off a bit when I saw you on the shore, but would you believe me if I told you I thought mostly about you when I was in the little boat?"

She turned away again. "I don't know what to believe," she said over her shoulder. "Sometimes I think you regard me as the same as your other women down in Clooneys."

"Now that's unfair. I have no women down in Clooneys or anywhere else."

"Except that I come cheaper," she added ruefully. The children had wandered away again, bored with an argument which they could not understand. He took her by the shoulders and turned her towards him again.

"Now listen to me. There are no other women. Since I first laid eyes on you I haven't been interested in anyone else."

"I've heard all about you," she was teasing now but he knew that she believed him. "They say you're a great favourite with herself and all the young ones."

"Well they say wrong then, if it's any business of theirs," he replied in the same bantering tone.

"And what about her ladyship from Balcunnin? They say you're great with her too. Maybe you'll both be very snug together with all your new money." There was no sarcasm in her voice but there was a question there all the same.

"Well they seem to know a lot about my business whoever they are. And what do they say about us?"

"Nothing so far and that's the way we have to keep it." It was as if a cloud passed over her face again.

"When will I see you again?" asked Howlett. "I'm going back to the island for a few weeks at least."

"I'll give you a sign like I told you. I don't know what night yet." She reached out and took his hand. To anyone observing them it looked like an oddly formal gesture. "I just wanted to touch you again. I'm glad now I met you."

"I want to go on meeting you." He held her hand for a moment longer. "Listen at night. I'll play some music for you." He walked quickly away, not looking back. She started down the slope through the meadow, calling to the children. Her heart was light again. It was a beautiful morning. The sound of the millrace came to her ear like a song. She took her children by the hand and sauntered homeward, humming softly to herself. Yes, it was, indeed, a beautiful morning.

John was sitting in the sun by the gable end when they arrived home. He had not been to bed since returning from Dublin and was dozing in the mid-morning heat. It would be a pity to waste a good day, he had said, with the intention of digging some of the new potatoes, but the weather was more suited to leisure than work. Eileen looked down at him, squinting her eyes against the glare of the white-washed wall. "I met Peter Howlett over by the mill", she said casually.

He grunted noncommittally.

"He was talking about the schooner." There was a brief pause. She waited for some reaction.

"Ye know, I've been wonderin' about Pether."

"Oh yes?" Was there some inflection in his voice that wasn't there before?

"Yes. Now look at it this way. Himself and Tom have a schooner. Well they will have. We have the wagons and horses, at least we will have them soon, more than we have now."

"Well?"

"Well what? Isn't Pether goin' to build us a new harbour and aren't we goin' to carry the stone. Now why can't we all work together? If we played our cards right between the three of us we could carry everything that moves around here either on land or on water. We could make real money." He stood up, reinvigorated by his vision of commercial success. Eileen laughed in relief and in pleasure at his enthusiasm. It was great to see how wholeheartedly John attacked any project that captured his attention. He had the innocent optimism of a child. He refused to recognise difficulties. Maybe it would work too. Perhaps in time the pain and the longing would mellow into friendship and the guilt fade to a dim memory, receding and dwindling into the past.

"Wonderful! Marvellous! So we're all goin' to be rich. But first let's look at the potatoes." She kicked off her shoes and wriggled her toes in the hot sandy soil. John pulled off his shirt. Great clusters of freckles stood out through the reddish hair on his shoulders and chest. He reached for the fork. "Isn't it always the way? Here I am about to conquer the world and I have to go and dig spuds." He put his arm around her shoulders. "It wouldn't surprise me if himself over on Elba is diggin' spuds right now too, but I doubt if he has such good lookin' help." She leaned against him affectionately and tugged at the hair on his back. "After dinner you can conquer the world but first things first."

"No, seriously." John had a grip on an idea and wanted to explore it. "Everything in Ireland comes back to spuds. That's what's wrong with the country. It's not kings or politics that matters. It's not even the laws on religion that keeps us down. It's all got to do with wages. Not enough people earn money for their work. The whole country works to get a bit o' land to grow spuds. It's goin' nowhere. I want to break out of all that."

There was a new intensity and urgency in his voice that surprised Eileen. "You're a deep one all right. I don't understand all you say, but it sounds like good sense all the same. Why not have a word with the others about your plan and see what they think."

"I will all right." He laughed, "just as soon as we dig the spuds." He stuck the fork into the first bed and levered the stalks upwards. "Get the childer to pick the little hazards and we'll boil them with a bit o' mint."

Eileen set the two little ones to work picking the smallest potatoes into a basket. She followed them along shaking out the stalks and selecting the larger potatoes some of which she would sell to Mrs Morris in the Square. It was nice to talk of business ventures and making money, but just now she would settle for delving her potato garden with her husband and children, where cares and problems were kept at bay by the hum of insects and the rhythm of the work.

As he looked down from the tower the sergeant wondered what Bateson was up to. The heavy set gunner lay prone on his belly in the long grass on the rim of the island with his musket beside him, watching intently some activity that was out of Howlett's line of vision. The gunner had been there almost an hour without moving and curiosity was beginning to get the better of Howlett. What could he possibly be stalking so intently? What could he possibly hope to hit with a brown bess at more than twenty feet? He could wait no longer and descended the spiral stairway. The guardroom door stood open and the late summer sunlight streamed into the high vaulted room. It had been both home and exile to him on and off for over a year and every detail of the solid ungraceful structure was familiar. Soon he figured they would be leaving it, probably forever, a monument to a war that had not left so much as a scratch on it. Indeed the only scratches were those inflicted by its defenders, a word or two of a scatological nature and some crude attempts at obscene drawings. Laidlaw and Thurston lounged on the steps of the ladder enjoying the heat.

"What's Bateson at?" asked Howlett. "I've been observing him for almost an hour." Laidlaw laid a finger on his temple, indicating the nature of the problem. Bateson had finally taken leave of his senses. "No," interjected Thurston "he's not daft at all. He's doin' what any man would do, protectin' his family."

This information was little help to Howlett. "What do you mean?" he asked, puzzled. "Go and see for yourself sergeant," said the young fellow. "Bateson's on sentry go." Howlett began to walk towards the edge of the slope where the gunner lay motionless. He crouched to avoid startling the quarry whatever it might be. Bateson turned his head and gestured to him to come forward.

"Don't fear sergeant. Us'll not alarm 'im." Howlett crawled forward. "What is it?" he asked, parting the long grass carefully. "See that bastard there, that herring gull. He be waitin' for my chicks to come out. He bin there every day for nigh on a week now." The herring gull, a dirty spotted evil looking bird, perched motionless on a rock-ledge, its basilisk eye unmoving. "My guillemots be in that 'ole there," said Bateson pointing to a small cleft in the side of the cliff. "There be two of 'em and they be ready for to come out soon. If they can get into the water they'll be all right but he'll try to grab one sure as anythin'."

"Why don't you shoot him now?" whispered Howlett, intrigued by the drama. "No need to whisper sergeant. He ain't interested in us. I be givin' 'im a fair chance but if'n 'e makes one move I'll blast 'im. Anyway they have to come out and take their chances in the world sometime."

"I can see them now," whispered Howlett again, fearful of alarming the chicks. Two small black heads peered from the safety of the nest. There was no sign of the parent guillemots.

"Aye, they be slow enough on land but once they hit the water it's a different matter. They flies with their wings under the water like." They were joined by the cat. It came creeping towards them with a professional interest in what was going on. Sometimes it gave a little playful dance sideways or sprang stiff-legged into the air with its back arched. Its tail twitched nervously as it advanced, sending little clouds of down from the dandelion clocks. Bateson advanced the musket quietly and rested it on a tussock. Slowly and carefully he pulled back the hammer with an almost inaudible click. The gull's eye flickered and the feathers at the base of its neck ruffled. Howlett held his breath. The two guillemot chicks inched forward from the nest, urged on presumably by an unseen parent. The gull marked time awkwardly as if on painful feet and prepared to pounce. His patience was about to be rewarded.

The chicks suddenly stumbled clear of the hole and hurled themselves downwards, propelled by their stumpy wings. They rolled and tumbled towards the water below and the gull gave a great leap.

Bateson squeezed the trigger at the same instant and the powder exploded with what seemed a shattering noise in the stillness of the afternoon. Through the cloud of acrid smoke Howlett saw the gull disintegrate into a shapeless bundle of bloody feathers under the impact of the heavy ball. Clouds of gulls arose screaming from the rocks, their shrill metallic cries adding to the noise of the shot which still echoed across the water. The cat fled to the safety of the ladder from which it glared in anger, all its hairs standing on end. Bateson grinned broadly, an unusual sight.

"Look," he said, pointing. The two parent birds had appeared as from nowhere and were shepherding their offspring towards the deep water with much splashing and flapping of their stubby wings. They were safe now and would not risk the terrors of the land for another year until the time came again to build their nest in the cleft and hatch another small brood to run the gauntlet of the gulls.

"That was a good shot for a musket," contratulated Howlett.

"Aye, I were lucky. I've seen 'em dash the young terns to bits an' eat 'em but I couldn't let 'em have my guillemots." Bateson felt the need to justify his interference with the natural order. A sombre thought struck Howlett. "But you won't be here next year to protect them, will you?"

"Nay. I don't know what may become of 'em when I be gone, but bain't that always the way sergeant? Us does what us can for them as needs us till they can fare for themselves." A silence descended between them. Howlett looked involuntarily towards the white line of cottages on the Kybe. There was precious little he could do for anyone, he thought, except cause them pain. Was he a bit like the herring gull, watching and waiting for his opportunity? No, the thought was absurd. The cat returned and rubbed its forehead against his arm. Idly he patted the animal's head. If he were the gull would not John Mullen take the part played by Bateson? Their motives would be just the same. He could see the justification in either case, although he admitted to himself that the gull was less culpable, being only a brute beast.

Bateson sat up and began, like the good soldier he was, to clean his musket. Howlett left him and scrambled down the slope to the little beach. The cat followed him, pacing behind him by the edge of the tide. The flooding tide ripped over the hidden dorn, the glassy surface disguising the danger beneath. Howlett sat and flicked pebbles into the fast moving water. His mind was in a turmoil. It was hopeless to seek a peaceful ending to their predicament, he realised, unless he was prepared to go away and forget Eileen for good. That way, he thought, she would have nothing to fear, but he would have nothing to hope for.

Eileen heard the shot on the island from where she lay on the sand below the breakwater. It roused her from her thoughts and she cast her eyes around to reassure herself that the children had not strayed too far. They were still there with two or three of the younger Donovans, industriously digging canals and letting the coming tide flood into their networks, surrounding their castles with impassable moats and eating away at their dams with relentless force. Nothing in her life had engaged her love like these two small children she thought, watching them. From the time each of them had come into the world it had been her greatest joy to see them growing strong and healthy and bright-eyed with intelligence. She thought of the nights that she and John had sat up with one or other of them, nursing them through their childhood illnesses or the pains of teething. At other times she would watch them sleeping, listening to the steady rhythm of their breathing. They were secure and she was happy.

What had happened to throw a cloud over all this? Why did she sometimes find herself thinking that she could leave them and the big capable man who watched over them, for a stranger whom she hardly knew? The loss and the guilt would kill her; of this she was certain. No matter where she might go and no matter what kind of happiness she might find with Peter Howlett, their voices would follow her and their eyes innocent and hurt, would haunt her for the rest of her days. She propped herself on one elbow and looked out at the tower. She could barely see the figures moving on the island. The heat of the sun burned through her light blouse. She wondered what it would be like to lie with him openly in the sunlight. The thought was involuntary and she felt her body reacting. She ran her hand through the fine sand, watching the white grains slip from her fingers in miniature avalanches. The image of his body possessed her, blotting out the present. She had only seen him ghostly white by moonlight. They had made love secretly, like thieves in the night. She resented this furtiveness but could think of no alternative.

"I said are ye not talking to anyone today." Nora Donovan sat down beside her.

"Oh! Nora. I was just thinkin'. I didn't hear ye."

"Aye, well. I thought I could do with a bit of a rest with that Larry out o' the way for the day."

"Oh aye. Is he workin' then?"

"That he is. Your father-in-law has him drivin' over to the coach inn two days a week. He won't get rich but it's somethin'. And the eldest lad is on a boat for the summer."

"Ye'll be rich someday Nora, when they're all out workin' for ye." Eileen thought it kinder to make light of Nora's constant battle with penury than to offer unwanted sympathy.

"Ah sure doesn't it all keep me occupied. I don't have the time to worry. And what about yourself?"

"How do ye mean? What about me? I'm all right."

"Do ye tell me now? Don't I know ye since we were childer and I can tell when there's somethin' up." Eileen said nothing. She drew circles in the sand. "Ye haven't been yourself this long time and don't tell me lies. I'm a bit worried about ye."

"It's nothin'," said Eileen, "nothin' at all."

"Have ye been goin' bathin' at night again? I thought ye was mad that night when ye came home wringin' wet. We thought you was lost."

"Oh no, that was just a bit o' fun like when we were young."

Nora looked at her sharply. "Has your mother been down at all?"

"Don't ye know very well she was and didn't I see the two of ye colloguin' together when ye thought I wasn't around?" Nora blushed but looked at her defiantly: "Well?"

"Well, what?"

"Well, is it true?"

"Yes it is."

"Aye well that explains the way ye've been lookin' lately but ye better look after yourself from now on. What does John say?"

"He's very pleased or so he says. I only told him a few days ago. He'd never notice a thing like that until it kicked him in the bed."

"I think your John notices lots o' things." A pause. "Not that I would say anythin' to him but he'd have to be blind not to see the way you've been wastin' away."

Eileen was touched by her friend's obvious concern but alarmed at the tone of her remarks. It was impossible that Nora could know of her night meetings with Peter, although there had been the awkward business of explaining her midnight swim on the night of the bonfire. She had arrived home to find Nora sitting by the fire anxiously waiting for her, having sent her two girls home hours before. She had explained it all lightly at the time, but all the same extracted a promise that John would not be told. Since then she had claimed to be visiting Mrs Morris or John's father who was laid up, so that her excursions passed without comment. "Oh, don't worry about me. I'm as strong as a horse."

Nora changed the subject abruptly. "Did ye hear shootin' abroad on the island a while back?"

"I did, I suppose they were after some game. Ducks or somethin' like that."

"There'd be no ducks at this time o' year. Maybe they're all murderin' each other. Wouldn't surprise me one bit." Nora sniffed disparagingly.

"Why do you say that?" Eileen thought she caught a strange inflection in the remark.

"Well it's obvious isn't it. Men stuck out there for months on end with nothin' to do. They probably all go mad after a while."

"Oh I don't know" replied Eileen casually. "They seem normal enough to me."

"You know what I mean," insisted Nora. "They're not all saints like, but then I'm not that well acquainted with them."

"If ye mean I am," said Eileen, feeling a blush beginning to spread. "I know sergeant Howlett to some extent and he seems to be a decent sort of fellow." She might as well brazen it out.

"Oh I don't mean him," responded Nora. "Everyone says he's a good type, for a soldier, but the others seem a very peculiar lot." There was nothing in her tone to suggest any ulterior design in her remarks and Eileen felt the blush receding, although her ears still burned. The hot sun would serve as an excuse for that, she hoped. "Look, here's Father Clare comin'. I don't want to meet him," she said seeing the portly figure of the priest approaching along the break-water. Father Clare was an inveterate walker, always accompanied by his setter, Rufus, and always armed with a walking stick. It was commonly held that Rufus was needed to put up sinners and the stick to beat them back into the ways of righteousnes.

"Oh don't leave me here on me own," said Nora plaintively. "I'll be here for ages."

"It's just that he does be on at me about havin' more children and souls for God's feast and that I don't want to give him the satisfaction of tellin' him right now." This small act of defiance would explain her anxiety to avoid the priest and Nora smiled conspiratorially.

"Off ye go then," she said. "Leave the childer with me and pretend ye don't see him." It would be hard not to notice the approaching pair, with Rufus barking and leaping among the shrieking children and scattering their sand-castles and the priest waving his stick at the dog, and uttering such imprecations as were not inconsistent with the sanctity of his calling. Eileen made good her escape in the confusion. It was a relief not to be tackled about attendance at the sacraments or to be reminded of her wifely duties. She looked briefly back from the corner of the fence to see Nora standing deferentially, nodding in agreement with whatever the little man was saying. Nora needed no advice on the performance of her wifely duties, she thought. The day of reckoning would have to come sometime, but for the present she would duck the issue and avoid the good priest for as long as she could.

CHAPTER 16

Tom Morris pulled back the sacking from the bundle on the floor of the trap to expose the bell. "There ye are Father. Now what do ye say? Will we put it up for ye?"

"Now men, let's talk about this for a minute," replied the priest, scratching the stubble on his chin apprehensively.

"What's there to talk about?" interjected John Mullen. "Isn't it time we had a proper bell on the church?"

"Aye but the law is still the law."

"Now Father don't ye say yourself that the law is wrong and that it will have to change soon and here we are in this day an' age bangin' gongs like heathen bloody Chinamen, savin' your presence." John was impatient to get on with the job and could see no problems. "Look Father, it's all very simple," put in Tom again in his reasonable tone. "It's a very fine bell, much too fine for a schooner and if I choose to give it to yourself who's to stop me? I'll put it up in the yard o' the church on a nice cross-tree and to hell with the law."

"It's not always as easy as that Tom, but the idea appeals to me I must admit." The priest's round face wrinkled in a mischievous grin.

"That's the style Father," said John. "Let's put it up an' to hell with them."

Again, Tom intervened. "Put it like this Father. It's not a mass bell at all but a bell that'll be rung to tell the time and sure what if yourself rings it on Sundays now an' again? What harm can that do?"

"Aye, leave the writin' on it and say it's in memory of the poor sailors that perished if anyone asks." John was warming more and more to the idea. Father Clare rubbed his hands. "Lads," he said, hopping from one foot to the other, "ye have me persuaded, and God bless the work. Now when do ye hope to set about it?"

"Give us a week or two when the case is heard. I wouldn't want to cut up any of the timber till we have the papers in our hands. I'm not worried about the bell since it came sort of adrift if ye know what I mean." Despite his tender years Tom Morris had a sound business head on his shoulders. He'll go far, the priest thought to himself. "What about your partner, the sergeant? He's not one of us, is he?"

"The way it is Father," said John, "the sergeant is so glad to be alive he'd give his share o' the bell to any clergyman that wanted it – not that I'm including yourself with that other lot," dismissing all denominations into the same fog of heresy as the heathen Chinese.

"Aye well. It will be something to hear a bell in my own church. Maybe they'll stop referring to the mass house then."

"Do ye know what we'll do then Father," said John, heaving the heavy bell out of the trap. The pony skittered friskily as the weight was removed. "We'll build ye a proper bell tower, made o' stone an' put this bell right up on the top. Every man in the town will work on it for nothin' or I'll have somethin' to say."

"Ah John you're a dreamer or a revolutionary, I don't know which. Next you'll be collecting the tithes for meself and tellin' the proctor to go hang."

"That day will come too sooner or later," growled John hefting the bell onto his shoulder. "Where will I leave this?"

"Bring it into the house John and I'd like a word with you if you have the time. Tom, I'm obliged to you for givin' an old man somethin' to cheer about."

"In a way it's a small return for me own good fortune. I'll be back in a few days, please God and we'll get the job done." Tom departed, striding out jauntily and whistling in satisfaction with his good deed.

"Now John," said the priest, closing the door. "I want to come straight to the point. It's about yourself and Eileen."

"Aye Father and what's troublin' ye there?" John had an idea of what was coming.

"Well is everythin' all right between ye? I'm askin' because I don't see her comin' to the altar rails like she used to and that usually means somethin' wrong."

"I'd only say it to yourself Father, but I was a bit worried about her durin' the winter but there's not a bother on her since the summer came in. We have the odd row but sure that's only to be expected."

"You're sure everythin' is all right then. Did ye ever consider havin' more of a family? I mean you're doin' reasonably well in business like. You could afford another child I'm sure." John laughed. "Since ye're on that oul line again ye can put your mind easy. There'll be another little Mullen raisin' the roof in the new year."

"Do ye tell me now. And isn't that good news?" The priest was pleased that his remedy had been anticipated. "She'll be well able for it, of course. I'll expect to see ye both at the sacraments a bit more often in the future. Don't let yourself get into bad habits." He put his hand on the big man's shoulder and escorted him to the door. "Off ye go now John and look after her. The women are a bit difficult at these times, or so I'm told." He laughed briefly at the incongruity of his offering advice, "but I suppose you know more about that than I do."

"When I know all there is to know about women, Father, I'll set meself up as an authority and give lectures at a guinea a time. There's many a lad would be glad to pay for that kind o' knowledge."

"It's true for ye John but you're not doin' too badly. I'll give an extra ring on the bell for Eileen. Tell her I'll look in some time soon."

John thought to himself that Eileen wouldn't be too pleased at that news and decided to limit himself to conveying Father Clare's kind regards. Eileen was a grown woman and would sort out her views on religion for herself. He turned his mind to other matters. He and his father were in the process of expanding the business. They needed some more horses and drays. The old man wasn't able for heavy work any more but he was still the best judge of a horse in the district. They had already started to put in more stables in the yard in anticipation of the increased business. All this cost money and they would have to have a bit coming in soon from the harbour works. Larry would make a good driver if he could be trained to regular work. John smiled to himself at the thought of his disreputable friend trying to load rocks in the quarry. It wouldn't do to overdo things with Larry at first or he might be frightened off his incipient career before he really got started.

He turned in at the yard and unhitched the pony. His father emerged from the shadows of the big shed. He was tall and gaunt with leathery brown skin. He moved slowly because of the rheumatics, a legacy of long wet nights on the road. The inevitable clay pipe protruded from below his straggling white moustache. He reached for the pony's head and turned away without a word.

"Work's goin' well," remarked John indicating the stone walls that were rising at the end of the yard. "Aye." His father's taciturn manner didn't bother him. They communicated without words most of the time and when the business required verbal negotiations John automatically took charge. He had never had a serious disagreement with his father in all the years they had worked together. "How are the pains?"

"Not too bad. Still gettin' around." The old man began to rub the pony down, his hands moving rhythmically bringing up the shine on the glossy coat.

"We should go to Balcunnin soon to look at a few horses and have a word with the agent."

"Aye."

"Maybe next week then or thereabouts? I'll bring Eileen and the childer."

"Do that". His father stooped for a handful of straw. "It'll do her good."

"Now don't you start. Everyone talks as if I was starvin' her to death. All she's doin' is carryin' another baby. That's nothing new."

"Is she now? Good." He made no further comment but stood back to survey his handiwork. "Good." It was unclear whether this referred to the baby or to the pony.

"Do ye think we should take Larry on full time? How is he doin' for you?"

"He'll do."

"Aye good. Well I'm away home now. I'll see ye in the mornin'. It'll be heavy goin' from now on till we get everythin' sorted out." He turned at the gate. "What about a week o' Monday then, we'll look at the horses?"

"Right so." The old man always enjoyed a trip to the stables at Balcunnin. It would make quite a holiday for him and for Eileen and the childer too, thought John. There was a chill in the air now that the nights were starting to draw in. It would be nice to spend a quiet evening by the fireside discussing their plans for the future. There would be more than enough work but it would be worth it in the end. One of the days he thought he would build a fine stone house on the Kybe with cellars and stairs and all. That might have to wait a bit but John Mullen the carrier was going to be a big man in the neighbourhood and his wife would be a grand lady who could hold her head up in any company.

CHAPTER 17

Captain Osgood let his gaze wander around the room. It had been his home for so long that the thought of leaving wrenched at him with unaccustomed pain. In military life one should be used to being uprooted at short notice but he found that middle age had come upon him stealthily making the thought of a move repugnant. For almost twenty years he had been stationed along this east coast and had got to know the area intimately as the maps could testify. He had had time to pursue his other interests without too much interference and had looked forward confidently to some reward for his services, perhaps even directorship of the Ordnance Survey. Had this come about he would have transformed that office from a political sinecure into a reality. The Osgood survey, he thought wistfully, would have become the model for the whole United Kingdom. Every inch of the realm could have been charted and surveyed with a greater precision than ever before. All he had to show for his efforts was a letter from the director to the effect that no major survey was justified now that peace was restored. His obdt. servt. sent his complmts. on the work already done and felt sure that at some future time etcetera.

Now, God blast it, he was faced with dismantling all military installations in the area and withdrawing his men. It was a strange kind of peace with Dutch-Belgium garrisoned and relations deteriorating between His Majesty's government and the restored regime in Paris. He wondered what lay ahead. In one sense it would be a relief to retire to his lands at Milverton in Somerset although his wife had become almost a stranger to him despite their frequent correspondence, but the thought of the conflict between her obsessive tidiness and his mania for collecting scientific specimens gave him pause. Perhaps there would be a posting to the Low Countries for a time to postpone the hour of decision. Meanwhile there was a delay in releasing men from the service until the peace conference at Vienna had concluded its deliberations. This would raise a problem for young Howlett he thought and possibly delay the work here. A meticulous man, he had already fulfilled his undertaking to his lordship. The maps and charts lay ready on the table, showing the extent of the sea wall and break-waters stretching from the harbour and diverging to protect the town on both sides. The breakwater appeared in elevation and sections, its massive foundations and skirts of interlocking limestone blocks designed to withstand the heaviest seas. A pity, he thought that I shall probably never see it built. He particularly hoped that priority would be given to the mouth of the stream where his plan indicated how the waters would be deflected so that the high tide could not flow directly upstream. This done, large tracts of land could be transformed from swamp and sedge into productive agricultural land as was done frequently by the Dutch.

He bent to give the drawings a final inspection and then carefully rolled them into a cylinder and tied them with a tape. These he would deliver to the agent as his lordship was in England. It would be safer than giving them to Mr Ned who would not appreciate the finer points. As for that young scalawag, he thought, his ship is still in drydock and I shall have to dispose of the guns. Osgood swore silently at the inconvenience of the whole thing. Peace was certainly far more disruptive than war. The stray thought struck him as interesting in a general way. Certainly patriotic feelings were enhanced by war and the spirit of cooperation and selflessness by and large prevailed, whereas in peacetime malconents found willing audiences and imaginary grievances became inflated into major injustices.

He sat for a while and propped his boots on the ledge of the oriel window. Pensively he regarded his gleaming footwear. Perhaps in one way, it was no bad time to be leaving Ireland, he thought. This country is a breeding ground for malcontents. They could be suppressed by draconian means during a war but in peacetime that British passion for freedom of speech and fair play allowed every demagogue and fanatic a forum or more likely a pulpit to expound his philosophy of reform or democracy. A twinge of sadness struck him at this bleak glimpse of the future. He had become quite fond in his reserved way, of these people, an ignorant and excitable breed certainly but with much good in them. It would be a great pity to see them driven yet again into rebellion by selfish and ambitious men. Even in England he knew, the doctrine of reform was disturbing people and making political life unstable while agrarian unrest had come in the wake of the peace. It is not right that a man of my advanced years, he thought with conscious self mockery, should be uprooted from such a comfortable billet and pitchforked into the great unknown. This little backwater suited me admirably.

He could see the *Kittiwake* rounding the cross rock with the spray bursting over its graceful bow. Two men pulled briskly on the oars while the familiar figure of Howlett sat in the stern. Warm work on this cold October morning although the sergeant must be feeling the chill. It would be warmer work to swing the guns down from the towers and stow them with the coastguards until the cutter put in again. There was something undignified, thought Osgood, in the army having to borrow guns from the navy and then hire the local carter to carry them around for them. Howlett could arrange with Mullen about the hire of a dray, particularly to take the gun from the island. Apparently only the major ports would be protected from now on. Whatever enemy might wish to invade the country in the future would have to be content with engaging the Pigeon House or the guns of Haulbowline.

There was a knock on the door and Howlett entered, and saluted. "Stand over by the fire sergeant," said Osgood, "and warm yourself. It's a chilly morning for boating."

"Aye sir, it is that." Howlett was curious to know the reason for the peremptory signal summoning him to the mainland. "Your signal said urgent sir." He felt a cold chill of fear grip him as Osgood explained what had to be done. He was trapped in the system. This could not be happening. It was impossible. It was like having swum towards the land only to be borne back by the undertow. The sweat broke out on his forehead and the blood roared in his ears. Osgood's voice came faintly to him, "and embark by the end of the month."

"May I sit down sir?" he asked. His legs felt weak and he thought that he would begin to tremble.

"Of course, of course. You don't look at all well. I'm afraid that this will disrupt your plans for the time being. But that's all part of the business of soldiering." Instinctively he understood the younger man's disappointment and assumed a brusque and businesslike manner. "On the other hand your health has improved and a change might not be a bad thing at this stage. You can always take up your civilian job when things settle down again. It's hardly likely that there will be any serious trouble again in our time."

Howlett felt his colour returning and his pulse began to ease off. He stood up. "Beg pardon sir. It must have been the cold." He composed himself with an effort while a confusion of thoughts raced through his mind. Could he ask her to come away with him? What could he offer her if she did? He could not see her taking to the poverty and squalor of barracks life. What if they were separated by war? No, she would never leave her children. He was certain of that. Mullen would try to kill him and would undoubtedly hang for it. He needed time to think. What was the captain saying about wagons? "Yes sir, I'll see to it directly. About a dozen men. As soon as the tide permits sir."

A small shamefaced thought knocked persistently at the back of his mind as if trying to gain an entry. He pushed the thought away but it returned bringing a kind of relief. "Go away," it said. "Postpone your life. Make no decision and maybe in time . . . " Maybe in time what? It was not a very noble idea to do nothing and hope for the best but what else could he do. He felt the sense of helpless fury rising in him. Damn the army and damn Mullen too, though not for anything he had done. If the salvage case had been settled perhaps he could have bought himself out before the restrictions. He would have to make some arrangement with Morris. Howlett wondered if in some way there were two of him. One side of him was numb with shock at the thought of leaving the sight of the woman and the other half was already making preparations for departure and mentally putting his affairs in order. This person was taking charge, rationally preparing for whatever was to come and ushering the other half of him along, as he had so often seen on the battlefield a man supporting a maimed and bleeding comrade. The rational Howlett must keep the other one under control or he would break out and make matters worse. Casualties must be kept to a minimum. He would have to see her to explain. It would not be for ever and yet the little voice kept telling him that it would. There was no other way. He would go now and negotiate with Mullen for his horses. God damn the man, his friend. How he wished him dead and gone or that he had never existed. It's a warped world where something good begets something bad and the bad devours the good. She would hear of the evacuation before he could see her and would form her own conclusions. What did it matter? the voice insisted. When you are gone it will make no difference. You will forget and so will she. There would never be any point in coming back like a ghost to disturb the living. He began to feel the cold closing on him and he shivered with foreboding. If he could think like that already he was as good as dead.

In his official position as acting head of the family Mr Ned conducted his niece to church on Sundays, a task which he found irksome enough at the best of times. He had no taste for the niceties of theological investigation and the Reverend Keble's soporific drone appreciably raised his blood pressure, causing him to shuffle his feet and clear his throat with vehemence. At the same time he never questioned the value of Divine Worship for the good of one's soul, regarding it as the spiritual equivalent of a good dose of salts. Also it was necessary to give good example to one's neighbours. On this particular Sunday his orisons were interrupted by the pealing of the papist bell. The sound came thin and clear through the still October air causing the Reverend Keble to pause momentarily in his monologue, one hand held aloft to pluck the obscure point of theology as from the air. Being a tolerant and charitable man he chose to ignore the interruption after the initial surprise had subsided. One did not pretend to be irritated by the caperings and superstition of the peasantry.

Mr Ned frowned with annoyance and shuffled even more violently. It was unreasonable that a man's devotions should be interrupted, especially in one's family pew in a church endowed for over a century and a half by one's family, at considerable expense, be it said. Was not that the Balcunnin window through which the sun shone in a blaze of purple green and gold? Damn, this isn't good enough. The ringing ceased suddenly and the congregation visibly relaxed. By God this would have to be investigated. He slapped his hymn book impatiently into the palm of his left hand.

The coachman pulled the two magnificent greys to a halt outside the Mass house and Mr Ned alighted impatiently. The vehicle righted itself and rocked on its springs. "Uncle don't be silly," Alicia called quietly after him. "There's no law against it and hasn't been for over thirty years. Not since they stopped registering priests."

"And a damn bad day's work that was too," growled her uncle, glaring about him and tapping his boot with his walking cane. "Damned discourteous, that's what it is." He indicated the shining schooner bell which hung from a cross tree on two strong uprights, about ten feet from the ground. The inscription was clearly visible, *Star of Runcorn* to which had been added *Requiescant in Pace* giving the instrument a religious and decidedly papist gloss. "I'll speak to Mr Clare about this," he conceded in a more conciliatory tone. "I think he should have had the courtesy to ask permission of his landlord."

"Please uncle, don't make a scene," pleaded Alicia. People had begun to emerge from Mass and were standing around in little groups,

watching with undisguised interest. Ned wondered if there was a
suggestion of insolence in the elaborate touching of forelocks and the
broad smiles and the "Mornin' Mr Ned, Sir, a grand day thank God"
and similar pietistic claptrap.

"Ah, Mr Clare, a word with you sir." The priest had emerged,
beaming benignly with his round cherubic face. "God save you sir;
God save you but isn't it a beautiful mornin' thanks be to the Good
Lord."

More of the same stuff from the clergyman. "Pray tell me where
you acquired this bell Mr Clare. It hasn't been the custom you know."

"Ah the bell your honour. Hasn't it the grand tone and to think of
those poor seamen . . . God rest them." The priest crossed himself.

Really, these people had the most embarrassing habit of dragging
their religious practices out into the public street. Ned restrained his
impatience heroically. "I think you might have had the goodness to
consult my brother or myself on the matter."

"But sure we never thought there'd be any objection, seein' as how
the poor men were of our persuasion and wouldn't it be a handy thing
to have if there was a fire or an invasion or such like and we could ring
it to call yourself and the mileetia?" The priest beamed with pride at
the manifold uses of the bell and the gathering ring of onlookers
nodded in vigorous agreement. "Who's to say Napoleon is bet? he
could be back yet." "Aye, aye." A few agreed judiciously that this
could not be ruled out.

Ned began to suspect that he was not stating his views particularly
well. "I'll speak to you again on the matter, Mr Clare and in the
meantime be more sparing in its use." He turned abruptly, making his
way through the obsequious groups, conscious of the blood rising
hotly to his cheeks. "Drive on," he snapped to the coachman as he
swung himself aboard. He would most certainly speak to Mr Clare
again and wipe the smile off the faces of those grinning oafs. Alicia,
seeing his annoyance attempted to mollify his anger. "I imagine father
would not take the matter too seriously either," suggesting that they
were both men of eniment good sense. "As his representative my dear
I feel that these people should not be allowed to presume too much on
his generosity. However I shall let the matter rest until I have
ascertained the legal position." This seemed like the best plan for the
moment.

"What I would do would be to pay for the building of a fine
belfry," suggested the girl, "and in that way everyone would be
satisfied and, if you like, we would be stealing their thunder." Ned

laughed. "You are a very Machiavellian young lady but that is not the way to deal with these people. A firm hand at all times, firm but just. That's the way. Firm but just." He nodded a couple of times in agreement. "Nothing precipitate of course." He nodded again pleased with his assessment of the situation. His niece looked at him sideways. It would be a strange departure for Ned if he stopped doing things precipitately.

It seemed, in the following week, that the blasted fellow spent all his time ringing the bell, obviously to provoke some reaction. Apparently there was the Angelus at six in the morning, just for a start. On his early morning canter Ned could hear the distant chimes echoing across the rolling, frost-covered stubble fields. Then there was morning mass with more tintinabulation. Then the Angelus at midday and in the evening, not to mention a plethora of holy hours, devotions, benedictions and so forth. No wonder the blasted people were impoverished if they spent all their time on their knees. By God, this ostentatious show of piety would have to stop. "I'll have the thing cut down," Ned muttered to himself, "and then, by God, he can ask politely. What the devil is the law anyway?" He determined to write to his brother about this insult to the family's position. As long as king George was alive there would be no capitulation to Popery and the Balcunnin family would not shirk in its duty.

Peter Howlett tapped softly on the door of the cottage. Except for the dim candlelight from a window here and there the Kybe was in darkness. The moon was not yet up. Even so he felt that eyes were watching him and his pulse raced violently. There was a shuffling sound within and he heard her voice for the first time in weeks.

"Who is it?"

"It's me, Peter," he called low and urgently. "Let me in for a minute." There was a long pause during which he expected her to tell him to go away but with mingled fear and relief he heard the latch being lifted and the bolt drawn back. She opened the door and he was aghast at the pallor of her face. Her long hair hung in matted strands on either side of her face. Her eyes, huge and glistening in the faint light looked up at him. They were dark and devoid of expression. "So you're going." There was no note of accusation in her voice, only a kind of hopeless resignation. "Come in then." It was the first time he had stood in the room since the night he had played cards and the contrast to that cheerful scene struck him with heart-rending sadness.

There was no fire in the hearth. The flagged floor looked as if it had not been swept for days. Soiled dishes stood on the table.

Eileen stood disconsolate with a shawl gathered around her shoulders. It was obvious that she had been weeping but now she seemed to have wept herself to a state of mute misery. Howlett felt a pain in his throat and had difficulty in speaking. "It may not be for too long." It sounded lame and unconvincing. She came towards him reaching out blindly and he held her. The tears came with low animal sounds and he felt the stinging in his own eyes and a sense of total helplessness. At length her convulsive weeping began to abate and he became aware of the coldness of the room. "What can I say?" He had never felt so inadequate.

"I knew it would happen like this some day," she said, the hopelessness coming through, leaving little room for consolation. "Don't pretend that you will come back." He made no reply. Even the faintest hope was to be cut away. He held her at arms' length and looked at her as if to imprint her forever on his mind. He had no words. "What are you thinking?" There was just the ghost of a smile on her lips. It recalled to his mind the times they had been together, a few hours out of a whole lifetime, when she had laughed at him and he had felt happier than he could ever have imagined possible.

"I'm not thinking," he replied truthfully. "I'm just looking at you. You are the most beautiful person I have ever known." This was an extravagant speech for such a time. "Are you well?" It seemed a stupid question, gormless, she would have said. Again she smiled with a little more animation this time. "As well as can be expected, considering."

Of course. That explained something different about her. "You are carrying a child." Irrationally he felt a stab of jealousy at the thought.

"Yes" she replied directly. "It's yours. I'm sure of that but that can't make any difference." Howlett felt his head reeling. How could this be happening and how could she be so matter of fact about it?

"It will be a boy – in February and he will be called after you. I'm entitled to that much of you."

"How can you be so sure?"

"I just know."

Again he could think of nothing to say. The immensity of the idea frightened him – that here was a being that had taken its life from him, someone who would go on for years into the future a stranger to him, for whom he could not raise a finger to help. Maybe he would be hungry sometimes, or cold or in danger. Howlett felt his guts contract at the idea. "There must be something I can do."

"Well you could help me to light the fire maybe." She made an effort to be light about it.

"Aye." It was something practical at least. He groped in his pocket for the tinder box and opened it with fumbling fingers. He knelt beside her at the hearth as she thrust paper and sticks into the grate. With difficulty he struck a spark into the dried coltsfoot and blew on it to produce a flame. Soon the fire crackled brightly, cheering the room and they knelt together, staring into the flames, without speaking, thinking their own private thoughts. They could not have said how long they remained there silently.

"I have to go," he said after a while. "There is no other way."

"Aye, I know that. You mustn't worry about me. I'll be all right."

He knew that she was saying it for him. It would have been easier to have parted in anger or in hatred but this was unbearable. The wild notion of desertion crossed his mind but he put it aside. There was nowhere they could go and she would not leave her family anyway. This pain was something to be borne in secret. He fed some turf to the fire. It would warm her for a little while after he was gone. A small act of kindness in consolation for the life that he could not give her. Mullen would look after her. It hurt to admit it. If only her husband had been a scoundrel he thought again, but he was a fine fellow. "I must get back before the tide flows," he said rising to his feet and dusting the knees of his breeches.

She remained kneeling. "We can't be together tonight, not here, and the children are above."

"I didn't come for that," he said hastily although the hope had been there all the time. "We have to move everything tomorrow at low tide." She stood up and took his hand in hers. Her eyes were dry.

"Goodbye," she said, "my friend. And God bless you."

"Goodbye Eileen." He hardly ever used her name. It sounded strange. There was nothing more to say. He touched her cheek with the back of his hand.

"Goodbye." She stood at the open door until he reached the corner of the house. He looked back once for a glimpse of her, dark against the lighted interior and then he was gone.

The moon was up in all its brilliance and a silvery path guided him over the wet sand to the island. Cold and gloom descended on him as he walked and again he felt like the small boy whose parents had abandoned him to the parish. He had not thought about them for years but now he found himself asking why. He had wanted to die then though physically he was better off with the cold parish charity but the pain of loss was unbearable. Now he too had lost a child, one he could never claim as his, and the child's mother. The curlews called in the darkness and the insistent 'chink chink' of the oyster catchers came to him like a chorus of condemnation. The wind was freshening from the south east and the rising tide reached almost to his knees as he gained the dorn. Tomorrow would see an end to the occupation of the island. The gulls would reassert their dominion, building their nests on the tower itself. He thought of Bateson and his guillemots. Where would the stolid gunner find himself in the spring? Howlett sat on the withered grass for a time, overcome with sadness. He was reluctant to face the men in the tower, a work detail of twelve men sleeping rough on the guardroom floor. Eventually the chill in the wind, rising now to a half gale, drove him indoors. The tide was flowing strongly and the criss-crossing waves whipped over the dorn.

CHAPTER 18

On the rise beyond Tyrrelstown John Mullen halted the cart and swore vehemently. If he went on like this the horse would be lamed for good and the oul fella would never forgive him. "Jasus, Pompey, but ye pick yer time for it." There was no use in blaming the horse.

The Mullen horses had always rejoiced in classical names, a legacy of the old man's early schooling with itinerant schoolmasters. Old Mullen was proud of his education and was inclined to drop the occasional Latin tag in his rare moments of loquacity. More importantly he had learned to gauge, as he called it and calculate weights and measures with precision. He had worked out the bill of quantities for the new stables to a nicety but there would be no point in having stables if his son went laming his horses under loads of herring.

John examined the shoe. There was nothing to be done. There was no damage to the hoof as yet but there was nothing for it but to lead the horse gently back to the stable. He took out his pipe and lit it, standing in the lee of the cart. There would be others along soon enough and they could take the boxes between them without overloading. No harm in an early night, he thought to himself, with all the heavin' and haulin' on the island tomorrow. In a funny way he felt sorry to see the soldiers going. They had been part of the town since he was a boy. It would be strange not seeing their red and blue coats around the place, especially the sergeant. He hoped that Peter would be able to get out of the army fairly soon. What was it Eileen had said when he told her they were going? Something very bitter about deserters. Didn't make sense. She was a funny one sometimes. Never a good word for the soldiers and yet she was fond enough of Peter, though she never said much about him.

Funny too the way the oul black mood has come back all of a

sudden. She was grand there for a while with the new baby and all. His thoughts were interrupted as a convoy of five or six carts trundled towards him. "A bit o' trouble here lads," he called. "The oul horse has slipped a shoe. Ye wouldn't mind a few extra boxes I suppose."

"No bother at all John," replied one of the men. "Throw a few up here and we'll look after them." In this manner he disposed of the cargo and turned towards home, leading Pompey by the bridle. It's goin' to be cold enough tonight. I'm not sorry to be on the way home, he thought. It was restful to be strolling along in the dark with Pompey sending clouds of steam from his nostrils and plodding stolidly along. Soon he came in sight of the town and the gleaming line of sea behind it. He remembered how, when he was a boy, the oul fella used to exclaim always when he got to the top of this rise, "Thalassa." A bit of a poet there somewhere. It had somethin' to do with the Greeks or the Romans getting their first sight of the sea after a long march. "Thalassa," he said aloud. "Thalassa," he shouted again and the echo came back to him from the dark trees and the dark fields, "Thalassa, Thalaaasa," fading away and away. he knew what the oul Greeks meant right enough. There's nothing like comin' home even after a couple of hours on the road.

"Aye that's right sir, Nothin' like comin' home at all at all." The voice startled him. He must have been thinking out loud. "Who's there?" he called, feeling the hairs prickling on the back of his neck.

"Sure it's only meself yer honour, a poor fear siúil that hasn't a home to go to this holy and blessed night." A wrinkled little man detached himself from the shadows of the ditch.

"Be Jasus but you put the heart crossways in me." John laughed in relief. "And what were ye doin' there?"

"Just keepin' out o' the wind and the weather, yer honour. It does be could enough this time o' year. Ye wouldn't have a sup on ye, would ye, to keep body and soul together?" The voice wheedled with the practised pathos of the professional beggar. "Well it just so happens that there might be a drop in the jar." John felt that expansiveness was the best disguise for the fright he had felt at this strange apparition. He fetched a small stone jar from the cart. "The blessin's of Jasus and His Holy Mother on ye sir," said the little man taking a long and skilful pull from the jar. Piety and drink would keep the cold at bay. John felt it was only manners to take a couple of pulls himself. "Ah that's the stuff all right" said the little man appreciatively. "Sure maybe I'll walk a step o' the road with yerself."

"And why not?" said John warming to the company. "The poor

horse won't hurry us. He's lame ye see," by way of explanation. "The divil mend it but it's a hard road right enough," averred the stranger, "and I should know, that's walked every inch of it these many long years."

"And what might your name be then?" John phrased the question obliquely after the courteous manner of the country people. "Haven't I seen ye around here before?"

"Oh aye I'm well known enough around Fingal. Jack the Stick they call me. I'm well known all around Ireland. And aren't you the big carter fella that does be in the football games, gettin' yourself bet for the glory of yer homeland."

"That's me right enough," chuckled the big man, pleased in a childish way, that his fame had spread.

"The man with the fine soncey wife with the big green eyes," added the little fellow. A chill descended on the carrier. "And what would you know about my wife?"

"No disrespect now sir but who wouldn't notice a fine young woman like herself and sure didn't I see the pair of ye dancin' in the new year abroad in Balcunnin. Oh the finest woman in the barony and no mistake."

Well that was true enough. "Now I remember you. You were one o' the wran boys."

"Ah ye have me now sir. And didn't I get a shillin' from yer fine friend the soldier. Now there's a dacent man. Him with the music. A real gintleman." He wheezed as if stifling a laugh. "Now there's a man ye could trust with your life, I'll be bound."

Peter again. Why did he keep coming to mind?

"I've no time for the military, the curse o' Crummel on them all, but I'd make an exception for the sergeant. Sure I thought to meself at the time if anythin' ever happened to yerself, God between us an' all harm, there's a man she could turn to for help."

John said nothing. Dark and formless ideas squirmed and writhed in the back of his mind. No, it was ridiculous. This was only a garrulous tramp with a few drinks on him. They plodded on as far as the big tree where the little man took his leave. "Good luck to ye now sir and the missus and sure won't it be grand to have another babby in the house." John turned in astonishment but there was no sign of the man. He seemed to have disappeared without trace. What was all that about? he mused. I suppose tramps know everyone's business. He remembered now the New Year's ball and the wren boys and suddenly with great clarity he could see them together, the soldier and his wife and the way they watched each other and he understood. All these months he had been blind. By Jasus Christ he had been blind and they laughing at him. The whole town probably laughing about it. That explained the moods and the tempers and the long misery of the winter and now the soldiers were leaving and the clouds had settled on her again. Now where do we stand? He had no idea what to do. I can't put her out with the child comin' and anyway I wouldn't want to. Where would I be without her? What about the childer? But by Christ I'll have a word with the sergeant, the lyin', sleeveen bastard. I'll swing for him if there's any truth in it. Doubts assailed him and the fury began to subside. No, it couldn't be true. It must be the loneliness and the few jars.

He quickened his step, jerking Pompey to a faster pace. As abruptly as it came the suspicion faded. Jasus I must be goin' soft in the brain. Sure what's wrong with havin' friends? He laughed aloud with relief and was aware of the cold sweat on his forehead. He tossed the empty jug into the ditch and stopped to relieve himself. It's time I thought of givin' up the jar. "Isn't that so Pompey?" The horse nodded in agreement and snorted derisively. "We'll take a short cut through the mill fields and give her a surprise eh? Ye won't mind waitin' around for yer supper," he continued, speaking over his shoulder to the horse. "Ye know, maybe it was all the long nights on the road that made the oul fella so morose. I'll have to watch that."

They bore to the right of the mill and cut across the low swampy fields towards the outline of the Kybe. The rising wind stirred the branches of the trees around the church, silhouetted now against the full moon.

It was a surprise to John to find her still up after midnight and a pleasant surprise to see the bright fire on the hearth and the room tidy and swept. The table too looked as if it had recently been scrubbed. So there y'are, he thought, an I was worried about her. Eileen sat quietly in her chair by the fire with her hands joined on her lap. She was not asleep but she looked tired.

"Have ye been workin' till now, lass?" he asked overcome with tenderness. "Ye should be in bed."

"There was a few things to be cleared away. What brings ye home so soon?" She continued to look into the fire with that faraway look.

"Oul Pompey thrun a shoe so we had to come back. Are ye all right? Ye should be mindin' yerself now."

"Aye, aye I was just tidyin' up a few bits an' pieces. I'll get ye somethin to eat."

"Ah don't worry about that. I'll just warm meself for a minute and take the poor horse down to the yards." He stood by the fire warming his hands. "An' the childer. They're all right?"

"Aye fine. I was about to go to bed when I heard the horse."

"We had a grand chat on the way home, Pompey an' me about how things is goin' to be from now on. I'm tellin' ye there'll be a few changes now and maybe that big house I've been talkin' about." he stooped to add a few sods of turf to the fire. A metallic glint caught his eye.

"What's this?" He picked up the tinder box and looked at her enquiringly. She was white with shock and her hands flew involuntarily to her face.

"Who was here? Was it Skip? Larry?" She nodded at him, staring desperately as if pleading with him not to make her tell him a lie. "It wasn't them, was it? It was Pether." He said it quietly, not questioning and from the fear in her eyes he knew it was true. So he hadn't imagined it after all. The beggar man had only been telling him what he had begun to realise for himself. "Well wasn't it?" She nodded, numb with misery. He felt a cold clear murderous rage take hold of him as he straightened up. "How many times has he been here?"

"Never, never, except the once't with yerself and Skip." He remembered the night. "There's more to this than sayin' goodbye isn't there?" He had to know the truth no matter how painful. She hung her head and he restrained himself with an effort from striking her. "Isn't there?" His voice was hard and merciless. He caught her hair and pulled her head back so that she was looking at him. She winced with the pain. "Please John, you're hurting me." Never before had she appeared so beautiful or so desirable, the tears starting from her enormous eyes. "Please John. It's over. We'll never see him again. I'm begging you." Her voice broke. "Let it go please, let it go."

"And raise a soldier's get for me own, isn't that so?" The words were wrenched from him in pain. "Oh Jasus, Eileen, I'd a' gone on me knees to ye –". He gestured blindly in front of him and started for the door. Desperately she clutched at his coat, her voice rising in terror. "John please wait, please wait. I'll make it up to ye –", but he brushed her aside, consumed with a blind implacable rage. She fell heavily, hitting her head a glancing blow on the doorframe. With startling clarity, as she lay unable to move, she heard the metallic chime of the gevell on the step. She heard the horse scooching the loose shoe on the pathway and its uneven gait as the man whipped it into a trot. She knew that she must stop him but her limbs refused to move. No sounds came when she screamed and she wondered if she were dreaming the whole thing.

Mullen set the horse at the shallows at a fast trot, driving him headlong through a curtain of spray until the deeper water began to slow him down. Pompey breasted the waves, thrusting forwards with all his massive strength and driven relentlessly onwards by the urging of his driver. All John could see was the black outline of the island and the jagged white breakers on the dorn. He had no plan but to force his way onwards till he reached the soldier. His fingers tightened on the gevell.

The waves began to break into Pompey's face and the spray whipped back from his tossing mane. They were still a long way from the dorn. John could feel the cart beginning to lift and swing in the tide-race and at times the horse lost contact with the gravelly bottom. He began to realise his danger as the waves came stronger and higher from both sides, lifting and rocking the cart and threatening to turn it right over. The horse whinnied in terror as the water broke over its head. "Oh Jasus, Eileen what am I doin' here?" he called aloud. I must get back, he thought. I must get back and mind Eileen. "Poor Eileen." He was talking aloud as he hauled on the reins but Pompey would not answer. "Eileen," he shouted and the wind whipped his words away. The enormous hooves threshed in the air as the horse and cart tipped over and John felt himself falling, falling into the cold dark wetness. Desperately he reached for a handhold but there was nothing there. He gasped for breath and the water flooded into his lungs. Eileen could swim for it, he thought. Eileen could swim to me. Weighed down by his boots and heavy clothes he struggled in vain to rise. The current clutched at him and dragged him over the submerged dorn. He felt the barnacles on the hidden stones scraping the side of his face and the soft caress of the swirling bootlace weed.

Eileen struggled slowly to her feet. Her dress front was covered with vomit and she could feel a hot sticky wetness on her temple. She put her hand to it and looked at the dark stain on her fingers. There's blood on my hands, she thought in a detached way. She must get help. She staggered towards the Donovan cottage and leaned against the door, beating feebly with both hands. A candle flickered inside and almost immediately Nora Donovan appeared at the door. "In the name o' God what's happened?" She reached for the stricken woman and helped her inside. "Larry get up, get up an' lend a hand. Now what is it child?" Already her capable hands were at work swabbing the blood with a damp cloth and cleaning the filth from her friend's clothing.

"He's gone Nora, he's gone to the island and I'll never see him again." That was all she could say. Nora thought she understood but when she questioned her further the story made less sense.

"It's John I mean. He's gone to the island." There was a frantic helplessness in her voice.

"Get some boats Larry, Get some boats." She clutched at the little man's sleeve. "We must find him."

"Go on ye fool" said Nora. "Don't stand there with your mouth hangin' open," and Larry was gone, stuffing his shirt tails into his trousers as he ran.

"I must go an' look for him," said Eileen starting out into the darknes. "Will you come with me?"

"Aye, I'll stay with ye child," said her friend as she took a shawl from the back of the door, "and you tell me what happened and not a word to anyone else."

The moon was still high and its white and pitiless light shone down on the waves that crept closer and closer to the breakwater. From far away they could hear the shouts of men aroused from slumber as they ran towards the small black boats on the beach.

"Sergeant," said the soldier, "you'ld better come and have a look at this. There's summat strange goin' on."

"Well what is it man?" Howlett was not pleased to be aroused even from such a disturbed sleep. The room was fetid with the odours of the men strewn around the floor.

"There's boats, sergeant, with lanthorns on' em. I don't know what to make of it." Howlett felt again the chill of foreboding and scrambled up to the parapet. Between the island and the mainland lights were bobbing on the water although it was still too dark to see what boats they were. "Get two men and stand by to launch the *Kittiwake* at first light," he said, "and bring muskets." It was strange considering that the water was too rough for night fishing and this was the wrong time of year. Deep down in his heart he knew that it had something to do with Eileen Mullen.

He went down by the ladder and began to walk carefully towards the beach. Even straining his eyes he could see nothing except the bobbing lights moving back and forth beyond the tide-race. I'll try to

get within hailing distance, he thought as he descended the slope. A
dark shape loomed in front of him and he drew back in alarm. He
heard the familiar tearing sound of a horse cropping the rough salty
grass and he moved cautiously forwards. He could see the horse now
and the cart behind it. There was no sign of anyone around. It was
Mullen's cart. He must be on the island and if so it could only be for one
reason. He felt for his sabre and remembered that he had left it behind
in his haste. If Mullen caught him unarmed there could only be one
outcome. "John," he called. "John Mullen. Where are you?" He
began to search back and forth calling. "It's me, John Mullen. Where
are you?" He felt no fear for himself to his surprise but no answer
came to him from the darkness. He began with a sinking feeling to
fear that the carrier was not on the island, that he must have perished
in the tide-race and that that was the explanation for the bobbing
lights, but still he stumbled on through the long grass, calling and
stopping to listen.

The cold grey light of dawn began to spread from the east and the
gulls rose with raucous cries of protest. Their ghostly white shapes
wheeled in the dim light and the small boats ventured through the
slackening tide-race and beached on the island. Howlett went down,
with his shirt sticking to him with sweat, to meet the group of anxious
men who stood by the cart. The familiar figure of Garrigan came
towards him, his face grey with exhaustion and grief.

"He's not here is he Pether? We've dragged back and forth on the
way over with no sign."

"No Skip. I found his horse and I've looked all over."

"He's drownded then Pether. The poor boy is drownded," and his
old voice broke. The tears ran down the ancient grizzled face and he
turned away in shame.

"What happened Larry?" said Howlett turning away from the old
man. Again he felt like Judas but he had to know.

"Aw Jasus Pether, I don't know. He had a few drinks on him, Nora
says, and had a bit of a barney with Eileen. So he said he was comin'
over here for the night seein' as how he had to be here today anyway.
Aw Jasus Pether." Larry sniveled and wiped his nose with his sleeve.

"Let's scour all the way round lads," said Skip recovering his
composure. "There's still a chance that he might have made it to the
rocks." It was a forlorn hope but groups set off on foot and in boats to
make a circuit of the whole island but to no avail. By mid morning the
townsmen had departed to continue their search along by the coast and
the tide dropped to allow Captain Osgood to ride across accompanied

by Mullen's dray driven by a soldier. They set about swinging the great gun over the parapet and loading their scanty belongings onto the wagon. There was little talk among them as a gloom had descended on everyone, partly at the thought of the change in their routine but mainly because of the tragedy of the night before. It was sad to think that the tower, built as a link in a great chain of defence, had never been used and would probably never be required again, that all the years of watching and waiting had been unnecessary. Sadder too that their day of departure should have begun with such a bad omen.

"Sergeant, you will take the dray and bring this gun to the coast-guard station."

"Yes sir," It was as well to be fully occupied.

"And take Mullen's horse in tow too. Someone had better look after him." Pompey was still hitched to the cart, almost forgotten in the confusion of the morning. Howlett looked up at the tower where Laidlaw was fixing a heavy padlock to the door. It would be a relief to get away from there he thought. He had felt too much pain there and some blinding moments of joy at times, particularly when the sun was shining and he could see the houses on the Kybe gleaming white in the haze. Too much feeling, he mused. The dark menacing cloud scudded over the tower as if the sky were spinning around it.

"Sir, sergeant." Laidlaw's voice startled him back to the present. "On the rocks doon there." He was pointing towards the weed covered ledges of rock recently exposed by the dropping tide, where a cluster of gulls had begun to gather. With surprising agility the little Scotsman leaped from the ladder and began to run, shouting and waving his arms, with most of the soldiers in hot pursuit. Once or twice he stooped to snatch a stone and send the birds squawking and screaming into the air. There was no doubt about it. The carrier's body lay in a cleft, rising and falling with the waves. Long fronds of weed washed backwards and forwards over him. Laidlaw had dragged him out onto the dry rock by the time the others came up to him and was kneeling beside him gently removing scraps of weed from the hair and beard. "Och the puir bugger," he said obviously moved. "A gye hasty mon, but tae end like that!"

Howlett looked at his friend's face, strangely peaceful and unmarked except for a few scratches on one side. He could find no words to express what he felt.

"It's a guid thing we got tae him afore the crabs or the birds. I wouldnae like tae bring him hame tae his woman after them had got through wi' him."

"You're right there gunner," cut in Osgood. "Some of you men fetch a tarpaulin and we'll bring him home to his people and let's be shut of this island." He turned his back abruptly and strode back to his horse.

And so the procession set off along the causeway, the dray creaking under the weight of the gun and Pompey limping behind with the cart, bearing its tarpaulin-shrouded burden. The men walked in silence and few of them looked back. Of those only Bateson had a wistful look in his eyes. The people came out to meet them from the Kybe, flowing onto the beach, a silent crowd of dark-clothed figures led by Osgood, walking now beside the priest and the widow supported by her neighbour.

Howlett dismounted to unhitch Pompey. What was there to say? He walked towards the group of people, holding the reins in one hand and removing his cap.

"I'm sorry Eileen," he said "I'm so sorry –"

She looked at him directly but there was no sign of recognition as she took the reins from him.

"I thank you sergeant, for bringing him home," and she turned away with Pompey hobbling beside her. There was a general muttering as the crowd parted to let her through and the soldiers waited a decent interval before resuming their trek across the wet sand. The cart tracks diverged from those of the dray in an ever widening vee. Howlett stood still watching the retreating crowd for a long while and then set off after his men, moving mechanically, hardly seeing where he was going. Soon he was the only one on the beach, a small blue-coated figure isolated against the grey October sky.

CHAPTER 19

The crowd of sombrely dressed mourners turned at the sound and saw the detachment of horsemen clattering into Church Street at a rapid trot. In front rode the familiar figure of the major, his face almost as scarlet as his uniform in the biting wind. It was unthinkable that he would try to antagonise the townspeople on this of all days. Over the sound of the hooves on the cobblestones the bell rang out, slow and mournful as the body of John Mullen was being borne on his last journey from his home to the church. A dense crowd converged on the church, huddling behind the coffin as it was shouldered along the glistening wet street.

The boy, who tugged slowly on the rope, paused to watch the militiamen converging on the funeral procession. Like so many others in the crowd he was at once curious and apprehensive, aware of tension in the air. A huge hand reached over his head and grasped the rope. "Move aside lad. I'll see to it." He looked up and towering above him stood a gigantic seaman, almost it seemed, blotting out the sky. The man, he noticed with increased interest had only one arm. The bell rang out again and again slowly as the procession shuffled to a halt and the coffin was lowered and carried through the opened doors. Some followed as the family and close friends filed inside but a great many remained in the churchyard, moving together wordlessly to form an impenetrable throng around the bell.

"Detail, halt!" The major raised his hand. "Move aside there," he snapped to the men on the outside as he urged his horse into the crowd. There was no smirking this time, he noted with satisfaction. The passage closed behind him cutting him off from his four troopers, who sat looking about them, sheepish and embarrassed. Farmers or minor gentry, they had known Mullen themselves and respected him and had it not been for differences of religion they would have been here as mourners themselves. Major Ned had a way of complicating matters with his headlong approach to everything. Pray God his obsession with the papist bell would not lead to violence. In a crowd of this size, already emotional as a result of the tragedy, feelings would quickly be inflamed. The men realised that if they were to be unhorsed, they would stand little chance of escaping with their lives. What in God's name was he up to?

The major glared down at the one armed man. Again the bell rang its insistent knell. Their eyes met and in the seaman's face the major saw a cold hatred that chilled him to the core. "Ye wanted somethin' major?" the man asked quietly.

There was no going back now in any sense, Ned realised. "I want that bell silenced once and for all. My men will remove it." He turned and realised with a shock that his hapless troopers were beyond reach and that he also was surrounded by the silent menacing crowd. This was not a situation familiar to him. Normally these people would have drawn back respectfully.

"Major, sir," the seaman replied, holding his gaze steadily, "let me put it this way. This is the first time this bell has rung for a funeral and at that, for one o' the finest men that ever walked. So it will ring and neither you nor your Hessians will stop it." He pulled again on the rope and the bell tolled in the silent churchyard. The sound of the priest's voice carried from the church as he intoned: *"averte faciem tuam a peccatis meis: et omnes iniquitates meas dele."* The voice was whipped away in the gusting wind.

The major shifted uneasily, feeling perspiration cooling on his forehead. He was outnumbered and anyway violence was the one thing his brother abhorred. How had he got himself into this situation? This strange one-armed man frightened him as no one had ever been able to before. The choice was simple. He could preserve either his dignity of his life. "Ah yes of course, Mullen. One of our own people." He should have left it for some other time. "Of course, of course, carry on then." He assumed an air of quiet solemnity and attempted to swing his horse around but this proved impossible in the close packed press of bodies. He was forced to back out slowly conscious all the time of the sea of upturned faces and of their cold contempt. There was no exultation or gloating, no laughter or mockery as they rejected him. He was of no further importance to them as they waited in their grief, *et os meum annuntiabit laudem tuam,* came the voice of the priest.

The troopers drew back in grateful relief as their major wheeled about. They could feel eyes boring into their backs as they retreated along the street with the major cold and tightlipped from humiliation. It was not that he had been defeated or downfaced in front of everyone but somehow he felt that he had made himself small in some inexplicable way. With relief the small party of horsemen turned the corner and broke once again into a trot.

They buried John Mullen next morning on the rise below the old church. The rain fell steadily and trickled into the open grave, carrying small avalanches of clay and gravel with it. Overhead the bare branches of the sycamores swayed, clashing their gnarled twigs like ancient hands plying their beads and the fir trees whispered a soft sighing sound at the onset of winter.

Gradually the people drifted away, filtering past the small group of family who stood still by the closed grave. They murmured the few awkward condolences to assuage their feelings, grief, inadequacy, guilt even, that they had escaped while this fine, strong, young man had been taken. There were some who marvelled at the widow's composure. She did not cry out. Nor were there tears. She stood stock still, staring at the freshly turned clay and replying to all who spoke to her, in the same lifeless monotone. She stood unaided and there were some who resented her, felt cheated of the spectacle of grief, while some confided to one another that the full impact of events had not struck home yet. Nodding wisely they averred that it would hit her all the harder in time.

The men drifted away to drink and to speak their inarticulate eulogies as is customary on such occasions. There was no one but had a good word to say, a reminiscence to offer or a kindness to remember. What made the event almost unique was the fact that people had been accustomed to hearing John Mullen's praises spoken even when he was alive. There was none of the dredging of the memory for something good to say about him, but a genuine outpouring of affection and regard for him that was gone. And for Eileen and the children too there was concern. How would she ever get over it? Who would look after them now? It takes time for the widow to become the object of winks and innuendo. No one had the bad grace to offer, on this day, any of the remarks that in a few months' time would give rise to guffaws and slaps on the back. It was said that she was with child too, a bad business altogether.

But what in the name of sweet sufferin' Jasus possessed him to head for the island with the tide on the flood? The question was asked for the thousandth time and no satisfactory answer was forthcoming. He was a good man to drink but he never did anything stupid after it. Nor did he need the soldiers' money that bad that he would risk his neck for it. They said there was a row but sure that was only Eileen trying to stop him going, what else? There was never a cross word betwixt or between them, even though she could be a bit moody when it suited her. Aye it was a strange business all right. Yes, he was very great with the sergeant, that Howlett fellow. John never felt ill will towards the soldiers. Live and let live, that's what he always said. Sure didn't ye see the sergeant and the captain there at the back o' the crowd with faces on them as long as a wet week as if they had lost one o' their own. Of course he did have words with the Scotchman, a malicious little hoor. Maybe the few drinks got him worked up and the soldiers leavin' and that.

And so the talk went on, drifting away to other topics, primarily the fishing, farming, work on the new pier and who would oversee the whole thing, but inevitably it came back abruptly to the crushing sadness, the injustice of the tragedy and the misery that made the man throw his life away in a fit of bad temper. And the funny thing about it, though not funny do ye understand, was that the horse was lame the whole time. Not like a Mullen to drive a lame horse like that. In fact they say it will have to be put down. He must have been powerful angry to overlook a thing like that. All very strange. The old man is takin' it bad.

And so he was. Taciturn at the best of times, he had hardly spoken a dozen words since his son's death. For most of the time he sat staring into the fire, rising only to feed the horses. How can a man who has lost the habit of conversation express the feeling of desolation that gnaws inside him? He recalled the joy of watching his amiable boy growing stronger and standing on his own feet; the understanding that had grown between them as the boy took more and more of the work off his shoulders, sketching in his plans for the future. He had been at it a day or two before he died, showing how the Mullen name would be on every wagon and coach in the county, feeling his strength like a young colt and glorying in it. How good it had felt to give him his head always, to let him meet and overcome obstacles in his own way. If he allowed it his old heart would break but it was not yet time. There were things to be done, one immediate and one that would take time.

He must say goodbye to Pompey. He must look into those trusting brown eyes for the last time and put him out of his misery. It was the least he could do in payment for a lifetime of service. It was more than a man could bear to see the proud animal crippled and hobbling like that. He would not like to see the spirit broken too.

Then there was Eileen. He must help her in some way now that she was at war with herself. She reminded him always of John's mother, dead these many years and he felt the loneliness again as sharp as the day she died. Whatever blame Eileen attached to herself, he must not allow it to destroy her and the children. It must not warp and corrode her spirit either. John would have expected him to help her no matter what difference was between them, but how could he begin? It was not easy to start again at his age.

"It's not in character," muttered Mrs Clooney, employing a phrase she had picked up in her long and varied career. "Not in character at all." She watched disapprovingly and not a little disappointed as the sergeant swayed towards the bar and banged a handful of pewter mugs on the slop-stained board. "And another round for my brave lads Mrs Clooney, me darlin'," he bellowed with a heavy attempt at an Irish brogue. "Another round before we leave ye all to the tender mercies of the French or anyone else who wants to have your delightful country." Again he swayed unsteadily trying to focus on her disapproving face. "And don't be lookin' at me like that me fine lady. Haven't we the right to a few jars before we go off to defend – to defend," he groped for a phrase, gesticulating vaguely to take in everyone around, "whoever has to be defended," he ended with a laugh.

"That's what ye're paid for I'm sure and no doubt we're all very grateful," she said tartly, "but let ye take yer drink now without any more andremarkins."

This retort confused his fuddled brain, leaving him at a loss for words. He took the refilled tankards and made his way carefully back to the table where a group of four gunners, among them Laidlaw, was waiting, all in good form as the locals would say. The locals however and the usual complement of seamen, although drinking as much, were not noticably in good form themselves. With the exception of the soldiers a kind of gloom pervaded the room. Men looked resentfully towards the noisy group. They'd be gone in a day or two and no loss. Old Skip Garrigan had withdrawn to a corner to drink by himself. He pulled pensively on the ever present pipe. There's no point in sayin' any more, he thought. I asked Pether to keep the men quiet but sure he's worse than any o' them. Not like him at all and the lads are a bit upset. Maybe they'll have had enough soon. He looked around at the glowering faces. There could be trouble here if they don't watch it. Oul Roche there and the two lads have been at it since the funeral and them two Nolan lads.

Howlett lurched to his feet again and swayed towards the bar. Mrs Clooney pre-empted him.

"I'd be obliged if you would take your men out of here before there's any trouble. This is a respectable house." She added her usual clinching remark.

"With respect Mrs Clooney," said Howlett seizing on the word "with the greatest respect," he drew himself up to his full height, holding on to the counter with both hands, "I wish to enquire for my friend Bridie." He had some difficulty with the words. "Perhaps you would convey my compliments to her."

"Bridie's gone," she replied tersely, "and I wish you would go too. You're welcome here any time provided you can conduct yourself proper."

"Where'sh Bridie?" He slurred over the words and looked around the room. The faces turned towards him in the spinning room. Desperately he tried to focus on some stationary object, the hanging lantern, a shining pewter dish, anything to stop the motion. "Wheresh Bridie?" he shouted again and somebody laughed. "Bridie's gone", he informed the woman, as if he had just made the discovery for himself.

"Aye she's gone right enough, the ungrateful strap." Mrs Clooney was talking more to herself than to Howlett. "Gone off to Spain she told me. Gone with Luke do ye mind." She set her mouth in a tight straight line. "No good will come of that carry on, mark my words."

"So Bridie's gone". He accepted the fact and slumped down on a stool beside old Garrigan. "Goin' to live in a white house with Luke. That's nice. Isn't that nice Skip?"

"Aye Pether, that's nice as ye say." Garrigan wondered how he could get his friend away before he made a further fool of himself. "Would ye have a bed we could put him in?" he muttered aside to Mrs Clooney. "He's not himself this weather since poor John was drownded."

"Aye," she said, relenting. "We'll do that. Take his arm Skip." Howlett made no protest as he was guided to the stairs to the ribald cheers of his drinking companions. "Ye'd nae be able for Bridie the nicht sergeant," called Laidlaw, his voice ringing through the murmur from the bar. The sounds faded as they reached the landing and they propped him against the wall while the proprietress produced her keys.

"Pether," said the old man, "I was asked to return this to ye." Tactfully he mentioned no names as he held out the tinder box. Howlett looked down at the box and the events of that night came back to him with unbearable clarity. She's clearing me out like rubbish. Getting rid of even the smallest trace. It hurt him to think that she could not bear even this small reminder of him. "You keep it Skip," he said. "Old friend. Keep it for a reminder of the good days we had."

The old man was touched. "I thank ye Pether. I will keep it and gladly. It's a pity the way things worked out." He took the younger man by the arm. "In ye go now an' lie down. Ye'll be a deal better after a sleep."

Howlett collapsed onto the low bed and the room began to move again. They left him in the dark with nothing to focus on. The pain returned unbidden and overwhelmed him. They say that the amputee still feels the pain in the missing limb, he thought, even till the day he dies. How do you amputate the pain? How does the limb feel about it? he wondered irrelevantly. He drifted into a fitful sleep in which he was troubled by strange dreams, and what seemed like far away shouting. A great limping horse threatened to trample him where he lay and crabs scuttled towards him, their claws rattling and reaching for his eyes. He cried out in his sleep but no sound would come from his parched throat. He tried to run but the water held him back.

Laidlaw picked his way carefully along the dark street. There's no doubt he thought but your Scotsman is the only man to hold his grog. They had all gone under the table except himself. As for the sergeant, he wouldn't be seen till morning. Aye it's time to be away from this hole of a town. He paused at a narrow lane to empty his bladder, leaning his head against the wall and groaning with relief. "That's all this toon is guid for," he muttered to himself as he buttoned up again. "Laidlaw?" a voice beside him asked. He looked around at the three shapes looming out of the darkness. "Maybe," he answered, shaking his head to clear it. Alarm bells rang in his brain. He recognised the one armed man.

"You're the Scotchman aren't ye?"

"Scotsman. Aye I'm a Scot." He could not resist the correction, which in the circumstances he knew to be unwise but he would be hanged if some ignorant bog-trotter would get away with it. Fear warned him to watch his tongue and he reached carefully for the haft of his bayonet.

"We're friends o' John Mullen," said one of the other men.

"It seems ye had some unfinished business together."

"I had nae business wi' your friend except for closin' his een."

There was a pause. "Ye were on the island then when he was found?"

"Aye I found him myself."

"And it was yourself he was goin' to see, wasn't it?"

"That would surprise me. We had little to say to each other and that was nae too friendly."

One of the men peered closer. "This is the lad Da. This is the one John pointed out to us that time."

"One redcoat is as good as another. We're holdin' you responsible for our friend drownin'."

Laidlaw knew from experience when a fight was inevitable. "Bluecoat. Are you blind as weel, ye lopsided bastard?" Might as well be hanged for a sheep. With a roar the big man lunged for him swinging his one fist wildly but Laidlaw leapt nimbly aside. The bayonet glinted dully in his hand as the other two came at him. He felt the blade go home in soft flesh and heard the scream as the man went down. He twisted the blade and pulled but a blow caught him on the side of the head and he fell backwards, tripping over the prone body. He rose to his knees, noticing the wetness on his hands. He heard a voice rising to hysteria and beginning to blubber, "Jesus Da, he's kilt me. I'm bleedin' all over." Dimly he saw the man on the ground clutching at his belly with both hands. The bayonet had worked free and lay on the ground.

What do ye expect? thought Laidlaw as he felt the heavy boots crashing into his ribs, sending him sprawling again. Only two to one now. Where's me musket? It had clattered to the ground somewhere. His right arm would not obey him. Must be broken he thought detachedly. Call for help. He shouted, strangled shapeless noises. Where's me mates? They'll come runnin'. The boots pounded into his face but he was beyond noticing by then. Savagely the men worked on him venting their fury until they stopped from exhaustion. There was no move from the broken little body, no more caustic answers or provocative jibes. They looked at each other in dread. The third man still lay groaning and clutching at his guts. "We'd best get him aboard lad and raise sail. There'll be hell to pay over this."

Peter Howlett sat up suddenly. Someone was shaking him. For a moment he could not recall where he was. "Come on sergeant for God's sake." He recognised the face of Mrs Clooney, eerie and frightened in the light of the candle. "Someone's been murdered." He stumbled to his feet. He was still fully dressed, he noted. "Who? Where?" His brain was beginning to clear. The cold night air refreshed him. At the entrance to the lane a small group of people had gathered. Someone was holding a lantern. Howlett pushed his way through. An onlooker remarked in awed tones: "Be God he gave a good account of himself judgin' be all the blood." There was blood everywhere and a trail of dark drops led away in the direction of the harbour. He looked down at the body lying in the pool of yellow light. It was Laidlaw, lying on his side, his face almost unrecognisable. His legs were crossed and his arms spread at impossible angles. On Howlett's mind flashed the picture of the little broken body of the wren. "Take him up men. He's beyond help now." He sent one of the bleary eyed soldiers to sound the alarm and call out the coastguard but it proved too late. The Roches were already under sail and well beyond reach of the hue and cry, the younger son's lifeblood ebbing away with the tide. A stiff north-westerly would take them out of reach of pursuit for the moment but there would be no safe haven for them on the east coast ever again.

His lordship was in foul temper by the time he arrived home to Balcunnin House. He had failed to obtain any subvention for the harbour works during his sojourn in London. This was not too bad as he was prepared to go ahead at his own expense anyway but it irritated him to have two sons lounging about the London house, kicking their heels on half pay when they should have been out making their names and fortunes in some profitable war. Damn the peace anyway, he thought, and damn the fact that he was losing a good engineer in Osgood and the best works foreman he could have got.

All the way across in the pacquet boat he had felt his irritation coming to a head and concentrating on that damn silly letter from his brother about a bell. He had started by asking for advice and ended by announcing his intention of cutting it down. The fellow hadn't even been there to meet him and he had to wait several hours until Ned condescended to put in an appearance. Now he looked at his brother's florid face, obviously the result of a few post-prandial brandies and his anger boiled up afresh. "Be so good Ned, as to explain what the devil has been going on in my absence." He did not wait for a reply. "It's not enough that my plans have been set back by those incompetents in London but I find my carrier drowned and the people inflamed against my authority. Now I must start taking depositions concerning this murder."

Ned made to interrupt. Was it possible that his brother was suggesting that he was responsible in some way?

"And I'm holding you responsible, at least to some extent, for this antagonism." Balcunnin pointed an accusing finger.

"How dare you sir?" Years of taking his brother's orders and putting up with his patronising ways proved too much for Ned.

"This idiotic business of the bell and on the day of the man's funeral too. Do you realise that you have done more for the cause of sedition than all the street corner orators and hole and corner revolutionaries could have accomplished in a lifetime?"

Ned had never seen him so angry but he did not have to put up with this kind of accusation. A vein throbbed in his temple. He should have pressed ahead with cutting down that bell. The fact that he had retreated weakened his argument but the certainty of being right goaded him on. "Nonsense. Absolute nonsense. You've never been firm enough in your approach to these people. If you had given me a free hand all along they would have more respect."

"God's blood man, you go too far. Your buffoonery has humiliated us in public – not for the first time and your complete lack of judgement probably precipitated the murder of one of His Majesty's soldiers." He stalked to the window of his study and stood, with hands clasped behind him, looking out at the bleak wintry garden.

With difficulty Ned refrained from striking his brother. "I've taken all I'm prepared to take from you sir. You have persistently undermined my position here. I shall leave you to mollycoddle the peasantry and take myself off to Mayo at the earliest opportunity." Balcunnin turned from the window. He had reached a decision. His rage had subsided now and his voice was cold and cut like a lash. "Mayo has enough troubles, sir. You shall not add to them. I have decided to give you one last chance to make something of your life."

"You have never done anything but impede me," interrupted Ned. "Why should you change now?" But his brother had passed beyond anger. "I shall supply you with funds and letters of introduction to some business associates in the Americas and from then on you must make your own way in the world." It was too good to be true. At last deliverance, after all these years of taking orders as an unpaid servant in his brother's house. His mind spun at the prospect of being at last his own master but he tried to hide his pleasure with an aggrieved air. "Brother, you may cast me off as you see fit but I warn you that some day those people will pull this house down around your ears and this entire country will fall prey to a rabble of jacobins and democrats." With this dire prophecy he pounded from the room and pulled the door to with a sound like thunder.

Balcunnin let his shoulders droop with a sigh of relief. It had been a long time coming and had proved easier than he had anticipated. In his present mood Ned would lose no time in departing and meanwhile there were other things to be done. He must swear out a warrant for the arrest of those sailors, whatever their names were and see them hang as expeditiously as possible. And something would have to be done about that young woman whose husband was drowned. Really there was no end to the problems one had to face in his position. In a way Ned was to be envied. Most likely he would make a protracted holiday of his American exploits and then return like the prodigal to plague him in his old age. He smiled wanly at the idea of two octogenarians locked in mortal combat over the governance of the Balcunnin estates.

It was a great pity about Mullen. His family had always been associated with Balcunnin and had shared his own interest in horses. He made a mental note to call on Eileen's mother at the earliest opportunity and express his condolences and to send Alicia to call on Eileen. He looked at the rolled bundle of maps on his desk. At least Osgood proved reliable, he thought, unrolling them. There was nothing for it but to oversee the work himself and get someone else to take charge of the blasting. No doubt old Mullen would still be able to arrange haulage. He became absorbed in the drawings, intrigued by the painstaking detail and by the terse explanatory notes. The fellow had even included preliminary drawings for a lighthouse on the Abel Rock with sections showing how the stones should be cut to lock together like a series of keystones. Was there no end to his ingenuity? It saddened him to think that this man, a minor Leonardo, whose mind delighted in invention and solving problems, should be packed off at such short notice, possibly to spend his time hurling iron balls at sundry murderous Frenchmen or whatever. I owe it to him, he thought with renewed determination, to put these plans into operation. Whether he would ever know it or not, Osgood's contribution to the town would be immense.

His thoughts were interrupted by the soft touch of his daughter's hand on his shoulder and he turned and embraced her. This wise and gentle girl had always been a joy to him and he was touched to see her pleasure at his return and at the same time the sadness in her eyes. "Oh Papa" she said, "I'm glad to see you home. Everything has been going wrong since you went away."

"Yes, I know," he replied gently, "but we must do our best to set things to rights."

"Uncle Ned tells me he's leaving. Is it true?" She had always had an affection for her scapegrace uncle but she could appreciate the advantages of his emigrating to foreign parts.

"Well yes. He feels that perhaps it is time to spread his wings a little and see something of the world."

She did not press him further. "I've been to see Eileen Mullen. Mrs Eavers is staying with her. It's very very sad." She could not find words to express what she had found. Never had she seen the life so go out of a person as it had fled from Eileen.

"Ah good. We must do what we can to help." He patted her shoulder.

"And the townspeople turned their backs on me," she added, "why would they do that? I fear Uncle Ned upset them over their bell." Her voice broke with the hurt of it.

"Let me see, let me see. I think we may be able to do something there. I shall have a word with the reverend Mr Clare on a certain matter. You know I think the people have a genuine grievance about their religious disabilities." Alicia felt her spirits lighten at his words. She knew that he could always see a way out of difficulties. She recalled her words to Ned. Perhaps he would in fact endow a proper belfry. She put the suggestion to him. "I see that you have inherited something of my devious political nature," he laughed. "I have something along those lines in mind but you must be patient for a while." He took her arm. "Now let us go and find your mother. She will have all the news about your brothers for you and of course all the latest London scandals."

CHAPTER 20

It might have been better had there been a band to march to, with drum and fife and flags flying, but it would have been difficult to invest the occasion with glamour. The artillerymen were leaving lock, stock and barrel as the old saying appropriately has it. It was by no means an impressive parade of men that fell in by the coastguard station, some two dozen assorted blue coats, middle aged most of them and uncomfortable at being disturbed. For some this was the end of service life but for the few younger and fitter men it was a new departure to places as yet unknown. Howlett called them to attention as the captain emerged. He was not in the best of tempers at the disruption of his routine. Cursorily he addressed the men. Their orders were to proceed directly to Dublin by sea, courtesy of the coastguard, and there await suitable transport to England where their future would be decided by those set above them. He sounded as if he reposed little faith in the wisdom of those set above him, petulance no doubt.

Howlett marched the men down to the pier, each man with his few personal effects stuffed into his knapsack. There was an air of pathos about the small procession, accentuated by the flurries of rain borne on the carping southerly wind. A small crowd of locals had gathered to watch what was to them a piece of history, an insignificant sideshow to the great events of Europe but a milestone in the quiet history of their uneventful lives. For years afterwards arguments would be settled by reference to the day the gunners left or the day the man was drowned or the time the soldier was murdered. Old men would play the game of remembering events beyond the ken of their younger drinking companions. "Do ye mind the time?" or "that was before your time – the year of the wreck" or "you wouldn't remember John Mullen", to which the younger men would have to concede how little they had lived and how impoverished was their experience. Children who stood by would recall the blue coats and white webbing etched on their memories against the background of limewashed harbour walls and would wonder in later years if they had seen it or had only imagined it from the descriptions of the event.

The cutter had come alongside and the men, long accustomed to the land, stepped warily on the wet and slippery deck. The vessel rose and fell imperceptibly with a movement like gentle breathing. Old Garrigan stood by the steps waiting for a word with the sergeant. He put out his hand. "So you're finally leavin' us sergeant."

The occasion was too momentous for familiarity. Howlett grasped the gnarled hand in his. "I am Skip. There's nothing else for it, it seems."

"Aye well I'm that sorry to see ye go. It's a sad time for old friends."

"It is that Skip." He could think of nothing more to say.

"Is there any danger you'd be back this way at all?" The query was couched in the peculiarly inverted form that Howlett had come to enjoy. He smiled briefly.

"I doubt it Skip. It's never the same to come back."

"Ah there you are Garrigan." It was Osgood tying up a few loose ends. "About *Kittiwake*. She's still army property but I've left instructions that you should have first refusal if the coastguards have no use for her."

"She's a brave little craft, captain, and I wouldn't mind havin' her at all, thank ye kindly." Garrigan touched his cap. Osgood turned to Howlett. "I've had to leave all my specimens behind – too heavy. It's a damned nuisance." He shrugged resignedly. "We must get aboard."

Howlett shook the old man's hand again. "You'll hear from me again sometime Skip and," he paused, "keep an eye on Mrs Mullen and her children if you can."

"Aye, I'll do that. I'll do that" Garrigan looked at him and understood what he saw in his eyes. "Good luck to ye now me son." He began to occupy himself with his pipe and Howlett went aboard. From the poop deck he watched as the land fell away behind him. Once the lines were cast off the process was inexorable. Harbour and headland with its squat tower fell behind. The surf over the Cross Rock lay astern and the buildings of the town dwindled into the gloom of the winter's afternoon. The cutter went about and beat between the whale backed islands and suddenly they were to seaward of his own island with its grey martello tower and beyond it the low line of white cottages, the familiar outline of the Kybe.

The rain beat in his face as he stood holding onto the shrouds but he could not take his eyes from the distant shoreline. He felt no urge to look ahead. There was nowhere he wanted to go. He had nothing to say to the officer of the watch or to the men, some of whom had gone below while others huddled in the well seeking shelter while they watched Fingal receding into the rain. For a moment a shaft of sunlight broke through the overcast, throwing the Kybe into high relief. But he was not sure at that distance if he could make out the long cottage.

In time they rounded Lambay and the skyline of Howth and Wicklow stood before them. Howlett was unaware of the change. His eyes watched the seething wake, a white track leading back to where he had found and lost the meaning of existence. There would never be any going back now he knew. They could never face each other again without the guilt. It would eat at them and probably destroy them both. The birds dipped and dived into the path of the wake and rose again to wing their way landward. He watched them enviously. A sneaking hope whispered to him that maybe someday, but he knew it was a delusion. He was dead to her now, more dead than her lost husband. It was unlikely that she would ever think of him again.

As darkness fell he watched the lights appear here and there on the land. A beacon flickered, guiding them to the harbour at Howth with its fine new breakwater. A kind of peace descended on him as he contemplated the emptiness of his future. She did not want him but she could not prevent his feelings for her. He could carry the memories with him into the darkness. No one could prevent him from loving her, as no one could ever know. It is no bad achievement to find complete happiness in life if only for the space of an hour. To a man without a future there was nothing to keep the warmth in him but memories, a little hoard of nuggets to be taken out and looked at to remind him that once he had been alive.

The primal picture that came to him was the sight of her walking over the windmill hill on a sunny morning, the way her body swung to her rhythmic walk, the animal vitality of her. It was unbearable to think. Unbidden, the warm smoothness of her stole into his mind and overwhelmed him. He was again in the little bay on the still summer nights where they had met and loved so briefly. He thought of the nights when he had stood by the parapet and wished her husband dead. Anger surged in him against his friend. He was gone and should not set his dead hand against them now.

The anger gave him a sort of strength and the resolve to win her. Time would dull the hurt and the guilt and she would warm to him again. He was young enough still and alive. She must be made to see that it was inevitable, that their lives were inextricably locked together, that one could not survive without the other, even that Mullen had realised this in his last moments and that the loss, not they, had destroyed him. It made some sense to him when he construed it that way. It made more sense than the thought that what they had shared had been wrong, that two souls here on this stormswept reef, in the dark ocean of eternity should not have turned to each other and given themselves in recognition and in mutual joy.

"Let go the anchor," the voice of the lieutenant brought him back to the present and the chain rattled into the still waters of the harbour. There was a flurry of activity as canvas was furled and clewed up and suddenly the cutter swung gently on her anchor under the lee of the hill. Lights approached from the land accompanied by the creaking of rowlocks. Activity, thought Howlett, activity would dull the pain and put in the time until he was free to formulate a definite plan and put together the fragile fabric of their lives.

Mrs Eavers went to the cottage door. There was the noise again. She opened the door apprehensively and was struck by a cold blast off the sea. She felt something brush against her skirts and looked down. It was a cat, a large tawny creature which stalked past her and went directly to the fire where it curled up in proprietorial fashion without by your leave to anyone.

She looked at the scene presented by the firelight. It should have been cheerful and domestic. Eileen sat in her usual place with a shawl thrown around her shoulders while the children lay on the floor playing idly with whatever came to hand. The cat's arrival threw them into wild excitement. There had been little enough to cheer them during the past weeks. They were still too small to feel the full impact of the tragedy or to understand the change that had come over their mother. Gran with her practical ways had kept them occupied and answered their plaintive questions as best she could, trying to deflect them from tiring their mother too much. Now they jumped at Eileen trying to climb on her lap. "Look at the cat, Mam. Can we have a cat like that? It's mine. I saw it first." Eileen patted them absently and nodded, "Of course, of course," without conviction until Gran lifted them gently down. She was glad of the cat as a distraction for the poor little creatures.

"Of course ye can have a cat. If this one goes away I'll get ye one from Balcunnin." They fell to stroking the strange intruder who purred and stretched, making himself quite at home.

"Rub butter on his paws and he'll never leave." It was Eileen who spoke, to her mother's surprise. This was the first remark she had volunteered for weeks, over and above her perfunctory replies to enquiries after her health. For a moment some animation showed in her face but it faded soon and she turned her face to the fire. "Aye he'll never leave you then," but she seemed to have forgotten the cat.

It had been like this for weeks. The doctor assured her that there was no danger to the baby. Eileen was physically strong and her pregnancy was well advanced but he did advise activity and company. Eileen should move out and speak to people in the interests of her own well-being. This she could not do. She sat for hours saying nothing, with fingers picking idly at the threads of her shawl. People who called on her became uneasy or embarrassed and soon found an excuse to leave. Only Nora persisted and seemed to have entered into a conspiracy with the grandmother not to allow Eileen to give in. They kept her informed of what was happening in the town, talking to each other of trivial matters in the hope of striking a spark of interest. Even the news that the soldiers had all embarked had not roused her from her torpor.

"Sure God help the poor craturs," said Nora. "Where will they all end up?"

"Aye it's sad for them sure enough," Mrs Eavers had agreed motioning her towards the door. She had wanted to discuss her daughter's condition and her own anxiety beyond Eileen's hearing. When she had re-entered she was surprised to find her daughter standing at the window, gazing seaward. A small speck of white sail was beating southward towards Lambay. Eileen had watched it until it had faded from sight in the dying afternoon light. For a brief second the sunlight had caught the sails and illuminated them in a flash of gold against the dark backdrop of the island and then they were gone. Eileen had stayed motionless until she had taken her by the shoulders and brought her back to the fire.

It was like nursing a stranger. Gone was the old familiar chatter, the laughter at a shared joke or the mutual interest in the doings of their menfolk. It hurt like a knife in her heart to see her daughter in pain and the spirit dying inside her. If only she could let it out, she thought it would be better but there had been no tears. It was bottled up inside her, something more than grief and it was killing her.

The children played with the cat, rubbing generous quantities of butter on the paws, which the cat licked appreciatively.

"It's strange the way he came in like that" remarked the grandmother. "Don't you think so Eileen?" Her daughter nodded. "Aye, it's strange the way he came in," but again she was not thinking of the cat. She returned to her perusal of the fire, her gaze wandering into the glowing caverns, red and white hot like the corridors of hell but her face felt cold, lifeless, paralysed. Events were going on around her but she could not reach out. She could see and hear but words did not touch her. She was inert, powerless, numb to all feeling. Voices came to her muted and distorted, like voices from an adjoining room and she had difficulty in apprehending what they said. She answered involuntarily as if an intermediary spoke for her, using unfamiliar phrases over which she had no control. Why could she not feel anything, the voice inside her screamed.

Sleep gave no respite. There were no nightmares or agonies of guilt. No spectral voices came to accuse her. Instead she dreamt of lying on the ground feeling the coldness of the wet street on her face and listening to the voices of the people coming from far above but all the time she was unable to move or speak. Unable to say "I'm alive", or "Help me", while they discussed her plight and made decisions on what to do with her. Her voice screamed in her brain, "I'm alive. Don't put me away." But still they talked on and their boots shuffled and moved in and out of her line of vision. Then she would wake in fear and feel the cold still lingering from the dream and her aloneness would sweep in with the dawn to engulf her again.

The nights drew in around the Kybe as winter tightened its grip on the town and the cat stayed, curled by the fire for most of the time. At night he departed on some hunting expedition but he made it quite clear that this was his home from then on. The wind howled in the chimneys and the pounding surf again hurled its burden of woar onto the beach. The men came with carts to collect it but nobody stopped at Mullens' cottage to ask for a hand. Only Jem called, with some of his older children behind him on the cart. He was cheerful and brought sweets for the children and all the news from the big house but the pain in his eyes was nakedly visible at the sight of his dejected sister. Eileen felt a stirring of gratitude to him and even something like pity for her brother who tried so hard to make everything seem like normal. Jem, for his part, was saddened to see how his mother had aged and grown gaunt from the task of providing the warmth and attention to bring his sister back into the world. You're never finished with childer, he thought, not till you're carried out in the box yourself. But he did not put the thought into words.

The old man came, diffident and awkward, to speak to Eileen. He had rarely come to the house in John's time and looked around shyly for somewhere to sit. He held his hat in his hand and gestured once or twice as if reluctant to leave it down. Mrs Eavers took it and laid it on the table. "I have a few little errands to do," she said, taking the children by the hand, "so I'll leave ye in peace for a little while." She left quietly, pulling the door to. The old man coughed, searching for somewhere to begin. Eileen waited, thinking: he's come to blame me for his son. And what can I say?

"He was a good lad Eileen," he began, "but he wouldn't want you to take on like this."

She lowered her head. "I know that grandfather," she said. "He was a good lad but I can't help what happened."

"Aye, well." He joined his hands, lacing the fingers together and stared into the fire. He spoke, not looking directly at her. "It's a random class of a world Eileen, a random world." It was a strange word but he used so few that it was his way to search for the right one before expressing his thoughts. "I know that things weren't always right with John and yourself but ye can't be responsible for everythin' that happens. No one said life has to be simple or easy. Nor can we always choose the way we want things to be." He stopped, embarrassed by the length of his speech. She made no reply, nor did she look up. "I want ye to know that the business is yours and the childers' and I'll keep it goin' till you're ready to take it so you're not to fret on that account."

"That's good of you, grandfather," she replied.

"It's what he would have wanted," said the old man. "John would have mourned for the dead but he'd have carried on."

"He would want no tears from me grandfather," she whispered and he was struck by the bleakness in her voice.

"In time, child, in time. What was good between ye need not die. Forget the bad." He felt his heart reaching out to her and he could scarcely trust himself to speak. "I never cared for anyone the way I cared for John but he's dead now and I'm still alive and there's things I can do for him that he would want me to do and there's plenty for yourself to be doin' too."

"I'm sorry grandfather," her voice sounded hollow and defeated. "I'm sorry but there's nothing I can do."

The priest's house was attached to the chapel, as the law required him to live on the premises. He preferred to call it the church although most people spoke of the chapel. It irked him to have to entertain visitors in the sacristy which also served as his kitchen. It was particularly embarrassing to be caught halfway through his dinner by his lordship himself. There was nowhere else to entertain his distinguished visitor, who insisted that he finish his meal. If he has come to argue with me, thought Father Clare, I am at a distinct disadvantage, sitting here with my bacon and cabbage. He felt slightly ridiculous.

"Father Clare," began Balcunnin, graciously using the courtesy title, "I'll come straight to the point. I require your assistance."

This came as a surprise to the priest and he paused in the act of spearing a nice piece of salty fat. He had expected a thinly veiled reprimand over the incident of the bell. "My assistance?" the surprise was obvious in his voice.

"Yes father. You see, I need a good number of your parishioners to work on some schemes I have in mind. For instance you know about the harbour works but to be blunt I find the people discontented and unwilling to cooperate with me even for good wages. Perhaps you can enlighten me as to why."

"Your lordship will permit me to be equally blunt, I trust." Such opportunities did not come very often. He explained how the whole town had been upset by the death of John Mullen and the soldier and particularly by the attempt of the militia to remove the bell on the day of the funeral. Out of manners he refrained from mentioning Ned by name. His lordship nodded without comment. "Now this has drawn attention to the grievances people feel over the religious question and with respect, they see yourself sir, as the representative of the government in these parts. The bell has become a kind of symbol to them."

"Tell me more about the bell, father."

"Well it came off the schooner that was salvaged by young Morris and the sergeant. In fact I've heard it referred to as Howlett's bell. He was a musical kind of fellow apparently."

"Howlett's bell. Now that is curious."

"Of course I'll admit when I was a student in Spain," went on the priest, "the same kind of restrictions were applied to Jews and Protestants and even more severely, no bells or steeples and so on, though I don't think the Jews go in for that sort of thing. But that was more in the line of keeping down heresy rather than a political thing." He looked levelly at the peer when he spoke the word heresy. The truth must never be watered down even to one as powerful as Balcunnin.

"And do you think, father, that this country would prosper if these disabilities were to be removed? Might it not lead to further demands and the destruction of the social order?"

"I'm not so foolish as to think that the streets would be paved with gold or that we would all grow instantly rich after Emancipation. Personally I always thought Virgil slightly ridiculous in *The Pollio*, parti-coloured sheep and all that, but the denial of full rights serves only to turn good god-fearing men into dangerous malcontents."

Balcunnin looked at the priest with a new respect. This level-headed man was not the shambling idiot described by Ned or the semi-literate simian, spouting his garbled Latin, so beloved of the cartoonists in the English popular press. "I take your point father. Now I have a proposition to put to you. What would you say to a proper church and a proper belfry for Howlett's bell? There would be work in plenty for everyone and I would meet half of the expense as well as granting the land – freehold."

The priest was speechless. He laid down his knife and fork, his appetite gone. "But . . . but the law. Would you not be placing yourself in an invidious position?"

"My dear man were you not prepared to circumvent the law when you put up your bell?" It was a fair comment. "My concern is for the future prosperity of this town. I could bring five hundred hungry men from Mayo to work for me but that might excite even more discontent. No. I want my people to work with me and for my town for our mutual benefit."

"But how will it be construed if you endow a Catholic church?"

"Firstly I am the interpreter of the law hereabouts and secondly I shall explain, to those who may ask, that I am providing monies and employing men primarily to knock down a Catholic chapel. Even the most bigoted can hardly argue with that. The same men may be retained to build your church, incidentally at my expense, but you and your people must provide the money for the stone. As this comes from my quarries I shall gain in some quarters a reputation for philanthropy and, in others, enhanced respect for my business acumen. You see I cannot lose." He smiled frankly at the simplicity of the plan. "If you agree, I assure you the financial burden shall not weigh too heavily on you."

You realise my lord that there are those who would see this as a bribe to gain my assistance."

"Yes I do. No matter how we proceed we are bound to antagonise someone but we must seek the greater good, must we not?"

"My lord your offer is most generous. I think it will be received in the spirit in which you have made it." A belfry, he thought and his eyes misted over with emotion. A real belfry where a man could climb and look out over the town – from whence the sound would be broadcast to call people to prayer for miles around. In his memory, as from far away, he heard again the bells of Salamanca. Beware of pride, he thought hastily – but to have a belfry! Surely this could not be the work of Satan. He would accept it no matter what detractors might say. In humility he would accept this offer not in vain glory and not as a mendicant.

Balcunnin saw that the priest was moved and withdrawn into his thoughts. "I'll take my leave of you, father. I'm sorry to have spoiled your dinner."

"Ah yes" said the priest, rising. "Rufus will appreciate it. My dog you see."

"Of course, the setter. I encountered him on my way in." Balcunnin extended his hand. "We have work to do father. We have a new century to build. It's time we started."

"Aye my lord. We cannot afford to wait for the politicians in London to see the light." They shook hands. Extraordinary man, thought the priest. Have I been manipulated? Childishly he grinned at the thought of the belfry and then went into his chapel and got on his knees to pray for humility, but his mind wandered to the great cathedral bells of Spain echoing over the tawny countryside and the memory of the people stopping in the streets and fields to pray. Perhaps even a weather cock on top he thought. It was useless. He could not concentrate. Already he could hear the masons cutting and shaping the grey-blue limestone and could see the scaffolding rising into the sky. He rose and went to find Rufus.

CHAPTER 21

It was midwinter when the old man came again. He saw the toll that
had been taken of the grandmother and the near despair in her eyes.
She was a fine woman still though, and he recalled the standing family
joke. No, he was too old to accommodate himself to another human
being. He sat stiffly in front of the fire. "And how have things been
ma'am?" he enquired, knowing the answer. "She's still the same Mr
Mullen, taking it very hard." The old woman felt a twinge of shame as
if admitting to a hidden weakness on her side of the family, the stigma
of bad blood. She felt her cheeks warming at the thought but in truth
there had never been even the suggestion of blame or recrimination,
nothing but the most courteously expressed concern. "She's inside in
the bed yet," she said nodding towards the inner room, "but she
should be with us soon."

In truth there were times when it was almost impossible to keep her
patience, when she wanted to scream and beat her daughter for her
lack of response. There were times when she longed guiltily to be back
at Balcunnin in her comfortable busy routine among the chatter of
voices and the shrieks of children. Only Nora Donovan kept her going
when the sight of Eileen moving about like an automation, rearranging
things or staring blankly out of the window, drove her to the limits of
endurance.

"She's just having a little lie down."

"Aye. Well I just wanted to let her know how we're doin' below."
He spoke deliberately in the manner of one partner to another and
began to explain how he was buying horses and wagons in preparation
for the harbour works. He paused as the door opened behind him and
Eileen entered. She had got thin and pale and her eyes were lack-
lustre, almost vacant. She sat in her accustomed place and her face
twitched in a mechanical smile of greeting. "How are you grandfather?"

"Fine, fine. And you're lookin' better yourself." He paused, averting his eyes. "I've been tellin' your mother about our plans for the business." He began again to explain about the haulage contract for stone and the extra horses and the extension to the stables, now nearing completion, and his voice became lively with excitement. It was in a way like being young again, like when he had told his own wife about his plans for the future, but this time there was no answering excitement, no unspoken contract to tackle the world together as equal partners. She nodded, apparently understanding, but he wondered who would really look after things when he was gone. There was nothing else he could do but carry on. "I've taken Larry Donovan on full time," he continued. "He's good with horses but no great man to load or unload." A flicker of a smile passed across her face. He paused, wondering if she would ask him about anything. He felt no rebuff when she did not. Instinctively he knew that he must continue on this road, wearing down her resistance, like a wheel bumping over new ground, cutting a groove, deeper at every journey so that some day the rut would control the wheel and direct it unerringly on its way. Someday Eileen would find her way again if the groove was cut for her. "Aye, and we'll be carryin' stone for the new chapel too of course."

"It's going to be a real church they say," put in the grandmother, "with a house for himself." Eileen winced at the mention of the priest. His had been the most difficult visit of all with his questioning and advice, hectoring her to put her trust in Providence. She had lost a good husband but hadn't she the blessing of his child to look forward to and more in the same vein, but to no avail. No doubt his intentions were good but his words fell on stony ground.

"Aye, it'll be a different town again they're finished. We won't know ourselves at all, at all." He paused, wondering whether or not to continue but he also needed to confide in someone. "I had to have Pompey put down," he said abruptly. "He wouldn't mend." He heard again the single report and could see the great animal crumple and fall, kicking its legs feebly in its final throes. How could he explain the loss of a friend, one who had borne his burdens for so many years?

"Oh no, not Pompey too!" Eileen was crying. The tears streamed down her face. "Not poor Pompey." Her voice caught in her throat and grief possessed her, obliterating everything around her. "Oh no," she sobbed and buried her face in her hands. The suddenness and force of her grief alarmed the old people but she was unaware of their presence. She was unaware of being held and helped from her chair like an invalid or of being led into the bedroom. Something had snapped inside her and she could not stem the flood.

The old people sat and waited with hardly a word. They knew that something significant had occurred but could not guess at the outcome. By tacit agreement they felt it better to leave her until she quietened down. Gradually the light began to fade and the sounds in the bedroom began to subside changing from the low animal moaning to a softer whimper and eventually to silence. At length the grandmother stole quietly into the bedroom. Her daughter, gaunt and hollow eyed, was asleep with tear-stained face and her hair lank and unkempt. She was, nonetheless, breathing quietly and sleeping more peacefully than she had for a long time. She covered her carefully with a blanket and went out.

The children came in from Donovans with their constant companion, the cat. The grandparents fed them, warning them that Mam was asleep and not to make noise. They seemed to sense that something important was happening and tried to be quiet, sitting at the fire with bread and butter. It was a bit like a picnic but much too quiet. Darkness came and they lit candles.

The door opened. Eileen had washed her face and made some attempt to comb her hair. "I'm sorry," she said, "I must have gone to sleep." There was something new in her voice, a hesitancy that suggested embarrassment. "I didn't mean to."

"Never mind child. You were very tired." Her mother pretended to poke at the fire. The old man stood as if to leave.

"Sit down please grandfather. You must have something to eat. Did you give these babies anything Mam?"

Gently, thought her mother. Don't rush anything. "You're feeling better then?"

"Yes I am. I'm a bit hungry too." She went to the table and began to cut herself some soda-bread. "There's just one thing I want to ask, Grandfather. You didn't send him to the hounds?"

"No lass. That I couldn't do." He couldn't have taken the thought of jaws slavering and snarling over the bloodied limbs. The hollow sound of crunching bones would have haunted him like an accusation. "No lass, I buried him in the yard fornenst the south wall."

"I'm glad," she said briefly and put her hand on his shoulder. He said nothing about planting a vine over Pompey as the doctor had suggested, saying that it was the best way to grow them. Some might be repelled by the notion, while others might think him foolishly sentimental. But the doctor had given him the vine and there it stood, a bare and withered looking twig. Eileen wolfed on the bread. There was more colour in her face than before, enhanced by the warm glow of the candles. "Mam," she said, "I've been a trial to you this long time, haven't I?"

"But sure what else would I do?" Her mother was at a loss. "You'll be yourself again soon enough," – more in hope than in certainty.

"No Mam. It will never be the same again but I won't go away from ye like that ever again." They were gone, she thought, both of them and nothing could ever bring them back but she had their children to care for and in this way she could make some amends. Now she could mourn their loss and maybe survive, mourn for the big kindly man whose voice had resounded through most of her years and for the awkward vulnerable waif who had been both child and lover to her. She felt the sadness of future years like a naked cut. Is the intensity of awareness a compensation for the pain? Anything was preferable to the numbness that had imprisoned her for so long. "I think we'll put these children to bed," she said gathering the feebly protesting young ones to her, "and then we must talk about Christmas. I'll have to see about a goose."

"We can do all that tomorrow Eileen. Let's put the children up now." Her mother felt a weight shifting from her heart. It might be that the worst was past. The old man rose to go. "And grandfather, will you bring the pony and trap for us on Sunday? It's time I got out again. Anyway I want to see the chapel before they pull it down."

"God, and I'd be proud to Eileen." It was more than he had hoped for. "And I'll give it an extra polish for the occasion." That would silence any malicious tongues, he thought, when they see the Mullen family drivin' to mass in style again. He left the two women there and stepped it out along the Kybe. He felt younger than he had for years and soon he began to whistle, the tuneless whistle that had accompanied him for so many nights on the road. He'd make that pony shine too, . . . for Eileen . . . bright enough to bring the light back to her eyes. She had a hard road ahead of her, he knew but he felt that he had a few years left in him to help her on the way.

"Do ye know what it is Tom, but I think it's near time I moved on." Old Garrigan was sitting hunched on a bollard by the slipway with his collar turned up against the thin January wind.

"And why would you say that, Skip, and you bred, born and rared in the town?" Tom had come upon him in a moment of pensive contemplation.

"Ah sure it's not like me own place anymore with all them changes." He indicated the embryonic harbour works with a sweep of his pipestem. "Incomaires all over the place takin' the wages out of our mouths." He spat contemptuously and wrung out the pipe. Hardly a justified remark coming from Skip, thought Tom, since he was not noted as a wage earner at the best of times. Inevitably however, there had been some resentment of the Mayomen who had come, hungry for wages, though not in great numbers. They were prepared to do the work of convicts in the quarry in preference to starving on their native mountains but their number did not exceed twenty or so and generally they were civil enough, for strangers. Still the suspicion was there as in any small community that every stranger might prove to be the thin end of some wedge that would throw the locals into penury and hunger. The fact that there was work in abundance for all who wanted it did not allay the suspicion.

"Don't tell me you're lookin' a job breakin' stones Skip. I'd come and see that for meself."

"It's not that at all Tom. It's just all the changes that's gettin' to me. It doesn't seem right to be pullin' everythin' down and buildin' things up so fast."

"They call it progress." Tom liked the sound of the new word. Everything was for progress and he wanted to be part of this progress.

"Progress me arse!" Skip dismissed the concept violently. "I'd rather have the military back instead of them bogtrotters. Ye could understand what they were sayin' at least. Them fellas! Ye couldn't hold a conversation with them, with their 'shticks and shtones' and their 'fuiskey'." It was true that the Mayomen fell short of Fingallian standards in the matter of elocution. His little face wrinkled in contempt.

"They're not such bad people and sure aren't they only tryin' to make a livin' like the rest of us?" insisted Tom.

"Maybe so, maybe so. I don't know at all, at all." He looked wistfully at the line of the pier. It had begun to grow imperceptibly where piles had been driven in, testing the bottom, and the dumping of massive rocks for the breakwater had commenced. A wagon drawn up by a team of six snorting horses was creaking along the pier. Two men walked in front holding the leading animals. The wagon groaned under the weight of several enormous limestone blocks. God alone knew how many similar wagonloads would be required before his lordship was satisfied but it seemed as if the noise of wheels trundling through the town was to be a permanent feature of their lives. Old Mullen had pulled off a coup in securing the contract and as well as his own teams he had men sub-contracting to him from all over the barony. "It's not that, Tom. It's just if I could see John in charge of the job I wouldn't mind at all. I can't get used to the idea that he isn't around to handle the horses. And the sergeant – I was sorry to see him go."

"Aye, I know what you mean." The young man, though little more than a boy, caught a glimpse of what he meant. Time sundered friendships and things were never the same again. "You know the sergeant and meself are partners now. We have full ownership of the schooner."

"I heard that. What do ye intend to do with her?"

"I'll fix her up and put a skipper on her. She'll do well enough in the coastal trade."

"But what about the sergeant?" He wondered if there was any chance of him coming back. It would be good to see him again. The sergeant had had a kind of feeling for the place and for boats and the sea. Maybe he could bring back some of the old times like when the town had still been theirs.

"He told me to look after everything and manage his share till I heard from him. If there's any money due to him I'll bank it with me da. He knows about money. I'd say he'll get out of the army soon enough and I'll probably buy his share out. Soldiers don't settle down for long."

"I wouldn't be too sure about any o'that. They say there'll be more trouble in France. They don't like their new king all that much an' they don't like the British bayonets that's keepin' him there."

"Well I hope the sergeant makes up his mind fairly soon one way or the other."

"A dacent lad he was. Not like the usual run. He took John's death very bad." A silence descended between them, each busy with his thoughts. Tom coughed, sensing the old man's gloom. "They tell me Eileen is in better form these days."

"Aye. She's started goin' out again. I'm glad to say. She does be doin' tallyman somedays for the oul man and drivin' herself and the childer around in the trap." They paused again watching with interest as the team of horses turned on the narrow pier with the now unloaded wagon. Gently does it. There was no room for rearing or kicking in the confined space. The operation was concluded without mishap.

"I'm glad to hear that, but she should be more careful. Isn't there a baby on the way soon?" Tom had always admired Eileen, from the days when she had worked in his parents' shop. She had always managed to slip him a little treat when his mother chased him from behind the counter.

"Next month or thereabouts so they say, but I wouldn't know much about them matters."

"Do ye not call at the house these days? Ye might do yerself a bit o' good there with Mrs Eavers." Tom grinned slyly to himself. Skip gave a little chuckle, his mood improving. "Be the jings she's a fine woman but the oul memory isn't what it was. I wouldn't know what to do if I got a hoult of her."

"I'll bet you'ld think o' somethin' soon enough," laughed Tom.

"To tell the truth I'd be more afraid of that woman than I was of Pether Howlett an' his gun. I haven't been near the place but I do meet Eileen now an' again in the street. She'll be all right but the laughter has gone out of her all the same."

"Still an' all she's done well to come through her troubles like she did."

There was no denying that.

But it wasn't quite as simple as all that. Activity wasn't the solution to everything, although it helped to keep her mind off things. She was glad to be able to help the old man in whatever way she could. She helped him to keep his books in order and relayed his instructions to the men at the quarry or at the harbour. Gradually she began to feel that she was coming to be regarded as his representative and the men began to defer to her. She began to enjoy driving her pony and trap with the children beside her and the sharp winter air began to bring the colour into her cheeks. Her mother was anxious that she should not overdo things and went in constant fear of her taking a tumble. She had visions of premature labour somewhere in the ditch on the Balcunnin road but she knew that there was little use in talking. She would stay for a while after the baby and then go back to Balcunnin herself. Eileen would manage all right without her.

Eileen did however worry about the baby. Could the shock have harmed him? It was still to be a boy. Worse still, are the sins of the parents really visited on the child? If so it was a strange God who would afflict the innocent for the crimes of the guilty. Was it wrong to think like that? Was it tempting fate? She knew that she should go to the priest and ask forgiveness for her sin. And do you repent of your sin my child? No. Where was the point in that? And have you a purpose of amendment? No. If he came back tomorrow I would go on my knees to him. But he won't ever come back. He has forgotten by now. No, the sin was not loving the stranger. It was in turning away from John and still wanting the other man even while John was dying. How do I confess that? No priest would understand or give absolution for that. There must be a punishment reserved for people who throw away what is good in a selfish search for something they hope will be better. The punishment must be to have everything taken away. All right God, whoever You are, do what You want to with me but please let the baby be well. She realised that she was not in a very strong bargaining position. If only there was someone she could talk to but nobody in the world must ever know.

Once or twice she met old Skip Garrigan in the street, maybe outside the shop in the square or at the yard. She was glad to see an old friend and his pleasure at seeing her looking better was evident. He was, in a way, a link with the past. "By the way," he had said on one occasion, "Pether Howlett asked me to give you his best regards and asked me to see if there was anythin' I could do for ye." Her heart thumped with alarm at the mention of the name. Had he said anything else? She set her face into what she imagined to be a noncommital expression, a mask of impassivity. "That was kind of him." Maybe you could raise his child for him or give me back my husband, she thought bitterly. "He was a nice man in his way." And he was in his way. There was no point or release in bitterness. It had come involuntarily. But still she wondered if that had salved his conscience. Did it wipe everything out to say, Oh by the way, see if you can do anything, there's a good fellow, and walk away? Did he toss you a guinea for your pains? No, that wasn't fair and not fair to Skip. Skip was as astute a businessman as you could meet, but nobody, least of all Peter Howlett, would be so crass as to insult him with a guinea for his trouble. She must not give way to blaming others. "Thank you Skip. You've always been a good friend to us and I know I can turn to you at any time." The old man blushed with pleasure and pride. He would have given his life for her at that moment and cheerfully too. Without guile or calculation she could draw people to her and even malice turned its point aside when confronted by her gaze, he thought but lacked the words to express his perception.

Eileen felt like a hypocrite. If only people knew how false appearances were! No one would walk on the same side of the street as she. Even her family would turn away from her in shame. Her own children would recoil from her.

Skip removed his cap, an infrequent occurrence. "Good day to ye Eileen. I must go and haul me cages. We can't all be pullin' the town apart." She watched him going on his way, his shoulders stooped with age and she felt a surge of affection towards him. She owed something to friends like Skip. She could not let them down. People are entitled to their illusions.

"Let me explain to you what they're about father." Balcunnin took the priest by the arm and conducted him through the piles of rock that littered the floor of the quarry. The priest called Rufus to heel sharply, with no visible success. "Don't worry about him. There's no blasting today. No harm can come to him." Father Clare threw up his hands. "I had hoped to make a gun dog of him but he had contracted too many bad habits by the time he came to me." The dog went foraging again through the rockpiles sniffing excitedly and wagging his tail. Men were working in groups, some breaking stones for road metal and others levering boulders into position for raising onto the wagons. They stopped as the two men approached and raised their caps respectfully to the peer and to the priest.

"Now do you see the new face that's been opened." Balcunnin pointed to the fresh scar of bare rock.

"Yes. I suppose that's where all the stone for the church is to come from."

"Not quite. My engineer tells me that the first twenty feet or so is no good for anything but the roads. Too much faulting. Here he is now, let him explain." A tall thin man in his fifties or thereabouts was coming hastily towards them. He was covered with a fine film of white dust which accentuated the wrinkles on his weatherbeaten face. "Ah Gorman, I want you to meet Father Clare, an important customer of ours. Gorman came to me at short notice," he added by way of explanation.

"Good day to you father," the engineer touched his cap. "I've been looking at the drawings for your church and I think we have just the thing for it."

"We are in your hands Mr Gorman," said the priest. "You have built churches before, I take it."

"Aye, I have but not so many for your persuasion. This will make a change for me." He smiled briefly. "Now do you see that layer of dark grey about twenty foot down. That's what I intend to give you."

"I see," the priest nodded.

"Aye, dark blue-grey, that's what I like for churches. Dress that right and it will stand for a thousand years. Though I prefer granite, so long as they don't put fiddly little borders of sandstone all around it." A personal prejudice obviously.

"Well I don't know a lot about that," admitted the priest. "Will there be enough?"

"Ah yes, the layer gets wider as we work eastward, no problem at all. We'll have it all dressed here and put your church up in no time at all."

"And the sea wall, Gorman? Is there sufficient for that?"

"No doubt about it me lord. We're taking the pier from over there." He pointed to the looming dark wall of the west side," but we'll face it from the best stone and the sea wall too as well as the ashlar for the church. Any amount of it."

"You know your own business best, Gorman. I suggest we leave you to it."

"If you gentlemen would care to wait we'll be blasting in about half an hour. I'm speeding things up a bit to get the masons started."

"Splendid," said the peer. "You know Osgood would have enjoyed this."

"Osgood? Oh yes, the artillery man. Have you heard anything of him since he left us sir?"

"Not exactly, father, but I gather that there is quite a concentration of our forces in the Low Countries. They are afraid of hostilities starting up again."

Gorman came back from where he had been shouting instructions to the men on the cliff face. "We'd do well to move back gentlemen. The charges are in position." The men were descending, spider-like by means of ropes. A bugle sounded and the area was cleared. The watchers moved back and the priest found himself standing beside Eileen Mullen. He nodded to her and she smiled at him but he had turned back, anxious not to miss the show. "Look at the dog," cried somebody as the sparks of the fuses began to climb the face of the rock. Of course it was Rufus sniffing along the base of the cliff following some erratic trail. A chorus of shouts and whistles greeted him and he stopped to listen, wagging his tail in pleasure. The priest started forward but hands gripped his sleeves. "Rufus, Rufus," he cried but his voice was drowned by a dull rumbling as the charges exploded. The ground trembled under their feet and the upper section of the cliff began to bulge like a brick wall coming apart. The people watched, hypnotised by the scene but Rufus had realised the danger. With the acceleration of a greyhound and his tail between his legs he streaked for safety as the massive blocks hurtled downwards. Within seconds he was clear and heading for the delighted crowd. He lost his footing once or twice but was back on his feet immediately, never pausing until he had gained the safety of the crowd. Father Clare, with uncharacteristic demonstrativeness, knelt down and put his arms around the dog. The animal trembled and its skin twitched in spasmodic ripples. The priest laughed in relief and looked up to find himself face to face with Eileen.

"That was close father."

"Aye. You don't get many chances like that. Ah Rufus what am I going to do with you?"

Eileen straightened and suddenly a spasm of pain went through her body. It was time. "Excuse me, father, I must go." She moved awkwardly and heavily and the pain hit her again. "Can you help me to the trap?" she said quietly. "There isn't much time." The priest guided her unobtrusively through the group of men. She would not want to draw attention to herself in front of the men. Gorman nodded to him, "It's crowbar work from now on, father," he said incongruously. "We don't want to damage it too much." The stone of course. He hoped Eileen hadn't noticed his puzzled expression. He'd He offered a silent prayer and slapped the pony into a steady trot. painfully into the trap. He offered to drive her and she did not refuse. What a predicament! He felt sweat breaking out on his forehead. If I go too fast I may precipitate matters; too slow and I may be too late. He olffered a silent prayer and slapped the pony into a steady trot. Every bump on the road, every lurch of the wheels went through him. He could feel his stomach contracting with every jolt. "Don't worry Mrs Mullen. We're nearly there," but he was not convinced. The road stretched before him league after league and with difficulty he refrained from increasing the pace. Eileen sat gripping the brass rail, each spasm of pain registering on her face but she said not a word. 'In pain shall she bring forth children' – but why must I be there to witness it? That was a cowardly thought. It was his duty to help those in distress, not run away.

"Oh father hurry, please." It was the first thing she had said in almost two miles.

"Hang on Mrs Mullen. Have no fear. I've brought more babies into the world . . . " It was only a small lie and with God's grace he would not have to admit it. He tried a smile of encouragement, a ghastly rictus which moved Eileen to laughter which in turn caused another searing contraction. This baby was impatient to come into the world. No shipwrecked mariner clinging to a spar ever saw land come into view with more gratitude than the priest hailed the cottage on the Kybe. Salvation at last. Mrs Eavers was at the door as if by instinct. "Let's get her inside Father if you please. Have the waters broken?"

"The waters? I don't know."

"Not you father. Oh never mind. We'll get her to bed." Now that Eileen was safe Father Clare took command again. There was nothing to be alarmed about. "Look after things here Mrs Eavers and I'll send for the doctor."

"Doctor is it? And what would I need doctors for? Take the childer out of here and get me Nora Donovan and be quick about it". It wasn't often you got the chance to order the priest about but he went and quickly too. Nora bustled past him at her door. "Will you watch these childer, father, till we're finished?" There was nothing else for it. The women had taken over and he was relegated to the more mundane tasks without any recognition of the fact that he alone, singlehanded had brought her two miles of the road. Let no one forget that, he thought in pique. So he watched the small Mullens and the small Donovans rolling on the floor and squabbling as children do and was moved to bless his bachelor status. Childbirth was a momentous thing but the ensuing years must be a process of attrition on the fabric of the home and the strength of the parents. Was there no end to the energy of these little . . . he groped for the word, his patience wearing thin. Perhaps one could entertain them with conversation but that did not work. A defensive action was the best ploy. Prevent actual bloodshed, particularly his own. And there a few yards away another child was coming into the world. It was so sad really, the poor woman without a husband to help her or to acknowledge the infant.

The pains had gripped Eileen and were coming relentlessly in waves of indescribable agony with blessed moments of release. She gripped the bars of the bed and pushed. Damn you Howlett. God damn you to hell for this. She focussed on the rafters. It was interesting the way the grain ran crossways in the wood. A blinding curtain of red pain and the womens' voices coming from somewhere and she cried out in relief. A cold wet cloth on the forehead. Was there ever anything so welcome and her mother smiling with tears running down her face. She held the baby, wet and shining with patches of bright blood on the head which she was wiping with a warm wet cloth.

"It's a little boy, love."

"Of course it's a little boy! Didn't I tell him it would be a little boy." Oh God, where are you now Howlett? "Let me see him." The baby gave a hacking cry and the grandmother wrapped him quickly in a cloth and laid him beside her, a little sallow fellow with black hair and blue eyes which stared up at her knowingly. I wish John was here to see him. He always had a softness for babies. The baby frowned and puckered his tiny mouth, wrinkling the white lips in puzzlement. Nora was gazing down at him. "He's beautiful Eileen," and her eyes glistened. "He is, isn't he?" she agreed. She was tired and wanted to see the baby's father but he was not there. "I wish John was here Mam," she said weakly. "Aye love, but we'll look after ye. Nora would you make a cup o' tea and I'll tidy up here. Then ye can have a little rest." She began to busy herself with clean sheets and towels. "And Nora I suppose ye'd better go and inform his reverence beyond."

"A boy," the priest exclaimed. "I knew we'd do it," and he swelled with pride. "A fine son to carry the family name. Great news Mrs Donovan. May I go and offer my congratulations?" Nora led the way but Eileen was already asleep with the infant in the crook of her arm. Mrs Eavers put her finger to her lips and the priest silently made the sign of the cross over the sleeping pair. "Thank you Father for all your help," whispered the grandmother, "We couldn't have managed without you." Father Clare strode homeward briskly, swinging his cane. If his chest protruded just a little more than usual, it was in justifiable pride. Rufus emerged from nowhere and fell in behind him. They made a striking pair.

CHAPTER 22

The first day of March 1815 broke bright and clear. It was the day, according to tradition, when the crows began to build and the trees around the old church resounded to their raucous cries as last year's bedraggled nests were furbished for the new brood. From their perilous vantage points the crows could see what events of moment were going on, the wagons straggling down from Balcunnin, the occasional sail making for the harbour or Master Peter James Mullen travelling in style to the chapel to be christened, the latest addition to the parish family. They could see his god-parents, Larry and Nora Donovan driving proudly in the trap and splashing flamboyantly through the little stream, bearing their tiny charge like a small bundle of washing in his immaculate white christening robe.

The crows however could not see how the ceremony was conducted by Father Clare, beaming in avuncular fashion as he expelled Satan from the infant in sonorous and resounding Latin. Oil and salt sealed the bargain and Father Clare commented approvingly on the excellent choice of names. Peter was of course the rock, denoting constancy and firmness of character, appropriate to his own behaviour on the day this infant was born, though this thought he kept to himself.

Another event beyond the view of the crows on that fateful day was the landing of just over a thousand men from a small flotilla at Cap d'Antibes in the south of France. There were men of the Old Guard, some Polish lancers with saddles but no horses and some Corsican and Elban volunteers. Their leader, a low sized rather portly figure wore a red, white and blue cockade in his hat. He attempted to make a short speech but the cheers of the wildly enthusiastic little army drowned his words. The Emperor had returned to claim his own.

Had they been able to witness these comic-opera goings on it is doubtful whether the crows would have done anything other than continue with their vital task while protesting harshly at being disturbed by the march of history. They protested loudly enough at the Donovans returning from the chapel, clattering over the cobblestones, sending the birds flapping into the air like tattered black rags but soon they alighted again in their windy colony and resumed their work.

There was the necessity of wetting the baby's head and neighbours felt obliged to come in and take a drop or two and wish him luck. It was good for Eileen to be busy attending to them and for a time it had the makings of a good party but at that time of day people had too many things to do to think of settling in. Larry reluctantly acceded to his wife's suggestion that they leave people to get on with their business and go home. He was in the mood for a chat and a few jars. It had been a long time since there had been any fun at all in Mullens' and he felt the whiskey putting a fine edge on his justly renowned wit. The best he could manage however was a lewd wink to all and sundry as Nora extricated him from the company and a thinly veiled suggestion that the baby had put the longin' on her. And so with reputation intact, Larry went home, hands in pockets and whistling to show that nobody ordered Larry Donovan around.

Now what the hell was wrong? The skilled observer can detect an atmosphere in a house before he even crosses the threshold. There was something about the way the knife flashed as she cut up the big potatoes and slung them into the black pot. There is a menacing ring to the way a spud hits the pot on an occasion like this. Play for time. See if any o' the childer are around as a kind of buffer. The knife chopped again and a half potato spiralled off the table onto the floor. "Begod missus but aren't we well off to be throwin' the good food away." Nothing like a little joke to lighten the atmosphere, thought Larry, bending to pick it up. He straightened his back. The knife-point pricked his throat just under the chin. Jasus, she's gone mad. The fumes of alcohol vanished in the cold blast of fear. She's lost her wits this time. Nora's eyes were blazing and Larry felt the sweat breaking out on his brow. There was a crawling sensation in his groin. "What in the name o' God?"

"Oh, you're the funny man all right." She swallowed, almost incoherent with fury. "You're the funny man Larry Donovan."

It was sad. The injustice of it. "What have I done now for Christ's sake? I only had the couple o' drinks." The knife point moved and Larry drew back in relief but he watched her warily. Women are queer fish and no doubt. "All right. Maybe I shouldn't 'a said that about puttin' the longin' on ye." He spread his hands, appealing to an invisible jury. "Vulgar, is that what you're thinkin'?"

"That's not it at all but you're too stupid even to remember."

"What in the name o' Jasus are ye on about? Wasn't I politeness itself and me in me official capacity? Sure haven't godfathers got certain privileges. And havin' a few jars on the babby's head is one o' them." Case proved.

Nora sighed. "You are an eejit. Your mouth runs away with ye after a few drinks." She spoke slowly and emphatically as if explaining to the simple minded. Larry's heart sank. There was more to this than met the eye. "Right so. What did I say?" Nora looked at him. He would insult a lifelong friend rather than forego a well turned quip but there was no ingrained malice in the man. He suffered from being a recognised character, obliged to trot out the chat on all occasions. He had sunk dejectedly onto a stool. Nobody appreciated Larry Donovan. "What did I say?" The clown's mask was gone.

"Nothin' much. Just remarked on your godson's colour and asked Eileen if she'd been talkin' to some Lascar off a schooner."

"Oh Christ." His shoulder drooped further.

"Or maybe one o' the soldiers." Her voice crackled like breaking ice. Larry looked up with the eyes of a drowning man.

"Aw Jasus, Nora, it was only a joke."

"A joke is it? Did ye take a good look at the child ye stupid man?"

"Of course I looked at the child. What do ye mean did I look at the child?"

"Now listen to what I'm sayin' and don't ever let a word of it outside these four walls." She's definitely mad. Larry looked at her and began to understand. "Ah now Nora . . ."

"That child is the sergeant's bastard, as sure as I'm standin' here. For God's sake just look at him."

Larry shook his head. It couldn't be true – and yet . . . He tried to imagine the infant with a black moustache. Right enough. A grin of astonishment began to spread across his face. "Well, be the holy fly." He rose and looked out through the small square of window. "Be the holy fly. That explains –" He wasn't sure what it explained. he sat down again exhausted by the act of comprehension. "Be the holy." He gave vent to a small chuckle of appreciation. "Wasn't she the dark one?"

"That's right. Laugh. It'll make a grand story for your cronies, won't it."

Be God but she's fierce when she's riz. "Ah now Nora. Ye don't think I'd go around spreadin' that kind o' talk about Eileen do ye?" What kind of a friend did she take him for?

"No I don't Larry and will I tell ye why? Because if ye did I'd come after ye with this knife." The blade flicked dangerously close to his face again. "And it's not your face you'd have to worry about. I swear to ye Larry Donovan, on me own mother's grave, that you'll never bed me or any other woman neither if ye breathe a word about this to a sinner. Do ye get me drift?" Larry shifted uncomfortably on the stool. He got her drift all right. "And just one other thing while I'm about it. I've had a few good laughs with you Larry but this is one subject that isn't for laughin' about – here or anywhere else."

Larry swore inwardly that drunk or sober he would never be the one to draw attention to Eileen Mullen's sallow faced baby. After all what else are friends for but to protect the good name? He paced the room again. My godson, he thought. A dig in the mouth is what they'd get if they make remarks about my godson. By God they would and no mistake. "You're right Nora." He flexed his arms, prepared for action. "We'll have none o' that class o' talk while I'm around. Just refer them to me". Larry was in command again. Still it was a queer one all the same.

So the baby throve and no one put any pass on him to Eileen's relief. He lay comfortably in the fold of her shawl when she went out of doors and people stopped to admire him and say how well she was looking. Mrs Eavers made guarded references to overdoing things and getting her strength back and Eileen knew well what she meant. Eventually the priest came again, not so much in his avuncular as in his pastoral role. She had been expecting him for some time but she still was not sure what to say.

"Mrs Mullen, it's fresh and well you're looking; and how are the children?"

"They're well father, like meself, and thank you for asking."

"I was just hoping you weren't overdoing things too soon."

There it was again. "No, not a bit of it father. I like to be busy and the fresh air does the children good."

"Quite so, quite so. It's just that you don't really get your strength back till you've been properly churched." There was a silence.

"Well the way it is father, I was thinking I wouldn't get churched this time at all."

"And why not?" There was an edge to his voice. "Didn't you go after the other two?"

"Well that should be enough then," she replied as if the matter was closed. The priest felt a pulse throbbing in his temple. Calmly now. Who did this young woman think she was to dictate which of the Church's practices she would accept and which she would not? "And don't you think Eileen, that you should go and give thanks for this fine little son?" Put like that she could hardly object.

"I give thanks for him father, and for the fact that he is strong and healthy but I won't kneel outside your chapel again like some dirt off the street waiting to be purified." Her voice rose perceptibly and an angry flush came to her cheeks. "Where are the fathers then? I don't see them on their knees bein' cleansed." She gave the word an ironic emphasis.

"It's not like that Eileen," but he was thrown off balance by her vehemence. "Maybe in St Paul's time they talked about vessels of impurity but not nowadays."

She interrupted: "Saving your presence father, you're a man. You wouldn't understand."

This was too much. "Indeed I do not. You choose to set yourself up against the age old practice of the Holy Church. This cannot be allowed."

"Like all men," she retorted. "They can do what they like with us and then go off." Her voice broke with bitterness. "They just go off and it's all a joke to them, a laugh with their friends. Go and church them and then come back to me."

"I can see that you are blind to your error at the moment" said the priest stiffly. "I will pray that your eyes may be opened."

"Aye do that. Pray me off the altar if you like, like any whore." She rounded on him. His complacent certainties infuriated her. "But answer me this, when did you ever pray for any man, any stinking sailor off the colliers that can buy a young girl with a shillin' or any pox-ridden soldier?"

There was no tolerating this. Even if the woman had had a hard time she could not be allowed to insult the cloth with that kind of language. "Mrs Mullen, when you return to your senses I'll expect an apology and then we'll arrange the matter of your churching."

"Father Clare. I'll cope with my own impurity if you don't mind. You must pray for more charity." She intended no insolence. "There's two sides to every question you know."

Father Clare took his departure with feathers considerably ruffled. The impertinence of the woman! He had never encountered anything like it before. Obviously she was in need of prayer. He had a good mind to – but perhaps it was the result of being left on her own. He relented but only for a while of course. He would use the threat of public prayer at the appropriate time. Something in what she had said perplexed him for days afterwards but he could not put his finger on it. It was ridiculous to suggest that he lacked charity but there could be no compromise with disobedience. What had she meant about the fathers going away? John Mullen was dead and buried. He would have to go back to St Paul for guidance. He put the matter aside and thought about his sermon. Perhaps the renewed threat of war with France could supply him with a starting point. The reports from France were suitably apocalyptic. The beast had come forth from his lair in no uncertain terms. It would be a good theme to remind sinners that we know not the hour.

The chasuble made a pleasing swish as he turned from the altar and placed his hands on the lectern. With God's grace he would soon have a proper pulpit from which to expound the word of the Lord. He swept the congregation with his gaze. "In the Name of the Father." The hands moved in unison, "and of the Son." He looked directly into the eyes of Eileen Mullen. She sat with her mother and children watching him calmly. Her eyes contained neither fear nor mockery but there was a challenge there. He faltered for a second; "and of the Holy Ghost," and he knew that this was no ordinary sinner to be beaten back into the ways of righteousness with blackthorn stick or threats of public humiliation. Something was troubling her, he knew, but it must not be driven underground. It must be allowed to find its way out in its own time and he must do what he could to help. "Amen" replied the people and he began to speak.

It always seemed to be raining in Belgium. Even a day that gave every appearance of starting fine could turn suddenly to a succession of torrential downpours leaving the newly ploughed land like a seething morass. To Howlett, nothing much had changed since his first time in the Low Countries almost twenty years before when a British expedition had, with the greatest difficulty, extricated itself from a similar quagmire. His abiding memory of that time was of rain and misery and he hoped with all his heart that the experience would not be repeated.

It was certain that there would be action at some stage but most assumed that it would be an invasion of France. Nothing else made sense and it was hardly likely that Napoleon, although restored to power, would be in any position to take the offensive for a very long time yet. Certainly there was no air of urgency in the cantonments and bivouacs of the variegated army of the Prince of Orange. How else could a situation have arisen where the horse artillery sent to stiffen his forces could allow the teams to be separated from their guns by some administrative whim? Nowhere in his experience could Howlett recall such a rag-bag force so ineptly led. The few Peninsular veterans regarded the rest of the Anglo-Dutch force with tolerant amusement laced with a little graveyard humour.

It was some consolation to Howlett to know that Captain Osgood was attached to the staff with responsibility for mapping and surveying the area as a likely theatre of operations. At least one officer in that top heavy collection of aristocrats and minor princelings knew what he was about. Less reassuring was the presence of young Thurston in his gun crew, still yearning after the glory that had eluded him on the draughty coast of north Fingal. Old Bateson was there too, still as stolid and resigned as ever, with no particular desire to be anywhere else as long as the army would have him.

He found that he was impatient for the situation to resolve itself one way or another. Action would cauterise the festering sore inside him and give him an identifiable enemy on whom he could work off the rage that consumed him. The dull routine of inactivity corroded his spirit driving him in upon himself, hating his own sense of helplessness. By now he knew he was father of a child who would never know him and would probably be brought up to resent him by a mother who never wanted to see him again. There must be some way by God, that he could take his revenge on her for turning away and blotting him out. No, revenge was not the word. It was not revenge to want to be part of her life in some way and to do something for his own child. In a way it was the only chance he had for survival. The schooner! He had hardly thought of it for months. He could sign over his share to the child. It was no use to him now. At least it would be something. He wondered what the child might look like. Was it a boy? She had been so sure. Perhaps it was a girl, a copy of the mother. He had no name to cling to to help him form a picture. He determined to see to it at once.

He stepped out into the incessant rain, his boots squelching in the rutted track of the village. In civilian life 'soaked to the skin' was a condition to be remedied at the earliest opportunity whereas to a soldier it was a constant state. A kind of warmth was generated when the inner layers became saturated and clung to the body, steaming under the uniform coat. In this weather there was no point in longing for the luxury of a dry shirt or stockings. Liberal quantities of cheap Dutch gin however went a long way towards keeping out the weather. He ducked in under the broad overhanging farmhouse eaves and knocked on the door. The rain fell in a curtain behind him and he shivered. The door was opened by a large French-Belgian woman who looked at his bedraggled appearance without any visible sign of friendship. "Captain Osgood?" She nodded, not deigning to address the foreigner. Osgood had remarked that most of the population were more Bonapartist than the French themselves and had no great love for their liberators. She gestured towards an inner room from which came the murmur of English voices.

Captain Osgood, as always, was examining one of a bundle of maps spread out on the rough kitchen table. Several officers stood around a large metal stove. Their uniforms were more flamboyant than Osgood's and they were obviously not particularly interested in his maps or in the sergeant who was removing his cap as he ducked under the low ceiling beams. "Sir," began Howlett "I come to ask for your advice."

"Yes of course sargeant. I'm sure I can spare you a minute. Let us walk into the other room. These gentlemen, I'm sure, can spare us for a little while." There was no sarcasm in his voice, just a tinge of irony. "Now what can I do for you on this auspicious day?"

"Auspicious, why auspicious sir?" It was not a word Howlett used very often.

"Why, haven't you heard the news? We have a new commander in chief."

Howlett looked again for sarcasm. "No sir, I haven't heard anything." Probably another outrageous prince or duke or some such.

"Wellington, man. Old Nosey himself is to take command of the army. That should please an old Spanish hand like yourself, I imagine."

The great duke himself. This was too good to be true. Surely this must mean that they would march into France. All the world would watch the contest between the two greatest men of the age. Howlett was almost speechless. He felt a twinge of dark foreboding. There must be a war now and this lent a new urgency to his errand. "In a way, sir, I came about the possibility of war."

"Rest assured sergeant, we shall see a battle that will decide the fate of the world." Momentous words.

"I want to make my will sir. I would be obliged to you for some paper and a pen and your signature as witness."

"A will, sergeant? That's a gloomy thought on this day of great news."

"It's important to me sir all the same. There are some things I would like to dispose of."

"Of course, of course. As far as within me lies I shall act as your executor but remember, I may perish in whatever cataclysm is coming too." He laughed to dispel the look of concern on the younger man's face. "I'm joking of course. We elevated personages of the staff bear charmed lives. Paper and pen then and I'll leave you to it."

"I'm no great hand at writing sir. Perhaps you could give me some guidance as to what to say."

"Yes, yes, let me see." The captain spread a sheet in front of him. "I'll jot down the main outlines and you can fill in the details." Howlett settled down at the table and addressed himself to the task. It was a long time since he had laboured so hard over any document and his tongue moved involuntarily as he formed the letters. The metal nib snagged occasionally sending little spurts of ink across the white surface, like tiny black shrapnel bursts on the page. He was aware of the scratching sound in the silent room and of the officer watching him unobtrusively. A jug on the table wobbled with each movement of his wrist. Osgood perused the document, nodding in understanding and signed his name underneath. "You may want to add a codicil sergeant. An additional clause or two," he explained to Howlett's blank look. "Oh I see. Yes. I'll write a letter to accompany this." He bent his head again to the task and Osgood tactfully withdrew. It was half an hour before he reappeared and Howlett handed him an envelope. The Captain's name was written on it in a spidery hand and the instruction to forward the contents to his lordship of Balcunnin if anything should befall the undersigned P. Howlett Sgt.

"I shall see that it doesn't go astray sergeant." The captain returned with animation to the subject of their new commander. "You've served under him before so you have the advantage of me. I'm afraid I am looked upon more as a surveyor than a gunnery officer nowadays so I don't expect to see much action except in the role of spectator." He sounded disappointed that he would not be an active participant in the great events.

"I wouldn't be too sure sir. His Grace has a way of involving his staff in the thick of battle. He likes to keep a close eye on things as I remember." Howlett did not like to see the older man looking dejected. He had grown to trust and like Osgood over the years. Osgood brightened at these words. "You would be advised sir, to keep a good horse under you at all times."

"You are attached to G troop, I understand," mused the captain. "That's Mercer's lot. He'll give you a lively time, given half a chance."

"Anything would be better than this damned rain sir. It must be interfering with your work too."

"It is indeed, sergeant. I have instructions to survey south of Brussels as far as Ligny and insofar as is possible bring our maps up to date but it has proved very difficult. So far I have only ventured south to Quatre Bras a couple of miles down the road."

"I'm sure Captain Mercer would have no objection to releasing some of us to lend a hand. It would be like old times again." Osgood smiled at the memory. "Except for the fossils," he said, "and the bird. No thank you sergeant. It's not chain and staff surveying at this stage. Just checking those odd looking French maps with their peculiar scales." He grimaced with the distaste of a purist in such matters. "There wouldn't be time to draw up our own."

"Very good sir. It was just a thought. And thank you for the help with my letters." He replaced his cap and saluted. Osgood returned his salute. "I'll bear in mind what you said about a good horse." He returned to his work. By all accounts His Grace expected instant answers to questions and maps to be up to date. He felt satisfaction at the thought that somebody appreciated his skills and expertise sufficiently to have asked for him.

CHAPTER 23

Captain Mercer gave them a lively time as predicted. With the dexterity of a skilled boxer the Emperor feinted to the East and then struck northwards towards Brussels, leaving Ney with two army corps to pound the Anglo-Dutch force into the mud of Quatre Bras, while he himself engaged the much more formidable Prussians. By the late afternoon of June the 16th the gunners had seen enough blood and glory to last them a lifetime. Thurston, black-faced from powder smoke, whooped with excitement, scarcely waiting for the shot to be discharged before leaping forward with his sponge. Bateson, calm as always rammed the charges home, cannister or grape as directed, to scythe down the men and horses that came against them in wave after wave. The air reverberated to the thunder of the guns and to the groans of the dying men. Horses kicked and screamed in pools of blood or blue-green skeins of their own entrails.

The Emperor's beautiful daughters, his twelve pounders, took an horrendous toll of the red-coated infantry and cavalry as they arrived in haste along the narrow Brussels road and took up their positions amid the waist high corn. Again and again the waves of brilliantly coloured imperial uniforms broke on the isolated farm buildings and washed backwards in a welter of smoke and flame. By nightfall the exhausted armies drew apart, tacitly agreeing to a draw and those who could, lit fires to cook something hot for themselves, while others were content to gnaw on whatever came to hand. Wagon loads of wounded began the long journey to Brussels, too long a journey for many whose bodies were left by the roadside. Surgeons plied their grisly trade in the mud of the campsites, working by lantern and candle, cutting, extracting lumps of iron from torn flesh and stitching together what was left where the patient did not succumb under the shock.

The arrival of this sorry procession in the city was to provoke a panic among the civilian populace where the rumour ran that Wellington had been annihilated. As the creaking wagons and the long file of stumbling bandaged men entered the city from the south a stream of refugees began to pour along the road to the coast, looking fearfully over their shoulders in the full expectation of seeing Ney's cuirassiers thundering up the road with murder in their hearts.

In truth many of Ney's fine horsemen had found their metal breast-plates and crested helmets no protection against musket balls or Colonel Shrapnel's shells. The Marshal himself smarted under a wounding reprimand from his emperor. Tomorrow would be his last opportunity to save France and his own honour. He looked towards the dark ridge behind which the enemy lay. Green lightning flickered on the horizon. Tomorrow he would overcome, if he had to lead every charge himself.

Wrapped in his blanket under the limber, Peter Howlett dozed through the short summer darkness. He would have welcomed a wash and a shave more than anything else but the effort was too much. Without a fire the chill of the night air penetrated to the bone and he shivered uncontrollably at times. The cold matched his spirits admirably. He had seen men die that day and had emerged unscathed. He had fought like a machine, caring nothing for his safety and yet, amid the storm of shot, he had not sustained so much as a nick. The thought struck him as odd when he reflected that men who had valued their lives sufficiently to cower from the cannonade had been blown apart or skewered by lance or sabre. He took a nip from the gin bottle and passed it to the man beside him. The clear fiery liquid burned a comfortable track down into his belly.

Far away to the west in a long white cottage an exhausted and lonely young woman rocked her baby on her breast and waited anxiously for the dawn. The baby whimpered in the half light and struggled against her. He was feverish and would not feed. She saw the lightning flicker far out to sea and felt the atmosphere in the house growing close and sultry. There would be a storm, she knew, and longed for the rain to cool the air. Please God the child would be cooler too. She sponged his forehead with a damp cloth and he protested with small hacking cries. If only Mam was here, she thought, to help me. If only somebody was here to tell me that he will be all right. He was such a small mite to have to fight his way in the world so soon. The thunder grumbled its long-delayed answer to the flickering lightning. It was a long way off.

Retreat! It was unthinkable that the hero of Spain, the greatest of all the allied commanders would contemplate such a move. To the newcomers and raw recruits it seemed to bear out what they had heard at home. Wellington would only fight from a commanding position and with overwhelming forces. The gentlemen of the Opposition would have been on their feet, waving their order papers, clamouring for his dismissal yet again had they known his orders for June 17th. The veterans of Spain smiled knowingly, sharing a secret confidence. Don't worry, they implied, he knows what he's about.

In the chill morning air the Commander in Chief gave orders to his staff where they stood around a small brushwood fire. Many had spent the night in the open and were stamping to loosen their cramped limbs.

"Captain Osgood, let me have your excellent map." That diligent officer unfolded the appropriate sheet from his map case. It was annotated with the usual meticulous care. The dispositions of yesterday's battle had already been pencilled in. The Duke studied it approvingly. "This gentlemen, is our route and this is where we stand." He drew his thumb in a semi-circle from the Forest of Soignes across the Brussels road between the villages of Waterloo and the farm at La Haye Sainte. "I picked this site a year ago. Blucher will join us from here." He indicated the village of Wavre. "With his help we should make an end of the business tomorrow."

Osgood felt a flush of pleasure that his work should be so central to the campaign. He was pleased too that he had observed the advantages of the Waterloo ground from an artillery point of view but he knew better than to intrude his opinions.

"Have the men on the move by ten o'clock, artillery to the rear and some of those damned rockets but keep them away from me. Captain Osgood, have you reconnoitred anywhere along the route where my officers may get a decent lunch?"

"Yes Your Grace. As a matter of fact I have had occasion to enjoy the hospitality at *The King of Spain* in Genappe. I recommend the cold plate." Everybody laughed at the release of tension.

"Very likely beef on the menu for lunch and frogs' legs for dinner," remarked the Duke wryly.

The wagons rolled towards Brussels, many bearing a cargo of wounded. At first there was an air of haste but no panic and detachments jostled for space on the badly broken up road. Cavalry and infantry moved steadily across country trampling the ripening corn. The morning sun glinted on bayonets and helmet badges as the men strode doggedly along. Detachments of light dragoons swept back and forth guarding the rear and the guns jounced and jolted over the rutted ground. The Duke seemed to be everywhere. Accompanied by members of his staff he rode back and forth causing repeated ragged outbursts of cheering. Howlett saw him lounging by the roadside, stretched out on the grass verge, regaling his companions with choice snippets from the London newspapers. He recognised the characteristic raucous laugh and was pleased to recognise Osgood among the group. The retreat was well under way.

By early afternoon the sky had darkened. A massive thundercloud towered twenty thousand feet high dominating the scene. Like a great anvil it dwarfed all other natural objects and cast its inky shadow on the land. Briefly the sun picked out the silver of lances against the dark backdrop and the British guns wheeled into position and opened fire. The very sky seemed to reverberate and the thunder cloud released its pent up violence drenching both pursuers and quarry in a torrential downpour. Rockets described erratic patterns across the sky putting Osgood in mind of his idea for rescuing shipwrecked mariners. It did not look like such a feasible idea just then. No concerted engagement was possible in these conditions and the retreat continued in orderly fashion save at the rear where the march was interrupted by stoppages, rapid salvoes and then hitching up to plod onwards through the mud. In the downpour lancers and hussars collided, hacking blindly at each other, slipping and splashing in the soaking fields until the pursuit petered out and the artillery took over. But it was obvious that Napoleon had left it too late. By evening he knew that his empire would stand or fall on one last desperate gambler's throw. This enemy must be eliminated before the Prussians could reach them.

The rain continued and the thunder crashed overhead reducing the mightiest armies the world had ever seen to puny dimensions. Lightning turned night into eerie day and men crouched where they could, trying to rest. The air was warm and heavy and sleep came fitfully even to men who lay in inches of water.

Howlett sat on his pack with his back to the wheel of the gun. He had nothing to say to anyone. The lightning illuminated the silvery wet backs of the horses hobbled nearby. He thought of the waves breaking over Pompey. He could visualise Mullen's last glimpse of his horse's back in the moonlight. How long ago was that? It seemed a world away. And yet somewhere in that world there was part of him now, some small being to perpetuate him; someone to remind her of him forever. In this way he had never left. He nipped at his flask. The gin warmed his innards. He felt a kind of peace. If only he could know for sure about the child. He had done what he could and now even his own fate was out of his hands. Strangely he noticed that he no longer felt a sense of guilt. Neither did he resent her rejection. He wondered what he would say to her if he could see her just then. How could he encapsulate what he felt in a few phrases? She would never understand.

It must be because of the battle that he was giving way to these thoughts, or maybe the liquor. He realised that he had been talking out loud. If anyone had heard they would have assumed it was the gin, he told himself but in fact each man was too preoccupied with his own thoughts or his own misery to notice a poor soldier mumbling to himself as he faced the imminent prospect of meeting his Maker.

In the heat of the night Eileen sponged the little body with cold water. The doctor had said to keep him cool at all costs. There was nothing for it but to let the fever run its course. She swabbed under the arms and over the little heaving chest, hour after hour, while he protested with heart-rending sobs. Occasionally he drifted off into what seemed a comfortable sleep but at every sound, every distant rumble of thunder, he awoke, twitching convulsively with his eyes rolling upwards till only the whites could be seen. "Oh God," she prayed, recalling her prayers before he was born, "let him be all right." She thought of his father and prayed for him too. "I can't help it Lord. Wherever he is look after him." She asked nothing for herself.

Nora came soundlessly to help her, with Larry following close behind, his eyes showing large with concern in the candle light. Together they sat through the dead hours sponging and swabbing, walking the thin line between fever and chill, holding on desperately to the little struggling spirit. Larry, while no expert nurse, made encouraging sounds and longed for a drink for his parched throat, but still he stayed, not prepared to leave his godson to fight on his own. Jasus, he thought. Doctors, with their 'I'll look in tomorrow.' If you're not dead be then ye'll probably live anyway. The sweat broke out on his forehead as the little fellow twitched again and another convulsion began. Wordlessly he poured more cold water into the basin. Would this night never end?

It was a sight either to freeze or to stir the blood depending on your point of view. For several hours the rivers of brilliant uniforms had poured down the opposite slope, regiments that had conquered all Europe and had held the world at bay. They flowed downwards to the insistent drumming and the strident blasts of trumpets. Cheering resounded to the sky as they passed their emperor. On they swarmed, riflemen, infantry, chasseurs, guardsmen, dragoons, artillery until the rye fields were hidden by the host.

Answering them, the assorted allied regiments, less gorgeous perhaps in panoply, took up their positions in businesslike fashion, a chequerboard line of squares, bristling with bayonets, as yet unbroken in any conflict and a total of one hundred and fifty six guns, the pride of the English and Scottish armourers. By nightfall one third of a million men would decide the fate of the world in this bloody crucible.

A half an hour before noon the cannonade began. Lethal iron and lead descended on the allied lines and the British guns in emplacements all along the line roared in reply. Clouds of dense smoke obscured the field and the acrid smell of cordite pervaded the atmosphere, filling mens' lungs and stinging their eyes. The guns leaped on their carriages and sweating cursing men with mud plastered leggings, wrestled them back into position for the layers to find their targets. Men dropped where they stood in their squares and the ranks closed immediately as the bodies were dragged back inside. Gunners crumpled over their guns or sank to the ground torn apart by the whistling grape. Cannonballs tore through the corn like invisible, frenzied beasts, emerging to ricochet into the waiting ranks. Still the squares held. Not an inch was given under the appalling onslaught.

At La Haye Sainte the gunners, under Howlett, could see some distance away, the ferocity of the attack on Hougoumont. Wave after wave of variegated uniforms broke on this bastion in much the same manner as they had dashed themselves to pieces on the whitewashed farmhouses two days before. It seemed impossible that they would not carry the position but miraculously it held, draining the life from the French like a massive haemorrhage. As yet Howlett's men had experienced only the cannonade. The worst was to come. Ney had to avenge the failure at Quatre Bras and punch his way through the centre, breaking the back of Wellington's force.

A battery of over eighty guns opened up with renewed vigour on the British line which fell back to the reverse slope. La Haye Sainte, like Hougoumont, was now far forward of the line, an obstacle to be cleared out of the way of Ney's thunderous advance. On swarmed the dense phalanxes of gigantic infantrymen unchecked by the storm of cannister and grape, driving the small force of defenders back behind the walls and hastily thrown up breastworks, until it seemed that the position must surely be over run. Howlett's crews worked in a controlled frenzy, loading, ramming, firing, sponging, loading again, cutting swathes through the oncoming formations. It was an artist's dream, dark grey smoke thinning to sepia, white clouds from the incessant fusilades, uniforms, helmets gleaming against the green and blue of a Flanders summer and suddenly the flashing tartans of the Highlanders, hurling themselves upon the labouring Frenchmen as they fought their way uphill through the sucking, clinging mud.

From somewhere came the imperative sound of the charge, and like a roaring avalanche the heavy cavalry was upon them, imploding with irresistible force into infantry and lighter French cavalry. The French were borne back amid indescribable din until the hillside was cleared of all but the dead and wounded men and animals. On they thrust deeper and deeper into the heart of the emperor's army, the force diminishing as they were pulled down and overwhelmed. Only a pathetic number returned but they had dealt a terrible blow. Six thousand red uniformed men lay dead after this terrible onslaught and half as many again of the French littered the hillside and the valley below.

The gunners paused for a respite. The barrels were too hot to touch. Howlett wiped his face with his sleeve. Amazingly he was untouched. He grinned, showing his teeth, white in the smoke blackened face. Three of his gunners lay dead by the guns. Flies had begun to gather on the raw flesh of their wounds. Howlett rinsed his mouth from the canteen and spat. Thurston sat on an ammunition box, his head between his knees, coughing in racking paroxysms.

"How do you like this sport now lad?" Howlett felt elated by the action. His mind had cleared as if the smoke had acted as an astringent. Thurston looked up without reply. He could not catch his breath. He gave a feeble thumbs-up and struggled to his feet. There was a livid weal on his temple, a close one by the look of it. "Reckon us b'aint finished yet lads," interjected Bateson removing a strand of straw from his teeth. Thurston wiped his watering eyes. They peered down the rise at the distant French. "Still plenty o' they fellows below." Howlett laughed. He felt a surge of confidence. They had beaten off the most concerted attack of the day. "We're going to win lads. I guarantee that." There could only be one outcome.

The afternoon was bright. A fresh wind came off the sea. It tossed the curtains of the open window and the baby's fever broke. Eileen saw the perspiration break out on his forehead and the heaving of his chest eased perceptibly. The flush began to fade from his cheeks. She looked at Nora without a word. Her eyes were red and gritty with exhaustion but she knew that it was over. Thank you God, she thought. What else was there to say? She took up the child and dried the damp little body in a fresh towel. The convulsions had ceased and he looked at peace. It was like waking from a nightmare. The doctor had predicted it but she had not really believed him. Now it was true and he was going to be well. She felt her heart swelling with unbearable emotion. The baby turned his head to her, making little pecking motions with his mouth. He was hungry. With relief she unbuttoned her blouse and put him to her distended breast. The veins showed blue against the taut white skin. He began to feed ravenously. Hungry little bastard, she thought with an inward smile, just like his father. A feeling of peace came over her and she lay back in the chair and closed her eyes.

The French cannon erupted again with apocalyptic savagery. The sky was darkened by the smoke and the British and Allied ranks were decimated by the multiplicity of missiles that descended upon them. Cavalry moved forward, first at the trot and then at what passed for a gallop, lurching through the debris-strewn mud of the hillside. Dead and wounded were trodden underfoot as the British batteries replied. Hearing was reduced to a buzzing sound as firing rose to a crescendo. Through the confusion the horsemen saw to their delighted astonishment the unbelievable happening. The British gunners were running away; abandoning their guns and scurrying into the safety of the bristling infantry squares. It was as it always had been – the irresistible Napoleonic machine sweeping all before it. The guns were canted sideways, with wheels missing from their carriages – out of action. Volleys of musketry struck the riders, cutting them down. Horses impaled themselves on the hedges of bayonets but the squares did not give. The cavalry faltered, turned in confusion and began to fall back, driven downhill by the counterattacking British horse.

Gunners sprinted from the squares bowling the missing wheels before them. Howlett laughed like an urchin with a hoop. Amazingly the guns were untouched and within moments were pouring shot into the shattered and retreating columns. Madness had gripped the armies. Another attack was launched with the same impetuous courage. Again

Howlett's crews took refuge in the diminishing squares. All along the line the charge milled about. The carnage was frightful. The churned up earth turned red with blood. The onslaught faltered again and receded. Again the untouched guns came to bear on the retreating columns. It was clear to Howlett that Napoleon had lost. The initiative was slipping away from the French.

He knew that he could not be killed. He had been singled out to survive. Nothing would make sense if he did not go back to the woman who had borne his child. Like an unfinished rope ravels into an amorphous skein of useless fibres the very point of their existence would be lost if he did not go back. No presiding intelligence could allow such a thing. He strained like a greyhound on a leash, waiting to get back to his guns. Thurston broke from the square leaving his mates to trundle the wheel. Howlett saw the retreating dragoon riding the boy down. The horse struck him, sending him flying. Thurston struggled to his feet holding the rod of the sponge in front of him but the heavy sabre took him in the face, cleaving half his features away. He fell forwards without a cry.

Howlett reached the guns. A blind rage seized him. He swore at the crews as they righted the carriages and loaded again. His mind was consumed with the urge to destroy, to destroy the evil before him, to sweep the enemy from his path, to make the world safe for those he loved. After this there would be peace and he could go home. Eileen would understand why he had gone. He understood why she had to let him go but all that was in the past. The day was almost over. Victory would soon be theirs. The conquering hero. She would be so proud. He heard voices telling him to run, saw the anxious face of Bateson turned back towards him as the heavy-set fellow plodded to the rear. Just one more round of grape. He rammed it home and leaped back. Where in hell is the match?

He felt a blow on the back, just below the ribs and a searing pain shot through him. The blade of the lance protruded from his belly. He heard the crack as the shaft snapped and the horseman swept by. He clutched at the red, obscene protrusion but it would not move. He sank to his knees in the mud. Crawl under the limber. That was the safest place. Hooves churned around him and darkness swarmed in front of his eyes. He could hear the roaring of the surf over the dorn, the rhythmic thumping of the waves. White flecks swam in his vision, a flight of kittiwakes spiralling down to nest on the Abel Rock. Of course. It's June. Time for them to come back. Terns too, dropping like white lightning on the glittering shoals of fry. The swell bore him landwards and the boat answered to the oar. He stood up in the stern, sculling with a single sweep. He could see her now walking down from the Kybe with an infant in her arms. A little dark haired fellow. Two others followed at her heels. She was smiling and waving, happy to see him back. This was how it had always been meant to be. The wave lifted the boat and it ran softly onto the beach. No more loneliness. He walked towards her, reaching out for the warm softness of her. No more pain.

He was cold by the time Bateson found him. The guns roared again and rocked backwards on their carriages. There was still work to be done.

CHAPTER 24

Stone by stone the pier stretched out into the deep water, firm on its foundation of Balcunnin limestone. The important business of the town went on uninterrupted by the sideshow of the rise and fall of empires and the redrawing of the map of Europe. The summer resounded to the chink of masons' chisels as blocks were shaped and fitted into place. In like manner the new church began to grow beside the old chapel making the old building look very much the poor relation. Father Clare haunted the site as if he could speed the workmen by his presence but there were some who did not rejoice as fully at the prospect of change. Of these Skip was among the most vocal. "We'll all be losin' the run of ourselves with all this grandeur," he confided to Eileen on meeting her near the site. As usual she was seated in her trap, drawn by her favourite pony, with her three young children beside her. The wee fella was looking better and better, thought the old man.

"Now Skip, don't you be one of those diehards always talkin' about the old days. Sure don't we have to improve things."

This was the same old cant about progress. "But it's a bit o'meself they'll be knockin' down when the oul chapel goes and I'm just not pleased about it, that's all."

"I know what you mean. Wasn't I married there too but we can't live in the past."

He wondered that she could put it all behind her like that. "When I was an altar-boy in there years ago, do ye know what?"

"You were an altar boy!" She laughed at the idea, old Skip in his soutane, serving Mass.

"Now don't you laugh miss. It's a fair while ago, but I remember the girls kneelin' at the rails could put their hands through and catch us be the toes. That'd give ye a quare start in the middle o'Mass. Many's the time I got a hidin' from the priest for lettin' a yelp out o'me." He chuckled and his eyes glazed over at the memory of sixty or more years before. "Now they're comin' to Mass in shoes, would ye believe!" The absurdity of it was almost too much for him. "The grandeur will be the ruination of us all." He assumed the ominous air of a minor Old Testament prophet.

Eileen pressed him further. "I just can't see you as an altar boy in a soutane."

"Soutane nothin'. Luck enough to have a pair o' breeks and an oul shirt in them days. It was still again the law to have Mass at all. That was why we had it. It was the Mass-house then and no talk o' churches and chapels. I'm telling ye Eileen, the grandeur will be the end of us."

"But don't you think that God should have a proper house?"

"It's not God I'm objectin' to." He rolled his eyes reverently upwards just to put the Deity at His ease on that point. "It's just when everything gets too easy for Catholics they'll just lose interest and give up the religion altogether. When the laws is all changed and the priests has their way in everythin', it'll be like makin' a pet of a dog. He'll be no use for nothin' afterwards and neither will the Catholics o' this country." There was something in his inverted logic. Take away their rights . . . and the people would climb to high windy mountaintops to repeat the sacrifice of Calvary, but make it easy for them in a fine new church and at best they might shuffle in at the last minute and lurk with an ill grace by the door.

"I hope you're not right Skip," she said thinking of her children's future. "But the law is wrong to keep us out of things like professions and government." This was one of the commonest topics for argument in the country and she felt slightly embarrassed at advancing this hackneyed line of reasoning.

"Would ye go 'way outa that with yer govermint," snorted the old man derisively. "And what would the likes of us be doin' in govermint? When would I drop me cages? Wouldn't you look well sittin' up there with all them lords and your babby in the shawl? Have sense woman." She had to admit that he had a point. The picture he painted amused her. "No, woman. Govermint is for the likes of his lordship that knows about such matters."

"But sure isn't his lordship behind the buildin' of the church." She felt she had scored a point but could not be sure what it was. Skip was silent for a moment, considering a change of tack. There was no way to refute her remark. "Ah the poor gentleman. Wasn't it bad luck to lose his boy in the war?" Indeed, the eldest son, heir to the Balcunnin estate had fallen gloriously at Waterloo as befitted an officer and gentleman. This was the only repercussion from that titanic conflict to penetrate as far as their peaceful backwater. Still there was the younger lad, the sailor, who would do just as well no doubt.

Eileen felt the chill close round her as if a cloud had passed over the sun. It was almost a year since John had died and the soldiers had left but there was never a day that she didn't wake up thinking about them. If he was alive she knew that Peter would come back someday but there had been a great battle in which many thousands had died and she had heard nothing. Perhaps he was dead. It would be better to know. Perhaps he was crippled or blinded somewhere, in need of help, left to beg for a living by the roadside. This thought she pushed aside when she could but sometimes it intruded on her dreams and she could see him hobbling the road from village to village, the butt of everyone's abuse, mocked by the children and barked at by the dogs. At such times she prayed for him as she had prayed for his son, asking nothing for herself but to be let know one way or another. Perhaps he had been nowhere near the battle and was well and prosperous somewhere in England, remembering her only as a casual dalliance, one of a long series in a soldier's career. She would not believe this. She longed for him to come back. In some way they could be together again and their love would help them to make amends and wipe away the old pain. Still there was no word and the fears remained.

There was the other matter of the priest to occupy her mind too. They had settled into a war of attrition in which Father Clare showed surprising flashes of good-nature. When he warned her about pride she countered by accusing him of rash judgement. He might laugh and retreat, lest he be judged in turn. There was no denying that she was a worthy opponent. Despite her lack of learning there was a logical commonsense about her that impressed him. Dire threats of terrible retribution were met by her appeal to his charity. It made a nonsense of his calling if he did not practise the precepts of his Master. Christ, she pointed out, did not condemn the woman taken in adultery. Unfairly, he thought that there were disadvantages in allowing the laity too much access to sacred writings but he could see that she was not merely quoting as an intellectual exercise. There was too much real suffering haunting her wide green eyes.

Still she would not be churched. She would regain her strength in her own time and in her own way. She would not submit to any kind of blackmail, despite his warning that she was flying in the face of God. These encounters left her exhausted and anxious but still she clung to the belief that God was not vengeful or capricious, waiting to pull the trapdoor out from under the struggling, fallible creatures of His Own making.

Old Skip coughed, interrupting her reverie. There was something on his mind. "I do be afeared sometimes that the sergeant must 'a been in the battle. We would 'a heard from him before now." She had got used to hearing him spoken of without flinching but she said nothing. Sometimes she wondered if people guessed the truth about the baby but nobody had ever given the slightest reason for her suspicion. "I do say the odd prayer for him, even if he wasn't one of our own. It can't do him a bit o' harm wherever he is, though God knows I'm not much of a hand at the prayers this past fifty year."

"I'm sure he'd appreciate it if he knew. It worked for him before as I remember, when he had the sickness in his eyes."

"Aye, that's right, so they did," agreed Skip, brightening at the thought, "so they did. And ye know in a way I like to think that he's prayin' for us too when his bell rings of a Sunday."

The pony had grown restive during their long and desultory conversation. The children had begun to complain but she felt no irritation. Skip had shown her a way of remembering that lessened the pain. It was his bell that had rung for John as if in gratitude for the kindness shown to him and his bell would ring to unite the many strands of their lives for generations to come. In a sense he had never entirely gone away.

Where Bateson stood he could see the sheep flowing down the side of the valley like a wave. The dog skirmished behind them, sweeping to the left and right, nipping at heels, gathering in the stragglers. A ripple ran through the flock as they swerved, like a cloud of sanderlings turning and jinking in the sky as if the flight were composed of a single composite creature. Pheep, he whistled, phip, phip, pheep. The shrill insistent notes carried to the distant animal directing him to turn the flock towards the pen. It was early morning and the Levels away to the east lay still under a blanket of fog. The sun shone orange through the mist on the hills and rime-frost clung to every twig in the hedgerows. Copses of beech and elm stood out against the sunrise, mauve and purple skeletons of trees on the rolling upland.

He reflected on the strange sequence of events that had brought him to this quiet outcrop of the Quantock hills where it looked as if he might spend the rest of his days in reasonable contentment. He had risen before dawn to gather in the sheep and ice crackled under his boots as he left the little stone-built cottage with its low beams and high broad-eaved thatch. He had to get to Milverton fair and secure the best possible price for the Captain's sheep. Duty had always been his guiding light and his support in times of uncertainty and as long as the Captain needed him, he was glad to be able to serve him.

It wasn't a bad life either, very like what he had been used to as a lad, before drifting into the army. It was a pity about the Captain but otherwise Bateson had been content these past few years although sometimes at night, by the candlelight, when he took out his book of birds, he remembered wistfully the cry of the gulls and the long swish of the waves on the beach. The only gulls he ever saw now were those that followed the plough when the ground was broken for corn but they foraged for mere worms with the humble jackdaws. They lacked the haughty poise of the island birds. Although he reckoned he was a shade older than Osgood, the Captain, in the artillery tradition, had always adopted a paternalistic attitude to his men. It had been natural then to try to seek him out after the battle to report what had become of his former company. Bateson alone, of the men who had served in the towers, had survived the carnage of Waterloo. He wanted desperately to find one familiar face in the exhilarated throng of men who stamped their way into Brussels chanting the news of their victory to the enthusiastic populace. It was two days before he found his Captain.

Osgood lay in an overcrowded hospital ward reserved for the many wounded officers. He was horribly maimed, apparently by an exploding shell which had blown the horse from under him. The left side of his face was severely mutilated and his left arm was almost severed by the flying shrapnel. The doctor had done his best but expressed a fear of gangrene. There was no light of recognition in the Captain's eyes, severe, perhaps irreparable concussion, the doctor said. "Lucky to be alive in a way. It seems the horse was killed outright," he went on. "We'll do what we can for him but he won't see any more active service." Gangrene did not set in as it happened, but the Captain showed no great improvement during the following weeks. The sutures were successfully removed but he uttered not a word. The arm hung lifeless by his side. The Duke himself had sent to find out about his condition and Mercer had no difficulty in acceding to Bateson's request to be detailed as the injured man's servant. The hysteria of victory subsided gradually and the heroes moved to other stages to receive the plaudits of a grateful nation. Bateson waited patiently in Brussels, watching over his Captain and generally making himself useful to the hospital authorities. There was no shortage of work.

This was the inglorious side of the coin, men screaming in fear or agony under the surgeon's knife, or rambling incoherently in fever during the dark small hours of the night when nameless terrors assailed them in their sleep. Bateson removed baskets of amputated members to the furnace and helped to carry out the bodies of those who could fight no more. These patients were officers with money to support them and people to care for them when they were released but the wards of the enlisted men were charnel houses of hopeless suffering where men went mad in their pain and desolation. For many there would be no future but the charity of the parish as they stumbled, mutilated and blind, into the darkness of age and decrepitude. The glory of Waterloo had been purchased at a price.

Captain Osgood recovered through Bateson's careful nursing to the point where he could walk with the aid of a stick but he had no recollection of recent events nor could he express any plans for his future. Again Mercer intervened, securing a passage home for them on a frigate leaving Antwerp for Plymouth, on the grounds that Osgood would not be able to survive a long journey overland. Bateson recalled that October journey through Exeter and the rolling Somerset countryside, surprisingly through the village of Wellington, a co-incidence, and their arrival at last at the Osgood house, a small unpretentious country house of warm yellow sandstone.

The Captain's brisk and capable wife had taken on the task of looking after the invalid without surprise or complaint as if it were the most natural thing for soldiers to return shattered from the wars. Bateson had removed the Captain's trunks and boxes of accumulated papers from the hired gig and had settled into civilian life on the estate. There was nowhere else for him to go and Mrs Osgood was anxious to repay him for his attention to her husband.

It was October again and as he had done for several years now, he was taking sheep to Milverton fair and would subsequently give an account of his stewardship to the manager or the mistress herself. Hoggetts would fetch a fair price now, fat with the grass of summer. He felt a justifiable pride in his work despite the discontent that was rife in the land. There would be agitators at the fair no doubt, circulating among drovers, shepherds and labouring men but Bateson had no time for them. A few glasses of good ale and a hearty meal was all he asked of a fair day and maybe a bit of a chat with his peers, but conversation was never his strong point.

Mrs Osgood was perturbed by her husband's restlessness. Since he had begun to improve something seemed to have disturbed his peace. She had got used to having him around in his state of placid torpor although it grieved her to see so active a mind reduced to nothing. But lately he had begun to talk more and he fidgeted and muttered incessantly, looking around as if he had mislaid something. He fretted constantly at his useless withered arm. Mercifully his right arm had not been impaired and gradually he began to feed himself, inexpertly at first, like a child, but as the skill returned he began to be impatient, spilling his food and muttering the more in an agony of frustration. She could see the desperation in his eyes but he could not explain what was troubling him. At times she even feared for his sanity but gradually he was recovering control of himself. He began to draw again with painful difficulty.

Now it was fair day, October the tenth, 1818, three years almost to the day since he had arrived home. He had asked hesitantly for his old military chests to be brought downstairs. This in itself was a momentous event but the trembling avidity with which he shuffled through the contents disturbed her. Papers littered her normally spotless drawing room floor and furniture, rolls of maps and charts and bound bundles of pages and letters. She was touched to recognise many of her own letters among them and distressed to see the difficulty with which he tried to open the maps, one-handed, on the floor. The vellum, rolled for so many years, sprang back into a cylinder until she suggested weighting the edges with his instrument box and the black case that appeared to contain a musical instrument, some souvenir of his travels no doubt. Her husband had never boasted of any musical accomplishments. He looked at her with gratitude and fell to studying the map on the floor. It appeared to be of a small triangular settlement with a promontory shaped like a doorhandle and several small islands. She left him to it, glad to see his mind occupied although he looked more puzzled than interested by the paper spread in front of him. Perhaps it may be good for him and help him to get a grip on the past again. The shepherd Bateson would be coming in the evening and she always took special pains to see that he was provided for. Regular as the seasons Bateson made his report on fair days and asked after the Captain's health. To him he was always the Captain, never Mr Osgood or the Squire as he was variously known.

Bateson, Bateson? The name had a familiar ring to it. Ah yes! Been with them for some time now. Always glad to see Bateson. "Show him in please." Osgood was drawing again, strange shapes, the pen moving out and around from the centre until the page was filled with black spirals which he shaded with elaborate care, or myriad-legged insects, swarm upon swarm of them filling page after page. Osgood searched the drawings as if for a clue.

"Bateson sir." The shepherd stood by the door with his broad brimmed hat in his hand. He saluted in military fashion unlike the customary tug of the forelock, and shifted his heavy boots awkwardly on the polished boards. He waited for his employer to speak, until the silence became obvious, accentuated by the ticking of the black marble clock on the mantlepiece. Still the Captain said nothing. Bateson coughed. "I see thee still has the sergeant's fife there sir."

"Fife? Oh this thing. I don't know anything about that." He returned to his drawing. "You've had something to eat?"

"Aye sir. The sergeant sir. Sergeant Howlett as served under 'ee in Fingal. He used to play on that pipe sir."

"I don't know anything about that. Do you play?"

"No sir. It were the sergeant as played it."

Osgood picked up the case and opened it. It intrigued him. He put the mouthpiece to his lips and blew. A low mellow sound emerged and he moved his fingers experimentally. A new sound reverberated around the room and a look of perplexity passed over his face. Bateson tried again. "Sergeant Howlett. The boat sir. He had a boat. He were with us at Waterloo." Osgood shook his head, dismissing the topic. "Thank you Bateson. You've done well I gather. That will be all." Why must people explain things to him when he was not interested? He looked down at his drawing. His hand had described a bird, spreadeagled like some sombre coat of arms with skull and vertebrae showing and wing and tail feathers spread like bedraggled fans. He could see something emerging from the mists, soldiers in blue, grey rocks swept by the spray, a man standing with a staff against the skyline, a young fellow. Music! There was his sergeant Peter Howlett. Pictures began to flood back. My god! How long ago was that? Was it all in some other existence? Had he ever been away from this comfortable house? "Hannah," he shouted. She had not heard him utter her name for years. "Hannah." She collided with him as he wrenched open the door. "Bring that man Bateson back. I must speak with him." His eyes were alive with recognition. She did not notice the litter of papers in the room as her heart lurched with hope and relief.

CHAPTER 25

Alicia hesitated at the study door. There was a stranger talking to her father. He was a large man in the rough clothes of a countryman but not one of their own workmen. He stood, clutching the broad brim of his hat in both hands but there was no air of servility about him. Her father had his back to the fire. The cold afternoon light highlighted the expression of concern on his face. He looked up and noticed the girl and his expression lightened. "Come in my dear. Mr Bateson has brought us news of some old friends." Who she wondered, was Mr Bateson? The man saluted in reply to her greeting.

"You had better read this. It will explain things better than I can." Her father handed her the letter that he had been studying in the fading light. "I have, it seems, become a beneficiary, but read it for yourself."

The writing was in sepia ink in a stylish cursive hand but it looked as if the hand had trembled from age or ague. 'My Lord' it began, 'I beg leave to trouble you after the lapse of several years in the matter of my late sergeant Peter Howlett.' She felt a pang of sadness at the abruptness of the news. She had assumed long since that he must have lost interest in their offer of employment and drifted away into some other walk of life. There was not much call for soldiers nowadays. She read on:

> In extenuation of my tardiness in acquainting you with the following, may I plead certain serious injuries sustained by myself at Waterloo, which left me an invalid for several years. Peter Howlett served with distinction in the same engagement where regrettably he was slain. Some time beforehand he consulted me concerning the disposal of his property, to wit, his share in a salvaged schooner, a small amount of money in specie

and his clarinet, in the event of his losing his life. He expressed
the hope that you might accept the clarinet as an addition to your
collection of instruments in return for your kindness to him. The
money he left to Captain Denis Garrigan to enable him to
purchase the boat *Kittiwake,* formerly the property of the army
and his share of the schooner is dealt with specifically in the will
witnessed by myself, which I enclose herewith. I recommend to
you the bearer of this letter as an honest and sturdy fellow. He
has expressed a desire to settle in your country where he served
for several years. I am indebted to him for his kindness and
loyalty and shall be sorry to lose him.

I should be grateful if Your Lordship would acquaint me with
the progress of the several schemes for which I had the honour
to draw up plans.

In conclusion I ask you to accept, with my compliments, some
small drawings which may be of interest to you. These were
executed at different periods during my service in Fingal and
during my recent indisposiiton.

I remain

Your Lordship's Most Humble and Obedient

Henry Osgood (Captain Retd.)

Immediately she thought of the clarinet, remembering how the music
had soared on that New Year's Eve so long ago and her eyes blurred at
the memory. "Oh father," she said and her voice caught in her throat.
"I'm so sorry to hear this. He was such a pleasant man," but pleasant
was not the word she was seeking.

"Yes indeed he was. I had hopes for him my dear but that is a
soldier's lot I suppose." He paused reflectively. "Not the usual run of
the mill though. I'm touched by the gift of the instrument although I
know of no one who could play it."

"I'm sure I could master it," she said impulsively. "It would be a
pity if it were never to be played again."

"By all means," he agreed, mildly amused by her sentimentality.
"Our friend will be remembered both for his bell and in the wood-
wind section." The idea of Howlett living on in the music of the town
appealed to him. It seemed somehow appropriate. "Now Bateson, we
must see you provided for. I can always use an experienced man.
You've been a shepherd with Osgood I understand."

"Aye sir. That I 'ave. An' gave satisfaction if I may say so."

"So he says. So he says. I intend to run sheep on more of my land and on the islands too." Bateson looked up from his study of the patterned Indian rug. There was more animation than usual in his eyes. "The islands sir? They could do right well there sir." His lordship continued, unperturbed by the interruption. "Yes they should. In my father's day we always grazed sheep there. The mutton was incomparable."

Bateson gave the slightest of shrugs. He had no idea what that word meant but the whole idea struck him as attractive.

"Perhaps my manager would have something for you in that line. I'll send you to him with a note." Balcunnin picked up a piece of writing paper and reached for a pen. Bateson watched him, thinking that he had never been the subject of so much correspondence in all his life. It gave him an inward sense of importance that two gentlemen had seen fit to write about him and entrust him with letters.

Alicia waited impatiently, hoping that her father would divulge the contents of the other documents. It struck her that her father was getting a trifle absent-minded. He was easily sidetracked or so it seemed, and lost the thread of his thought. He had even begun to speak kindly of his brother from whom they had heard only once since his precipitate departure. They had no idea how he was faring in the New World but she suspected that somehow her father missed him. There was never an argument or raised voice in the house nowadays but some of the mirth had gone out of it too. Balcunnin scattered some sand on the paper and shook it down. "Now my good fellow. Take this along to Eavers at the gate lodge and he'll see that you are looked after."

Bateson gave his abridged version of the military salute to both of them and quietly took his leave.

"Poor Osgood was very bad you know. Lost his memory completely for years it seems. Have a look at these drawings he sent me." He handed her a manila envelope which contained over a dozen drawings, executed both with pen and brush, some of familiar local scenes, working men, sailing vessels, horses, and some more difficult to understand, pieces of stone with strange whirling shapes and swarming insect-like creatures embedded in them. There were some sections of diagrams for the sloping breakwater wall and one small map of the island with the tower. "Osgood wouldn't approve of course but I don't intend to bring the wall along the Kybe. People would be unable to draw up their boats. The old breakwater will have to suffice there. Gorman assures me that there is no danger." He was off again, engrossed in the technicalities of his shore defences, with a

tinge of guilt at adulterating Osgood's original sweeping concept. "I
shall write to him of course and express my satisfaction at hearing of
his return to health. I should really offer him some consideration for
all his work but I fear he would be insulted. I shall endeavour to put
some preferment his way at the earliest opportunity."

"Father," Alicia scolded, "You really are most exasperating. I feel
you are doing it deliberately."

"What's that?" he asked with just a hint of mischief.

"The other documents. What about the sergeant's share in the
schooner? You can't leave me with only half of the story." She was
surprised by her own curiosity. It was not quite ladylike to wish to pry
into another's private affairs.

"Ah yes. The will. You shall accompany me in the morning to call
upon the people concerned and then perhaps your curiosity will be
laid to rest." He would say no more on the matter, savouring the little
drama. "I want to cast an eye on Mr Clare's new church while we are
in town. It will be a very fine edifice indeed when the belfry is
completed. I feel almost obliged to worship there on alternate
Sundays," he added wryly "to be sure of getting my money's worth."

Alicia's eyes strayed again to the drawings scattered on the desk.
The flowing white stripe on the side of a small fishing smack glowed
in the late afternoon light and the firelight flickered so that the vessels
at the pier seemed to rock gently on their moorings. She felt the
sadness of things changing and slipping irretrievably into the past
although why it should affect her so deeply she could not say. "I
should like to keep these if you don't mind father," she said, replacing
the sheets in the envelope. "Whatever you like my dear," he assented.
"I shall send them to be framed for you if you like. Remind me to
write to him about, eh, you know, the buildings and so forth."
Balcunnin's mind had moved on to other matters, perhaps a little
music after dinner before retiring. He cracked his knuckles in
anticipation. Stiffening up. They say the sea air penetrates the joints. A
scherzo and brandy should loosen things up a bit. The only dependable
pleasure left to a man really. Unbidden, he thought of island mutton,
boiled with whole onions and covered in parsley sauce. Plain ordinary
food. Good to be alive to enjoy it. Good fellow Howlett. Made a
damn fine end too. Yes, Waterloo cost us dear. "Dinner," he said
aloud. "Yes of course, my dear. You keep the drawings. Most
interesting. Good heavens. Why are we standing here in the dark? Let
us go and cheer ourselves up a little. These winter evenings are
inclined to make one melancholy."

The bare branches stood out black against the pale November twilight and the wind gusted in the chimney. Alicia shivered and drew her shawl around her shoulders.

Eileen turned the envelope over, undecided whether to open it or not. Her visit from Balcunnin and his daughter had left her thoughts in a turmoil. By any reckoning it was a stroke of good fortune to have come into such an inheritance, half shares in one of the finest schooners in the harbour, to be held in trust for her children, and a tidy sum in the bank already earned in Peter Howlett's name. She remembered vividly the morning of the wreck and the sight of himself and Tom scrambling like two bedraggled monkeys on the sloping deck. That was less than five years ago but it seemed like another age. They were all so much younger then when there was laughter in the world. She thought of John and his warmth and strength and the sense of loss came to her as sharply as when he died. There was never a message from John, like this one coming from the dead. He had never an opportunity to sort things out or put his books in order before he was taken. Why then should Peter Howlett be given a chance to plead his case or disturb the tenor of her life when she had come to terms with herself? It was too late to undo the damage so why reopen an old wound?

She had prayed for them both many times, asking God's blessing on them but always on her own terms. She wondered not for the first time if He would punish them because she refused to accept the rules of His church. It seemed too hard a reckoning for a merciful God. For herself she could not be sorry for what Father Clare would have called her greatest sin if she had confided in him, although she regretted more than anything the tragic outcome of it. Recognising fully her selective attitude towards right and wrong she had made survival her moral code. In a small town such as this she knew that she and her children would be picked to death by gossip and envy and so she held her head up and made a success of what she attempted.

She worked several days a week with Mrs Morris and on the other days she helped John's father with his book-keeping. Things were going well. The children were healthy and happy although the older ones, Lucy and Matt, sometimes asked for their father. She would gather them close to her and tell them all about him, how big he was and how strong and how he was the best footballer in the barony, until their eyes shone with pride. Little Peter would get very excited then and jump on his brother's back or try to wrestle him to the ground shouting that he was John Mullen the strongest man in Fingal. Nothing that I have done, she thought, must ever hurt them. This apparent good fortune must be accepted in such a way that their future would not be invalidated. Her children must not be exposed to jibes or innuendo from people whose sole pleasure in life was in trying to reduce others to their own miserable level.

Peter must have been thinking along the same lines when he phrased his will in favour of the widow and children of his late friend John Mullen who had shown him such kindness. Discreet as always, almost invisible at times, she thought and felt a spurt of gratitude to him for not exposing her to the gaze of the curious. She smiled to think that this legacy would quicken Tom Morris in the interest he had shown in her in the past few years. Tom, sprouting his new whiskers, had become quite gallant towards her to the amusement of old Skip Garrigan, who intimated on his occasional visits that she could do worse than given him some encouragement. But she knew Tom for the calculating businessman he was and parried such suggestions with the remark that she was not yet reduced to robbing cradles. Now Tom would see the advantages of cementing their partnership even more closely and she must prepare for a siege.

She tore open the envelope and spread the sheet of yellowing paper on the table. The writing was carefully executed but inexpert with words crossed out here and there. The lines she noticed had a tendency to slope downhill to the right and blank wedges appeared where an effort had been made to get back on an even keel. Poor little man, she reflected. He was never entirely in control of any situation. He did not open with her name. She was not surprised as he had rarely addressed her by her name anyway.

I am writing this in the village of Genappe in Belgium. Captain Osgood says it is an auspicious day (I asked him to spell the word) because the Duke of Wellington has taken command of the army. Soon we shall go into action. If you receive this letter it will mean that I am dead as I have determined to come back to you if I survive and there will be no need of letters.

Maybe you would not wish to see me again but I cannot believe this unless you tell me to my face. For my part I know there is no other life for me without you.

I regret the injury done by me to your husband who was the best man I have ever known and beyond that I regret the loss caused to you and your children.

If this letter is the last you ever hear of me know that for a time with you I was happy and for that I thank you.

I am doing what little I can to make emends and hope that you will remember kindly one who loved you without apology and with very little hope.

Your servant,
P. Howlett. Sgt.

'Emends'. Surely it should be 'amends', she thought inconsequentially. So he had not forgotten after all. Like an old ballad it was all so sad and yet so good to know that what they had felt for each other was still intact. He was safe with her now where no vicissitudes could separate them again, no more misunderstandings or jealousy, but underneath it all like a great ocean swell building up and flowing relentlessly over her was the realisation that never again would she feel the touch of his hand on her cheek or the shivering of his long spare body as he sank into the warmth of her, where they lay together on the moonlit beach. The wave passed over her. There was a roaring in her ears and she sank her head on the table. She felt her body hunger agonisingly at the thought of him but there was nothing to do but hold on while the room darkened and spun around her.

After what seemed an age she became aware of the musty smell of the paper on which her cheek lay and little by little she returned to the present. What was to be done? Something had to be tidied up. She rose and went into the garden. The waves foamed white below the breakwater and the grey bleak line of the island swam in her tears. She began to pick at the rag of cloth on the fence. It had once been red but now it was almost colourless and tangled in the branches of the weather beaten thorn that slanted away from the sea wind. The dawks tore at her hand but she paid no heed, pulling the faded threads from the twigs and gathering them into a useless bundle. She would not need them again. No one on the island would ever again look landward to the Kybe searching for a flapping red signal. Fold it away. Put it out of sight. She hurried indoors and thrust the damp bundle into the fire. The flames struggled with the wetness of it and gradually took hold. She felt someone tugging at her skirts. "Mam, Mam, your hands are all bleedy." It was Peter, the wee fellow as Skip called him, his brown eyes large with alarm. "So they are pet," she agreed looking at the white scratches and spots of red. "So they are."

"Did the cat scratch you? He's wicked."

"No pet I was just in the wars." She lifted him and hugged him to

her. "I was in the wars but I'm home now. I'll tell you about it
someday." She picked up the letter and folding it carefully, she put it
in the box with the five guineas from Luke and the silver half-crown,
Georgius III, that John had given for her on their wedding day. What
was that word again? Auspicious. What a beautiful name for a
schooner!

"Run and get your sister and brother. We must go and see your
uncle Tom about a new name for our ship." She twitched her best
shawl from the back of a chair and swung it round her shoulders,
suddenly looking forward to the outing. "And tell them to hurry. We
have things to do."

The sun reflected a blinding whiteness from the limewashed harbour
wall. Skip squinted reflectively against the glare and sucked on his
pipe. "Be the jings Larry but it's a comical oul world."

"Oh aye?" Larry pricked up his ears. Skip had the advantage of him
of nigh on forty years, but all going well, by listening attentively and
deferentially Larry could succeed to the position of chronicler and
chorus to the doings of the town bringing to the task the accumulated
wisdom of several generations – and there were one or two things that
even Skip didn't know.

"Aye we've seen it all, yerself and meself," a generous
acknowledgement to one so much his junior. "The poor divil of an
emperor after dyin' away out there on his island and a few years ago
the whole world goin' in fear and dread of him. And who gives a damn
now?"

"Aye it's comical, all right Skip, comical." Not funny mind you,
but comical like. They looked down at their glasses watching the
bubbles rising slowly to the surface, expanding and vanishing with the
slightest of sounds.

"Ye know over the other side they have wagons that run by
themselves. No horses, only steam."

"Go 'long outa that now. The only decent job I ever had and you're
tryin' to tell me they'll be doin' away with horses. Do ye take me for
an eejit?"

"It's progress Larry." Skip chuckled at a private joke. "Ye can't stop
progress. Listen to that now." Clear and vibrant on the sharp southerly
breeze came the sound of the angelus bell. "Landlords breakin' the law
buildin' belfries for papists. Now there's a comical one."

"Aye." A pause. "You're not fishin' at all this weather," tactfully so as not to suggest any deterioriation.

"The way it is Larry I think I'm gettin' a bit too ould for haulin' cages. Me partner looks after them now."

"Is he right in the head? They say he's a bit touched."

"He's all right, I mean for an Englishman." That explained a lot. "I lend him the boat when he needs it and he hauls me cages in return. Never asks for any money. He just prefers animals and birds to people an' sure maybe he's right. I'm just keepin' the boat for Eileen's childer."

Another pause. That was a story that could wait for a generation or two. "There she goes now Skip. Ye know John would have been proud of her the way she came through it all. She has me godson on board this trip ye know." Larry had to admit to a feeling of envy at times. Nobody went around giving poor Nora, that worked hard every day of her life, schooners and the like but still he felt a vicarious pride in the good fortune of his employer.

"Aye he'd have been the proud man all right."

The crack of the unfurled mains'l carried to them over the water. *Auspicious* fell back from her mooring. The orange-brown jib bellied out swinging her round to port and the mains'l became taut. A white wave formed at her bow as she headed for the open sea and she began to rise and fall rhythmically as she breasted the incoming swell of the darker water beyond the harbour.